Australian author **Ally Blake** coffee, porch swings and dappled sunshine, beautiful notebooks and soft, dark pencils. Her inquisitive, rumbunctious, spectacular children are her exquisite delight. And she adores writing love stories so much she'd write them even if nobody read them. No wonder, then, having sold over four million copies of her romance novels worldwide, Ally is living her bliss. Find out more about Ally's books at www.allyblake.com.

A frequent name on bestseller lists, **Allison Leigh**'s high point as a writer is hearing from readers that they laughed, cried or lost sleep while reading her books. She credits her family with great patience for the time she's parked at her computer, and for blessing her with the kind of love she wants her readers to share with the characters living in the pages of her books. Contact her at www.allisonleigh.com.

Also by Ally Blake

Millionaire to the Rescue
Falling for the Rebel Heir
Hired: The Boss's Bride
Dating the Rebel Tycoon
Millionaire Dad's SOS

The Royals of Vallemont miniseries

Rescuing the Royal Runaway Bride
Amber and the Rogue Prince

Also by Allison Leigh

Yuletide Baby Bargain
A Child Under His Tree
The BFF Bride
One Night in Weaver...
A Weaver Christmas Gift
A Weaver Beginning
A Weaver Vow
A Weaver Proposal
Courtney's Baby Plan
The Rancher's Dance

AMBER AND THE ROGUE PRINCE

ALLY BLAKE

FORTUNE'S HOMECOMING

ALLISON LEIGH

MILLS & BOON

First Published in Great Britain 2018
by Mills & Boon, an imprint of HarperCollinsPublishers,
1 London Bridge Street, London, SE1 9GF

Special thanks and acknowledgement to Allison Leigh for her contribution to the Fortunes of Texas: The Rulebreakers continuity.

ISBN: 978-0-263-26500-2

38-0618

MIX
Paper from
responsible sources
FSC™ C007454

This book is produced from independently certified FSC™ paper to ensure responsible forest management.

For more information visit: www.harpercollins.co.uk/green

Printed and bound in Spain
by CPI, Barcelona

AMBER AND THE ROGUE PRINCE

ALLY BLAKE

For all the women dreaming
about their next chapters.

And Bec, who leapt into hers with enthusiasm,
fortitude, grace, humour and style, taking her
first steps alongside me, and naming
Ned the dog along the way.

CHAPTER ONE

AMBER PLONKED HERSELF onto the rickety stairs out front of the shack hovering on the edge of Serenity Hill. Stretching her arms over her head, she blinked sleepily at the view.

A misty glow slithered over the acres of wild lavender carpeting the hillside. The first hint of morning sun peeked between the hilly mounds beyond, creating a starburst of gold on the horizon and making silhouettes of the willows meandering along the banks of Serenity Creek below.

"Could do with some rain," said Amber. "That said, can't we always?"

Ned stared fondly up at her from his mismatched eyes. She gave the mottled fur behind his good ear a thorough rub.

Then, nabbing her bright yellow gumboots, Amber tugged them on over faded pyjama bottoms. She rubbed a smudge of mud from one of the bees that Sunflower—who lived in the bright purple caravan up on the hill—had painted on them for her. Then she twirled her heavy hair into a low bun and ducked her head into her fencing-style veil. Last came elasticised gloves, then, finally ready, she pushed herself to her feet.

"You ready?"

Ned answered with a wag of his tail.

"Then let's do this."

But Amber only made it down one more step before

she spied Sunflower hustling down the hill behind the shack towards her.

With her fluffy strawberry-blonde hair and pixie face, her feet bare beneath her long paisley skirt, Sunflower looked as if she'd fallen to earth on a sunbeam. But like everyone in Serenity she'd come in search of sanctuary.

Amber pulled off her veil and tucked it under her arm before wiping the dislodged strands of hair from her eyes. Not used to seeing anyone else out and about this early, Amber called out, "Everything okay?"

Sunflower waved a hand while she caught her breath. "I have news."

"For you to be out from under your blanket this early it must be pretty good news."

The look Sunflower shot her was thick with meaning.

"Not so good, then."

Sunflower shielded her face against the rising sun and said, "I'm actually not sure. The news is they've opened up the Big House."

Amber glanced up the hill, even though Hinterland House—the big, deserted, Tuscan-style villa that everyone in the area simply referred to as the Big House—was perched too far over the other side to be seen.

"Grim mentioned seeing smoke coming from the chimney a couple of weeks back. But considering Grim lives in a cloud of smoke, I ignored it. Then Daphne claimed she saw sheets on the clothesline and I began to wonder. Last night, when he was taking one of his wanders, my Johnno saw a fancy black car barrelling up the drive and pulling into the garage." She paused for effect, then announced, "It seems the family is back."

"What family? The way the place was always kept so well-tended I'd figured it was a tax write-off for some overseas conglomerate."

"Oh, no," said Sunflower, her eyes now dancing. "It

belongs to the Van Halprins. A family as famous for their money and power as their terrible bad luck. As the story goes, they all died off, in one tragic manner after another, until only one remained—the youngest daughter, Anna, who was very beautiful. Twenty-one and all alone in that big house—the townspeople feared what might become of her. Then, in a fairy-tale ending, she married a prince from some far-off land and the place has been barren ever since."

"And now this fairy-tale princess is back?"

Sunflower shook her head, her eyes sparking. "The person my Johnno saw driving the car was a man. City haircut. Deadly handsome. They say it's *him*."

Amber knew she was meant to say, *Him who?* but her throat had gone dry. Her earlier frisson of concern now bore the hallmarks of fully fledged anxiety: sweaty palms; ringing in her ears; a strong desire to run inside and bar the door.

But the door to her shack was barely holding onto its hinges as it was, so what would be the point?

Oblivious, sweet Sunflower went on. "It *has* to be Anna's son! Anna's *royal* son. Prince Alessandro Giordano himself."

Not one to follow that kind of thing, Amber didn't know Prince Alessandro from Prince Charming.

Only, she had an awful feeling she did.

"Don't you see?" Sunflower went on. "As heir to the Van Halprin estate, Prince Alessandro owns Hinterland House, which means he also owns pretty much every bit of land you can see. From one side of the hill to the other, from the river to the township. Including the land you and I are standing on."

Amber found she had to swallow before asking, "Whoa. Back up a little. I assumed the commune owned this land. Or that the township simply let them stay." So deeply grateful had she been for a place to stay, she'd never thought to ask. "Are you saying that this *Prince* owns Serenity Hill?"

Sunflower nodded slowly. "And there are more rumours."

There were always rumours. Especially in a town this size. Having had parents whose chief personality trait was "being deeply involved", Amber had developed a sincere lack of interest in knowing other people's business.

Sunflower said, "Apparently a man fitting that description—tall, citified, handsome, *and* with an accent—has been seen meeting with the town council. And the only reason for an outsider to meet with the council is—"

"Town planning."

The wind had picked up, creating eerie paths through the field of lavender. And despite the sun lifting into the air, Amber shivered. She wriggled her toes in her gumboots in order to keep the blood flowing.

Unlike some of the old-timers living in tents, wigwams, caravans and Kombi vans up the hill, Amber was a relative newcomer to Serenity. But, while her history of the area was sketchy, her experience with the law was sharp and clear.

"The commune has been occupying this land for years. Decades, right? Long enough to build structures. To hook in plumbing. Electricity. To have signs pointing the way. It's even noted as a point of interest on the tourist map. Surely that gives us rights."

Sunflower blinked. "Rights?"

Before Amber could take the thought further, something banged inside her shack. Both women turned to see what it was. Amber took a subtle step back up onto the porch.

"Probably Ned demanding breakfast."

Sunflower backed away. "Of course. I'm off to spread the news to the rest of the morning folk. See what else we can unearth. Feel free to fill everyone in yourself. Fire-pit meeting tonight. At sunset."

Another bang came from inside Amber's shack. She took another step nearer her front door. Said, "You bet. See you then. I'd better check on Ned."

Of course, at that moment Ned came running out of the fields below, purple flowers caught in his fur.

Amber madly ushered Ned inside the shack, then yanked the door shut behind her before leaning against it, holding the doorknob tight.

In the quiet her heart thumped against her ribs.

All she had to do was lean forward to see past the cupboard-cum-kitchen wall and into her small bedroom. To spot the crumpled sheets. The colourful crocheted blanket kicked into a pile on the floor.

And the masculine shape of the stranger in her bed.

A chop of sun-kissed hair slid over one eye. Broad shoulders lifted and fell as he breathed. The profile cast against her pillow was achingly handsome. Even now. Even with the indignation building inside of her.

To think, she'd only slipped out from under the warm, heavy weight of his arm ten minutes before, smiling at what a deep sleeper he was. And the reason why.

He'd said his name was Hugo. And she'd believed him.

That particular something in his eyes—directness, authority, unflappability—had allowed her the rare luxury of taking everything he'd said at face value. No doubt the foreign accent had helped too. Not only was it devastatingly sexy, but it also meant he was a tourist, just passing through. There was no point worrying too much about details when their dalliance was only ever going to be short-term.

And yet, it sounded like the man she'd just indulged in a clandestine three-week affair with was none other than

Prince Alessandro Giordano—and he was also known as the owner of the land on which she and her friends lived illegally!

Three weeks earlier...

Amber breathed in the scent of lavender as she looked out over Serenity Hill.

There had been a chill in the air that morning. Like the blast of an open fridge door on a hot summer's day.

It was the sign she had been waiting for. Time to harvest her bumper honey crop for the year. Collect at the right time and the honey would be ripe, sweet, in its prime. Leave it much longer and the colony would start eating the wares or moving it lower into the hive, making it near impossible to collect.

By late afternoon there was no need for the smoker. Warmth had settled over the valley and crept up onto the hills, meaning the honey would be warm, running easily, and the bees would be calm.

Dolled up in her veil, overalls and gloves, gumboots slapping against the stairs, she realised Ned was not at her side. No point whistling for him—he was nearly deaf.

She tipped up onto her toes to see if she could spy his fluffy tail cutting through the field. No luck. Maybe he'd headed up the hill to visit the others. But that wasn't like him. They knew better than to feed him scraps. Amber had made it clear that he was her responsibility, nobody else's. That in taking him on she wouldn't put undue pressure on the commune's resources.

About to give up and head off alone, she saw him by the pair of trees down the hill, watching the hammock slung between them with great interest.

As Amber neared she realised why.

A stranger in fact was lying therein. Asleep.

Not just a stranger…a man. A *long* man. Longer than the hammock, his big feet poking out of the end. His T-shirt had twisted to cling to a sculpted chest. The bottom edge lifted to reveal a tanned stomach, and a dark arrow of hair leading to…jeans that left little to the imagination.

Even in sleep he was riveting. Deep-set eyes beneath dashing, slashing brows, and overlong hair that fell across a brow furrowed as if he was dreaming important dreams. The rest of his face was rough-hewn, but handsome with it—a stubble-shadowed jaw and cheeks that appeared carved from rock. A veritable modern-day Viking.

Not from around here, or she'd have noticed. A tourist, then. Not the seasonal fruit-picking kind. Or the type who came to Serenity looking for enlightenment. Or absolution. His clothes were too nice. His aura too crisp. But people didn't just happen to pass through Serenity. They came with a purpose. So what was his?

Her gaze running over every inch of him as if she was committing him to memory, Amber realised with excruciating discomfort just how long she'd been living in this patch of pretty wilderness dotted with leisurely artisans and gentle hippies, none of whom had made her nerves twang. Not like this.

She swallowed the thirst pooling in her cheeks and reached out for Ned.

Ned looked at her with his contented face.

"What are you grinning at?"

Forgetting the fact that in all likelihood the stranger was not as deaf as Ned, Amber hadn't thought to lower her voice.

The stranger sprang to sitting as if he were spring-loaded. His feet hit the ground, his hands gripping the edges of the hammock, the muscles of his arms bunching as the hammock threatened to swing out from under him.

He was even bigger sitting up. Well over six feet. Strong with it. Yet Amber felt compelled to stay. To watch. To wait.

A few beats later, the stranger shook his hair from his eyes before palming the heels of his hands deep into the sockets. With a heavy breath he dropped his hands, opened his eyes, took one look at Amber and leapt out of the hammock so fast he nearly tripped over his own feet.

A string of words poured from his mouth. Italian? French? Who cared? It was the sexiest sound Amber had ever heard. Raw and deep, it scraped against her insides like a long, slow, rough-tongued lick.

Ned loved it too, what little he could hear of it. He bounded to his feet and ran around in a circle, barking at the sky.

The stranger looked over his shoulder, then back at Amber. He looked down at Ned, then back at her again. This time his gaze caught. And stayed. A beat slunk by in which deep breaths were hard to come by.

Then, in lightly accented English, "Please tell me you come in peace."

She reached up and slowly pulled her bee-keeping hat and veil from her head. As usual, the mesh caught on her hair, pulling long blonde strands free of her bun until it fell over her face in a wispy curtain. She tried wiping them away but the heavy glove made it next to impossible.

In the end, she threw her veil to the ground, slid off both gloves and threw them down too. Feeling overheated, she unzipped her overalls, pulling them down to her hips, the arms flapping about her thighs. She fixed her tank top, pushed her hair back off her face, and—hands on hips—stared the stranger down.

The effect somewhat lessened when Ned saw his chance and went for her gloves. He managed to get both, but dropped one about a metre away as he took off into the lavender with the score in his delighted teeth.

Not that the stranger seemed to notice. His eyes never left hers. In fact, they had warmed, distinctly, the edge of a very fine mouth tilting at one side as he took her in.

Flustered, Amber pressed her shoulders back, angled her chin at him and said, "I might ask the same of you."

"Me?" He stretched his arms overhead, once again revealing his flat, tanned belly, and Amber gritted her teeth as she looked determinedly anywhere else. "I am all about the peace."

"Well, next time keep your peace far from my hammock. *Capiche?*"

"If I said I really needed a nap at the exact moment I came upon it, would that help?" One side of his mouth kicked up, and her tummy tumbled over on itself in response.

"What do you think?" she deadpanned.

"I think perhaps not," he mumbled, running a hand through his hair. It was a little rumpled from sleep on one side. He wore it well.

He took a step her way, and Amber took an equal step back, which was ridiculous. If she screamed, a dozen hippies would rush down the hill to check on her. Well, maybe not rush. Amble with intent.

She pressed her gumboots into the ground. It wasn't concern for her safety that had her on edge. It was concern for her hazy judgement.

He stepped sideways, picked up the glove Ned had dropped and ran his thumb over the honeycomb stitching. "How about if I said I tripped and fell into the hammock, knocking myself out?"

"I'd think you were an idiot."

A smile tugging at the corner of that mouth, he looked out over the lavender, all the while taking a step closer to her. "Then here's the unvarnished truth: a wicked witch lured me here with a peach. I took one bite and fell into a deep sleep."

As punctuation, he held out her glove. Naturally, she reached out to take it. Only he did not let go, capturing her gaze right along with it.

His eyes were a deep, intelligent hazel, his mouth on the constant verge of a smile. The fact that his nose appeared to have been broken at some time only added to his stunning good looks.

"It was an apple," said Amber, her voice breaking on the last syllable.

"Hmm?" he said, gently letting the glove go.

"Sleeping Beauty was felled by an apple."

Again with the devastating half-smile. "Wasn't that Eve with the apple? Tempting poor Adam."

"Forbidden fruit. No mention of an apple, specifically."

"Right. I stand corrected."

At some point in the past few minutes, the sun had begun to set, stretching shadows over the stranger's arresting face.

But it was the words that had her transfixed. The locals were so earnest she couldn't remember the last time she'd indulged in spicy banter. It felt good. Really good. Like slipping into a freshly made bed after a long day on her feet.

"Who are you?" she asked, the desire to know far too obvious in her tone.

He held out a hand. "Hugo. And you are?"

Feeling as if she was about to step off a cliff, she took his hand. His fingers were long and strong. His grip dry and warm. The tingle that zapped up her arm had her shaking once and letting go.

"Amber."

"It's a very great pleasure to meet you, Amber."

"I'll bet."

At that he laughed.

The sound tumbling about inside her belly made her feel empty. Hungry. She breathed through it. “Wicked witch or no, this is private property, so you’d best get moving on. It doesn’t get fully dark for another hour. If you walk with pace you’ll make it to the village in time. There you’ll find somewhere else to sleep.”

The man slid his hands into his pockets and rocked back on his heels, going nowhere.

Amber crossed her arms and shook her head at the guy. But he only smiled back, the directness in his eyes telling her she wasn’t the only one having an “interested at first sight” moment. She rolled her eyes, turned on her heel and beckoned to him over her shoulder.

“Come on, then, Hugo. This way.”

CHAPTER TWO

HUGO TWISTED AND stretched, enjoying the creaks and cracks of muscles well-used.

Still half-asleep, he couldn't be sure if the images skirting the edges of his brain were real, or the remnants of a very good dream. Then slowly, like drops of mercury melting together, he recalled slippery limbs sliding over each other. Warmth easing towards heat. Sighs, laughter, a gasp.

No dream. Just Amber.

A bump to the bed echoed through him, as if it wasn't the first.

He dragged his eyes open, battling the sharp morning sunshine, to find Amber no longer tucked into his side. Instead, she stood by the other side of her bed, glaring at him.

And he found himself riding a wave of déjà-vu.

The first time he'd laid eyes on her she'd worn the white veiled hat and the long, chunky gloves, the bulky overalls and those wild yellow boots. She'd looked like something from a nineteen-fifties space comic. Then she'd stripped down in front of him, all sun-browned shoulders, wildly tangled lashes over whisky-brown bedroom eyes, full lips, her long hair a halo of honeyed gold falling halfway down her back.

The difference this time: her lips were pursed. Her hands white-knuckled on her hips. And her narrowed eyes shot daggers his way.

That didn't stop him from weighing up the likelihood of dragging her back to bed. He deemed the chances slim.

Brought up never to readily surrender the advantage of position, Hugo sat up, the sheet dragging with him. His feet curled as they hit the rough wooden floor. Then he pulled himself to standing.

Amber's gaze flickered to his bare chest and she sucked in a sharp breath. The chances looked slightly more promising.

But then her arm lifted, one pointed finger aimed towards her front door, and she said, "Get out."

"Excuse me?"

"I said, get out. Do you not understand what that means? Were you raised by wolves?"

"Nannies. Mostly."

"Of course you were. Get out of my bed. Get out of my shack. Now."

Hugo ran both hands over his face, hard and fast. Better to be fully awake for this. "Start at the beginning. You're not making any sense."

"Then look at my face. Look deep into my eyes so that you see I am serious. I want you to get out."

Well, this was new. Her voice rose with each word, rare emotion tinging her words. She was genuinely upset.

"I will go. Of course. If that's what you want. Look, I'm already out of your bed." The sheet at his hips slipped as he reached up to scratch his chest.

Her tongue darted out to wet her lips, which alleviated his concern, at least a little.

"In the spirit of fair play, I deserve to know why. What has changed in the world since you fell asleep while trying to convince me that honey was better than peanut butter?"

Her hand dropped, just a fraction. Then she regrouped, pointing her finger towards the door with renewed conviction. "Nothing has changed. Not a single thing. Apart from the fact that I now know who you really are."

Time stood still for the merest fraction of a second, but when it resumed, everything seemed to sit a little off from where it had before.

He nodded, dropped the sheet back onto the bed and ambled over to the metal chair in the corner to gather his clothes. His underwear was nowhere to be seen, and, not about to go searching, he went commando, pulling on his jeans, taking care with the fly.

He'd known their liaison would end. They both had. That had been the underlying beauty of it.

In the first few days it had been diverting, watching things unfold from a safe mental distance. Distance was his usual state of being and Amber had seemed glad of it. The guiltless pleasure, the ease of transaction, the lack of desire on both sides to pry deeper than what the other might like for lunch had led to a beautifully contained affair.

Somehow, in all the hazy sunshine, with the cicadas a constant background hum, the clear edges of their association had begun to blur...until he'd found reasons to come to her earlier, to stay longer. They'd fallen into a rhythm of days lit bright and nights lost to exquisite, immoderate pleasure and murmured nothings in the dark.

As he pushed one arm through his shirt, then the other, he no longer felt distant. The dissatisfaction he felt was real.

But only a fool would have expected the halcyon days to remain that way—like a bug trapped in amber. So to speak. And Hugo was no fool.

"Is that it?" Amber's words hit his back like bullets. "You don't have anything to say for yourself?"

He patted his jeans pockets in search of his wallet, phone, keys—then remembered he didn't carry any. Not here. So he snapped the top button before looking up at her. "What would you like me to say, Amber?"

"I don't know, that I'm acting crazy? That I've been duped—by someone other than you, I mean. That it's not true."

She looked so incorruptible, like a force of nature. But something he'd learned in his month in this part of the world—nobody came to Serenity without a good reason. Or a bad one.

He opened his mouth to call her on it, but he stopped himself in time.

He'd never known someone to wear their absoluteness like a badge of honour the way she did. The moment she'd decided to let him into her house she'd decided to let him into her bed. No coquettish equivocation. Only firm decision.

This was the first time he'd seen it waver. Enough for him to take heed. To hold out his hands in conciliation. "I never lied to you, Amber. I am Hugo to my friends, my closest family."

"To everyone else?"

"I am Prince Alessandro Hugo Giordano, sixth in line to the principality of Vallemont."

The quiet that followed his statement wasn't new. The rare times Hugo found himself in a conversation with someone who wasn't aware of who he was, what he was worth, and who his relatives were, it was clear when the penny dropped.

Though this might have been the first time he was half-dressed when that realisation occurred, he thought ruefully.

A hippy beekeeper on the Central Coast of Australia had not been in the plan, meaning it was taking him a little longer to decide upon the appropriate protocol with which to navigate this moment.

Meanwhile, Amber's nostrils flared, fury dancing behind her bedroom eyes. He imagined she was finding it hard not to climb over the bed and tackle him. As unmoved by convention as she was, she could do it too.

For a man whose entire life had been ruled by ritual, no wonder she'd been impossible to resist.

"Wait," he said. "Fifth. I'm fifth in line. My uncle's recently abdicated all rights and moved to California to produce movies. Not that it matters. I am a prince in name only. I will never rule."

She blinked and it was enough to snap her from her red haze. "I don't give a flying hoot if you are set to be Master of the Universe. Don't even think about turning us out on our ears."

"Excuse me?"

"These people are special. The community needs this place. The commune is Serenity's heart. If you mess with that you will kill it dead."

That was what had her so het up? Not *who* he was, but the plans he had for this land?

What the hell had she found out? And how? This wasn't his first rodeo. He'd been discreet. Painstakingly so. Who had talked?

He did up a couple of quick buttons on his shirt before re-rolling the sleeves to his elbows. Then he moved slowly around the bed, hands out, palms up.

"Amber, until this point in time, we have been having a nice time together. I'd go so far as to say very nice. With that in mind, I suggest we sit down, have a cup of coffee and discuss any concerns you might have."

He could still fix this.

"I don't want to discuss anything with you. I just want you to tell me, right here, right now, if the rumours are true."

"Which rumours might they be, exactly?"

"That you have been meeting with the local town council. Discussing plans…development plans that may or may not put the commune in danger."

"Would that be such a bad thing?"

Emotion flickered behind her eyes. Deep, frantic, fierce. "Yes," she managed. "It would be a terrible thing."

"Look at this place, Amber. It's falling down around your ears."

"Not every home has to be a castle."

Touché. "And yet if you have the chance to sleep somewhere that doesn't whistle, drip, or threaten to fall down the hill every time you step onto the porch, it's worth considering."

"My sleeping arrangements are none of your business."

"They became my business when I began sleeping here too."

"Lucky for you that is not a problem you'll have to face again."

Hugo breathed out hard, while emotion darted and flashed behind her big brown eyes. With the tension sparking in the air between them, it was all he could do to keep from going to her and letting the slow burn of her fill the empty places inside.

"Tell me, right now, if we have made incorrect assumptions. Are you planning on developing the land? Should we be concerned?"

A muscle ticked beneath his eye. And she took it for the admission it was.

Amber slumped onto the corner of the bed, her face falling into her hands. "This can't be happening."

"I hope you understand that until anything is concrete I can't discuss the details."

She looked up at him, beseeching. "Understand? I don't understand any of this. Like why, if you are so offended by my home, you kept coming back. Was I reconnaissance? Were you hoping to create an ally in your devious plans?"

"Of course not, Amber." Hugo's stomach dropped and he came around the bed, crouching before her. "Amber, you know why I came back. And back. And back. For the same reason you took me in."

He lifted a hand and closed it around hers. Her soft brown eyes begged him to stop. Heat sat high and pink on her cheeks. Her wild waves of hair caught on a breeze coming through one of the many cracks in the woebegone shack in which she lived.

Then her fingers softened as she curled them into his.

A moment later, she whipped her hand away and gave him a shove that had him rocking onto his backside with a thump that shook the foundations, raining dust over his head as she scrambled over him and into clear space.

As he cleared the dust from his hair, his eyes, Hugo wondered how his life had come to this.

The downward spiral had begun several months earlier when he'd agreed to his uncle's sovereign command to enter into a marriage of convenience. His former fiancée—and long-time best friend—Sadie, had come to her senses and fled before they'd said *I do*, bringing about a PR nightmare for the royal family…and freedom for Hugo. The fact that he would likely have gone through with it had been a wake-up call. What had he been thinking? Where was his moral compass? Not that that should be much of a shock—he was his father's son after all.

Afterwards he'd needed to get away. Clear his head. Recalibrate. He'd never have imagined that would lead him away from a life of luxury to camping out in a small, lumpy bed in a country town in the middle of nowhere, Australia, tangled up with a woman he barely knew.

He'd not hidden his position on purpose, she'd simply never asked. Their affair had been lived in the moment, fulfilling basic needs of hunger and sleep and sex while talking about everything from *Game of Thrones* to Eastern philosophy…but nothing truly personal. His family had not come up. Nor, for that matter, had hers. He'd been so grateful to avoid talking about his own that he had given no thought as to why she might also be glad of it. Perhaps he was not the only one for whom that question opened Pandora's box. Either way, after a while, the privacy had felt like a true luxury.

"I need you to leave, Hugo," said Amber, yanking him back to the present, only this time she added, "Please."

It was enough for Hugo to push to standing. He looked around the small, dilapidated room, but he'd left nothing behind bar the impression of his head on the pillow. It didn't seem like enough.

Too late to rectify that now, he turned to walk out.

"Wait," she called, grabbing him by the arm. Before he even had the chance to feel relief she pressed past him and headed out onto her wonky porch, causing the area around her shack to tremble in response.

Ned nuzzled against his hand. And Hugo lost his fingers in the dog's soft fur, taking a moment to work out a burr.

"All clear," Amber called.

"Wouldn't want your friends to know you've been harbouring the enemy."

She glanced back at him, the morning sun turning her hair to gold, her eyes to fire. When she saw Ned at his side her mouth pursed. "Away," she called. But Ned didn't move, whether because of his deafness or his obstinacy. She clicked her fingers and with a *harumph* the dog jogged to her side.

He joined them on the porch. The old wood creaked and groaned. A handmade wooden wind chime pealed prettily in the morning breeze.

"Is that why you came to Serenity?"

Now, there was a question. One she might have thought to ask at any point during the last few weeks if she'd had a care to know anything at all about the man she'd been sleeping with. "You really want to know what I came to Serenity hoping to find?"

She only nodded mutely.

"Absolution. How about you?"

She snapped her mouth shut tight.

He raised an eyebrow. *Now, what do you have to say about that?*

Nothing, it seemed. He'd finally managed to render Amber speechless.

With that, Hugo left her there in her bright yellow gumboots, her tank top clinging to her lovely body, her hair a wild, sexy mess. He jogged down the steps and headed down the hill, past the hammock, through the field of lavender to the small dead-end dirt road on which he'd parked his car.

The urge to look back was acute but he kept his cool. Because he had the feeling that it wouldn't be the last he saw of Amber.

She might be done with him, but he wasn't done with Serenity. For he did indeed have plans for his mother's ancestral home—plans which had him excited for the first time since the debacle of the wedding that never was. He might even go so far as to say they excited him more than any other development he had ever actualised.

For Hugo was renowned for taking underused or overlooked tracts of land that others would deem too remote or too challenging, and turning them into stunning holiday playgrounds for diplomats, royalty, the rich and famous, and families alike. His series of Vallemontian resorts—including a palatial masterpiece tucked into the side of Mont Enchante and an award-winning titan overlooking Lake Glace—had been a revelation for the local economy, making him invaluable to his uncle in terms of commerce if not in terms of the line of succession.

But this one, this place…it would be all his.

When he reached the bottom of the lavender field he did look back; Amber's shack and the rest of the commune relegated to glimpses of purple and red and orange obscured by copses of gum trees.

He'd keep the natural landscape as much as possible, but the caravans, tents and shanties would of course have to go to make way for the bungalows, tennis courts, lagoon-style pool and a peach grove where Amber's shack now wobbled.

Hugo wasn't some monstrous land baron. With the council's help, he would assist them in their relocation. Help them find safer places to live.

And he would create something beautiful, something lasting, something personal to break the cycle of tragedy in his mother's family.

He would make his very personal mark on the world without trading on his family name, a constant reminder of the top job for which he and his heirs would only ever be back-ups.

Amber would just have to lump it.

Serenity's Town Hall was packed to the rafters, with people lining the walls and spilling out through the open doors. It was late enough that young ones would normally be home in bed, but nobody was missing this meeting, so they sat in messy rows on the floor at the front, making occasional mad dashes across the stage, followed by their harassed parents.

There was only one reason for the big turnout: the news had spread. Nothing this momentous had happened in Serenity since Anna had been swept away to an exotic foreign land.

Amber slumped on her bench in the third row, her legs jiggling, her thumbs dancing over her fingertips. There was a good portion of the commune lined up beside her, including Sunflower, who was humming happily despite the cacophony of white noise, and Johnno, who was staring out into space.

Only, Amber wasn't here in the hope of spotting the exotic stranger. She'd seen enough of him already, from the scar above his right eyebrow to the birthmark on the base of his left big toe—and everything in between. She shifted on her seat and cleared her throat.

She was here in case the Hinterland House plans—whatever they might be—were on the agenda in the hope she could see with her own eyes as someone shouted it down. Then Hugo would leave and things could go back to normal. Or as normal as things ever got in Serenity.

Someone, but not her.

It hadn't passed her by that her parents would have loved this kind of David and Goliath fight—though nobody would have mistaken them for David in their Gucci suits and Mercedes four-wheel drives. It made them great lawyers, but terrible parents.

How could they be expected to nurse a "difficult" baby when there was so much injustice to stamp down? Enough that Australia's most infamous human rights lawyers put the care of their only child into the hands of daycare and night nannies from six weeks of age. Their work was far too important for them to abide the distraction.

The smack of a gavel split the silence and Amber flinched, reminded of the number of courtrooms she'd been in as a child. Well, she didn't have the mental space to think about her parents today. Or ever, if at all possible. She sat taller, stopped her nervous fidgets and waited.

"Squeeze up," called a voice as someone managed to squash into the end of Amber's row, the rickety wooden bench wobbling as the crowd sardined. When she looked back to the stage, Councillor Paulina Pinkerton—the leader of the seven-member local council—and her cohorts trailed onto the stage then took their seats.

The gavel struck a second time. Amber flinched again. It was a conditioned response, like Pavlov's ruddy dog. The twitters settled to a hush, chairs scratched against the wooden floor, a teenaged boy laughed. Somebody coughed. A baby started to fret. And the town of Serenity held its breath.

"Nice to see so many of you here today. I might choose to think it's because you've heard around the traps how darned interesting our meetings are, but I fear there is some issue that has you all aflutter. So let's get through the necessaries."

The councilwoman swept through the minutes and old business with alacrity. Then she opened the floor.

"Any new business?"

The hum started up again. Whispers, murmurs, the shuffle of bottoms turning on seats. But nobody said a word.

"Fine. Next meeting will be…next Tuesday at— Ms Hartley? Did you have something to add?"

Amber blinked to hear her name being called from the councillors' table, only to realise she was on her feet. Did she have something to add? No! Legally emancipated from her indifferent parents at sixteen in a legal battle that had become a national story in a slow news week, she'd spent her life living like dandelion fluff, flitting from place to place, *not* getting involved.

Until Serenity. Sunflower had taken one look at her empty backpack, her bedraggled state and offered the shack for a night, then another, and somehow she'd found herself stuck in this sweet place, with these kind people, none of whom had a clue what was about to befall them.

This place…it was her sanctuary. And she'd harboured the enemy—however unwittingly. She owed it to them to do whatever it took to protect them.

Damn him. Damn Hugo Prince Whatever-His-Name-Was and his whole crazy family for making her do this.

Amber scooted past the knees blocking her way down the bench. Once she had reached the small rostrum—a literal soapbox attached to a stand fashioned out of a fallen tree, which had been a gift to the town from Johnno, who was a pretty brilliant artist when he was in the right head-space—Amber squared her shoulders, looked each councilman and councilwoman in the eye and prayed her parents would never hear word of what she was about to do.

"Ms Hartley." Councillor Pinkerton gave Amber an encouraging smile. "The floor is yours."

"Thank you. I'll get right to it. I have come to understand that the owners of Hinterland House are back and I believe that they have plans to develop the land. Firstly, I'd like to know if the latter is true, and, if so, I put forward a motion to stop it."

Once she had started, the words poured out of her like water from a busted pipe. Energy surged through the crowd behind her like a snake. It was electric. And she hated it. Because the thrill of the fight was in her veins after all.

"Much of Serenity belongs to the Van Halprins, Ms Hartley, and, apart from the segments bequeathed to the township, they are within their rights to develop that land."

"Into what?"

The councillor paused, clearly thinking through how much she was legally allowed to say, and legally allowed to hold back. "The plans as they are will be up for local consideration soon enough. The Prince plans to build a resort."

Whispers broke out all over the room.

Amber breathed out hard. Sunflower's rumours were one thing, Hugo's indefinite admissions another. But having Councillor Pinkerton admit to as much had Amber feeling sick to the stomach. In fact, she had to breathe for a few seconds in order to keep her stomach from turning over completely.

She glanced over her shoulder and saw Johnno grinning serenely back at her; found Sunflower watching her like a proud sister. Her gaze landed on another dozen members of their collective community—all of whom had come to Serenity in search of acceptance and kindness and peace.

Where would people like them, people like her, go if they had to move on?

She turned back to the front, her heart pumping so hard it seemed to be trying to escape her chest. The room was so still now, even the fretting baby had quieted, meaning her voice made it all the way to the rear of the room and out into the halls, hitting every ear as she said, "I ask that Council accept the inclusive community living on Serenity Hill has been in residence long enough to legally remain. I cry adverse possession."

The murmurs began in earnest. Most asking what the heck adverse possession was.

"For those who do not know the legalese," said Councillor Pinkerton into her microphone, "Ms Hartley is claiming squatter's rights."

At that, the town hall exploded as a hundred conversations began at once. Cheers came from some corners, jeers from others. The fretting baby began to cry in earnest.

The gavel smacked against the wooden table, quieting the crowd somewhat. And this time it rang through Amber like an old bell. Sweet and familiar and pure.

"Thank you, Ms Hartley. Your position has been noted. Does anyone else have anything to say on the matter?"

Amber glanced over her shoulder to find movement at the back of the hall.

A man had stepped into the aisle, a man with overlong

hair swept away from his striking face and dark hazel eyes that locked onto Amber. She didn't realise her lungs had stopped functioning until her chest began to ache.

Hugo. But not the Hugo she knew. Not the man in the worn jeans and button-downs who was happy rolling on the ground with Ned, watching her collect honey, or sitting on her stairs staring towards the horizon chewing on a blade of grass.

This was Hugo the Prince. His stark jaw was clean-shaven and he looked dashing in a slick three-piece suit with such bearing, composure and self-assurance he was barely human. Behind him stood a big, hulking bald man in black, watching over him like a hawk.

She hoped no one noticed how hard she clenched her fists.

"Your Highness, good evening, sir," said Councillor Pinkerton, the friendly note of her voice making it clear it was not the first time she'd set eyes on the man.

Hugo's deep voice rang out across the room. "If I may?"

Councillor Pinkerton waved a hurry-up hand. "Up you come, then. State your name for the record. And your purpose."

While Amber had had to climb over a tangle of legs to get to the lectern, the crowd parted for Hugo like the Red Sea.

He slowed as he neared, his head cocking ever so slightly in a private hello.

Amber hated the way her cheeks warmed at the sight of him, her heart thumping against her ribs as if giving the death throes of remembered desire. Nevertheless, she held her ground, waiting until the last moment to give up her position. Then, with an exaggerated bow from the waist, she swooshed out an arm, giving him the floor as she backed away.

Laughter coursed through the crowd.

Hugo's smile eased back, just a fraction. Enough for Amber to know she'd scored a hit.

All's fair, she thought, in love and war. And this was war.

"Councillor Pinkerton," he said, "Council members, good people of Serenity. I thank you for this opportunity to introduce myself to this community."

His hand went to his heart on the last few words, and Amber rolled her eyes.

But the crowd? They were hooked. Straining forward so as not to miss a word spoken in that deep, hypnotic, lilting voice. And he was ramping up the accent. Big time. Playing the dashing foreigner card for all it was worth.

"It has taken me far too long to return to the home of my mother's family, but in the days I have spent wandering the hills and vales your home has come to hold a special place in my heart. And I cannot wait to tell my friends and family about this gem of a place. To invite them here to meet all of you good people. To give the world a taste of Serenity."

Amber rolled her eyes again. But when she looked out over the crowd she saw even members of the commune listening with interest. Including Sunflower, who looked entranced. And then came a smattering of delighted applause.

Enough. Amber marched back up to the rostrum and gave Hugo a shove with her hip, ignoring the wave of heat that rocked through her at his touch. She grabbed the microphone so roughly that the feedback quieted the room.

"Really?" she said, her voice echoing darkly around the room. "*A taste of Serenity...?* It's like a cheesy brochure."

Hugo laughed. And she knew she had surprised him. He licked his lips, swallowing it back, but the light of it lingered in his eyes.

"He," said Amber, pointing an accusing finger towards

the Prince, "is *not* one of us. His words might be pretty but his plans are not. And I can't stand to—"

Something lodged in her throat then. Something that felt a lot like a swell of deep emotion, the kind that preceded tears.

Come on! She wasn't a crier! She breathed out hard. And managed to keep her cool.

"It would be a grave injustice to see Serenity lost under the overwhelming influx of tourism that would come by way of a resort. I hope, I *believe*, that you are with me on this point: Serenity's future must be allowed to evolve as it always has—organically."

If Hugo's words had been met with happy claps, Amber's were met with a standing ovation, and a cheer that all but lifted the roof off the place.

The gavel banged several times before Councillor Pinkerton regained control. "Assuming that's all the new business, we will keep further discussion to next week's town meeting. Date and time as mentioned earlier. Meeting adjourned."

With that, Councillor Pinkerton and the others made their way back behind their private closed door, leaving the people of Serenity to ease off their numb backsides, stretch their arms and talk excitedly amongst themselves.

Hugo stepped in and took Amber's elbow. Gently. Respectfully. But that didn't stop the sparks of heat from travelling up her arm and making a mess of her synapses as he tilted his head to murmur near her ear.

"You can't possibly believe I want Serenity to suffer."

"You have no idea what I believe. You don't know me at all."

His eyes didn't move but she imagined them sliding up and down her body as a slow smile tugged at the corners of his mouth. "You have a short memory, Ms Hartley. Or perhaps selective would be a better description."

"You want words? I can think of so many words to describe you right now, *Your Highness*. We could go on like this *all night long*."

Hugo's eyes darkened. And yep, she'd heard it too. Dragon fire gathered behind Amber's teeth as conflict and desire swirled through her like a maelstrom. But behind it all, the need to protect her town, her people, herself.

"Game on," said Hugo as he was swallowed by the crowd.

Bring it on, Amber thought as she crossed her arms and backed away. Bring. It. On.

CHAPTER THREE

HUGO TUGGED HIS cap lower over his eyes and hunched into his shoulders as he made his way up a gravel path winding through the quaint market town of Serenity. The kind of place where business hours varied daily and where as many animals sat behind counters as people.

Prospero—the bodyguard Hugo's uncle had insisted upon—was not happy about it. He did not like being in the open. Or moving slowly. Or places with tall buildings. Or cars with open windows. He particularly didn't like the fact that Hugo had ditched him in Vallemont a couple of months before and had only just made contact again, requesting his presence, now that he had been outed.

But for all the big guy's efforts at keeping Hugo safe, Hugo blamed him for the sideways glances and double-takes. The size of a telephone box, dressed in head-to-toe black, a clean-shaven head and *Men in Black* sunglasses, he looked like a soccer hooligan on steroids.

Otherwise there was no way the locals would make the connection between the guy in the ripped jeans, Yankees cap and skateboard shoes and the Prince in the three-piece suit from the meeting the night before.

Though it wouldn't take long for that to change. There was no doubt the story of Hugo's public life was being shared and spread.

A prince, fifth in line to the throne of the principality of Vallemont. An Australian mother, a father who had died when his son was fifteen, having infamously run his car off a cliff with his young mistress at the wheel. Now he was the black sheep: independently wealthy and single.

The official palace statement was that Hugo was back at work, but after the wedding debacle he'd needed to escape. Eventually he'd found himself in Serenity. Where his mother had been born.

Days had dissolved into nights, a blur of time and quiet and nothingness; of exploring the empty, echoing house which seemed uninspired by his presence as if he too were a ghost.

Until he'd walked over the other side of the hill and found a hammock strung between two trees in the shade. He'd sat down, kicked off his shoes and fallen asleep.

Upon waking, he'd looked into a pair of whisky-brown eyes. And seen colour for the first time in as long as he could rightly remember.

"Alessandro!"

Hugo followed his name to find Councillor Pinkerton sitting at a colourful wrought-iron table inside a place calling itself "Tansy's Tea Room", which looked like a middle-eastern opium den.

She waved him in and, since he needed her support to be granted planning permission for his resort, he entered, leaving Prospero at the door with a, "Stay. Good boy."

"Sit," said the councillor. "Have some tea. You look tired. A man as rich and good-looking as you should never look tired. It gives the rest of us nothing to aspire to." She clicked her fingers, called out, "A top-up on my 'Just Do It', and a 'Resurrection' for my friend, please."

"Should I be afraid?" he asked.

"It's just tea. Mostly chamomile. I'm on your side."

"Glad to hear it."

"Don't get me wrong, I'm on Ms Hartley's side too."

"I see."

"Do you?"

"You want what is best for Serenity."

"I do."

"Councillor?"

"Paulina, please."

"Paulina. Before the town meeting last night, your council had seemed extremely positive about my proposal."

"They were."

"And now? Is a green light still assured, or are we now leaning towards…khaki?"

The councillor smiled. "I can see that the resort would be good for us. An influx of tourists means an influx of the kind of money which cannot be sneezed at for a town of our size. But Ms Hartley had a point. The beauty of Serenity is its way of living. The openness, the quiet, the kindness and, most of all, the community. We are self-sufficient in the most important ways, in a great part thanks to the commune."

"I would have thought the presence of a commune has negative connotations in this day and age."

"Which is why we call it an 'Inclusive Community' on the brochures."

Two pots of tea landed on their table, slopping towards the rims as the unsteady table rocked.

Paulina poured. "So how is your mother?"

Hugo stilled at the unexpected turn of conversation. "My mother?"

"Anna. Yes. I knew her, you know. Before." She waggled her fingers as if about to go back in time. "We were good mates, in fact. Went through school together, met boys together. So how is she?"

Hugo went to say *Fine*, but something about this woman, her bluntness, the intelligence in her eyes, the fact she'd known Hugo's mother in the before, had him saying, "I think she's lonely."

"Hmm. She is remarried, no?"

"Yes."

"To a French businessman, I hear?"

"An importer, yes. He travels a great deal."

"Ah." The councillor nodded again. "Handsome though, I expect. Your father was a very handsome man. I might even go so far as to say, devastatingly so. Add the Giordano charm and…" Paulina pursed her lips and blew out a long, slow stream of air.

"So I have heard."

Paulina's eyes hardened. Then she slapped herself on the hand. "Sorry. Insensitive."

Hugo waved a hand, releasing her of any apology.

His father *had* been charming, famously so. His mother was only one of the women who'd loved him for it. The mistress who'd been driving the car that had killed him was another.

"I was there the day they met. Your mother and father. Would you care to hear the tale?"

Since Hinterland House, with its air of quiet slumber, had not yet given up any secrets, he found he cared a great deal.

"Your father was ostensibly in Australia to see the reef and the rock and forge relationships on behalf of his little-known country—but mostly to watch sports and try his fair share of our local beers. He came to our small corner to pick peaches. Your mother and I were working at the orchard that summer, handing out lemonade to the tourists. I remember so many long-limbed Germans, sweet-talking French, Americans full of bravado. And there was your father—the brooding Prince.

"A good girl, your mother. Seriously shy, she ignored his flirtation, which was a good part of why he kept it up.

He could have offered diamonds, played up his natural charisma, but he was cleverer than that. He brought her hand-picked wild flowers, notes scratched into sheaves of paper bark, the very best peach he picked every day. It took three days. When she fell, she fell hard. And I was glad to see his adoration didn't diminish for having her. They were so very much in love.

"He left for Sydney a week later. A week after that he came back for her with a ring and a proposal. And I never saw her again."

Paulina smiled. "I was sorry to hear of his passing, not only for your mother's sake. How old were you?"

"Fifteen," Hugo said without having to think about it. His headmaster had been the one to inform him, having been instructed by his uncle to wait until after the funeral. A decision had been made not to send Hugo home to keep him away from the scandal.

"Ah. A trying period in the life of a boy, at the best of times."

Hugo merely nodded.

"Ah," said the councillor, looking over Hugo's shoulder, a smile creasing the edges of her eyes as someone approached their table.

Hugo knew who it was before a word was said. The wild energy snapping at the air behind him disturbed the hairs on the back of his neck.

He let his voice travel as he said, "Now, Paulina, about that woman who stood up in front of the council last night—shall I buy the bag of lime and shovel or simply pay you back?"

The councillor's eyes widened in surprise before a smile creased her face. "Good morning, Ms Hartley."

A beat, then, "Good morning, Councillor Pinkerton."

"Paulina, please."

Hugo pressed back his chair and stood. Amber wore a

short summer dress that hung from her tanned shoulders by thin ribbons tied at her shoulders. A battered pork-pie hat sat atop her head, leaving her long honey-blonde hair to hang in waves over one shoulder.

But it was the eyes that got him every time. They were devastating. Fierce, wanton bedroom eyes that could lay civilisations to waste.

"Well, if it isn't my worthy adversary," he said.

Amber tilted her chin and looked only at Hugo's companion. "I'm so glad to have run into you, Paulina. I was hoping to have a word."

"Any time. Won't you join us?"

Amber's chin lifted. "Considering the subject, I don't think that's wise."

"I think quite the opposite. Did the two of you manage to meet properly last night?"

Hugo looked to Amber with a smile, allowing her to respond.

She gaped like a fish out of water before saying, slowly, "We did not meet last night."

"Then allow me. Amber, this is Prince Alessandro Giordano of Vallemont. Prince Alessandro, this is our supplier of all things sweet and honeyed, Amber Hartley."

"A pleasure to meet you." Hugo held out a hand. Amber's face was a concerto of emotion as she fought against the need to play nice, at least in front of others, so she didn't look like an ass.

Finally, Amber's eyes turned his way. "Prince *Alessandro*, was it?"

He nodded. "My friends call me Hugo."

"How nice for them." Then she took his hand, grabbed a hunk of skirt and curtseyed. Deeply. "Your Highness."

Until that moment Hugo hadn't realised a curtsey could be ironic. Laughter knocked against his windpipe, desperate to escape. Only years of maintaining a neutral countenance in affairs of state made it possible to swallow it down.

"Amber, sit," said Paulina. "I insist. Talk to the man. Work out your grievances. At least attempt to come up with a workable plan, for your sake and for the sake of the town. If you can't, well, you can tick 'having tea with a prince' off your bucket list."

Councillor Pinkerton pushed back her chair and stood. Hugo reached for his wallet.

"No," said the older woman. "My treat. Wouldn't want anyone thinking you'd bribed me with a pot of tea, now, would we?"

Then she held out her hand, offering the seat to Amber.

"No," said Amber, waving both hands to make it clear she meant it. "Thank you. But I couldn't."

"Your loss," said the councillor. Then, at the door she called, "She's got mettle, this one. Might take more than a peach."

Hugo's laugh left his throat before he even felt it coming. Then he ran a hand up the back of his neck, settling the hairs that were still on edge.

Amber continued to glare.

"Please join me. At the very least so that I don't have to stand here all day."

"You'd like that, wouldn't you, *Prince Alessandro*? Get some paparazzi shots of us hanging together so as to muddy the waters regarding my side of the case."

"It's Hugo. Paparazzi a fixture here in downtown Serenity?"

"Well, no. But now word is out that you are here I'm sure it won't be long."

Hugo was sure of it too, meaning his blissful few weeks of anonymity truly were over. And the time to get the plans put to bed was ticking down.

"I'm going to sit," he said. "The chair is yours if you want it."

Amber glanced around, found the table beside his was empty, and sat there instead. With her back to him.

She turned her head ever so slightly. "This isn't the first time for you, is it?"

"Hmm? I didn't catch that with you sitting all the way over there." First time for what? he wondered. Drinking tea that smelled like feet? Or locking horns with a stubborn woman he couldn't get out of his head? "First time for what?"

"Tearing the heart and soul out of a town and turning it into some fancy, homogenised getaway for the idle rich."

"Ah. I probably won't use that as the tagline of any future advertising, but yes, I have experience in this area. This will be my…seventh such resort." A beat, then, "Have you been Googling me, Amber?"

Her shoulders rolled. "It was a stab in the dark. The only semi-decent Wi-Fi around here is at Herb's Shiatsu Parlour. You can go grey waiting for a picture to load."

"But at least you'd feel relaxed while doing so."

Her mouth twitched before she turned her back on him again. He spotted the edge of the dandelion tattoo that curled delicately over her shoulder blade. He remembered the slight rise of it as he'd run a thumb over the area once. The way her muscles reacted, contracting under his touch.

"I've come up against people like you before," she said, "privileged, successful, glowing with an aura that says *don't worry, I've done this before, you're in good hands.* But just because you think you're in the right, doesn't mean that you are."

"I could say the same for you."

"I live in a shack, Your Highness. I collect and sell honey for a living. You and are I are not on the same playing field. But the biggest difference is that, while you think you are in the right, I know I am."

Hugo could have argued relativism till the cows came home. In fact, if they'd been rugged up in her bed, limbs curled around one another, it might even have been fun.

"What were you telling Councillor Pinkerton about me?" Amber asked, and Hugo gave up pretending he could focus on anything else while she was near.

He pushed his tea aside and turned back to face her. "Until the moment you arrived your name did not come up."

"I find that hard to believe."

"Are you a subject of much chatter around these parts?"

A pause. "No. Maybe. At one time. I was a newcomer too once."

"The councillor and I weren't talking about my plans at all. It turns out she knew my mother. And my father."

Talk of family? Talk of something personal? He half expected Amber to leap over the table and bolt. But her head turned a little further, giving Hugo a view of her profile. Full lips, neat nose, and a fine jaw disappearing into swathes of golden hair. When she lowered her eyes he was hit with the memory of her sleeping; hands curled under her ear, lips softly parted, lashes creating smudges of shadow against her cheeks.

She asked, "Was that a surprise?"

"It was. A good one, though."

She turned a fraction more on her chair, until her eyes found his. Big, brazen pools of whisky that he knew, from experience, darkened with desire and brightened when she laughed. "Prince Alessandro—"

"Don't do that." Hugo's voice dropped so that only she could hear. "Amber, I am still the same man you found sleeping in your hammock and took into your home. Into your bed. I am still Hugo."

Amber's throat worked as she swallowed. "Ah. But that's the name your friends call you. And I am not your friend."

"You could be." Hugo called upon years of royal conditioning to keep his messier emotions at bay, to keep himself apart. He leant towards her, close enough to see the creases now furrowing her brow, the single freckle on her neck, the way her lashes tangled as they curled. "I'd like it very much if you were."

Her chest rose and fell as her eyes darted between his. She licked her lips then glanced away. "You have history here, I understand that. But you're not the only one. Think on that as you sit in your big house, poring over your Machiavellian scheme to destroy this community."

"You paint quite the picture. You must have spent a great deal of time imagining what I've been up to since you threw me out."

Pink raced up her cheeks as her jaw clenched. "I can assure you, *Prince Alessandro*, the amount of time I have spent wondering about you is entirely proportional to my desire to figure out how to make you walk away for good."

"Hmm," he said, not believing it for a second. The deep breaths, the darkness in her eyes—she was still as aware of him as he was of her. As much as she might want to switch off the fascination they had in one another, it was still alive and well.

"Amber?"

Amber blinked several times before they both turned towards a man with raging red hair gelled into painful-looking spikes. "Tansy. Hi. Sorry, I'm taking up a table. I..."

Amber stopped when she realised that was clearly not Tansy's concern. For Tansy was staring at Hugo as if he were an alien who'd landed a spaceship inside his shop. And behind him Tansy had amassed a small crowd, a veritable sea of tie-dye and hemp.

"Is this…?" said Tansy. "Is he…?"

"Why, yes," said Amber, her voice nice and loud. "Tansy, this is Prince Alessandro Giordano, the man who is planning on stripping our hill bare."

Tansy shoved a hand between them. "So pleased to meet you, Your Highness."

"Hugo, please. My friends call me Hugo."

When the shake was done, Tansy's heavily tattooed hands fluttered to his heart. "A prince. In my tea room. I honestly don't know what to say."

"How about *Get out*?" said Amber as she hopped out of the seat and melted into the crowd. "How about *Leave our village be*? How about *We don't want your type here*?"

Hugo saw Prospero begin to head inside, clearly not liking the growing crowd. Hugo stayed him with a shake of the head.

"Will you be King?" asked a woman twirling her hair and looking at him as if he were a hot lunch.

Hugo searched the crowd until he saw Amber's profile. She was whispering to someone in the back, no doubt working them to her favour.

"No," said Hugo. "Vallemont is a principality, not a kingdom. It is protected and overseen by a royal family, the head of which is my uncle, the Sovereign Prince. There are several people between me and the crown."

A ripple of disappointment swept through the small crowd.

Hugo bit back a laugh. He heard that. But since his chance at a possible shot at the crown had been ripped away from him at the age of fifteen, he'd had to find other uses for himself. Building resorts gave his life meaning.

"Now, who here loves a lagoon? Tennis courts? Who thinks this town could do with a yoga studio?"

He no longer kept looking for Amber, but he could feel her glaring at him just fine.

* * *

Dying sunlight poured tracks of gold over the stone floor of the tiny little shopfront in Serenity she had inherited along with the beehives when she'd first arrived in town.

Honey-Honey was a teeny-tiny mud hut with a desk, an old-fashioned cash register that binged winningly as it opened, and a small back room behind a curtain. The shop floor boasted a handful of shelves filled to the brim with pots of honey and beeswaxy goodness. And Ned, who was curled up on his soft doggy bed in the sunniest corner, his face twitching as he dreamed of chasing dandelion fluff and finding an endless supply of used socks.

Amber's ancient broom tossed dust motes into the light as she swept the stone floor, preparing to close up shop for the day, when she looked up and saw a man in black as big as a house, the man she'd seen hovering around Hugo at the town meeting and again at Tansy's.

"Amber."

So busy gaping, Amber hadn't seen Hugo lurking behind him until it was too late.

Ned on the other hand was all over him—bouncing about on his back feet, nose nuzzling Hugo's hand, tail wagging as if he was in utter bliss. The big man with Hugo looked ready to take down the dog at the first sign of teeth.

"Ned, heel." She clicked her fingers, knowing he'd feel the vibration if he didn't hear her words, and Ned gave her a side eye before ambling to her feet and plopping to his haunches with a snort. His version of a doggy eye-roll. "We're closed."

"This is the honey we collected?"

She winced at the use of "we". "Some. Several local apiaries sell their wares in this space. Different bees, different flora, make for different tastes, different texture, different healing properties." Amber tugged the strap of her bag over her head until it angled across her body. Not as if it was some kind of shield. Righteousness was all the armour she needed. "What are you doing here? I said all I needed to say at the tea room."

"I didn't. Are those live bees in the wall?"

He peered through the dark hexagonal observation pane where a small hive of bees buzzed and worked. Huffing out a breath, Amber turned on the nearest lamp, creating a pool of gold on the floor and showcasing the sweet little hive in her wall.

Hugo pressed a finger towards the glass but didn't touch. The one person she'd ever seen think before leaving a fingerprint she'd have to clean.

Humming contentedly, he moved around the space, picking up tubs of wax, reading over the names of the several flavours of honey. "Amber, this is charming. Why didn't you tell me about this place when we were...?" Hugo waved a hand to intimate the rest.

"Hooking up?" she finished helpfully.

The man in black squeaked, then covered it with a manly cough.

Hugo turned, ignoring his big friend, his eyes only for Amber. "Is that what we were doing?"

"Sure. Why? What else would you call it?"

Amber tucked her hair behind her ear and feigned nonchalance, even while her knees started to tingle at the way he was looking at her. But he didn't offer an alternative. He did rub at his hand, no doubt aching from having shaken the hand of every person in town since his "disguise" had been blown. Traitors. Fawning over the enemy just because of an accident of birth. And charm. And those magnetic good looks.

She pressed her palm to her belly and rolled her shoulders.

The townsfolk might all be blinded by the trappings but

not her. She could take him down all on her own. They'd thank her for it later.

He rubbed at his hand again, wincing this time.

"Oh, for Pete's sake." Amber turned on her heel and went to the freezer behind the curtain in the back, grabbed a bucket and filled it with ice. She plonked the bucket onto her counter and clicked her fingers at Hugo.

He came as asked.

"Good boy."

A solitary eyebrow shot north. Amber tried her dandiest to remember that she didn't find the move seriously sexy. Not any more.

When Amber looked back at Hugo it was to find his gaze had dropped to her smile, where it stayed for a beat or two. Her lips tingled under the attention, remembering how that look usually ended. Heat trickled through her veins and she began to itch all over, her body wanting what it could no longer have.

"Give me your hand," she demanded, all business.

He looked at his hand, surprised to find he'd been rubbing it. Then he looked at the bucket of ice. "I don't think so."

"Don't be such a baby."

The big guy made another strangled noise in the doorway, though this one sounded more like a laugh.

"Have you never had this done before?"

"I'm usually better protected."

The laughter from the doorway came to an abrupt halt.

Amber took her chance, grabbed Hugo's hand, and before the warmth of his skin, the familiarity of his touch, overcame her she shoved it into the ice.

Hugo let forth a string of expletives, in multiple languages no less. Amber enjoyed every one. Hugo shifted from foot to foot and cleared his throat.

"You okay there, buddy?"

"Peachy," he muttered.

And she shoved his hand just a little deeper. "So who's the elephant in the room?"

"Hmm?"

"The giant who is trying very, very hard not to tackle me right now."

"That would be Prospero. My bodyguard."

"Why the heck do you need a bodyguard?"

Hugo raised the single eyebrow.

She raised one right back. "Seriously. If you were a president or a drug lord or something, sure. Are you afraid the townspeople will throw mantras at you? Or is this because of *me*? Wow. Does he have a dossier on me? What's my code name?"

Hugo's brow furrowed, reminding her of the Furrows of Important Dreams on the day they had first met. That gravity that had drawn her to him in the first place. It was almost enough for her to let it go. Almost.

"Why do you need a bodyguard? I really want to know."

"Last year my uncle and his family were having a picnic by a local waterfall when a band of masked men attacked. Whether to kidnap, scare or worse, it was never clear. The small security detail managed to fend them off but the perpetrators got away. The royal family upped security across the board. Prospero has been my devoted body man ever since. Though I believe he feels as if he must have done something terrible in a former life to end up on my detail. Right, big guy?"

Aw, crud. "Was anyone hurt?"

"Not physically, no. But my uncle has been hypervigilant ever since, making demands on the family no one in power should ever make."

Amber had a thought. "Is he the one making you turn Serenity into a resort?"

Hugo smiled. “No. In fact, when he finds out he will not be pleased.”

“Why?”

“Because every decision he makes is for the good of Vallemont. This decision is for the good of me.”

“No kidding.”

It was hard to get her head around. For Amber had known him before he was royal. Or at least before she’d *known* he was royal. The point was she’d known him when he was *Hugo*. A man of unremitting curiosity, acerbic wit and nothing but time. An avid listener with an easy smile. Smart as anyone she’d ever met, including her parents, who were called on to untangle the trickiest international laws on a daily basis. But, basically, a dissolute gadabout.

Yet he was a successful businessman in his own right. He accepted a bodyguard because he was deemed important to the crown and yet was content to stand up to his uncle if he believed it was the right thing to do.

While her brain understood the duality, a small part of her was still clinging on to the man who’d cleaned out her gutters when he’d seen grey clouds on the horizon; who’d rubbed her feet without being asked as they’d snuggled on her ancient couch.

She’d kicked that man out of her bed.

And created an adversary.

No. He’d done that. He wanted to build this resort of his for his own ends. She was merely standing up for what she believed was right.

Hugo made to lift his hand from the ice and she grabbed it. “Stop moving.” She wasn’t done with him just yet. “So this bodyguard of yours. Where was he when we were…?” She flapped a hand.

“I was playing hooky.”

“From?”

“Real life.”

"Seriously?"

"You keep questioning the veracity of my answers. I have no reason to lie to you, Amber. I never have. All you ever had to do was ask."

She shook her head, but didn't have a comeback. It wasn't the first time she'd been accused of avoiding intimacy, but it was the first time she stuck around to continue talking to the person who'd made the accusation.

She told herself it was a learning opportunity. How not to get fooled next time. Next time what? Next time she found a hot man in her hammock and dragged him back to her cave to have her way with him for a few weeks?

Cheeks heating, she gritted her teeth. "From the little I know of Vallemont, it sounds like one of the prettiest spots in Europe. All craggy mountains and verdant valleys? Am I right?"

Hugo nodded.

"So, as far as real life goes, being a prince of such a realm must have been terrible. And being rich and handsome and royal surely feels all the same after a while."

His smile turned to laughter—rough and soft, so that she felt it right deep down inside.

"Alas, now real life has found you again," she said, "you have to go back to princeing. Is that the right verb?"

"You done?"

"For now."

"Good. Because it's my turn. Are you ready to tell me how you ended up here yet?"

Amber flinched. And said nothing.

"Nothing? Really? I showed you mine, now you show me yours. Quid pro quo. Or else I'm no longer the bad guy for not sharing my life story."

Dammit. He had her there.

"So what were you running away from?"

"Who said I was running away?"

"Those of us who are not where we started are all running from something. Responsibility. Danger. Boredom. So which was it?"

"I didn't run," she said, the words feeling as though they were being pulled from her throat with pliers. "I had an honest-to-goodness chance at a fresh start so I took it. I wasn't running, I was exploring."

"To what end?"

"It didn't even matter. It was all new for me out there. And all mine."

She knew she wasn't making sense to anyone but herself, but Hugo didn't press. He had a way of knowing just how far to push before giving her breathing space. She'd never met anyone who could read her the way he did.

Feeling as if a spotlight was shining on her, about to give her deepest insecurities and darkest fears away, she glanced over Hugo's shoulder to the shadow in the doorway. "So how did he summon you, Prospero? Did he send up a bat signal? Or would that be a crown signal? One in the shape of a ceremonial sword, perhaps?"

"He used a telephone signal, ma'am."

"How modern. I hadn't realised he even had a phone. Or a title, for that matter."

Hugo laughed deep in his throat, only just loud enough for her to catch it. The way it was when they'd lain in bed at night. The way it was when he'd swept her hair from the back of her neck to find that kiss spot that brought her out in goosebumps, before murmuring all the things he planned to do to her the next moment he could get her naked.

In the quiet that followed, Amber held her breath, hoping Hugo had no clue where her thoughts had gone. His charm was dangerous. His likeability her liability. His power, his political and personal influence, a real, living thing.

People like Hugo, like her own parents, were used to getting their way.

Not this time.

Not on her watch.

"And what exactly did our friend *the Prince* tell you about where he had been, Prospero? And what he had been up to?"

Prospero shot a slightly panicked look to his boss. "His Highness does not kiss and tell."

Amber burst out laughing. "Meaning he did exactly that. I never mentioned kisses, and nobody else in town knew about any kisses, so that leaves him." Amber waggled a hand Hugo's way.

Hugo caught her gaze, held it. "You really didn't tell anyone about what had kept you so busy the last few weeks? Not a girlfriend? A shaman? A friendly possum?"

Amber folded her arms loosely across her chest and slowly shook her head.

"More's the pity. My reputation could do with some bolstering in this town."

She laughed again. "Not going to happen."

"Really? You haven't been fighting the desperate urge to drop into casual conversation that I am a man of experience."

"No."

"And taste." His gaze dropped to her mouth before lifting back to her eyes. His expression darkening, all touches of humour now gone. "And unparalleled skill?"

"Hugo."

He paused. A slow, warm smile spreading across his face and making her knees shiver. Because—dammit!—she'd called him Hugo. She'd been so determined to stick with *Your Highness*.

"Amber," he lobbied, with grave deliberation.

His deep voice, the crinkle around his eyes, did things

to her basic structure. Turning her bones to liquid. Quieting her worries. Until she felt as if she was floating just a little above the ground.

She cleared her throat. "How's your hand?"

"Numb."

Rolling her eyes, Amber dragged his hand from the ice, feeling a little bit better when he winced. "And now?"

Hugo wriggled his fingers, twisted his hand and grinned at her.

She grabbed a tea towel and threw it at him. "Try not to drip. I've just swept. Now, while this has been a delight, you really must leave. It's time Ned and I got home."

Hugo wiped his hand. And nodded. "Fine. But first, the reason I came by. I brought you this." He held out his hand and Prospero handed over a rolled-up sheaf of papers held together with a pink and gold ribbon.

Amber looked at it warily. "What is it?"

"Take it home. Look it over. We can talk about it tomorrow. Once you've had time to think."

"I've thought. I don't want to talk to you tomorrow. Unless it's to hear you say you were mistaken and you're sorry for causing our quiet little community such distress. And that you are leaving and never coming back."

Hugo's eyes darkened. And he took a step closer. Or maybe he didn't. Maybe he just looked at her in that intense, indulgent way she found so overwhelming. As if she'd been tumbled by a rogue wave, not sure if she'd find her feet ever again.

"Fine," she said, whipping out a hand to take the sheaf of paper. Taking care not to let her fingers touch his. Those fingers had a way of stripping her defences and right now those defences were all she had.

When Hugo stepped back she felt that too. As though someone had pulled a blanket from her shoulders, and a stone from her chest.

He turned to leave before looking back. "Amber."

Swallowing his name, she simply waited.

"Is fighting this what the town needs? Is it even what they want?"

Amber reeled. "Of course it is."

"They seemed pretty happy about the idea at the meeting."

"They were happy a real live prince was in their midst. And you knew they would be. Why else did you shave? And wear that slick suit? And give them your smile?"

"My smile?"

"You know the one. All teeth and charm and eye crinkles. You are well aware that it makes knees go wobbly from a thousand paces."

Amber found herself glad the light was low, otherwise the look in his eyes might have melted her on the spot.

"I know perfectly well how stubborn you are, Amber. And how much you care. Take care you don't lose yourself inside a blind crusade."

Amber flinched. Hugo could not have picked better words with which to cut her. Deep. The number of times she'd accused her parents of getting caught up in doing right, in fighting for the little people, in pursuing justice at all costs, without really stopping to imagine the consequences…

She stamped her foot so that Ned would come to her side and lost her hand in the familiar softness of his fur. "I know what I'm doing."

"Okay, then." He reached a hand to the doorjamb, breathed, and turned back to her one last time. "You were quite the sight up there at the town meeting. Banging on the lectern. Riling the masses. I was waiting for you to climb the thing and punch your hand in the air. If you had I am absolutely certain the council would have agreed to anything. Including running me out of town with flaming pitchforks."

Amber breathed. Or at least she tried. Her throat threatened to close down. She wasn't good at taking compliments, never having had reason to learn when she was a kid.

With that he tapped his knuckles on the counter, gave Prospero a look and left.

Leaving Amber all alone with her weak knees, her deaf dog and the insatiable hunger that was gnawing at her insides.

Though it wasn't for food. Not even a bit.

CHAPTER FOUR

"IS THAT A HELIPAD?" Johnno's voice hummed at the corner of Amber's brain as she sat back in one of Sunflower's straw-filled beanbags and rubbed at her temples, breathing in the scent of Sunflower's stew warming over the brazier near her feet.

"And stables. Look!" That was Sunflower, resident animal whisperer, her fey voice tinged with excitement.

But Amber didn't want to look. She wanted to figure out what it meant that Hugo had given her the architectural plans in the first place. Plans so detailed they had clearly been worked on for some time.

"Does he think I'll go all gooey at the fact he has given away a big chunk of advantage? Does he think I'm that easy?"

"Honey," said Sunflower. "Who are you talking about?"

She flung her arm away from her eyes and said, "Hugo!"

At the concerned faces of her friends, her comrades, these sweet, trusting souls, she remembered everyone else knew him as Prince Alessandro Giordano of Vallemont. "The Prince. The Prince gave them to me."

"Oh, my."

Amber sat forward as best she could in the lumpy home-made beanbag. Firelight sent long, scary shadows over Sunflower's brightly painted caravan beyond. "You all agree, right? That we need to fight this? I'm not on some kind of blind crusade."

"Oh, yes." Sunflower swayed side to side to the music in her head.

"Johnno?"

"Hmm? Sure thing. I only wish he was dastardly. It'd be easier to dislike the guy."

Sunflower leaned down to give her man a hug. Then shoved a bowl of stew under Amber's nose. "You look pale. Eat."

Knowing better than to argue, Amber ate, spooning mouthfuls of unexpected vegetables and some kind of gamey meat into her mouth.

While Sunflower said, "Everyone does seem to be stuck on how charming he is. And how handsome. Do you think he's handsome?"

Johnno nodded.

Amber loved these people with every recess of her stone-cold heart, but at times she wished they were a bit more commercially switched on.

"Don't you think he's handsome, Amber?" Sunflower asked.

She put the half-eaten stew on the ground. "Sure. I guess." *Handsome didn't even come close.* "But what that has to do with any of this, I have no idea."

"Don't you?"

Something in Sunflower's voice made Amber wonder exactly how much she had been paying attention. Was it possible she'd known Hugo was in Amber's bed the morning she'd come by? That Ned hadn't been the one making the banging noises?

If any of them knew she'd been the one feeding him and watering him while he made his devious plans she was sure they'd never look at her the same way again.

Then Sunflower grabbed a set of bowls to hold the corners of the plans down. "I just don't see it. Far too clean-cut for my taste. Not like my darling scruffy Johnno. Though it is hard to believe he was left at the altar."

"He was what, now?" said Amber.

"Left at the altar by a runaway bride."

Amber looked from one friend to the next to find them nodding along. "How did you even know about this?"

Johnno stuck a stick in the fire and sparks shot up into the sky. "Everyone knows."

Amber let out a breathy, "Jeez…"

Playing hooky from real life, my ass.

"So this was recent?"

"Oh, yes."

When he'd opened his eyes and looked into hers that very first day, she'd had to brace herself so as not to fall right into his gaze. For she'd felt his pain in that unguarded moment as if it had been her own.

Like a standing redwood suffering the notches of an axe. Not broken so much as wounded. Needing somewhere safe to hole up. To heal. It had been half the reason she'd thrown caution to the wind and invited him into her home.

Had she been a transition fling? Why the heck did it matter?

Because you're envious of some other woman who turfed him out, when you should be high-fiving her. Starting an exclusive club—women who've turned away the estimable right-royal Hugo.

Sunflower went on, oblivious, "As the story went, he handled it like a true gentleman, not saying a bad word about the girl. A few days later they did a television interview together. It was honest, forgiving. Turns out they're old friends and they both wished the very best to one another for the future."

Sadie. The fact that this mystery woman had a name felt like a dagger to Amber's stomach. Which was ridiculous.

Amber had no hold over Hugo. And he none over her. Her stomach would simply have to catch up.

"He might be the big bad wolf, but boy, does he make it look appealing."

Amber dropped her head into her hands and let out a sorry sob.

"Hey," said Johnno, back with them. "Doesn't this design remind you of a honeycomb shape?"

Of course she had noticed.

"Oh, my," Sunflower breathed, glancing at Amber. "How about that?"

"And did you also see where the buildings are situated? Right here, on this exact spot." The colourful caravans, shanties, tents, tree houses and demountables obliterated by the stroke of a pen. As if they'd never been.

Just about the only section of the hill which had been preserved were the two trees to which her hammock was hitched.

Rubbing the heels of her palms deep into her eyes, she tried to hold back the memory, but it came anyway.

It had been late afternoon. The air had been filled with pollen and that strange heaviness that heralded a storm.

She'd snapped off a chunk of honeycomb and given it to him. He'd carried it back through the forest to the shack, holding it up to the sun, rubbing it between his fingers, licking the thing till she'd tripped over her own feet.

Somehow they'd ended up at the hammock, then in the hammock. Together. It had been one of the most perfect moments of her entire life.

And then it hit her. *That* was why he'd given her the plans.

He knew she'd see that he'd saved those trees. *That manipulative bastard.*

She was furious she hadn't seen it straight away. She'd been raised by master manipulators after all.

Her parents, Bruce and Candace Grantley—OBEs—had been "influencers" before the term was popular. On the surface that seemed like a compliment. A sign of respect. But really it meant they knew how to sway, cajole, manoeuvre, distract, use bias to engineer outcomes to their liking.

Embroiled in an international child labour case, they'd begun bringing Amber along to newspaper photo shoots, on television interviews, using her as an example of a child of privilege. A counterpoint to the children they were representing in some far-off country. But only after taking her braces off five months early. She'd overheard her mother telling her father a bright white smile would "play better".

Now, at twenty-seven, she had bottom teeth that overlapped. Just a little. Just enough to remind her the lengths her parents had gone to in order to get their way.

"True gentleman my ass," Amber muttered, sweeping the plans up into her arms, shoving them under her arm and taking off up the hill.

Hugo sat on the large portico at the rear of Hinterland House, watching the dragonflies dance over the surface of the moonlit fountain beyond.

His phone buzzed. A quick check showed him it was from his aunt Marguerite.

He ignored it.

He'd been getting messages from the palace—mostly from his aunt—since he'd first taken off. He'd made it clear he had no intention of telling them where he was until he was ready.

He was a grown man. And not near enough to the throne for his whereabouts to matter to anyone but his mother. He was in one piece, he was keeping his head down, and after recent events he needed some time. And he would very much appreciate it if they'd leave him the hell alone.

When the phone buzzed again, he switched it off.

Prospero came outside with a green metal coil and a box of matches. He lit the end until a whirl of sweet-smelling smoke curled into the air.

"What is that?" Hugo asked.

"They call it a mozzie coil. One of the women in town gave it to me earlier when she saw my bites." Prospero tugged a black sleeve up to his elbow, revealing a handful of red welts.

"Do you need those seen to?"

The big man shook his head. "Just mosquitos. Saliva takes out the itch."

"Did the woman in town help you with that too?"

Even in the growing darkness Hugo saw the red creeping up the big man's throat.

He'd been in town a few days now. It would be worth getting his take on the situation. "So, Prospero, you have been paying attention." One could only hope. "What do you think of my plans?"

Prospero did his soldier poster move, looking out into the middle distance. "I couldn't say, Your Highness."

"You couldn't or you won't?"

"Yes, sir."

Smarter than he looked. "And what do you think of my opposition?"

"Sir?"

"Need I be worried about Amber Hartley?"

Prospero stilled. "In what way? Do you think she is dangerous? Has she threatened you again?"

"I don't think she is about to jump out of the bushes and attack me, if that's what you're worried about."

Prospero's face worked before he came to a decision. "You joke. I understand that. But you must know, Your Highness, that the possibility of someone jumping out of the bushes and attacking you is why I am here."

Hugo winced. Right. Bad choice of words.

As he had intimated to Amber, not that long ago his uncle, aunt and their multiple sets of twins had been near-victims of a targeted attack while on a family picnic within the palace grounds.

Hugo sat forward. "I am not blasé, Prospero. I promise. I have every intention of living a long and healthy life. If you feel that I am placed in any real danger, I will heed your concerns. Now, please tell me you understand I was joking. That Amber is not a physical threat."

A muscle twitched under Prospero's eye. "My observations suggest you do not see straight when it comes to Ms Hartley. You are not careful when you are with her."

Hugo blinked. "I believe you are right."

For Amber Hartley had been a safe haven when his life was in upheaval. A slip from reality when reality chased hot on his heels. No expectations, no burden, no demands. He could not have been more grateful that he had met her when he had. And that kind of thing left a mark.

Which didn't even begin to cover the way his blood still heated at the sight of her. How precisely he could remember the scent of her hair. The taste of her skin. How deeply satisfied he felt when he made her smile. Even fighting with her was the most fun he remembered having in years. *Years*.

Yes, Amber Hartley had left a mark on him. A brand.

But he would not change his mind about the resort because of it. No matter how much he wished he'd had one more week in her bed.

While his father had been Sovereign Prince, Hugo had been the next successor. But when his father died he'd been too young to take the throne and his uncle had acceded instead, shunting him to sixth in line as his uncle's children now took precedence. It had forced Hugo to reimagine his life. It had taken time. He'd been angry for a while, had acted up, thrown money around. Until one of his wild investments had paid off. And just like that he'd found purpose. His resorts had seen stupendous success, channelling millions into the Vallemont economy and projecting the small, quiet principality into the international consciousness.

Families in Vallemont had safer jobs and better incomes, in thriving townships because of him. It was no crown, but it was a fine legacy, something of which he was immensely proud.

One he planned to keep refining, perfecting, until he made a true name for himself, by himself. Until the loss of the crown no longer mattered at all.

"Fear not the beautiful blonde in our midst, my intrepid friend. Once the resort plans are through council, my work here will be done and the project team will take over from there. We will head home."

Prospero wasn't the sharpest tool in the shed. Slipping away from him in Vallemont had been far too easy. But, as Hugo was beginning to find, he was a genuinely nice fellow.

"Do you feel as if you are being punished for something, having ended up with me, Prospero?"

Prospero swallowed and said, "I won't leave you. Not again."

"No. Of course. I totally understand. I just thought it would be a good opportunity to case the place. Perhaps see if any…women have an insight into the seedy underbelly of the town once the sun goes down."

Prospero looked to the door, then to Hugo, then to the door. "You keep your phone near by and you answer if I call."

"Yes, sir!"

"I see how you ignore the phone when the palace calls. Promise me."

Right. "Promise. Cross my heart. Hope to die."

His face looked pained at the thought. Big guy needed to lighten up.

"Lock all the doors. I will be back in an hour."

"Why don't you make it two?"

Hugo sat and listened to the rustle of wind in the trees, breathed in the sweet scent of gum trees and red dirt and wondered how he'd gone thirty-some years without feeding the Australian half of his soul.

The patter of feet on stone caught Hugo's attention moments before Ned bounded up onto the patio.

"Hey, Ned," Hugo said, leaning forward and opening his arms to the dog who came in for a cuddle.

Meaning his owner wouldn't be far behind.

Like a ghost she emerged from the shadows, skin glowing in the moonlight, hair floating behind her. A sylph, ethereal, so beautiful, Hugo's heart stuttered.

"Down, boy," Hugo murmured, pulling himself to standing.

While Ned, lovely, near-deaf Ned, who could pick up on human emotion from a mile away, dropped to his haunches in response.

"Okay," Hugo said, releasing him, after which the dog happily trotted off inside the house, then, "Well, if it isn't Amber Hartley, local beekeeper, representative of the little people, and excellent cooker of pancakes."

She baulked at the reference to the one time she'd cooked him breakfast before their cocoon had imploded. But then she collected herself and jogged up the back stairs and slammed a bunch of scrunched-up paper on the table beside him.

"Would that be the plans I gave to you earlier, rolled up all neat and tidy?"

"Sorry," she said, clearly not sorry at all. "I hope you have spares."

Hugo poked a thumb over his shoulder and Amber followed with her gaze. Her eyes widened when she saw the state-of-the-art computer system he'd set up on the Queen Anne dining table, the plans open right now on one of the three forty-inch monitors.

"I can't believe your gall!"

"Which gall?"

"Tennis courts. Seriously? And a spa? As for us, you levelled our part of the hill. As if we never existed."

"You didn't like it, then?"

"Like it? It made me feel physically ill!" She even looked a little grey, but it could have been the moonlight.

"And your friends? I'm assuming you shared the plans with them."

She snorted. "Johnno now wants his own helipad."

Interesting. "So what didn't *you* like about it? Be specific."

"Apart from the fact you plan to wipe out the commune in one fell swoop?"

"*Move* the commune."

"Excuse me?"

"There is a tract of land on the other side of town I had the planners put aside with space to build a number of cottages. More than enough to relocate everyone."

She blinked. "Those were meant for the commune? With the vegetable gardens? And neat little paths? The window sills filled with lavender?"

"Yes." Hugo realised he'd crossed his arms.

"Have you actually visited the hill? Apart from my place, of course."

The two of them locked eyes a moment, a spark zapping between them as they both remembered. Amber looked away first, tucking her hair behind her ear before frowning at the floor.

"Willow's caravan broke down on the hill twenty-five

years ago. Tomas, her ex-husband, came down from Sydney to help her fix it and has lived in his tent next door ever since. Dozens of others have come and gone since. Sunflower and Johnno arrived a couple of years before I did. They'd been struggling to have kids for years, and coming here, to a place that was quiet and clean, helped them lick their wounds, to start afresh. Johnno lives in a tree house outside Sunflower's van. It could never be replicated. This community has been here long enough that nature has grown up around it. Grass and flowers and trees and shrubs connecting their homes to the earth. And you want to move them into matching cabins?"

"I'd be amenable to hearing input from the commune about the exact designs."

Amber ran a hand over her forehead, clearly not fine with it. And he knew that if he offered to move them an inch to the left but keep everything the same she'd still fight him.

"I don't have to make any concessions, Amber. The land is mine."

"I'm well aware—"

Hugo leaned forward. "I had my lawyers look into it. And by lawyers I mean the Sydney branch of the top firm in New York, so they are au fait with local law. Squatters' rights don't apply in your case."

She took so much time to speak he wondered how long she could hold her breath. "Why not?"

"I'm more than happy to give you a copy of their findings. It goes for over a hundred pages."

She held out a hand.

He coughed out a laugh. "I don't have one on me, but I promise I will get it to you."

Hugo pictured the plans for the estate. The vineyard that would sit so prettily on his side of the hill, the beautifully crafted structures taking advantage of the views on her side. The way his family's land, his mother's land, could be of use…his mother who had not felt much at all since his father's death, merely going through the motions of living her life. The way he could create something beautiful, functional, recreational and successful on his own. For her. And for himself. Without palace backing, palace oversight, or palace fingers delving into his financial pockets. He needed to do this. To create a legacy that was his alone.

With a growl, Amber plopped down in the cane chair beside his; legs stretched out in front of her, one arm bent behind her head, the other lying gently across her belly.

"That's it? You've given up? If I'd known it would be that easy I'd have got my lawyers onto you sooner."

"I come from a long line of lawyers; they do not scare me." She smiled from beneath the mask of her arm. "I'm just suddenly feeling very, very tired. Can we call a truce? For five minutes."

"Let's make it ten."

She held out her hand and he shook it. Holding on longer than necessary. Then again, she didn't let go either.

Finally, their hands parted, fingers sliding past one another, leaving tingles in their wake. And her hand once more moved to rest across her belly.

Watching her lie there, a picture of long-limbed, brown-skinned, earthy grace, he was well aware that there was something to be said for simply wanting *her.* She stirred and he dragged his hungry gaze away.

"Can you smell that?" she asked.

Hugo sniffed. "Cut grass? Night air?"

"Exactly. I don't know what it's like where you're from, but the cities I've lived in don't smell like this."

"No, they do not."

A pause, then, "What is it really like? Where you're from?"

"We have grass in Vallemont, like here. Night skies, like here."

"Fine…but—"

"Fine. It's…glorious! Tucked into a valley, surrounded by stunning mountains. Lakes like glass. Towns out of a Christmas card. With smart, sophisticated, friendly people. Last year we were also voted as having the cutest sheep on the planet."

"Sheep."

"Fluffy, white, say 'Baa' a lot."

The woman knew how to deadpan. "If it's so perfect over there, why did you really come here? And none of that 'playing hooky from real life' bull. Give me the unvarnished truth."

"So bolshie this evening." Her face was blank, but something—in her voice, in the shift of her body—alerted him. The town had been talking and she'd been listening. "You've visited Herb's Internet Café and Shiatsu Parlour, haven't you?"

She rolled her eyes. "I haven't Googled you! Why would I need to when you are right here?"

"Because you don't like asking hard questions when it might mean having to answer some of your own."

She growled again, this time shaking fists at the sky. "I thought princes were meant to be diplomatic."

"I thought hippies were meant to be mellow."

The growl turned to laughter. "You are infuriating, did you know that?"

"I've always thought myself rather charming."

"I'll bet." Her fists dropped, softening before her hands landed on her belly yet again. "The people in this place… For all its inherent loveliness, it's a small town. News travels fast and twists and turns as it goes. Whatever I might have heard, I'd prefer finding out the truth from the horse's mouth."

"Neigh."

She laughed again, then frowned at him as if she was struggling to figure him out. "Tell me about your wedding."

This time he had seen it coming. "You mean my non-wedding."

"If you like."

He sat forward, looked out into the dark night, and chose his words with care because this one wasn't all on him. "After the attack on my uncle he saw need to put his house in order, and so he offered me a deal. Marry or else."

"Or else what?"

"Being that she was born here, my mother is not of royal blood. After my father died, her link to the royal household diminished. Once I turn thirty-three, it diminishes further. If I am not married by that date my place in the line of succession will be forfeited and my royal rights depreciated, making my mother's rights non-existent. With no prince as her husband, no prince as a son, her title would no longer have meaning. The palace—her home for the past thirty years—would no longer be available to her."

"You can't mean that he intended to kick her out?"

Hugo could feel Amber's sense of righteousness kick in. It flowed from her pores like the electricity that rumbled through the air around here right before a storm. He fed off it, releasing his own indignation, which he had kept held down deep inside all this time.

"Most unfair but there you have it."

"That's scandalous. It's…it's blackmail."

"Pretty much."

She shook her head; livid, riled, she could have been a Valkyrie. "I thought my parents were master manipulators, but your uncle takes the crown."

"Literally."

She looked to him then, a moment passing before she

caught up. A smile passing over her bright eyes. "But you didn't marry."

"No, I did not."

"So, the girl. The woman. Your…" She flapped a hand at him, the way she did when she hit a thought she found too uncomfortable to voice. The fact that his ex-fiancée fell into that pile was interesting, to say the least.

"Sadie," Hugo said, "my intended, grew up in the palace, the daughter of a maid, and has been my best friend since as far back as I can remember. When I told her of my predicament she agreed to marry me out of the goodness of her heart, not for any romantic reason at all. But at the last she decided blackmail wasn't the best way to start a marriage. So she jumped out of a window at the palace and ran for the hills. On the way, a friend of mine—Will Darcy—found her on the side of the road, rescued her, whisked her away to safety, and the two of them fell madly in love."

"Oh. Wow. That news did *not* make it to Serenity."

"Small mercies."

"Were you—*are* you—okay with that?"

"Will and Sadie? I am immensely grateful they found one another. It let me off the hook big time."

He smiled, but she simply waited for him to stop joking and answer the question she'd asked.

"They are both wonderful people whom I care for very much. And I am truly happy for them both. Does that make me sound warm and generous, or a monster for not being broken-hearted?" It was a question he had asked of himself more than once in the weeks since it had all gone down.

She thought about it. "It sounds like not marrying her was the right decision. Happy ending."

Right. Okay, then. A weight he didn't even know he'd still been carrying lifted away from his shoulders.

"And what happened with your mother?" she asked.

"What with the PR disaster brought upon us by my runaway bride, Sadie and I managed to make a deal with my uncle that suited us all better. She promised not to marry me or anyone in my family and he would agree to leave our mothers alone and never to meddle in our love lives again."

A light lit Amber's eyes. "Sounds like a good deal."

"Sadie is a much better negotiator than I will ever be."

"I like the sound of her."

"I believe she'd like the sound of you too."

Hugo hadn't felt the words coming, but as soon as they were said he knew them to be true. Sadie would take one look at Amber and see a kindred spirit for sure. Something unlocked inside him at the thought.

"So you don't have to marry any more?" Amber asked, her voice now more careful.

"I do not." And then he understood the reason for her care and he felt another door open inside. If he didn't curb the unlocking soon he'd have nowhere left to hide. "I did not latch on to you hoping you might be my next victim, Amber. What happened between us…"

"Yes. Okay. No need to go there."

In the moonlight, this beautiful woman made of fight and fire lying within reach, he wasn't so sure any more.

But Amber went on. "And your mother is now safe. I'm glad for her. It must have been frightening, the prospect of being kicked out of her home for no reason other than the whim of one man."

Hugo went to nod…but caught himself in time. Clever girl. While he'd been trying to figure out ways of getting her to trust him again, she'd just tied him neatly in a big fat knot.

"Ironic, don't you think?" she went on. "That fear for the loss of home sent you rushing to marriage. Yet that is what you plan to inflict on all of us. On me."

His smile was without humour. "Ah, but I did not fear

the loss of my home for myself. My connection to the palace is tenuous. I could happily live anywhere. A four-poster bed in Paris. A tent in the Sahara. A hammock slung between two gum trees. As, I believe, would you."

He'd said it in jest. But beneath it, like a silver thread in a sea of black, it twisted through the night connecting them. Like a language only they knew. Secret stories, stolen moments that belonged only to them.

"So there's really no chance you might one day rule?"

"The succession plan is ancient and twisted. And if you ask Reynaldo, the current uncle in charge, he is going to live for ever." He sat forward on the chair, leaning towards her, now determined to find another way in. "It's just a title, Amber. A side note in my bio that refers to the family into which I was born. Just as you are a Hartley, I am a Giordano."

"Ah, but I was not born a Hartley."

Just when he began to feel comfortable, she knocked him sideways. Yet again. "You weren't?"

"I was born Amanda Grantley. But after I legally divorced my parents when I was sixteen I also changed my name."

"Excuse me, you divorced your parents?" His mind shot back to the rare times he'd been able to get anything out of her about them and all he came up with was lawyers and master manipulators.

"Separated. Emancipated. No longer governed by. Anyway, I picked a name near enough to instinctively respond in answer to it, but still wholly my own. Now it feels like Amanda was a poor, sad little girl I once knew."

Sixteen? Hugo had been in boarding school in Scotland at sixteen. His father had been gone a year, his connection to the palace now tenuous, his biggest concern how to sneak beer into the dorms. He'd barely been able to make a decision about which socks went with which pants at sixteen. Or what to do about his first crush, his oldest friend Will's sister, Clair. While Amber…

"You were declared an adult by the state. At sixteen."

She nodded. "For all intents and purposes. I was precocious. I had to be. My parents are in demand in the human rights field, and their work keeps them occupied. I was pretty much raised by nannies. When they opened their eyes one day and decided that they quite liked the young woman I had become I was suddenly of interest to them. When they began to bring me out at parties, showing off their daughter like I was one of their Picassos, I took them to court, proved my maturity, and their lack of parental care, and won."

"Hell, Amber."

"I've shocked you a little, haven't I?"

"I'll say."

"Good. I feel ever so slightly like I've just clawed back some ground."

Keep clawing, he thought. Maybe there was a chance they could meet back in the middle once more.

"How long has it been since you saw your parents?"

"I told you, not since I was sixteen. No, I lie. I was working in a bar in Sydney once when they came on the TV. Looking all sanctimonious as they talked about the children they had helped all over the world. I packed up and left. Not long after that I found my way here."

"So we both had a pretty regular upbringing, then?"

"Sure. Only yours had more tiaras." A smile hooked at the corner of Amber's mouth. A razor-sharp sense of humour, and just a little vicious…the way he liked it.

There was something still going on here, between them. Something rich and deep and untapped. If only he knew how to make her see.

She got in first. "One more question, then I will let this be."

"Ask away." The fact that they were talking, really talking, had him feeling better than he had in days.

"Do you wish you could one day be in charge?"

And just like that she cut right to the heart of things. "Once upon a time. But now? I am content with my contribution."

"Which is?"

He pulled himself to sitting, putting his feet to the ground. "I find tracts of royal land near towns that are enduring hardship because their industries—milling, mining, transport—have dried up. Families are struggling to support themselves without welfare. And I build—"

"Resorts. Of course you do." Amber hauled herself upright, her feet hitting the ground as well. Her face sank into her hands.

"I give families jobs; first in construction, then in services. My developments give struggling communities a future."

"Admirable."

"Thank you. I want to turn my mother's home into something workable, useful, beautiful too. To allow it to thrive I will put money into town infrastructure. Shopfronts such as yours can expand. Sunflower and Johnno will have access to top-notch medical attention. It will bring this place alive, giving back to the community that looked after it while my family was gone. It was you who gave me the idea, Amber. You woke me up."

They locked eyes in those few moments, connecting them in ways Hugo wasn't equipped to name.

The last time he'd felt anything close to this he'd been a young man. He'd not long lost his father. Barely able to control his thoughts, much less his hormones, he'd met Clair—Will's twin sister. They'd shared an unexpected summer in Vallemont while Will was stuck at home in London with a broken leg. He'd barely begun to know her before she'd fallen ill. And succumbed. On top of the loss of his father, the tragedy of losing Clair had emptied him.

For a long time, Clair had been his *what if?*. A valid reason not to get too close.

Until Amber.

Now he knew his attraction to Clair had been forged from limited supervision and adolescence, the memories drenched in the golden glow of youth.

With Amber he was a grown-up.

Those weeks in her shack—the long, lazy days, the soft, warm nights, the talk of nothing, the luxurious quiet—had put him back together in places he'd not even known he was still broken.

Now the world shrank around them. All he could see was Amber; fierce, tough and confused. About him. It was a start, he thought, a way back.

But then she pulled herself to her feet. "Truce over," she said. "Our ten minutes is up."

On his feet now too, Hugo said, "Amber, come on."

She held out a hand, as imperious as any princess he had ever known.

But he took a step towards her. Then another.

She looked spooked. "How dare you suggest the resort idea was my fault?"

"It was absolutely your fault." His next step brought them toe-to-toe. He hadn't been this close to her in days. The scent of her skin, the power in those eyes—he felt drunk on her nearness.

His voice was rough as he said, "Amber."

He didn't even realise his hand was on her cheek until she leant into it. The feel of her skin after missing it, missing her, for the past few days was like an elixir. His blood, sluggish before then, began to pump in earnest.

Amber pulled away, turning, holding both arms across her belly. "I don't feel good."

"Neither of us feels any good. The way things ended... it feels unfinished. We feel unfinished." His mouth suddenly dry, he pushed past it, knowing he'd never forgive himself if he didn't try. "I never had any expectation of our time together. I still don't. But I miss you, Amber. I miss waking up to find you've stolen all the pillows. I miss watching you dress in your spacesuit. I miss watching you get out of your spacesuit. I miss listening to your voice as you tell stories in the darkness."

Amber shook her head hard. "No, I mean I really don't feel good."

She pushed away from him then, ran to the nearest flowerpot and threw up into a rose bush.

CHAPTER FIVE

AMBER LEANT AGAINST the open door of her bathroom, relishing the feel of the cool wood against her cheek. Whatever had been in Sunflower's stew the night before had not agreed with her. And had continued not agreeing for many, many hours.

In fact, it had been a rough night all round.

After embarrassing herself in the flowerpot, Hugo had insisted on taking her home. But she'd been adamant, telling him she was not about to fall for his plan to muddy her case by being seen coming out of her place in the dark of night.

But the truth was she was mortified beyond belief. The thought of him being nice to her, looking after her, was too much.

She'd gone over there to put her foot down, to insist he make changes, or give up the idea wholesale. Instead she'd come over faint and had to lie down.

And in the quiet that followed, it had felt far too much like before—when talk had been easy, when they'd been… *together.* And then there had been a moment—if a long-drawn-out stretch of breathlessness and anticipation could ever be deemed a mere moment—when the space between them had contracted as if it was being sucked into a black hole.

Throwing up in the bushes had merely been the cherry on the cake.

When Prospero had arrived and Hugo had asked him to escort her in his stead, she'd wept with relief. Literally. And she wasn't a weeper. Just another level of mortification to add to the rest.

But Hugo had taken it in his stride. He'd been kind, protective and supportive. *A true gentleman.*

Her stomach roiled. She closed her eyes, placed a quieting hand on her abdomen and breathed. Maybe it wasn't food poisoning. Perhaps it was a stomach bug. Or—

Amber's eyes flew open and she stared into the middle distance, calculating madly in her head.

No. It couldn't be that.

She crawled back to bed and grabbed her phone, checking the app where she kept track of her periods, before sliding to her backside, extremities numb, sweat prickling all over her skin.

She was a little irregular, could be a few days out, here and there. But even she couldn't justify the great red "negative twelve" glaring back at her, meaning her period was nearly two weeks late.

An hour later, Amber sat on the corner of her bed, with Sunflower holding her hand, the two of them staring at the small white plastic doo-hickey resting on Amber's bathroom sink.

"I'm so sorry," Amber said for the thousandth time.

Sunflower squeezed her hand harder. "Shut up, okay? I'm glad you came to me. I'm happy to be here for this, as I know how terrifying this moment can feel."

Everyone knew. Sunflower and Johnno had been trying to have a baby for years. It was how they'd ended up in Serenity—in the hope a holistic life would make all the difference. Which was why Amber had called, begging one of the dozen pregnancy kits she kept on hand, just in case.

"But if it's good news for me it will only hurt you. Don't pretend. I know how much you want this."

Sunflower turned to her with a smile. "The fact that you'd consider it good news is good enough for me."

Good news.

Amber wondered if she'd used those words simply out of kindness for her friend. It couldn't possibly be how she really felt.

She was a nomad. An anonymous traveller, following her nose. Or she had been until she'd landed here.

Now she had a roof over her head. But Hugo was right—there was a bucket to catch the drip in the roof; air whistled through the walls; a very good blanket and Johnno's potent moonshine had kept her warm through winter.

A person could survive that way. But a baby?

She squeezed her eyes shut and for the hundredth time in half the amount of minutes tried to figure how it might have happened.

She wasn't on the pill—it always made her feel nauseous. But as fast as things had heated up, not once had she or Hugo forgotten to be careful. Meaning that if two little blue lines appeared on that stick, their protection had failed.

But good news?

Sunflower gripped her hand harder. "I'm going to ask, and you can tell me to shut it, but do you know who the..."

Amber nodded.

"Super. And, again, tell me if I'm overstepping, but if I were to hazard a guess, might he be a certain newcomer in our midst?"

Amber's gaze shot to Sunflower to find her sweet face warm and open.

"The sexual tension between the two of you is palpable.

The entire town saw it at that meeting. Electric! And, I'm happy to say, contagious. The entire commune is going through a red phase. Johnno and I have been at it like rabbits. While Willow and Tomas are back on for the first time in years, much to Tomas's delight. And—"

Amber held up a hand. "It's okay. I don't need the full run-down. Truly."

Sunflower laughed her fey laugh. "Okay. I just find visualisation helps. You know who the father is, and you clearly have a spark. You think a baby would be good news. All signs point to positive to me." She gave Amber a quick hug, leaning her head on Amber's shoulder. "Come on, baby," she whispered. "You can do this."

Amber looked at the ceiling in an effort to hold back tears as she tried to sort through the mess to see how she truly felt about this.

She had been conceived on purpose and her parents had failed miserably. If she was pregnant, it was very much an accident but that would not have to colour the child's life in any negative way. It would be all about the choices she made next.

Her hands were slippery with sweat, and they shook as she reached out for the indicator.

Time slowed. Her hearing turned to fuzz as blood rushed through her head. She lifted the white stick, turned it around and…

Her brain filled with so many thoughts she couldn't pin them down.

"Amber?" Sunflower called out.

"Hmm?"

"What news?"

Sunflower stood and came to her, looking down at the stick, breathing out a long sigh.

A knock banged so hard at the front door the entire

place vibrated, dust falling from a light fitting. And they both coughed and brushed dust from their eyes.

"What am I doing in this place? It's a death trap," Amber said, her throat tight.

Sunflower winced. "I did wonder if you'd ever notice."

"The railing wobbles. The front step is on the verge of snapping in two."

Another knock came and with a snap the door swung open by itself, as it tended to do.

And there stood Hugo, backlit, hand raised to knock, hair tumbling over his forehead in that way that made Amber feel all warm and fuzzy.

"Sorry about the door. I'll fix it, of course. I brought the papers from my lawyers that I promised. And I wanted to see if you were feeling…"

Even with his face in darkness she saw the moment his eyes saw the stick she was holding in her hand.

Sunflower placed a hand on Amber's shoulder. "I'll leave you be, honey. You two have a lot to talk about." She leant in and whispered, "Take it easy on the guy. A man with eyes that dreamy can't be all bad. Hey, Hugo."

Hugo nodded as Sunflower wafted past. He even found a smile. "Sunflower. Lovely to see you."

Sunflower put a hand to her heart and gave Amber a last look.

Then it was just the two of them, together in her shack for the first time since she'd kicked him out.

Well, the three of them. Amber, Hugo and The Stick.

He took a step inside, filling the space with his calm, his strength, the scent of him, so familiar, so delicious. "Is that what I think it is?"

She nodded.

"Are you pregnant?"

She held up the stick in answer.

He tore his gaze away from her to glance at it. "One

blue line. No, two. There's a second faint one, right? I don't know what that means. Yes? No? Boy? Twins?"

Despite the tension gripping her every cell, Amber somehow managed to laugh. "Yes, Hugo. It means yes."

He breathed out hard through his nose, and before he had the chance to say anything nausea rose thick and fast in her throat and she spun on her heel and ran to the bathroom, this time taking an extra second to shut the door.

Nothing came up as she had nothing left. Her stomach ached from her spasming muscles. Sweat streaked her hair.

She slowly sat on the floor, shaking, in shock, her future a blur.

"Amber? May I please come in?"

She closed her eyes. "I'd rather you didn't."

She listened hard for footsteps but heard none.

"Can I get you anything?" he asked, in that voice of his. Velvet, deep, sure. "Food? Water? A doctor?" A beat, then, "Prospero tells me he helped deliver one of his nephews."

Again she laughed, only this time tears fell freely down her face. "Tell Prospero I won't be in need of his services for a good few months."

A few months and there would be someone in her life *looking* to her for support, food, shelter. And love. Change was coming at her whether she was ready for it or not.

"Amber?" His voice was so close she imagined him sitting on the other side of the door, his head leaning back just as hers was. "May I ask...your intentions?"

Amber closed her eyes. For all the wild and crazy going on in her head right now, she hadn't stopped to think about how he must be feeling. Shocked, sure, but in limbo too, not knowing what she planned to do with this news.

"I'm keeping this baby, Hugo."

She heard the outshot of breath even through the old door. "That's good news."

Good news. Those funny two words again.

"Do you mean that?"

"I believe my brain has gone to its most primal basic state, and I do not have the wherewithal to say anything but the absolute truth."

"Mmm. I hear that."

A few breaths went by and her tummy seemed to settle. Her nerves too. As if not having to go through this momentous thing alone was a relief.

"Hugo?"

"Yes, Amber?"

"I didn't plan for this."

"I know, *miele*. Neither did I."

A beat, then, "I'm sorry."

"Don't be. Don't ever think you have to be…"

She'd heard the emotion rising in his voice before he'd cut himself off. She swallowed, cringing at the awful taste in her mouth.

Hugo said, "I wish… I wish I knew what to say. To do."

"I don't expect anything of you, Hugo." Ugh. That sounded like a line from a bad teen angst movie.

Then Hugo said something she was sure would haunt her for the rest of her days. "That's always been our problem, Amber, you never have."

Amber's hand went to her belly, only this time not to curb the pain therein. For the pain she felt was higher, deep behind her ribs. "I need some time. To get my head around this. To clean my teeth. To sleep. To recuperate."

It was a good while before he said, "Okay."

She heard him shift from the floor, heard his footsteps echo on her rickety floor. Heard him fiddle with the door until it was properly shut.

Then there was nothing but the sound of her breaths. And the knowledge that, no matter what, she would never be alone again.

* * *

Hugo lay on the couch in the library, arm slung over his eyes to block out the sun streaming through the huge windows. His gaze glanced over the paintings on the walls—gum trees and billabongs, red dirt and bushrangers. Alien scenes to anyone who'd never seen Australia.

Summer was in its final throes, bringing with it dry winds and temperatures in the high thirties. Prospero was wilting.

What he wouldn't give to be sprawled out in Amber's hammock.

Amber.

Who was pregnant.

With his baby. At least, he assumed it was his. He hadn't asked.

Of course it's yours. This is Amber we're talking about.

He hadn't said much at all, in fact, his subconscious having switched to basic survival mode. All those years of rigid princely training had come to the fore, forcing any feelings about the news into a watertight box while the diplomat took over.

Yes, Amber. Of course, Amber. Whatever you need, Amber.

When she'd asked him to go, he'd gone. Even though he was pretty sure Amber Hartley had no damn clue what she needed.

As for what he needed… For a man who could schmooze in several languages, negotiate multi-million-dollar developments, he was damn useless at intimate relationships.

His first crush, the lovely Clair, had died tragically not long after they'd met and he'd had no idea how to process that. Thus losing his best school friend—Clair's brother, Will—because he'd been too thoroughly schooled in not showing weakness.

As for Sadie… After his uncle had made it clear he

would marry or face the consequences, he'd truly thought marrying his great mate Sadie was a good plan. It would give her and her mother security. Never occurring to him that she might not be so emotionally detached as he, and actually hope to one day marry for love.

Thank the gods she had panicked.

And then had come Amber.

A different kettle of fish from any woman he'd ever dated. Any person he'd ever known.

Sadie had known him her entire life and hadn't realised that beneath his outward confidence, the practised ease, was an emotional wasteland.

Amber had seen right through him from the moment they met. Damaged, deliberately isolated, detached. And still she'd taken him in. Until over the weeks, with her, those darker parts of himself had begun to fade, to seem less irreversible, to heal.

And now he was about to become a father. He had no choice but to leap into the unknown.

Hugo pressed himself to sitting, all the better to think. And breathe.

Thankfully he had time. Months, in fact. Could his plan to leave Serenity be put on hold? He had excellent teams in Vallemont who could manage the Dwell Forest resort that was meant to break ground in the autumn. Maybe.

But that was logistics.

This was far bigger than dates and times on a calendar. He was going to be a father.

A father. Considering the lacklustre examples he'd had in his life, he found himself struggling to know what that really meant.

He loved his younger cousins. He'd taught Kit how to catch a ball, and Kane how to ski. He'd frightened off any number of the older twins' suitors, but he was smart enough to know that being an uncle was wildly different from being a father.

The big question hovering on the edge of his mind since he'd seen those two faint blue lines was what if he, like every other man in the Giordano family, found a way to screw it up?

But this wasn't theoretical. Soon, if everything went as it ought, there would be a baby. A child. He would be that boy or girl's father. And Amber would be its mother.

Somehow, amidst the dark quagmire of disquiet roiling inside of him, that was the one shining light. He might not have a clue what kind of father he would make, but Amber as a mother…?

He'd watched her tend her bees with careful fingers and a calm voice. He'd seen her interact with the townspeople over the last few days—never too busy to stop and listen; to offer advice; to lend a hand; to have a laugh. She drew people to her like a flame.

He'd also watched her stand up to a town council, and a *prince*, in order to protect people she cared about.

She was considerate, serious, presumptuous and fierce.

Hugo could not think of a single person he had ever met who was more qualified for the role of mother.

With it came some other feeling—intangible, slippery, warm. But he couldn't hold on to it long enough to know its name.

Feeling as if he was on the edge of some realisation that would glue it all together, Hugo started when Prospero cleared his throat.

"We have visitors." Prospero's voice had bite to it, as if he were a Doberman who smelled trouble.

Hugo moved to the window, shifting the heavy brocade curtains aside to find a nondescript black town car had pulled up in his front drive.

A pair of men in dark suits hopped out. Something in

the way they moved, slow, careful, on high alert, had Hugo shifting closer to the wall. "The men who attempted the attack on my uncle at the picnic—?"

"Were not dressed in suits, Your Highness."

And paparazzi never drove such clean cars.

One of the men went to the back door of the car and pulled it open. A black high heel with a red sole hit the cobblestones, followed by another. Then, out stepped Hugo's aunt, Marguerite—the wife of Sovereign Prince Reynaldo.

Hugo yanked the curtains closed and snapped out of his daydreams. This was no time for exploring his tender side. He had to have his game face on in order to deal with his aunt.

Hugo was out of the door and down the front steps before the car door shut. "Aunt Marguerite."

Adjusting her face away from the snarky bite of the shimmering summer sun, she offered her cheek for a kiss.

"To what do I owe the pleasure?" Hugo asked, taking in the sombre bodyguards. Four in total…meaning the unrest back home was not over and done with.

"To the fact you seem to have forgotten how to answer your phone."

Others might falter at his aunt's impressively imperious tone, but she'd chased him and his cousins around the backyard with a hose when they were young enough not to be able to outrun her. "I told you I was safe, which Prospero no doubt reiterated in clandestine missives sent back to the palace."

Marguerite looked at him then, really looked at him. As if trying to see him as something other than the half-naked little boy running from the hose water.

Crickets chirped in the dry grass near by.

"Anyway, welcome to Hinterland House." With its Italianate yellow stucco, towering conifers, lead-light windows and neat shrubbery, it could have been transplanted whole from Tuscany.

Marguerite flicked a speck of red Australian dirt from her white skirt. "Yes. I have been here before."

The shocks kept on coming. "When?"

"Reynaldo and I holidayed here with your father—secretly, mind you, as we were not yet married—when he dragged us to this place, claiming a hankering for peaches. Ironic, that."

Hugo kept whatever retort he might have made to himself. He didn't remember his father well enough to defend him, even if his actions had been defensible. Which they hadn't. Would his child judge his choices as harshly one day?

Hugo put the thought aside. For now. Marguerite was a consummate royal—she could sniff out weakness at a hundred paces.

"It's smaller than I remember," said Marguerite.

"You are such a snob."

"Yes, I am. Now, are you going to invite me in or am I to melt into a puddle in this infernal heat?"

Hugo led his aunt into the house. One of her bodyguards stayed by the car, another at the door, one proceeded to case the house and the other camped out in a spot mirroring Prospero, who hadn't moved from his position by the front door.

"Drink?" Hugo offered. "Something to eat?"

Marguerite had barely removed a glove when she said, "Hugo, this is not a social visit. I am here with news. Three days ago, your uncle died."

Hugo's brain froze. One shock too many. "Which uncle?"

She shot him a look, one that asked that he please keep up. "The Prince. Reynaldo. My husband. The Sovereign Prince of Vallemont."

Only then did he see her hands were shaking, how drawn she looked, the tightness around her eyes. "Marguerite—"

When she saw him coming in for a hug she stopped with a hand. "We have no time for that. It has been three days. There is much to be done."

"Three days?" While he'd been busy at town hall meetings, having cups of strange tea and trying to keep his hands off the local honey-seller, his uncle had gone. What the hell was wrong with his family? The way he'd learned of his own father's demise was staggering in its similarity, tearing open old wounds until anger spilled through him like poison.

"How did I not hear of this? And don't tell me it was because I wouldn't answer my phone. You could have left a message. Email. Overnight mail. You've clearly been in touch with Prospero. What's wrong with you?"

If Marguerite heard the anger in his voice she did not show it. "We could not release the news without letting the people know who their next ruler will be. Officially, he is in bed with the flu, while he is actually in a freezer in the local morgue." She coughed at the end, a gloved fist pressing against her mouth.

Hugo's heart felt as though it had been squeezed.

Everyone in the palace knew that she and Reynaldo had been married in name only for years. They kept separate apartments in the palace—but that was perfectly normal in the royal household. They also kept separate calendars and engagements—again normal. The fact that she openly detested the man hadn't helped Hugo's views on married life over the years.

Bluebirds and love hearts might not be the theme of their relationship, but they'd had a family. Shared a life. Whoever had led her to believe she had to be stoic at a time like this deserved to be shot.

Whether she wanted him to or not, he moved in and wrapped his arms around her, breathing deeply, encouraging her to do the same. Until her short, raspy breaths matched his and her trembling abated. "Tell me what happened."

"It was awful," she allowed. "Too awful."

"What happened? And the twins? Are they okay?"

"His heart gave way."

"His heart?"

Reynaldo had been a big man with a beard like a Viking's. He'd seemed indestructible. As if he could protect Vallemont by sheer force of will alone. Yet the last time Hugo had seen his uncle he'd been ashen, Hugo's non-wedding having taken its toll. He swore under his breath.

"Do not blame your absence. It was a weak constitution and a lifestyle of excess. The belief he could do it all on his own. He was a Giordano after all." Marguerite smiled with her eyes. "The men in your family have not proven themselves equipped for longevity, delegation or fidelity."

Hugo's eyebrow twitched. The fact he'd just been navel-gazing about this exact concern hit home hard.

"Except for you, of course," said Marguerite, looking at him strangely. "Unless that's why your little friend left you at the altar?"

Hugo stiffened. "It is not."

"No. I wouldn't think so. If our country has any hope of producing a truly admirable Giordano it is you."

Something in Marguerite's tone was beginning to rub against the grain. Hugo ran a hand up the back of his neck and stepped away.

"What did you mean by 'letting the people know who their next ruler will be'?" The members of the royal household were versed in the twisted intricacies of royal succession before they could walk. With Reynaldo and Marguerite's twin boys too young to rule, it fell to Reynaldo's younger brother, Prince Ralph. "Uncle Ralph is married. Of age. And more than capable."

But Marguerite shook her head.

"It has come to our attention that he is not actually married to your aunt, Esmeralda, as she never divorced her first husband. As it turns out, Reynaldo discovered the truth of it a few months ago. Assuming he would live to see his own son grow up and take the throne, he kept it to himself. Yet—"

"The marriage requirement is invalidated." Hugo swore beneath his breath. "So that also means that Jacob—"

"Is a bastard."

Hugo gave his aunt a deadpan stare, but she didn't flinch. "I would not have put it that way. But yes." Meaning the succession of Hugo's other of-age cousin had been nullified in one clerical swipe.

Hugo moved slowly to a window, his gaze unseeing as he looked out on the happy blue sky over Serenity. His voice sounded as though it came to him from another room as he said, "So, unless I am mistaken, you are here to inform me that I am to inherit the throne of Vallemont."

"You sound honestly surprised. Did you not have an inkling? Did you not wonder why your uncle encouraged you to marry our dear Sadie? He wanted you to be ready for this."

Hugo turned on his aunt. "He did not merely *encourage* me to marry Sadie. He blackmailed me into it."

Marguerite's gaze was calm, measured. She came to him, put a cool hand over his. "Watching your father self-destruct pained him. Watching you turn rogue and wander further from the family broke his heart."

"That does not excuse his actions. He threatened Sadie's mother's job. Threatened to throw my mother out of the country."

"This is not about him," said Marguerite, politically savvy to the last. "Not any more."

Hugo ran a hand down his face, scraping against the stubble that had grown back. "And if I refuse?"

"Cousin Constantine."

Hugo's hand dropped. "You are kidding."

Marguerite shook her head. "He's next after you."

"He's eighty-three. And a clown. Literally. I remember him performing at my eighth birthday party. He scared the living daylights out of me."

Marguerite's shrug was as elegant as it was possible for a shrug to be. "Your country is rudderless. And I for one can think of no one better than you to steer the ship."

When Hugo realised he was holding his breath he let it go.

His entire childhood he had been prepared for this moment. When his father had died, the opportunity to put his knowledge, his education, his ideas to use had been snatched from his grasp, sending him spinning out into the world, a royal rebel whose success had been both a revelation and a thorn in his uncle's side.

With his next breath he felt the last vestiges of that rebellion dissolve away.

"I will have my lawyers double-check everything you have told me."

"I'd be disappointed if you didn't."

"And if this turns out to be fact, it will not be announced until I have spoken personally with Kit."

Marguerite raised a single thin eyebrow. "My son is twelve, and mourning the loss of his father."

"That is not all he will mourn. Reynaldo's first-born son was brought up believing that one day he would rule. He has not only lost his father, but also the only version of a future he has ever considered. No one understands the pain of *that* loss more than me."

Marguerite nodded.

"What else needs to be done?" Hugo asked.

"You must return home immediately. The sooner the funeral, the better for the children and stability."

"Agreed. But I would have to return immediately afterwards. I have loose ends that need tying up."

Marguerite made to insist before changing tack. "What could possibly bring you back here?"

Plenty, he realised. In a short space of time he had made real connections, his Australian roots digging in fast. Then there was the resort. And there was Amber. Amber, who was pregnant with his child.

Hugo closed his eyes against what felt very much like a wave of despair. His hope of sticking around, of shifting things in his life to accommodate months of getting to know her, to see if their connection was worth exploring above and beyond the fact they would have a child together, had just been unduly snatched away.

It was time for him to go home.

Marguerite went on, "After which you must marry some lucky girl, and fast. I will write up a list of suitable young women. The coronation will occur right after."

With that, she curtseyed. His venerable aunt, a fierce, battle-hardened woman, bowed before him, and said, "Your Highness."

Hugo rolled his eyes. "Stand up, woman."

She glanced up at him. "Is that a yes?"

He took a deep breath, giving himself one last moment to be sure. But his answer had been written on his heart the moment things had become clear.

"Yes," he said, his shoulder blades snapping together. "My answer is yes. Now, come with me while I find you a drink. And a room. In that order."

"Bless you, dear boy." Marguerite slowly untwisted from her curtsey and slid him an unexpectedly watery smile. "I knew you would turn out to be the very best of them."

"We shall see."

When his aunt was settled—prostrate on a spare bed, snoring quietly, a carved wooden fan pushing the hot air around the room—Hugo headed back to the library to find Prospero still hadn't moved.

Though move he did when he spotted Hugo, bowing deeply, with a deep, proud, "Your Highness."

"Don't feel so punished now, do you, big guy?"

Prospero looked up, his smile wide and full of straight white teeth Hugo had never seen before.

"I need you to do something for me."

"Anything, Your Highness."

Hugo wanted to command the big guy to call him Hugo, but considering the change of circumstances it might give him an aneurism. So he went with, "Stay with my aunt. Let me know the moment she wakes up. There is something I must do alone."

CHAPTER SIX

When Amber wasn't to be found in her shack, Hugo went to look for her in the next logical place. Through the cool shade of the patchy trees to the north-east of the shack and then the darker depths of Serenity Forest.

This was where he'd imagined a string of secluded bungalows. Blond wood cladding, slate-grey roofs, muted colours to blend in with as much of the forest as they could save.

When the idea had first come to him, he'd called his uber-designer in Bern. Her response had been "nudes, taupes and creams" with "splashes of mossy green" to "effect an aura of calm, of solace, of rest". The woman could read minds. His dream had been to share the healing magic of this land with as many people as possible. And people would come. People needed a place like Serenity.

Stepping carefully now over fallen logs and random rocks, Hugo came upon her in a small glade.

Long shadows cast by saplings dappled in afternoon light cut across Amber's face, her loose white button-up shirt, her short denim cut-offs. Wild flowers brushed against her bare ankles. Her strangely beautiful dog sat lovingly at her feet.

Hugo kept to the shadows for a moment and took it all in. No wonder his embitterment had crumbled in this place. A person could only take so much light, and life, and exquisite beauty before he had to open up and let it in.

Amber stood by a hive he hadn't seen before. Where the others had been painted every colour under the sun, decorated with smiley faces, cartoony red mushrooms and star fields by Amber's friend Sunflower, this one was clean, white, new.

Bending over, peering into a hole at the front before moving to the back of the hive where she proceeded to attach a hunk of Styrofoam, Amber was tearing strips of tape from the roll with her teeth.

For all the time he'd spent with her—first in the quiet of the cabin and then the white noise of the public arena—the woman was still an enigma. She looked like a French film star. Spoke like a corporate lawyer. Pretended to be a flower child. And acted as though nothing and no one could ever hurt her.

But he'd hurt her. Having picked their relationship apart in his head over the past several hours, he knew that now.

He'd believed her when she'd acted as if her anger towards him was because of the resort, probably because it let him off the hook. But it had been more than that. Deeper. She'd been hurt because she cared. For him. He wasn't the only one whose life had been altered by their time together.

At least, that was what he was counting on. Because if he was wrong, if he was mistaken about her feelings for him, his plan would be defunct.

He ran a hand over his face. The fact that he'd had to choreograph a "plan" at all was less than ideal. If he had the luxury of time, things might be different. Hell, they'd *have* to be different. But none of this was normal. It hadn't been from the very start.

But the bigger truth was that there were bigger things at play now than her feelings. Or, for that matter, his.

A twig snapped, and then Amber bounced about, holding a bare foot.

Which was when Hugo realised something was very wrong.

Amber was tending her bees—meaning she ought to be covered head-to-toe in gloves, veil, overalls and those bright yellow gumboots.

Fear speared his guts like an arrow, panic swelling from the wound. And he was running before he even felt his feet move.

"Amber!" he called, rushing towards her, darting around saplings, waving his arms as if he might be able to distract the swarm before they touched her.

She quickly looked over her shoulder as if a bear might be behind her.

Then she turned to him, shoved her hands on her hips and shouted, "What the hell are you doing?"

"Saving you, you great fool!" Then he swept her into his arms and carried her away, bracing himself for the stings that would pierce his clothes any second. Not caring, as his caveman instincts had kicked in. *Protect woman. Protect child.*

"Let me down!" she said, wriggling like a fish on a boat deck.

"Not going to happen," he gritted out as he avoided getting smacked. And kicked. Bee stings had nothing on her. She was slippery too, sunscreen and sweat making her skin slick.

Hugo gritted his teeth and carried her until she was far enough away that he could be sure she was safe.

The second he stopped she wriggled free and pushed him away. She swept her hair from her face and stared him down. "Are you insane? Has the heat gone to your head?"

"I might ask the same of you." He waved an arm down her body, his gaze catching on the open neck of her shirt and the glimpse of a pink lace bra beneath. He knew that bra. He'd removed it with his teeth. And in the quick glance he saw that he'd left a tear.

Hot, mentally exhausted and turned on, Hugo's voice was a rumble as he said, "Where the hell is your gear, Amber? Are you trying to hurt yourself? And what about the…?"

The baby. He'd yet to say the word out loud. Even thinking it brought up more emotions than he could pin down.

Amber's eyes flickered at the missing word, but she didn't jump in to finish his sentence this time. Instead, she licked her lips, and said, "These are native Australian stingless bees, you idiot. Emphasis on the *stingless*."

"How can you be sure?" he asked. He felt like an idiot as soon as he asked. And yet, if pressed, he knew he'd have asked the same again. His need to protect her outweighed not looking like a fool by a long shot.

And he saw the moment she realised it too.

It was a rare sight, seeing her eyes soften that way. Her already pink cheeks darkening in abashment. He drank it in. Drank her in. She had feelings for him, all right. What he hadn't counted on was his crumbling control over his feelings for her.

"Come on," she said, taking a step towards the hive. Then, rolling her eyes, she grabbed him by the hand and dragged him through the forest.

Ned leapt between them, happy the gang was back together, while Hugo's synapses fired and misfired by turns at how good, how right, it felt to have Amber's hand in his. How much he hoped she wouldn't fly off the handle; that she'd listen to what he'd come there to say.

He curled his fingers tighter around hers. She looked back.

But then she very deliberately let go, her hands tucking together. "Hugo."

"Yes, Amber."

"I'd like you to meet my newest hive. I've been saving up for these guys for months. They're not cheap. But they are so very worth it."

"And stingless?"

"Stingless."

He watched the hive but saw nothing except a small area of tacky black near the opening. But as they stood in the quiet glade he heard the hum. The gentle buzz. And then…there. One. And another.

"They're smaller than the stingy bees so they produce less honey. But what they do produce is delicious with lots of healing properties. But the best bit is that they are amazing pollinators. These little sweeties might just save the world."

Hugo planned to step in and save his country. Amber wanted to save the world.

Then her hand went to her belly and Hugo's world shrank to about two square metres.

"Are you okay?" Hugo asked, stepping in. "Was that pain? Or a…kick?" Hell, he had no clue.

By the flat stare she shot him, she clearly did. "I'm a month along, Hugo. There will be no kicking for some time."

"Then why did you wince?"

"I've been throwing up most of the day. It's left me a little tender, that's all."

"Right," said Hugo.

And Amber gave him a look. A look that connected them. It was the first time they'd spoken with any sense about the fact that they were going to have a child together.

"It may be obvious," said Hugo, "but I've never been in this…situation before."

Her eyebrows shot towards her hairline. "Me neither, thank you very much."

Going on instinct, he took a risk, asking, "Does this all feel as strange to you as it does to me?"

"If you mean you feel like you're living outside of your body and yet are truly aware that you are a living, breathing, cell-duplicating body for the first time in your life, then yes."

"Exactly like that."

In the shade of the hot summer's day, the both of them wildly out of their comfort zones, they burst into laughter.

This woman, he thought. His deep subconscious adding, *Do not let her slip away or I will never forgive you.*

There was a moment when he thought about revealing himself to her, telling her how much he wished they could go back to the ease, the simplicity, the warmth before real life had intervened with such alacrity.

But it was a risk he wasn't willing to take.

He was about to become the sovereign ruler of a country. Every decision he made from here on in would affect the lives of tens of thousands of people.

His only choice in the matter was to leave emotion out of it; to make her an offer she couldn't refuse.

"Amber," he said.

As she heard the serious note in his voice, her laughter dried up. "Yes, Hugo."

"I'm going to say some things now and, before you leap in with thoughts and questions and concerns, I'd like you to let me finish."

She opened her mouth to retort, but he held up a finger. An inch from her mouth. The warmth of her breath rushed over his skin. But he would not be distracted.

"And, once I'm done, I would like to hear your thoughts, questions and concerns. Every single one."

The sass slipped a little then. As if she wasn't used to being offered the floor. As if she was used to having to fight for it. It was enough for her to acquiesce.

Hugo filled Amber in on the turn of events. And then, "A week ago I was fifth in line to the throne. In a few days I will return home to be crowned the Sovereign Prince of Vallemont."

Amber's hand slipped from her hip to her belly. As well it might. For the second in line to the throne might well be growing inside of her.

To that, Hugo added, "There are certain stipulations that must first be met. I must be of age. Which I am. I must be male—"

She opened her mouth. He held up the finger again. Her eyes crossed as she stared at it, then she closed her mouth.

"—a stipulation which I would hope to change when the job is mine. And I must be married."

At that she stilled. Only her honey-blonde waves shifted in the hot, dry breeze.

"Your turn," he said.

"You're not married, right?" she blurted.

"No."

She breathed out, muttering, "That would have been the real cherry on the cake."

He opened his mouth.

She held up a finger. "My turn."

He closed his mouth.

"There's a strong chance I'm wrong, but I have a feeling that I know where you are going with this. And I think you should stop now. Before either of us says something we can't take back."

"Marry me."

"Hugo!" Amber paced away a few steps before pacing back again. Ned followed, panting, happily thinking it was a game. "I just said—"

"I don't want to take it back." He stepped in close, took her by the hand—both hands—holding her gaze with everything he had. "Amber, you are pregnant with my child. I will not be an absentee father like mine was to me."

He saw a flicker then. Of understanding. Of empathy.

"I must go home. It's not a choice, it's necessary to the future of my country. To the people of my country. There is only the slightest tinge of arrogance in my stating that I am the best chance they have for a bright, prosperous, safe future. Having you near me, *with* me, when our child is born, is of the utmost importance to me."

He then saw the moment she shut that empathy down. Her head shook side to side. "I can't. Hugo, it's a ridiculous notion. We barely know one another."

"Not true. I know that your parents did not appreciate you. I know that you are fearless, and kind. I know that you doubt yourself at times. And that everyone who knows you respects and admires you."

He hung every hope on the fact that she didn't blink.

"These past few days have been a challenge, but the time we spent together in your shack, talking rubbish, making one another laugh, making love, proves that if we choose to we can get along just fine."

She swallowed, her gaze dropping to his mouth, and he wondered if her vision of "getting along" matched his.

"That does not mean I am under any illusion that our relationship will ever be that way again." Only then did he realise how much he wanted it to. But no, now was not the time to speculate. "You would be made comfortable. You would have your own apartment within the palace. You would have complete freedom to do as you please. You could rule at my side or in name only. You could champion any cause that speaks to you, with the backing of a royal name, royal funds, royal gravitas. And our child will have a family. A mother and a father."

"Hugo," she said, her voice a whisper, and he knew he was giving her more than he'd intended. But the words were coming from some place real. And raw. And open. And, while fighting with her had been fun, this felt far better.

But he knew it would be short-lived. For he hadn't played his trump card yet.

He reached up and tucked a swathe of hair behind her ear, relishing the feel of her, the warmth of her, for it might well be the last time she let him this close ever again.

"One more thing."

Gripped now, discombobulated by the ridiculous drama of it all, her voice was barely a whisper as she said, "What on earth else could there be?"

He looked into her eyes, remembering what it felt like to fall into the bright whisky depths as she fell apart in his arms, and said, "If you agree to come with me, marry me, be my Princess, and raise our child in the Palace of Vallemont, I will give up the plans to turn Hinterland House into a resort."

And like that the brightness went away as her eyes narrowed. A crease appeared above her nose. And she let go of his hand.

"Hinterland House has been in my mother's family for generations, so I will save it for my children, our children, as well as five acres to the west. But I will gift the rest of the land to the town of Serenity. Including the lavender fields, the forest…and I will sign over your hill to the commune."

Amber swallowed hard, even as a tear ran slowly down her cheek. She quickly swiped it away.

He wished he could take her in his arms, run a hand down her back, over her hair. Kiss away those tears. Kiss her until she sighed. Until they both forgot what the hell they were even talking about.

He'd had no idea how hard this would be. How physically brutal. It actually hurt. Deep inside his chest. But with the future of his beloved country at stake and a child on the way, he did not see that he could have gone about it any other way.

"I don't expect you to make a decision right now. But time is pressing. I am heading home immediately for my uncle's funeral. I will be back in time for the town meeting. I will need to know your decision by then."

A shiver rocked her body and she seemed to snap back to her old self, her eyes flashing, her fists curling into hard balls. It was far easier to handle than the tears.

"My decision?" she hissed. "Let me get this straight. If I agree to marry you…" she stopped to swallow the words "…and move to the other side of the world, raise the baby I only found out I was having today, in a palace, then you will not tear down my friends' homes. But if I say no then you will go ahead with the plan to build your resort. Just because you can."

"Yes."

She breathed out through a hole between her lips. Her eyes were bright, her face was pale and she was glorious. This woman to whom he had just proposed. Who, no matter what happened from here, would never fully trust him for the rest of her life. Hugo soaked in the sight of her like a man on his way to prison.

"I knew you were a bender of the truth. I knew you kept things close to your chest. Until this moment I had no idea you were an asshole."

Hugo kept his cool by reminding himself his family had not prospered for as long as they had by being the nice guys. "I'd rather think of my offer as knockout negotiation."

"I bet you would. This isn't normal, Hugo. You do realise that?"

He ran a hand through his hair, his cool hitting breaking point. "We have never been normal, Amber, not from the moment we met. We ended up in bed before we even knew one another's names. Time lost all meaning as we lost ourselves in one another. I had no idea what day it was, what date, whether it was morning or afternoon. It didn't matter. I can't presume to know what it meant to you, Amber, but for me those weeks..."

Too much. The moment he caught her eye again, he knew he'd said too much.

But then Amber breathed, the air shaking through her like an earthquake. And he knew it had been as transformative for her as it had been for him.

And he knew, in that moment, how to get the answer he wanted.

He had one chance to get this right. It was off plan, and risky as all hell, but he went for it.

Reaching out to her, Hugo took her hand and gently pulled her into his arms, an inch at a time. Her hands moved to rest against his chest but she didn't push him away. She was listening now.

"Amber, every person I have ever met has seen me as a prince first and Hugo second. But for those weeks, with you, I was simply a man. You were short with me if I was presumptuous. You were cool with me if I made you angry. You didn't laugh if my jokes weren't funny. You berated me if I made you wait. And I wouldn't give up a second of it."

He dropped his hand to her side then, his thumb resting against her belly. Beneath that warm skin his child was growing, a child created during one of those meandering days—or one of those decadent nights.

"Not a single one."

He'd meant to leave it there, but having her in his arms again, swamped in memories of their time together, he found he couldn't let her go. He pulled her closer still and she let him. Then, before he could stop himself, he leaned down and he kissed her.

In the back of his mind he imagined the moment as a place-holder, a precursor to the official sealing of a deal.

But muscle memory took over and soon his hands were in her hair; hers gripping his shirt for dear life. And the kiss took on its own life, pulling him under. Deep. His heart thundered hard enough to burst.

His senses reeled. Shadow and light played on the backs of his eyelids. The taste of her was sweet and fresh and familiar. Her softness gave under his touch.

Heaven and hell. Wanting her, while knowing that if he had her it would be due to a devil's bargain.

As if remembering the same, she broke the kiss. Sighing as her lips left his.

Their foreheads touched for just a moment, before Hugo lifted his head and found her eyes. Whisky-brown. Flecked with sunshine and gold. And trouble.

"Think about it," he said, his voice rough. "Whatever you decide I will accept your answer unequivocally. The next town meeting. Let me know your answer by then."

And then he let her go, aching at the way she had to catch herself, as if her knees had gone soft.

Then he turned and walked back through the forest, seeing nothing. It was a miracle he didn't walk into a tree.

The sweet warmth of her body was imprinted on his. The honeyed taste of her lips still flowing like hot treacle inside him.

His head hurt at what he had just done. His gut burned. Even his bones throbbed.

Was this how Reynaldo had felt when he "encouraged" him to marry Sadie, blanketed by his sureness that it was the right thing to do?

Was this what it meant to rule?

If so, Hugo knew he shouldn't be so concerned about getting through with his heart intact. He'd be lucky to get by without destroying his soul.

* * *

Three days later Amber stood at the podium in front of the town council.

She'd sucked on a lemon just before coming out, so the nausea was at about a four rather than its usual nine or nine and a half. The lights glaring down on her made her head hurt.

Though perhaps that might have had more to do with the fact that her time was up. She had a decision to make that would change her life, and the lives of the townspeople, no matter which way she went.

She glanced over her shoulder at her cheer squad. Sunflower waved and Johnno gave her a thumbs up. Looking at them, she wondered if she ought to have confided in them. Asked their opinion. But she was so used to relying on no one but herself, she'd had no clue where to start.

Raising a child here with these good people would be magical. But if she stayed, the commune would no longer exist, not in the form it kept now, so that made the option redundant.

Also, and this was the thing that had kept her awake at night, no matter how she had come to care for them, they weren't her family. People came, and people went. The ebb and flow of the commune's population was what kept it so vibrant.

On the other hand—there was Hugo. And grrrr, she was so mad at him right now! Madder than she'd ever been at anyone in her entire life—her parents included, which she hadn't thought possible.

Meaning she'd had no choice but to think about why that was.

Sure, his marriage proposal had amounted to extortion. But he hadn't *had* to offer to give up the resort. For all the sangfroid he'd shown making his proposition, she understood he was offering a sacrifice to balance her own.

It was the sentiment that confounded her. He'd said that being near his child was of the utmost importance, and that he would never be an absentee father. As if he knew exactly how to rip right to the heart of her. Unless, of course, he'd been telling the truth.

Then there was the kiss. It had come from nowhere. Yet at the same time it had been brewing for days.

For a little over three weeks she had experienced the closest thing to comfort she had ever known; waking with Hugo's arm draped over her, protective and warm; falling asleep with him caressing her hair; listening to the deep hum of his voice as he'd chatted to Ned.

She let her gaze drift to the far corner of the room, where Hugo stood with Prospero a hulking shadow at his back. They were mobbed, the centre of a dozen conversations. And yet Amber could feel Hugo's attention attuned to her.

Her tummy fluttered at the sight of him. Nausea. That was what that feeling was.

And anger. Because she was mad at him still. Deeply, hotly mad.

The gavel struck and Amber looked to the front table. Her heart hammered against her ribs. Her vision began to blur.

Before Councillor Pinkerton could call the meeting back to order, Amber held up a finger. "May I beg a minute?"

The councillor looked towards Hugo's corner. "We can spare two."

On unsteady feet Amber turned and walked towards the side glass doors. She waggled a finger at Hugo, motioning for him to follow her.

Outside she paced, the long skirt of her loose dress catching around her ankles every time she turned.

Hugo slid through the door, looking ridiculously handsome with his sexy stubble and his hair falling across one eye. In jeans and a jacket this time, he reminded her far more of the man she'd known than the man he'd turned out to be.

He looked tired, no doubt thanks to flying to the other side of the world and back in the past few days. Burying his uncle. All the while not knowing what her answer might be.

Or maybe it had never really been under contention. Maybe it had always been about giving her time to pretend she had a choice.

"Ned," she croaked. And tried again. "What about Ned?"

"What about Ned?" he said, the first time she'd heard his voice in days.

"He's not mine. Not officially. He was a stray. And he sort of…got attached to me."

"I know the type."

She shot him a look, felt the heat of his gaze slice through her like a knife through butter. "I should leave him behind. This place is all he knows. And what with his hearing…" She flapped her hands, which were suddenly going numb. Her toes were too. She closed her eyes and wriggled her toes.

She felt Hugo take her by the elbows. "Breathe, *miele*. Just breathe. I simply assumed he'd be coming with us. That is what you want, isn't it?"

Amber swallowed. "But what about Customs? Don't you need a vet check? Or immunisation records? Proof he's not going to infect your entire country with some weird Australian disease?"

Every word became harder to come by. She glared at Hugo and felt a little better. Though her righteousness would feel better still if he acted more like an ogre while holding her to ransom. If he'd blackmailed her for profit, not for good. If his super-prince sperm hadn't managed to break through every protection she'd put in place.

"I vouch for him," he said, with a very European scowl. "What is the point of being Sovereign Prince if one cannot take advantage every now and then?"

"Do you mean that?"

"Of course. I plan on taking advantage wherever and whenever I can."

"No, I..." A beat, an unexpected smile, then she said, "You're kidding."

"Much of the time. I have spoken to the relevant authorities already, as I am also thorough."

Amber's thought went to her belly. Didn't she know it?

"Are you ready to go inside? If not I can take your place. I can give the council the news, whatever it may be."

Amber shook her head. "I started this. I'll finish it." But she didn't move.

She looked up, made sure he was looking at her, really paying attention, when she said, "I don't want my baby to be raised by nannies. Or governesses. Or to go to boarding school. Or to sleep in another wing of the palace. I want him or her sleeping with me, if that's what works. I want to carry her and cuddle her and take her everywhere I go. And if anyone—anyone—suggests otherwise, I reserve the right to tell them to back the hell off. No committee. No PR agency. Every decision, whether it is the kind of foods she will eat, or the friends she has, will be up to us, and us only."

She'd been entirely ready to say "me" and "I". But as she looked into Hugo's solemn eyes it had come out "we". For they would be in this together. For real.

She expected him to make some kind of quip to lighten the mood, but he placed a hand on her cheek, looked deep into her eyes and said, "What level of hell did your parents put you through, *miele*?"

She flinched. “I don’t know what you—”

“Amber.”

She swallowed. “Enough.”

He said, “If that is what you wish then that is the way it will be. You have my word.”

She nodded. Then, without another word, she went back inside and gave the council the news.

The resort was no longer in play. The commune was saved.

And she was leaving town.

CHAPTER SEVEN

IT HAD ALL happened so fast.

Amber's pregnancy.

His uncle's death.

The trip home for the funeral. The hand-picked interviews announcing his upcoming succession. The chance to fulfil the destiny he had grown up believing would be his.

A very fast visit to see Sadie and her new fiancé, his old friend Will, who had brought him back to earth.

And then back to small-town Australia to get his bride. And to officially remove his resort plans from council consideration.

Used to working by the seat of his pants, he'd taken each revelation and rolled with it.

Only now, in the dark quiet of the private plane, the ocean sliding beneath them with a half-finished glass of Scotch in his hand, did Hugo have the chance to unpack the enormity of what had happened.

He *had* the chance, but he chose not to take it. Instead he twisted his Scotch back and forth, hypnotised by the play of light in the golden liquid.

Sovereign Prince. Father. Husband.

Husband. Father. Sovereign Prince.

Closing his eyes, he lifted the drink and downed it in one go. Wincing as the heat burned the back of his throat.

"Hey."

Hugo looked up, saw Amber leaning in the doorway. Her hair was up in a messy bun and the colourful crocheted blanket she'd used to have on the end of her bed was wrapped about her shoulders. Her eyes were puffy from sleep.

"Are you drunk?" she asked.

"Not yet."

"Is this something I need to worry about?"

Hugo laughed, running a hand up the back of his neck. "Not at all. I was raising a quiet glass to my uncle."

"It looked like you were drowning your sorrows."

"Same thing, I would think."

"Mmm."

Hugo shook off the funk, quickly moving the paperwork he had piled up on the chair opposite his. "Sorry, come in. Sit."

"What's all that?"

He readied himself to brush it off as "nothing", before remembering Marguerite's assertion that the men in his family had not proven themselves equipped for longevity, delegation or fidelity. He had no problem with the third, and the first was out of his hands. But the ability to see and use the resources at his disposal? That was his bag.

Amber was an outstanding natural resource. It would behove him to start as he meant to go on.

"Details of coronation plans," he said, pointing to the document printed on Marguerite's letterhead. "Articles of law currently before parliament. The notebooks are Reynaldo's private records. If there's anything you're keen to have a look through, feel free."

She blinked at him and shook her head. But after a beat she moved to sit in the chair across from his.

"Everything okay?" he asked. "Do you need food? There are more blankets…somewhere. The staff are all over that. Shall I call someone?"

She laughed softly, then pressed a fist over a yawn. "I'm fine. Just…antsy, I guess." She curled her feet beneath her. "You looked to be in deep thought just now. Took me a couple of tries to get your attention."

"I have things on my mind."

"You and me both." A beat, then, "Anything you'd like to talk about?"

"With you?"

"No, with the seatbelts. Yes, with me!"

"You must understand my shock. You've shown an aversion to talking about anything more personal than the weather up until now."

She quelled him with a look. "I'm exhausted. It's messing with my equilibrium. I probably won't even remember this conversation in the morning." She sank down deeper into the chair and let her eyes drift closed. "But sit there and stew. See if I care."

Hugo shifted in his seat, leaning an elbow against the arm rest, balancing his chin in his fingers of one hand. Was she serious? Or pulling his leg? Only one way to find out.

"I was thinking about my aunt and uncle. About what it was like for them when they first found themselves in our position."

Her eyes fluttered open.

"Unlike our exuberant expectation, Reynaldo and Marguerite started their family late. After trying for some time they fell pregnant to much rejoicing all over the land. Then they had twin girls."

"Alas."

"Reynaldo's thoughts exactly. Three years later? Another set of twin girls."

Amber's eyes sparked. "I'm starting to like this story. Still no heir for poor blackmaily Reynaldo. Go on."

"He was beginning to feel punished."

"And why wouldn't he?"

"Our succession laws are ancient and complex, and certainly different from other Royal houses of Europe. Like a house given extensions in different architectural styles over centuries until it no longer makes sense as a building. But there it is, filled with people."

Amber snuggled a little deeper into the chair and leant her head against the leather seat, her eyes sleepy but engaged. And so he went on.

"Growing up, my father was second in line. Charismatic, roguish, larger than life."

"Sounds familiar."

"Ah. But my father's behaviour declined, making it abundantly clear that he wasn't interested in the role of Sovereign and could not care less about playing the part of dutiful public servant. Meaning that, unless Reynaldo had a boy, I was next in line to the throne."

Amber watched him carefully now. Taking in every word. "And then?"

"My father died. I can't even remember much of that time. Flashes of pain. And anger. Mostly anger. For it was a one-two punch. Not only had he left my mother and me for ever, but also with his death I lost my place in the line, relegated down back behind my uncle and his sons. Reynaldo insisted I could still be of use. But I wasn't interested. I gave up on the family and put my energies into other pursuits. And succeeded.

"Reynaldo was not happy. He made life as difficult as possible for my mother as punishment. I never forgave him for that. And he never forgave me for walking away."

"My, what a twisty family you have."

"You have no idea."

"Apple doesn't fall far from the tree though, does it?"

Hugo looked up, his whole body tight. "Excuse me?"

But she didn't back down. The look in her eye was

sharp. And unforgiving. "Don't you see that you pretty much used the exact same move to get me on this plane?"

"That's not what I—"

"*Marry me or else I'll tear down your home*? What would you call it?"

Hugo ran a hand over his face.

"Relax. It's done now. I'm too tired to go another round tonight. So I'm giving you a free pass. A one-time deal. And only because I can't see how any normal person could take the amount of stuff that has been thrown at you in the past few days and glide through with ease and grace. It's a lot."

Sovereign Prince. Father. Husband.

Hugo blinked. "It is rather. And I fear there's more to come. I did some press when I came home earlier in the week but I didn't stay long enough to see how it played out. After the wedding that never happened, and my recent extended absence, I'm not sure how the people will take to a 'rebel prince' as their sovereign."

"What do you imagine they'll do? Protest? Picket? Riot?"

He turned to her with a gentle smile. "You'll find we are a seriously civilised nation. Protests would likely be more in the order of satire. Snarky journalism. A lower than usual crowd at the coronation."

"Wow. Harsh. Brace yourself."

"Quite. It's not violence I'm concerned about. It's ambivalence. We are a proud country and rightly so. It would…sadden me to know I'd had a hand in depleting that civic spirit."

"But that's not the only reason." Her feet dropped to the floor and she leant forward, elbows on thighs, hands falling gracefully over her knees. "You present as if you don't care about all that much—with your slow walk, easy smile, and always with the wry humour. But when you talk about Vallemont you become a different man. This place is truly important to you, isn't it?"

He breathed out hard. "It's who I am."

"And you want to do a good job and look after your people fairly, equitably."

"Yes."

"Then you will."

"You can't possibly know that for sure."

She looked him dead in the eye then. And said, "I've seen you at your worst now, Hugo. And I've seen you when you're on song. You can do this thing blindfolded and with one hand tied behind your back. And if I can get past my stubbornness to admit I think you won't suck, then it must be true."

He thought he'd believed it too, but hearing her say it with such conviction, for the first time it felt real. Doable. As if the challenge wasn't overwhelming, but his for the taking.

A smile started down deep before tugging at his mouth. "Will you write my coronation speech? Truly. That was beautiful."

"You bet." She nodded. "And you can do something for me in return. Don't you dare pull any more of that Reynaldo-style rubbish on me ever again, or I'll take it all back. Every word."

"I won't."

"Say it."

"I promise."

"Okay, then." She yawned. "What time is it?"

"Where?"

"Good point."

She pressed to her feet and padded back through the doorway, shooting him one last pink-cheeked smile before she was gone.

"Hot damn," Hugo said, feeling as if he'd been let off

the hook and given the greatest gift of his lifetime all in one go.

He sat back in his seat and looked out of the window, at the blanket of stars covering the dark night sky, finally ready to take on whatever came his way.

They flew into Vallemont under shadow of night.

After more than twenty-four hours in the air, constant nausea, close proximity to a man who made her twitch and itch, as well as having to deal with the enormity of what awaited her at the other end, Amber was ready to claw her way out of the plane.

Instead, she allowed the flight attendant to heave open the plane door. Then shivered at the icy air that slithered into the breach, up her legs and into her very bones.

The private airfield was quiet bar the driver of a serious-looking town car with blacked-out windows; engine humming, its exhaust fumes created clouds in the cold air.

Hugo pressed a gentling hand to the small of her back and her skin tingled in response. Not his fault. That kind of thing was bound to happen when she'd agreed to marry a wildly handsome, deeply sexy, powerful man who had swept her off her feet to rescue her from a swarm of stingless bees. *Marriage*. That felt even more strange to her than the fact she would live in a palace and become a princess.

"Everything okay, *miele*?" he asked.

Amber swallowed. The endearment he'd started using screwed with her feelings. But if she called him on it he'd know she *had* feelings. It was a Catch-22.

"Amber, look at me."

She did.

"I meant it when I said you can change your mind at any point. I've been jilted at the altar once already, remember, so if it happens again I'll take it in my stride." He smiled then, as if he did mean it. But she had seen the strain around his eyes. The Furrows of Important Dreams had become permanent the past few days.

Handsome, sexy, powerful and selfless. The guy genuinely wanted to be a good servant to his public. She was in big trouble.

But resist she would. To surround her baby with family it would be worth it.

She shook her head. "I'm fine. Just tired."

"Of course. Let's get you to bed."

Amber closed her eyes for a moment, trapping behind them the plethora of images his words brought forth.

Think of the baby. This is all for her. Or him. Or them. Twins were in the family after all. What have you let yourself in for?

Hugo led her down the stairs and towards the car.

Once the bags were squeezed into the boot, Prospero sat up front with the driver and began speaking animated Italian, leaving Hugo and Amber in the back.

Leaving behind the last throes of Australian summer, they'd hit the end of Vallemontian winter. Through the window, neatly tapered evergreens lined the roadside, mist reflected off glassy lakes, and, framing it all, craggy, snow-dusted mountains created an eerie, otherworldly feel to the place.

"Is that a village up ahead?"

"Not quite yet." Hugo glanced out of the window to check out the lights she'd seen. "It shouldn't be. Not yet."

But then the lights brightened, and she realised they were coming from the side of the road. First sporadically and then in clumps. "Hugo?"

"I see it." He pressed a button in a panel in the back of the limo. "Prospero?"

"Yes, Your Highness."

"The lights?"

"We were given forewarning, Your Highness, hence the armoured car."

Armoured? She reached her hand along the seat until it found Hugo's. He curled it into his warm grip in an instant.

"Should I be worried?"

Hugo opened his mouth to answer but Prospero got there first. "It's the people. They are lining the street, carrying lanterns which they have been making in all the local schools for days. They've come out to welcome you home."

"But it's three in the morning," Hugo said under his breath, as the groups on the side of the road got deeper and deeper the closer they got to a village. Streamers began to float over the car, sliding off the windows. And it had begun to rain what looked like rose petals.

Hugo rolled down the window, against Prospero's protests, and the noise of the crowd intensified tenfold. When he waved, the faces swimming through the darkness beamed and cheered and sang.

Amber laughed, the sound catching on the chilly air pouring into the car and floating away. "And you were worried they might pillage."

Hugo looked at her, surprise and delight etched into his handsome face. He brought her hand to his mouth and kissed it. Hard. Several times. Until she couldn't stop herself from beaming. As for the first time since this whole debacle had begun she realised it might actually be rather amazing.

"Amber?"

"Mmm?" Amber opened her eyes to find she'd fallen asleep. Her head rested on Hugo's shoulder. His arm was around her; his fingers smoothing her hair, distractedly, as if he'd been doing so for some time.

She gently disentangled herself from his arms, and surreptitiously scrubbed her fingers through her hair to get rid of the feel of him. Or maybe not so surreptitiously, as he laughed. His eyes were dark and loaded with understanding.

She looked away to find they'd pulled up outside a crumbling old building dripping with bougainvillea. Moonlight shone against an exoskeleton of scaffolding that seemed to be holding it together.

"Wow," she said. "I didn't imagine the palace to be so…quaint."

"We're not at the palace."

"We're not?"

Hugo grinned. He actually grinned. It reminded her of how he was before.

Careful, commanded the voice in her head. He might be a fixture in her life, which meant amity was more sensible than animosity, but this was an arrangement, not a relationship.

"This used to be a hotel called La Tulipe, but is now the headquarters of the new Royal Theatre, of which I am the lucky patron. Before throwing you on the mercy of the palace, I thought we'd spend our first night with friends."

"Friends?"

Before she'd even got the word out, the car door was whipped open and with the gust of icy air came a redhead in a pink beanie with a pom-pom on top.

"Hugo! You're late," she said in a lilting sing-song accent that reminded Amber of Hugo's. "It had better be because you stopped on the way for chocolate. Or wine. Or both." Then she leaned down to peer deeper into the car. As she spied Amber, her face broke out into a grin. "You must be Amber. I'm so happy you're here! Oh, Hugo, she's gorgeous. Why did you not tell us how gorgeous she was?"

"Maybe he doesn't think I'm gorgeous," Amber said, then regretted it instantly. "Forget I said that. Jet lag and catnaps, summer to winter—my brain has clearly not found its feet. Hi, I'm Amber."

"Sadie." Sadie grabbed her by the hand and all but dragged her out of the car, meaning she had to climb over Hugo, hands and elbows trying not to land anywhere precarious.

When their eyes locked for a split second he gave her the kind of smile that made thought scatter, bones melt, and strong women rethink their boundaries.

Amber spilled from the car and landed in a Sadie hug that squeezed the air from her lungs so fast it puffed out in a cloud of white. "I am so happy to meet you. You have no idea."

Sadie pulled back, looked into Amber's eyes and laughed. "Oh, no. What has Hugo said about me? It had better have been nice. For I have stories I can tell you—"

"Leo," said Hugo, now standing very close behind Amber. "It might surprise you to know that Amber and I haven't actually spent all our time together talking about you."

Sadie poked out her tongue and Hugo laughed.

Interesting. From the little that Amber had heard about this woman she hadn't imagined her to be so lovely, so charismatic and warm. Or for Hugo to be so easy with her after what she had done. But if Sadie was indeed a friend of Hugo's it only made sense.

Sadie looked from Amber to the man standing over her shoulder before a smile settled on her face. "You must be exhausted. Let's get you lovebirds inside. Prospero, you have the bags. Excellent. Follow me."

And then she was gone, Prospero in her wake.

"Wait," said Hugo when Amber went to follow. Taking her by the hand and drawing her close. "Don't let her run over the top of you."

"Excuse me?"

"I can see your mind ticking over. Trying to figure her out. Trying to figure *us* out. Leo—Sadie—is my very oldest friend. Which is why I am allowed to say that she is hyperactive, full of energy and opinions and a compulsive need to make everyone around her happy. I know you need your space, your quiet time. Don't be afraid to tell her to stop."

He knew she needed space. He knew she needed quiet time. He knew her.

Determined not to let him know how touched she was, how much that meant, Amber lifted her chin and said, "Do I look afraid?"

The hint of a smile. Then, "No."

"Okay, then."

"It's just… You got me to thinking on the plane. I don't want us to be like my aunt and uncle, so cold with one another they could barely make eye contact. I hope we can be better than that. Because we have a chance to do good here. Together. I am on your side, no matter what Sadie, or Will, or Aunt Marguerite, or the press, or ex-girlfriends who will no doubt come out of the woodwork have to say."

He reached up and pressed her hair behind her ear—a move that always sapped her breath.

Needing to hold on to her dignity before she did something stupid like fall for him, right then and there, in the moonlit darkness, she said, "You don't need a speechwriter, Hugo. You're a natural."

His face split into a smile. "Am I, now?"

"The way you put words together? I have chills."

"Then how's this for a speech? You know I think you're gorgeous, right?"

The cautious voice in her head threw its hands out in surrender. "Hugo, that was a stupid quip. Forget I ever said it."

"Can't. It's out there now. You are gorgeous. But above

and beyond that you are smart. Canny. And generous to a fault."

Amber pinched her leg to try to stop the trembles rocketing through her that had nothing to do with the cold. "You promised you wouldn't mess with me."

"On the contrary. If you were not aware of how much I appreciate your decision to accompany me, how much I appreciate you, then I have been remiss. And I apologise."

Desperate to get out of this conversation, she mumbled, "Apology accepted."

No such luck. Hugo moved closer, his voice dropping, the chill in the air nothing compared to his body heat, making her feel all warm and soft and molten. "Now it's your turn to say something nice about me. Quid pro quo."

She laughed despite herself. Better that than sighing, which was what her entire body was on the verge of doing. "My mother always said if I didn't have anything nice to say, not to say anything at all."

"From memory it's been quite some time since you've done anything your mother told you to do."

He was right. Damn him.

And as she looked into his eyes the memory of their first kiss swarmed over her. It had been inside her kitchen, mere moments after she'd invited him inside after finding him in her hammock. Like two lost souls desperate for warmth, for connection, finding recognition in one another's loneliness, they'd fallen together. After which they'd burned up the sheets.

Then something unexpected had happened over the days and weeks. The heat had expanded, allowing for warmth, loneliness giving way to comfort, to small acts of kindness and caring.

Whatever had gone down between them since—the white lies, the disagreements, the forced intimacy neither had asked for—that time had happened. It was a part of their story. A part of them.

Her hand fluttered to his chest to push him away. Or perhaps to give in to the feelings messing her up inside. To take a chance, and risk it all.

"Get a room!"

Hugo blinked, and came to, turning and smiling in the direction of the deep male voice behind Amber. "Will Darcy. Impeccable timing as always."

"Come on, mate. It's bloody freezing out here."

As the men bantered, relief and regret whirled inside of Amber, and she had to grip Hugo's shirt to keep herself from collapsing under the combined weight.

Once she felt able, she turned to meet Hugo's friend Will, a Clark Kent type, with curling dark hair, a cleft chin and bright, clever eyes.

He stepped forward. "You must be the famous Amber. Will Darcy. Pleasure to meet you."

She took his hand and was hit with a wave of familiarity. "Have we met?"

"I'm sure I'd remember." A smile. Neat white teeth. Dimple in one cheek. English accent. Again those bright, clever eyes.

Then it hit her. She clicked her fingers. "You spoke in a documentary I saw once. You're an astronomer, right?"

He nodded, and held out both hands as if to say, *Sprung.*

"I can't believe this. I was travelling at the time and you were so inspiring I actually decided on my next destination by following the Southern Cross. It's how I ended up in Serenity in the first place. Wow! Ha! This is amazing."

From behind her Hugo grumbled, "She was far less excited when she found out I was a prince."

Will laughed. "Smart woman." He then took her hand, placed it into the crook of his elbow and swept her away from Hugo, through a set of glass doors and inside the building, where they had to dodge drop-cloths and paint buckets.

In the low lamplight she saw crown mouldings, ancient wallpaper and more crumbling brick. It was like something out of a play.

They followed the sound of Sadie's voice to find her regaling Prospero with tales of refurbishment and *Much Ado About Nothing*.

Sadie looked up and saw Amber just as she yawned. "You poor love. Your rooms are right here. One each if you're sticklers for tradition, or share and share alike. Apologies that they are not yet finished. We are a work in progress."

Amber's thank-you was lost in another yawn.

Then Sadie's eyes darted to Amber's belly, before darting away.

And all the good, warm, mushy emotions she'd been feeling towards Hugo evaporated.

He'd told Sadie about the baby. Who else? Did the entire royal family know it was a shotgun wedding?

It doesn't matter, she tried to convince herself. *This was an arrangement, not a relationship.*

"Okay," said Sadie, "we'll head upstairs and leave you to it. Though I'll be fast asleep in two minutes flat, Will will be on the roof looking at his stars if you need anything. Oh, wait." She reached into the pocket of her gown and gave Hugo a small box. "That thing you wanted me to procure."

"Right. Thanks."

Will took Sadie by the hand and tucked her in behind him. "With that we'll take our leave. Goodnight. Sleep tight. See you when it's light." Then he pressed her ahead of him and into the darkness.

"If you don't have a preference I'll take the room on the left."

"Fine," said Hugo, spinning the box in his hand.

"Anyway, goodnight."

"Wait." Hugo put the box in his upturned palm and held it out to Amber, all remnants of playfulness gone. "I apologise in advance."

Amber took the box, opened it slowly and her jaw literally dropped when she saw what was inside.

It was a ring—a baguette half the size of her pinkie finger set with dozens of different-sized pink diamonds on a thick rose-gold band. "Is this for real?"

"I'm afraid it is. For that is the Ring of Vallemont. Handed down through the family for generations. My grandmother gave it to me after my father died. Quite contentious within the family, as usually it is given to the next in line to the throne. The woman was clearly psychic. When Reynaldo and Marguerite had the boys, I should have passed it on, but for some reason I couldn't. Funny, that."

"Well, it's big. And shiny. And very pink." She went to hand it back.

"No, Amber. It's yours."

"Excuse me?"

"It's your engagement ring."

She looked down at the ring again, this time with a different eye. It was huge. Cumbersome. Like something you saw in a museum, not something you wore for the rest of your married life. "But it must be worth millions."

"No. It's priceless."

She opened her mouth to protest but Hugo shut her down.

"Amber, I know my proposal was not…normal."

"Enough with the normal already."

"Yes. But no matter the circumstance, a woman should at least be given the respect of tradition."

In the near-darkness, it took a moment for Amber to

realise Hugo was making to get down on one knee. But Amber grabbed him by the shoulders and yanked him back to standing, her heart racing, blood rushing to her face.

Keeping her footing here meant not mistaking the situation even slightly. Their attraction was palpable, a constant hum that vibrated between them. Something might come of that. Who knew? But there was no room for *romance*. None.

"Look," she said, popping the ring out of the box and sliding it onto her finger. "All done."

And by gosh it fitted. Like a glove. The gold was warm and smooth, the pink the perfect tone for her skin. It didn't look nearly as big and gaudy on her finger as it had in the box. It looked pretty, elegant, right.

If she'd thought her heart was racing like a rogue train before, now it was about to jump the tracks.

"Amber," said Hugo, his voice rough, as if he'd noticed it too.

So she faked a yawn. "Sorry, but I really need some sleep."

Hugo nodded, moving into the open doorway of the unfinished room next to hers.

"What time is the thing in the morning?" she asked.

Hugo looked at his watch. "We thought about two in the afternoon. Give us time for a sleep-in and time to get ready. Do you need anything until then?"

"Someone to pinch me so I know this isn't all some strange dream."

"Sorry," he said, backing away. "I've had a dose of your reality; now it's time for you to get a dose of mine."

"Quid pro quo."

He smiled. "Exactly. I'll see you in the morning?"

Which was when Amber heard the question in his voice. No wonder. The last time Hugo had planned to marry he'd been the only one to turn up.

“I’ll be there,” she said, and meant it.

With a nod, and a furrow of the brow, Hugo slipped into his room and quietly shut the door.

Amber did the same. She glanced over her bag, then to the bed. It had been so long since she’d slept on a mattress that hadn’t been handed down a thousand times, she crawled from the end to the pillows and sank onto her back, her entire body groaning in pleasure.

She wished Ned were here now. She could do with something to cuddle. But he was in quarantine, hurrying through the requisite vet checks, and would hopefully be with them within the month.

A gentle knock rapped at her door. She sat up, heart thumping, expecting Hugo.

“Come in,” she said.

Her disappointment must have been obvious as Sadie’s face dropped before she glanced towards the wall connecting the two rooms.

“Sorry,” said Sadie. “I know you just want some privacy and sleep. But I was upstairs feeling awful about something… There was a moment earlier when I saw you touch your tummy, and you saw me see and…”

Sadie took the few steps into the room and sat next to Amber, before taking her by the hand. When she saw the ring she stopped, a smile tugging at the corners of her mouth. “Wow. I never thought that thing could suit anybody, but you rock the rock.”

Then she looked up and said, “Hugo came to visit us briefly when he was here for Reynaldo’s funeral. To tell us about you. And about the baby.”

Amber breathed out hard. Sadie shook Amber’s hands as if hoping to shake out the sigh.

“But not to embarrass you or make you feel uncomfortable. Only so that he could insist we were gentle with you. And so that we didn’t force you to stay up late and chat and tell us all about yourself, which I'd really love to do. And so I didn't try to force prawns or wine down your throat. Why prawns I have no idea. I can't remember the last time I even ate a prawn. And because he's so excited. In fact, I've never heard him talk the way he talked about you; words tripping over themselves, so many adjectives. I was actually a tad worried he'd been hypnotised until I saw you. Or, more specifically, saw him with you."

Amber had no idea what to say.

Sadie clearly took it as a sign to keep talking. "He's usually so cool. Nothing fazes him. Not even being ditched at the altar. He understood, he moved on. He can be frustratingly enlightened that way. But he followed you in here like a lost puppy. It's actually hilarious. I'm going to enjoy this very, very much."

"Well, I'm not so enlightened, just so you know. I'm rather overwhelmed right now."

"I'd be more worried if you weren't." Sadie patted her on the hand. "Just trust in Hugo, love Hugo, and you'll be right as rain."

Trust? Love? She might as well be asked to run to the moon. Amber managed to say, "Thanks for putting us up here tonight. And for organising tomorrow."

"My pleasure." With a wink Sadie was gone, leaving Amber to fall back onto the bed, splaying out like a star.

She stared at the ceiling, her mind whirling, wondering if she'd sleep at all...and was gone to the world less than three minutes later.

The next day, at just after two on a chilly winter's afternoon, with Will and Sadie as witnesses, and their office manager, Janine, throwing peony petals at their feet, Amber and Hugo were married.

CHAPTER EIGHT

"PLEASE TELL ME you are not married!"

Hugo had been reading about the measures that would be put in place to protect the royal family at the coronation, when his aunt barged into his office in the palace.

Because she'd recently lost her husband—and that barging into any room in her palace used to be within her rights—he let it go.

"I could. But that would be a lie."

"Oh, Hugo. What were you thinking?"

"Better for worse. Richer for poorer. That kind of thing."

"Hugo…"

Hugo reclined in his chair, the very picture of laid-back. "Aunt Marguerite, we didn't see the point in starting my reign with a costly wedding followed by a costly coronation, so we married atop the roof of La Tulipe with a view of the palace and friends bearing witness."

And it had been fun, of all things, everyone in a festive mood. The ceremony was a blur but afterwards they'd talked, laughed, told stories. And after the tumult of the past several months, watching that group of people get along, he felt an uncommonly large swell of pride at knowing the lot of them.

"*We?*" Marguerite looked around as if his wife might be hiding under the table.

"Her name is Amber. And you will be nice to her. Kind. Helpful. In fact, you will be her fairy godmother."

Marguerite looked as pained by the idea as he'd hoped she might. "At least tell me she can string a sentence together. That she has some semblance of class."

While he itched to tell her Amber was all that and more, Hugo folded his arms and admitted nothing. Let her sweat.

Marguerite sighed. "I had a number of lovely girls from good families lined up ready to meet you. I'd even sent out invitations for an intimate dinner party for tonight."

"Probably best you cancel."

Another sigh. "And her name is truly *Amber*?"

"Amber Giordano, Princess of Vallemont, no less." A beat, then he threw her a bone. "It was Grantley."

"I'm not sure I know the family."

Hugo laughed. "I'm sure you don't. Amber's parents are very well-respected lawyers out of Canberra." Hugo didn't know why he was building them up because Amber's background mattered not a jot to him. But it would be of interest to others. Something he hadn't considered in his hot-headed decision to throw her over his shoulder and bring her back to his cave.

"She is *Australian*?" She pressed a hand to her forehead.

"So dramatic. If you're looking to spice things up, Sadie could give you a role in one of her plays."

Marguerite lifted her head and levelled him with a look. "You look more and more like your father every year, you know. And now you have found a girl in that hot, dusty, hippy outback town and brought her here and for some reason you expect a different result."

Hugo didn't even realise he was standing until his hands hit the desk top. While it took every ounce of diplomacy he had not to erupt, his voice was like ice chips as he said, "That's enough. Amber is my wife. This time next week she will be the wife of your Sovereign Prince. And even if none of that were true, she still deserves your respect. When you meet her you will see that she is bright, articulate and lovely. She is also resolute. If you try to push her she will push back because she does not take bull from anyone. Not even me."

Marguerite kept eye contact for a long while before glancing away. "At least tell me she is beautiful."

Hugo moved around the desk and held out two hands to lift his aunt out of the chair. "Very."

"Brunette?"

"Blonde."

She winced. "At least it's better than red. Our Sadie, with that red hair of hers, would have been much harder to dress."

"I wouldn't count on it. Now go away. I am a busy man. And you have a coronation to plan."

"At least there is that." Marguerite nodded, angling her cheek for a kiss, then left.

It left Hugo feeling on edge, though quite honestly he'd been feeling on edge all day. He hadn't seen Amber since the palace chef had insisted on feeding them a private wedding banquet in the dining hall the night before. Amber had nearly fallen asleep in her dessert.

He wondered where she was right now, whether she was coping, if she was content. Though he feared he knew her well enough to know that without focus, without someone or something to look after, she would be bored out of her mind.

"Prospero?"

The big guy was through the door in a flash.

"Can you check if the package has arrived?"

Amber sat on the balcony of her rooms in the palace, huddled under a blanket, drinking ginger and honey tea to keep her nausea at bay and staring out into the very un-Australian wilderness in the distance.

To say she felt antsy would be an understatement.

While Sadie called daily and Hugo checked in as often as he could, she was used to keeping busy. Tending her bees, working at the shop, keeping Sunflower company while she painted, or taking Johnno into town to make sure he made it back again. She missed her friends. She missed Serenity. But, knowing they were only a plane flight away, mostly she missed being of use. At least Sunflower was looking after her bees.

She glanced at the side table where the pile of books Hugo had left in her room one night sat; books about princesses past. From ex-movie stars to kindergarten teachers. Women who had used their new platform to highlight children's diseases, women's rights, science, the arts, mental health.

All wrapped in an ostentatious big pink ribbon with little tiaras imprinted all over it, the gift had been given with a wink, but also a nudge. The man knew her too well.

She sat forward to read the back cover blurb when out of the corner of her eye she saw movement below…

No. It couldn't be. He wasn't due to get through quarantine for another few weeks.

But it was Ned, bounding across the grass!

Throwing off the blanket, she leaned as far over the balcony as she could without tumbling over the side to see if he had anyone with him. But he seemed to be galumphing around happily on his own. She called his name as loud as she could. But he wouldn't have heard her anyway.

So she had to go down there, find her way out of the maze of halls and staircases and wings and—

Hand to her throat, she stifled a scream. A woman cast a shadow in her doorway.

Something about her, several things in fact—the chignon, the long neck, the lean frame, the pale, elegant skirt suit, the legs locked straight on prohibitively high heels—

made Amber think of her mother and she came out in an instant sweat.

Then the woman stepped out onto the balcony and Amber's panic eased.

"I startled you," said the stranger.

You think?

"I'm Princess Marguerite."

"Amber," said Amber. She held out a hand and the other woman took it, as if expecting her ring to be kissed. But Amber hadn't come this far to be kissing anyone's ring. Amber shook and let go.

"How are you settling in, my dear?"

"Gradually."

"Hmm. You're a long way from small-town Australia."

Suddenly Hugo's promise to be "on her side" had resonance. For while the Princess was being perfectly civil, Amber was fluent in the language of passive-aggressive disappointment.

Amber casually leant her backside against the brick balustrade and said, "A whole twenty-four hours by plane, in fact."

A quick smile came and went, along with a flash of surprise. "And what did you do in Serenity, Amber?"

"I was a beekeeper. And I co-ran a honey shop." She let that sit a moment before adding, "How about you, Marguerite? What do you do around here?"

The woman's eyes widened, before a smile lit her face. "My nephew warned me that if I pressed you, you would press back. I'm rather glad to see he was right."

Amber felt herself begin to relax.

"He also said you were beautiful, but he didn't tell me I had all of that to work with. The man has always underplayed his achievements."

Amber opened her mouth to protest being labelled an achievement.

But Princess Marguerite waved her hand, stopping her. "I had come in here merely to have a look at you, but now that I have I think I can skip forward a few steps and we can have an honest conversation."

"Okay."

"I stood where you are before you were even born. On the precipice of being the wife of a ruling prince." She glanced down at the pile of books on the side table next to Amber's chair and made no comment. "It's a position that requires grace, diplomacy, style, self-assurance and temerity."

Amber laughed softly. "One out of five ain't bad." Then she heard a bark and turned to look over the balcony.

Only to find Ned was not alone after all.

Hugo was there, striding across the grass in suit trousers and a dress shirt, the wind ruffling his hair and the wintry sun glinting down upon him as if he was made of gold.

He stopped, brought a hand to his mouth, and whistled loud enough for all the forest animals to hear. It worked. Ned pricked his good ear, before bounding back.

But then Hugo reached down. He threw a towel over his shoulder and picked up a bucket and a sponge. And Ned stopped so fast he practically laid down smoke.

It fast became a case of chicken. Ned, standing like a statue, waiting for Hugo to creep up on him, then bolting the moment he got close. Leaving Hugo to place hands on hips and breathe so as not to lose all patience.

Amber laughed at the ridiculousness of the sight, bringing her hands to her mouth to hold in the waves of emotion lifting and rising inside of her.

Oh, Hugo. That's not playing fair.

"What on earth is he doing?" Marguerite had joined her.

"Trying to wash my dog and failing heroically."

Amber felt Marguerite's curious gaze on her but she didn't care. No one was about to burst this bubble. Ned was here, and Hugo had made that happen. She wanted to hug them both so hard.

She cupped her hands around her mouth and called Hugo's name, but her voice didn't carry nearly far enough. So instead she held her arms tight about her and watched, smiling so hard her cheeks ached.

"Where is Prospero? Shall I summon help?"

"Nah," said Amber. "Let him figure it out himself. It's character building."

By the time Hugo managed to catch his quarry he had wet patches on his dress shirt and soap bubbles in his hair. His cheeks were pink from the cold air, and the exertion. And Ned looked so happy with all that land, the cool sunshine and the man who'd given it to him that Amber's heart clutched. Squeezing so tight she groaned.

She'd never felt anything like it in her life. As if she was filled with air and breathless all at once. It was too much. And she could no longer hold it back.

Like a stone tossed into a lake, she was falling for him. Tripping and tumbling and sinking deeper and deeper.

Not that she could ever tell him so.

She wouldn't have a clue where to start. She couldn't remember a single time her parents had told her they cared, much less used the magic word. Meaning she never had either—not once. Not even to Ned.

But mostly because the thought of putting herself out there like that terrified her to the centre of her very bones. He wouldn't laugh in her face. That wasn't Hugo's style. But what if he was ambivalent? She couldn't face that again.

No. There was no quid pro quo for this. This was a secret to keep.

She breathed out a sigh as Hugo knelt in the wet grass and Ned's muddy paws landed on his shoulders. He gave the wet dog a big rub about the ears, looking more relaxed than he had since arriving at the palace.

He was so busy, which was to be expected, but she had a new job to do too. Sure, it would be a challenge, but she thrived on challenge. And, so long as she had that man *on* her side and *at* her side, then it might well be the adventure of her life.

"Marguerite, can I ask you a favour?"

"Of course, my dear. What is it?"

"I have a pretty important event coming up and I think I might need a new dress."

"Oh, you dear girl. I thought you'd never ask."

Hugo stood behind the doors leading to the ceremonial balcony.

Marguerite had given him a kiss on the cheek before heading off to schmooze with the invited guests. His mother had even come by to wish him luck before disappearing back into the sanctuary of her rooms.

Leaving him to stare at the gap between the doors leading outside, alone.

Memories of his childhood flittered and faded; running these roads till he knew every fallen log, every hidden stream, every badger sett; slicing open a knee jumping a fence or two—he still had the scar; climbing those trees and dropping seedpods on the ancestors of the sheep that roamed there today.

Today he would officially become Sovereign Prince of all that and more. No longer merely a finance whizz, but a master of policy, of protection. Open to new ways while respecting the methods of governance and social life that had worked for generations. Beholden to the people of his country until the day he died.

He could not wait.

"Hugo?"

Hugo turned to find Amber strolling towards him. And whatever he'd been thinking about dissolved into dust motes in his mind.

For she was a vision in a sparkling pink dress that shimmered as she moved. The top hugged her curves, the skirt a feast of silk peonies swishing about her legs as she walked. A small diamond tiara nestled in her long, honey-gold hair, she looked like the Queen of the fairy folk.

Hugo swore beneath his breath. Or perhaps a little louder than that, as she shot him a quick smile.

"I know, right?" she said, giving a little twirl. "I scrubbed up well."

"Understatement of the millennium," he said, his heart thundering at the sight of her. "In fact, who cares about the coronation? I'm sure there's a broom cupboard somewhere if you'd care for a quick five minutes in heaven."

A smile quirked at the edge of her mouth and she moved closer and fussed with the brocade of his royal uniform on one shoulder. "From what I remember, you can do better than five minutes."

The world slowed to a complete stop. His wife was flirting with him.

Not that he was about to complain. In fact… He slid his hand around her waist, tugging her closer, and she let him. His voice grew low, intimate, as he said, "I wanted to thank you for my coronation gift. It was terribly thoughtful."

"What do you get for the man who has everything? I know your library is extensive, so I hoped you didn't have it."

"No. It is my very first edition of *Dog Washing for Dummies* and I will treasure it always."

She laughed then. Her soft pink mouth twisting into a smile that made his head spin.

Then the trumpets blared and the murmur of the crowd reached a crescendo. And there was no time for broom cupboards. Or flirting. Or mooning over his wife. There were more important things—

Screw it.

He pulled her in and kissed her before he could think about it. There was no hesitation; she sank into him, tipped onto her toes, her arms going around his neck as she kissed him back.

Then, far too few seconds later, she pulled back in a rush. Her gaze going to his mouth.

"Oh, no, no, no. My lipstick. You're all pink." She slid down his front, and it was all he could do not to groan. And she frantically rubbed the edge of his mouth using her thumb.

"It *is* one of our national colours. Perhaps the people might even appreciate it."

She laughed, though it was slightly hysterical.

Then the doors pressed open, letting in the wintry sunlight, the fresh Vallemontian air, and the voice and song of his people.

He let Amber go but only so far as he needed to in order to take her by the hand.

"But Marguerite said I was only to go this far."

"And do you care what Marguerite says?"

Her eyes sparked and she tucked her hand between his and looked out to the hills, tipping onto her toes to see the size of the crowd. Tens of thousands. More than the entire population of the country. She laughed. "This is insane."

"No," he said, walking her out onto the balcony, "this is us."

The coronation went without a hitch.

With the head of parliament taking Hugo's oath, tens of thousands of Vallemontian nationals as well as many tourists cheered and waved flags.

Once it was all over, Hugo and Amber retired once more

to the relative quiet of the anteroom. Their gazes caught and they both burst into laughter. Then Hugo reached out to Amber, gathered her up and twirled her about, her honey-blonde waves swinging behind her.

When he put her down she smacked her fists against his chest. "Was that as much of a rush for you as it was for me? It was like a million-person love-in. They adore you, Hugo."

"Of course they do. I am adorable," he said, taking off his gloves, then undoing the buttons on his jacket and passing the accoutrements to a valet. Then, catching her eye, he said the first thing that came into his head. "I want to kiss you again very badly."

Her laughter faded, but the light remained in her eyes. "It's the dress."

"It's the woman inside the dress."

No comeback for that one.

"One of these days I'm going to crack that crotchety exterior of yours, Amber Giordano, and I'm going to find that your centre is as soft and gooey as they come."

"Dream on," she said.

"I plan on it." Then, "Do you want to get out of here?"

"More than anything."

Within half an hour they were in the palace garage.

Instructed to change into something more comfortable, Amber had taken him at his word, changing into her old jeans, boots, a jumper and a beanie.

Amber looked wide-eyed over the royal car collection; at least a small part thereof.

Hugo pointed to a small Fiat, bright yellow, laughing at how disappointed she was. "The last kind of car people would expect to see their Prince driving, so get in."

"Yes, Your Highness," she said. When she saw Ned

sitting in the back seat, panting happily, she brightened. "Hey, boy. Are you coming too?"

And they were off, with Prospero and a bolstered security team discreetly on their tail.

Soon they were driving up into the foothills, heading towards the rugged landscape of Folly Cascades—the site of Vallemont's most infamous waterfall.

"This was once a primary timber area," he said, when he noticed Amber craning to see out of every window. "Prosperous from milling and hydro-power."

It was now the location of Cascade Cabins. They were small by the standards of the places he built today. Quaint and rustic, but still extremely popular. Except right now, the place was empty, the guests having been "upgraded" to the elegant Lake Glace resort over the next rise so that he would not be disturbed. So that the security team felt more comfortable too.

Hugo pulled up by a log cabin, its age evident in the ivy climbing the walls, the damp, mossy rocks lining the path and the forest that had regrown around it.

Ned hopped out of the car first and sniffed all the lovely woodsy smells.

Amber followed close behind, rolling her shoulders, breathing deeply. "What is this place?"

"The first resort I ever built."

Her eyes swung to him. "You built this?"

His hands went into his pockets and he swung up onto his toes. "Not with my own bare hands, but yes, it was my design. My idea, my funding, my project. Validation I could be successful at something other than just a spare prince-in-waiting."

This place had been the making of him. The planning battles, the down-to-the-wire negotiations, the extreme physicality required to get a place such as this to fruition, had given him grit, built his fortitude, shown him how to deal with failure. He would be a better prince for it.

"This is what you had in mind for Serenity?"

Hugo's gaze swung back to Amber. "My style has evolved since I built this place, as well as my budget. But I imagine a similar kind of 'grown out of the environment' feeling to the place. This, but with every modern luxury."

She breathed out hard through her nose, then looked with a fresh eye, taking in lush surroundings, the quiet overlaid with sounds of birdsong, of forest animals, the comfortably rustic aesthetic.

Hugo knew the moment she found the sign. A couple of days back he'd had it made, the words "The Shack" burned into a piece of wood. It was now attached to the front door of the small cabin ahead.

She walked slowly up onto the porch, barely noticing when Ned ran past chasing a butterfly.

Hugo followed. "If you ever need a time-out, a break from the crazy goings-on of the palace, this cabin can be your escape. There's a spare room, which I thought we could set up as a nursery. Perhaps get a fold-out couch in case of visitors. But I'll leave all that up to you, since it is your coronation gift."

"My…? But I gave you a book."

"Which I will read from cover to cover. Now back to my gift. I asked Maintenance to take the door off its hinges, and to put a hammer to a couple of the walls to make it feel more like home, but—"

"Shut up," she said, her voice ragged. "Just shut up."

And then she threw herself at him. Literally. Her feet left the ground and he wrapped her up tight, right as her lips found his.

The soft, sweet taste of her was like an elixir, scrambling his thoughts. But not so much that he couldn't find the door. He yanked it open, carrying her inside using one arm.

He kicked the front door closed—his security team was out there somewhere and there they could stay—and together they stumbled into the main room, where a fire crackled in the hearth.

They backed into the room, narrowly missing couches and end tables, and bumping into a lamp that threatened to topple. Then Amber's toes caught on the floor or the rug, acting as a brake, and Hugo twisted to take the brunt of the fall. He rolled so that she was beneath him, her hair splayed out across the fur.

Her chest rose to meet his as she breathed heavily, her dark eyes looked unblinking into his. He lowered his face, achingly slowly, and brushed his lips across hers.

Then suddenly she scrunched her eyes shut tight. "This is too much."

For Hugo it wasn't nearly enough.

"I can't take all this…this romance."

"Is that what this is?"

"Come on, Hugo. The cars, the sign, the fireplace. You're romancing me." She stuck her left hand in his face, showing off the ring. "At this point in time, it's pretty much moot."

Hugo took her hand, kissed her knuckles and then turned her hand over and kissed her palm. "I beg to differ. We did this all backwards, you see."

She blinked. He kissed the tips of her fingers one by one.

"We fell into bed together. And then we fell out. Then we fell pregnant. And then we eloped. We missed this part, you see. The drives, the dates, the romance."

She breathed and said nothing.

"Now, will you shut up and let me woo my wife?"

He let her hand drop back to her chest and looked into

her eyes, where he saw hope, timid and shy; emotion, ragged and true; desire and slow sexual unfurling.

"No more talk," she said, her voice barely a whisper. "I've had enough talk. From Sadie and Marguerite. From the protocol people and the ladies-in-waiting. Even Prospero has found his voice. Did you know he has a thing for insects? I've never answered so many questions about bees as I have this week."

"No more talk," Hugo promised.

"I'm a girl of action."

"Then let's get you some." Hugo ran a hand down her side, holding himself together by the skin of his teeth as her body undulated beneath his touch.

"More," she said, and he wondered how he had gone this long without touching her, tasting her, revelling in her beautiful abandon.

He kissed the bottom of her jaw and the soft spot below her ear.

He knew her tells—like the way she nibbled at her bottom lip. But there was something new here too. A new tension that had her in its grip.

"It's okay if you're nervous."

She flung her eyes open. "I'm not nervous."

"I'd understand," he said, taking advantage of her open mouth and tugging on her lower lip until her eyes near rolled back in her head. Then, "The last time we did this, I was merely a man. This time you'll be making love to a prince."

It took a moment for her to come back to him, but when she did she burst into laughter. "If you believe it makes a difference, prove it."

"As you wish," Hugo murmured, and set about doing just that.

It was agony taking it slow. The sweetest agony there was. But he took his time undressing her, caressing her, stretching out her pleasure. Until her breaths grew ragged, her hands clung to him and she rolled and writhed beneath the touch of his fingers, his mouth.

When he kissed her belly he did so with all the gentleness he could manage. He kissed to the right of her belly button, then the left, breathing in the scent of her skin, letting the knowledge that a part of him grew inside of her wash over him.

He rose to kiss her. She lifted to catch the kiss.

When he pulled back her eyes caught on his—dark, sensual, nearly lost to pleasure.

He stopped torturing her—torturing himself—and joined her. Neither looked away as they rocked together. As they made love.

Then Amber gasped, gripping him, her fingers digging into his arms. Heat and pleasure and emotion collected inside his core, before flooding through him like a lava flow.

While a single tear travelled down the edge of her cheek, manifesting the stunning emotion welling behind her eyes. No hiding. No pretending. No secrets. As if he could see all the way to her soul.

It was sumptuous. It was undefended.

It was his.

"What does *miele* mean?" she asked, her voice sleepy.

"Hmmm?"

"You call me that sometimes."

Did he? He hadn't noticed. But then, it did suit her. "It means honey."

Amber smiled up at him before rolling onto her side and taking his arm to place it over her like a cage. She snuggled into the cradle of his body. Within moments her breathing slowed.

While Amber drifted gently to sleep, Hugo had never felt so awake in his entire life.

* * *

An hour later, Hugo stood by the window, looking unseeingly into the forest beyond, his mind still freewheeling.

He was married to the most compelling woman he had ever known. They had a child on the way, and he had just been crowned Sovereign Prince of the country he loved.

It was a strange and unexpectedly difficult moment to realise he had everything he could ever want.

Philosophically, he knew that he should be crowing. Instead he felt as if he was careening towards the edge of a cliff.

He glanced back at Amber, who lay asleep on the fluffy rug by the fire, curled up in a ball beneath the throw he'd laid over her, not quite covering her dandelion tattoo. Her face was gentled in sleep.

As if the things he had to face—the security threats, the debilitating weight of overwhelming bureaucracy that remained after such a long reign—had nothing to do with her. But they did, as she was his wife. Making it far harder to make clear decisions when how it would affect her was never far from his mind.

He could no longer pretend that this was a mere marriage of convenience; a prince in need of a princess, a child in need of a father. There were feelings here—deep, broad, twisty, ingrained, developing, reaching feelings.

It would not have concerned him nearly as much if it had been one-sided. He had been stuck on Amber from the moment they had met.

But now he was certain Amber felt something for him too. He'd seen it in her eyes. Felt it in her touch. He'd tasted it as he'd kissed away the tear as she'd fallen asleep in his arms.

He could not offer any more than he already had—a beautiful home, the opportunity to do real good in the world, and as much help raising their child as she desired. But truly tender feelings? Love?

At thirty-two years of age his growing was all done. His heart was as big as it was ever going to get.

And yet making love to Amber, as her husband, had created a shift inside of him, allowing an aching kind of regret to bleed through the cracks. Only proving that, while he would not bend, he could still break.

As Sovereign Prince of the great nation of Vallemont, breaking was not an option. He would not make the mistakes his father had made and screw it all up.

He crouched down, pressing her hair away from her face, and forced himself to ignore the heat rushing through him. “Amber. *Miele*, wake up.”

One eye opened, and then the other. Her hair was all messed up, her face pink with sleep, leaving him feeling disorientated with desire.

You can do this. You can resist. It’s the only way.

“Did I snore?” she asked. “I dreamt I was snoring.”

“Like an ogre,” he lied.

She breathed sleepily. Then she ruffled her hair and yawned and Hugo felt such a heady mix of affection and bone-deep attraction it threatened to take his legs out from under him.

It seemed that decades of protocol would no longer be enough. He would have to keep his wife at arm’s length in order not to slip again. It might well be the hardest thing he ever had to do, but it was the price he had to pay to take on the role for which he had prepared for his entire life.

“I just had the best dream,” she said, her words sliding into a yawn. “The best part? Waking up and knowing real life was better.”

Then she reached up to touch his face. Wound so tightly, he couldn’t help but flinch, his entire body physically recoiling from her touch.

Amber saw it too. She suddenly went stiff, as if the blood had drained out of her extremities. “Hugo?”

He squared his shoulders and stood. “It’s time to go.”

“Already?”

“I’m needed back at the palace.”

“Shortest honeymoon ever.” She tried for a joke, her brow furrowing when he didn’t smile. “But I guess the beauty of being married to the owner means we can come back any time.”

It was. But it could never happen. Not if he had any chance of being the kind of prince he’d always wanted to be.

“Come on.” He held out a hand. Hesitating, she took it, allowing him to help her to her feet.

Confusion flashed behind her eyes, as well it might. She searched his face for the reason for his reticence.

The urge to explain was near overwhelming. But confessing his feelings would only put the onus on her, which was entirely unfair.

In that moment, he found himself understanding his forebears. Keeping separate apartments wasn’t a simple matter of conflicting social hours, or full closets, or accommodating separate staff; it was a necessary form of self-protection.

Then Amber straightened her shoulders, pulled the blanket around her and said, “Okay, then. I guess that’s that. I’ll collect my things.”

He made to let her go, but then at the last—blaming the streak of self-destruction he could have inherited from either of his parents—he took her by the hand and twirled her into his arms and placed a gentle kiss on her lips.

She sank into him without hesitation, his beautiful, fierce, impossible Princess.

When she pulled back she looked into his eyes for a moment. And this time she pressed away. As if she was so used to being dismissed that closing herself off was the easier path for her too.

It was why he was sure this could work.

The both of them were so screwed up they would never let love get in the way of a good thing.

CHAPTER NINE

THE MORNING AFTER the coronation, Amber lay on the colossal bed in her private apartment feeling nothing.

Not sick. Not any more. The usual gnawing sensation had gone from her belly. She was simply…blank.

She stared at the canopy over her bed, her gaze skimming brocade and fringing, lace and…were those crystals? The workmanship was beautiful. Exquisite even. Sunflower would take one look at the detail and burst into happy tars.

But Amber couldn't seem to find the energy to care.

Perhaps it was because she'd grown up with money—with prestige, luxury, really nice bedding—and had turned her back on it.

That was the thing her friends had been so shocked about. Not the fact she felt misunderstood and overlooked to the point of legally emancipating herself, but that it had been enough for her to turn her back on the rewards.

Over the first few years she'd questioned her decision more than once—when she'd been hungry, broke, when she'd had every one of her meagre possessions stolen from a cheap motel.

Until she'd followed the Southern Cross and arrived in Serenity.

From the moment she'd looked up that hill, over that field of lavender, she'd felt vindicated in her choice to follow her own path. For she had found people who opened their arms to anyone. Heck, Hugo had planned to rearrange their entire existence and they'd welcomed him in and said, "Let's see what you have to say." Every decision they made came from a place of acceptance. Of love.

People were life's true reward. Having a community to rely on. Having a community rely on her.

She'd met Hugo while high on their goodness, in a single glance seeing him as worthy of her time, and over time finding him a man of honour and depth, of humour and heat. A man who truly seemed to value her, not for what she could do for him but because of the qualities he saw in her. The elusive something she'd been searching for her entire life.

It was their fault that she'd believed his promises.

Waking in front of the fire on their "honeymoon", she'd felt so happy. That a man as busy as he, with all the pressures he was under, had taken the time to create something private, something uniquely them. It had been a few seconds of pure and utter bliss.

And then she had opened her eyes.

There had been nothing in particular that she could put her finger on. Only that he'd seemed cool, detached; like a marble bust of a prince rather than flesh and blood.

On the drive back to the palace he'd asked her questions, answered hers; his hands had been relaxed on the wheel. But nothing was as it had seemed before. Nothing at all. Suddenly, the wintry cold outside was nothing compared to the chill within.

Which was when she'd realised it had all been in her head.

That she was so desperate for affection she'd believed the fairy tale. But it had been nothing but an illusion created by a broken, lonely girl.

Finding some deep reserve of energy, she pulled herself to sitting then padded over to the dressing table and sat.

The reflection in the mirror was of a woman she barely knew. Her hair was a mess, her eyes dark and sleepy; her cheeks a little leaner than usual, a result of barely keeping her food down for days. But that would change. She'd fill out, become smooth and rosy and plump.

The baby that had connected them in some quiet, magical way suddenly felt vulnerable. As if she hadn't been as diligent in her protection as she'd promised.

Amber put a hand over her belly and said, "Shh. It's all right. It's all going to be okay."

And then a knock came at the door.

Marguerite didn't wait for a response before entering. A plethora of strangers followed in her wake.

Amber grabbed the fine mohair throw from the back of the chair and wrapped it around her shoulders to cover her thin T-shirt and bare legs.

"Good morning, Your Highness."

"Good morning." She ran a quick hand over her bed hair and edged over to the Princess. "Marguerite? Who are these people?"

"My dear, I'd like to introduce you to your staff." One by one Marguerite pointed to the people in the line, listing hairdresser, make-up artist, stylist, linguists, personal planner, personal cook, and other positions she didn't quite catch.

She gave a double-take to the cook, who had the same wild strawberry-blonde waves as Sunflower, but the woman's smile was tight. Not like sunny Sunflower's at all.

So this was her new "community": a group of strangers whose job it was to tell her what to do, how to look, talk and dress, what to eat and where to go.

It didn't feel right. Not a bit. In fact, it felt horribly familiar.

She glanced towards the door, but what was she going to do? Complain to Hugo? He was so busy. And after the day before, she was no longer sure how firmly on her side he really was.

Instead, she turned to Marguerite, who looked positively buoyant as she pressed one last woman forward. In her fifties, with a tight grey bun and a stern countenance, she looked like the nasty principal from a Roald Dahl novel.

"Hi," said Amber as the woman loomed over her. "And you are…?"

"This," said Marguerite, "is Madame Brassard. She is the nanny."

Amber stilled. It took everything in Amber not to put a hand to her belly. "The what, now?"

"The nanny. For when the time comes, in the future, that you and Hugo are blessed with children, Madame Brassard will be assisting you in their day-to-day care. She has impeccable credentials, has worked with several important families, although non-disclosure agreements mean I cannot say who."

Having a breakdown was bad enough. Having one in front of a room full of strangers, some of whom probably didn't even understand a word she was saying, was a mortifying thought.

"Marguerite, may I please talk to you in private?"

"Dear girl, I'm afraid that the moment you become a Giordano there is no such thing as private any more. Especially from these good people."

"But I don't know these people."

"You will. In good time. They are your team, my dear."

Ah, no, she would not. Amber's hackles were now screaming.

"I actually prefer to build my own teams, if it's all right with you."

"Unfortunately, that is not possible. We have security to consider. Tradition. Royal protocol."

With every one of Marguerite's attempts to block her, Amber felt the walls closing in. She held up both hands in the international sign for stop. "I don't give a flying hoot about royal protocol. I truly don't."

Marguerite's eye twitched. "You married a prince, my dear. And not just any prince. The Sovereign Prince. It comes with responsibilities..."

Amber held up a finger to hush her, and the "team" all gasped in shock. But Amber's head was now buzzing so hard it might as well have been filled with bees. "Semantics aside, I did not marry a prince. I married a man. I married Hugo. A man who I may, one day, have children with. And if I do, it was made very clear that I will raise them myself." She added a belated, "With him."

Marguerite's expression was unreadable, though Amber could have sworn she saw a flicker of respect.

"Where's Hugo? I need Hugo."

Marguerite snapped her fingers, the lady-in-waiting leaping to her side. "Sofia, send word to the Prince that—"

"Wait! No. Thank you, Sofia, but you do not have to send word. I'm a smart woman with two feet and the ability to put one in front of the other. I can find the Prince myself."

With that she left her parody of a "commune" in her rooms. She tracked down Hugo in his apartment, which was down the hall and around a couple of bends. Seriously, who lived that way and called it a relationship? It was insane.

This whole thing was insane.

Her head spinning, her heart racing, she came to a halt in the open doorway when she saw Hugo was with his "team" too.

Prospero noticed her in an instant. "Your Highness?"

"Just a moment," said Hugo, sitting on the banquette at the end of his big bed, paper resting on his knee. Her heart squeezed at the sight of him, turning her into a mess of confusion and need.

"Hugo," Prospero said, his voice more insistent than Amber had ever heard it.

Hugo clearly felt the same way, as his gaze swung past his muscle man to Amber. Whatever he saw on her face brought him to his feet, eating up the floor and coming to her side.

"*Miele*, what is wrong? What happened? Is it—?"

His hands reached out to hold her before they stopped mid-air, as if a remote control had changed him from go to stop. The anxiety ramped from an eight to an eleven.

Then he stared at her belly as if an alien were about to explode out of her.

"No." She looked around at the half-dozen others in the room, each one looking out of the window or at their feet. "It's not that."

He breathed out hard. "Good. Excellent."

And then he took a step back and put his hands into his pockets, the disconnection as strong as if he had shut the door in her face.

And whatever anxiety she had felt at Marguerite's intrusion was nothing on the emotional wreck she became in that moment.

She somehow found words, saying, "I can see you are busy, but do you have a moment?"

He breathed out hard, and looked around at the dozen people all vying for his attention. He ran a hand through his hair and it stayed messy. He looked beleaguered. And it made her heart twist, just a smidge, to note that he was struggling too.

"Just one minute," she said, holding onto the very last hope that she was reading things wrong; giving him a chance to show her that she was wrong. That he *was* on her side. That he did care. That she could count on him as she'd thought.

Then he said, "Give me five minutes to finish up here and I'll come find you."

He hovered a hand near her back, ostensibly shooing her from the room. Once she was over the threshold he nodded at one of his lackeys, who closed the door in her face.

And something inside of her came away. Like a rowing boat snapping its moorings and drifting out to sea.

On numb feet she headed back to her room. Aware that, when it came down to it, it wasn't even really his fault. She'd never asked for affection. In fact, she'd made it clear she didn't want any of that kind of guff.

He'd given it anyway. And now she was used to it. To how it felt to be a part of something real, something warm. A community of two.

And she would never accept anything less than that again.

It was more like an hour before Hugo was finally able to drag himself away.

Unable to come up with a reason not to, he'd been forced to fire half the people on the board of the transport department for bad management bordering on state fraud. When he'd agreed to take on the position he'd never imagined his first week would be so onerous.

But it was compensated for by the security breakthrough. Prospero's compatriots had tracked down and rounded up the misanthropes who had orchestrated the attack on his uncle at the picnic all those months ago. The same ones who'd been causing strong headaches for Security since Hugo's return, a burr that had lived in the back of his head. And they were singing like canaries.

Still, starved and emotionally raw, his whole body felt like one big ache.

But he'd promised Amber some time. And the truth was, he could do with seeing her. Despite his best efforts at keeping his distance, for both their sakes, it turned out he couldn't function—not in the capacity he desired—without her keeping his head on straight.

His feet no longer dragged as he strode down the hall towards Amber's apartment.

"Amber?" he called from the open doorway.

No response.

He poked his head into her room to find it empty when he'd expected laughter and noise. And arguments, to be sure. For Marguerite had volunteered to get Amber acquainted with people who could guide her in the coming months. And, hoping to keep his aunt distracted from her woe, he'd agreed.

Where was everyone?

Where was Amber?

With security on his mind, he didn't like this one bit. "Amber?" he called more loudly this time, his ear straining, his heart thunderous.

"In here."

The sound of her voice, coming from her dressing room, brought a rush of relief.

But he pulled up short when he found her. She'd changed into warm clothes—boots, jeans, an oversized jumper that kept falling off one shoulder, and her hair fell in golden waves from beneath a beanie the colour of lavender that Sunflower had knitted for her before they'd left.

And she was folding clothes into a suitcase.

Ned sat at her feet, looking the way dogs looked when they thought they were in trouble. Only Hugo knew Ned wasn't the one Amber was mad at.

"Amber?"

She looked up. She seemed tired, fragile. He ached just looking at her.

"Amber, what's going on?"

"You said I could leave at any time."

The word *no* almost tore from deep inside, but he held it at bay. Just. He moved deeper into the room and said, "And I meant it."

He told his hands to go into his pockets so that he would not touch her, but one moved to her elbow, gently stopping her from packing. He turned her to face him, and she didn't even try to stop him. As if she was hollow. As if she had no fight left to give.

He placed a finger beneath her chin, lifting until he could see her face. As beautiful as the first time he'd seen her. More so now that he knew the mind that whirled behind it, the vast heart that held her together.

"Talk to me," he said, his voice raw.

She closed her eyes for a second before they fluttered open, hitting him with all that whisky-brown delight. "Do you need me here, Hugo?"

Hugo baulked. It wasn't what he'd been expecting. Or a side of her he'd ever seen before. She sounded almost brittle. It rang of Marguerite.

"Amber, please—"

"No. After meeting the vast number of people I apparently need to make me a palatable princess, I'm pretty sure I'll be nothing but a distraction." She threw a shirt into her bag. Then another. "A hindrance to your ability to do what you have to do. Especially in these early days of transitioning."

It was so close to what he'd been thinking the day before that he baulked again. Only she made it sound as if she was a burden when the truth was the polar opposite. "Amber, stop bloody packing, will you? I want you here. I would not have asked it of you unless I believed it was the right decision. If I didn't know that my country would benefit from your…" Heart, soul, fierce upstanding goodness.

She stopped, some item of clothing scrunched in her hand. "My what?"

"Your innate knack for ferreting out trouble."

Coward, his subconscious muttered.

No, he shot back. *The smart move.*

Because he knew what she wanted to know. He could see it in the set of her shoulders; hear it in the raw scrape of her voice. She wanted to know how he truly felt about her.

But he couldn't tell her what she wanted to hear. For, while he wanted her, while he cared for her so deeply it was disorienting, he didn't *need* anyone. He'd amputated that part of himself when he was a younger man.

And yet, with Amber, he wasn't even half as afraid of losing her as he was of loving her.

Which was how he managed to say, "I am married. I am of age. I am crowned. I needed you to ensure all that was possible. And for which I will be eternally grateful. But hereon in, whatever you decide to do will not affect that."

She blinked at him then, like a puppy who'd been kicked out of the house during a downpour. Marguerite had earned a reprieve. Now he wanted to throttle himself instead.

Amber grabbed a pile of clothes and threw them into the case without folding them, then she slammed the case shut, zipping with all her might. "That's just great. I hope you know how lucky you are, going through life so blithely unaffected. I hope the people of Vallemont know what a big-hearted leader they have."

She grabbed the bag, and hauled it past him into her bedroom.

"And where exactly are you planning to go?"

"I'm not sure."

"You can't just walk out the front door."

"You think so?" She turned on him then. She had her

fight back—thank goodness—her spirit so strong it burned in her eyes. “Watch me.”

Screw it, he thought. Screw holding back. Screw the job. Screw everything but this woman. He took the three steps to meet her and hauled her into his arms and kissed her.

She resisted for a fraction of a second, anger and hurt still raging inside her. Before tossing her suitcase to the floor and wrapping her arms about him and kissing him with such unbridled passion it took his breath away.

It felt like days since he’d touched her, not hours. All the energy spent thinking about keeping her at arm’s length only making the abandon more intense.

She tasted like honey and sunshine and everything good as she sank into him, and he into her. Basking, exploring, until the world contracted to the size of her.

He might not need her, not in the way she needed him to, but God how he wanted her. In his arms, in his bed, in his life.

He spread his hands over her back, sliding his thumbs up her sides, catching her sweater until he reached skin. Silken soft, hot from the inside.

She gasped, her head falling away, leaving him scope to trail kisses along her jaw, down her neck. As her body melted against him, he feared he might tell her whatever the hell she wanted to hear. So he wrapped his arms more tightly around her; holding on for dear life.

When the backs of her knees pressed into the bed, he lowered her down and they fell together. Landing in a mass of twisted limbs. Their ragged breaths snagged against the silence.

And Amber looked into his eyes, deep, searching. Her hair splayed out around her like waves of sunlight, her lips pink from kissing.

Hugo ran his thumb down her cheek and she turned her cheek to rub into his touch.

Then she lifted a hand as if about to run it through his hair…

Only at the last she stopped, pressing against his chest with her other hand to push him away and disentangling her legs so fast she nearly fell off the bed.

And she split the heavy silence with a growl. That turned into a roar. That had even near-deaf Ned jogging out of the dressing room to make sure she was all right.

"I can't do this! I won't. I spent my entire childhood collecting the rare drops of attention from my parents and waiting in agony for the next. Do you know why I divorced them? Really why?"

Hugo hooked his feet over the edge of the bed and ran a hand down his face. Still trying to collect his wits, he shook his head.

"That paperwork was physical proof that my life was mine. No one else's. That it would, from that moment on, be lived on my terms. Those terms were hard for a really long time. Scary at times. But I got through it, because I knew that, no matter what, my choices were mine. I won't do hot and cold, Hugo. Not now. Not ever."

Hugo had never felt more like a grown-up than he did in that moment. And it wasn't as much fun as the brochures had made out. "Are you saying you want a divorce?"

"What? No. I don't think so." A beat went by then she shook her head. "We had a contract and I plan to honour that contract. But I need some time away to come to terms with what we are. What we *really* are. I think I've been stuck on those two lonely people who shared a small, lumpy bed and talked in ridiculous streams of consciousness until three in the morning. But that was the fairy tale."

Finally her hands went to her belly. "We have a baby coming, Hugo, and that's as real as it gets. To be ready for that I need to shake this off. This feeling…" She glanced at him—a flash of hurt, a flash of heat—and something squeezed deep inside his chest.

"How much time?"

"As much as it takes."

Hugo ran a hand over his face. To think he knew a dozen perfectly lovely women who would have fallen over themselves to be Princess. Women who could have led a civil, courteous, undramatic life by his side. And he'd have been bored out of his mind.

Amber had never been the safe choice, or even the smart choice, but she had been his only choice. Choice being the important word. For the choice was also hers. To stay or to go.

For all his faults, he was no bastard. He wouldn't keep her if she wanted to go. Even with the possible future of his country growing inside of her. But once he had a handle on this behemoth job of his, he'd track her down wherever in the world she landed and bring her home.

"All right," he said. His mind was set, but his voice was raw. "On the proviso you allow me to assign security."

Her expression grew thunderous. "Hugo—"

"That's non-negotiable. I know you, Amber. I know you'd take on a dragon if it looked sideways at someone you cared about. I need to know that you are safe."

She swallowed, her eyes giving nothing away. Then she nodded.

"You must also promise you'll find appropriate housing—heated, with walls that actually keep out the wind."

At mention of the shack her expression softened. "No buckets to catch the drips?"

"Stairs that don't crack when you walk on them. Railings that don't wobble. Working plumbing."

She glanced towards the bathroom with its double

shower and claw-footed bathtub. "I do like working plumbing."

His voice was rough as he said, "You will have a bank account at your disposal. And access to the best doctors. For the baby."

"Thank you. Any other demands, Your Highness?"

The only words that made their way out of his mouth were, "Come back soon."

Then, aware of how close he'd come to completely giving himself away, he added, "You can do good here, Amber. So much good. I hope, in time, you find that level of service reward enough."

She swallowed. Nodded. And picked up her suitcase.

Even while Hugo's head hurt with the effort not to command her to stay, he did as so many princes had done before him and leant on history, on convention, on duty and said, "So be it."

He moved to the side of the bed and pressed a button in the panel. A knock came at the door moments later. "Come in."

Prospero entered.

"Prospero, could you please organise a car for Amber?"

The big man glanced at Amber, then Hugo, at Amber's suitcase, concern lighting his stern, solid features. "Where shall I say the car is to take her?"

"The airport. From there the family plane will take her wherever she wishes to go."

"If that is her wish."

"It is," Amber said. "I'll call. Let you know when I'm settled. Don't worry about me. I'll be fine."

Hugo wasn't worried about her. He was worried about himself.

But it was too late to do anything about it as she gave Hugo one last long look, then walked out of the bedroom door. Gone. For how long, he did not know. Where to? He did not know that either. He couldn't remember ever feeling this ineffective.

"Your Highness." Prospero's voice was tight.

Hugo held up a hand—he didn't want to hear it. When he saw his hand was shaking he shoved it into a pocket.

"Your Highness," Prospero insisted. Then, breaking protocol for the first time since they'd known one another, said, "What the hell happened?"

"Stay with her. Keep her safe. She's..." *Important*, he'd been about to say, but it felt so cold compared with how much she meant to him. "She's wily. Even more so than I was."

"I will protect her as if she's my own." Prospero nodded and then was gone, leaving Hugo feeling more alone than he remembered feeling his entire life.

As if sensing his loss, Ned padded over to Hugo and sat on his foot, looking up at him with his strange mismatched eyes. Hugo sank his hand into the dog's soft fur. "I know, buddy. But this is life. People come, people go. And some make such an impact they leave a crater that never quite heals."

Hugo gave Ned one last rub before the dog harrumphed and left to follow his girl out of the door. Then he looked around Amber's apartment, the unmade bed, the open door to the wardrobe she'd never had the chance to fill.

Everyone he cared for left. Died. Ran. Or slowly slipped away.

But now was not the time to be morose. It was time to focus. He would be the best damn prince they had ever seen.

All he'd ever wanted, deep down, was to follow the family tradition, to be a true Giordano.

Now he was prince of all he surveyed. Even as his private life lay in tatters.

"Well, what do you know?" he said out loud. "You're a Giordano, through and through."

CHAPTER TEN

"TOLD YOU WE'D find him here. What is he wearing? Is he drunk? Give him the coffee."

Hugo had smelled the warm, hazy scent before he heard Sadie's voice. He opened one eye just enough to see Will shrug. Good man.

"I don't think I've ever actually seen him drunk. Is he allowed to get drunk, being the leader of the country? What if he has to decide on the blue wire or the red wire and he's too drunk to remember which is which?"

Will gave Sadie a look. "I'm not sure nuclear launch codes are something you need to be concerned about in Vallemont."

"True. I'm just worried. I've never seen him like this."

Will pressed forward, his face darkening. "I have. The last two times his world fell apart. Mate!" he said, giving Hugo a shake.

"I'm awake." Awake enough to feel the press of a rogue stone from the wall of the tallest turret in the castle wall pressing into his back. "And I'm not drunk. I'm merely exhausted."

For he had barely slept a night since Amber had walked out of his door.

He'd worked. And worked. And worked. Wrangling with parliament. Sweeping through government departments, cleaning house like an avenging angel. And dealing with the reason behind the security threat that had dogged his family for months.

When there was no other work to be done he'd spent his time in the garden. Washing Ned—for all its challenges—had been therapeutic. On a whim, he'd had his staff install a kind of modified greenhouse. And he worked in it daily. It was so physically demanding it was the only thing that could send him into a dead sleep when he needed it most.

In fact, he'd been working in there before he'd followed his feet and ended up here.

The staff called it his Zen Garden. He wondered if it might yet kill him.

Will added, "Then stop eavesdropping and get the hell up. You're worrying my woman."

Hugo gave Sadie a look, realised she was truly worried, then pulled himself to standing.

He held out his hand for the mug and Will handed it over. Sadie moved to stand beside him, crossing her arms but near enough to nudge with her elbow. She gave him a once-over, her gaze stopping a moment on his torn jeans, battered sneakers, holey beanie. "This is a new look for you."

"I've been gardening."

"You what, now?"

Hugo took a long sip, closing his eyes against the bliss of the bitter taste. Strong, black. Laced with something medicinal. No wonder Will was his oldest friend.

Thankfully Sadie changed the subject, though it wasn't any easier. "How is Amber?"

"Safe," he said, which was the most important thing.

"Have you heard from her?"

"Prospero has been sending updates."

Hourly at times, good man.

Amber wasn't sleeping well. The nausea seemed to have abated. She looked pale. She laughed at a joke. She was reading children's books, making lists. Baking. She wasn't good at it and he hoped she'd give it up.

"Is she okay?"

He sipped on his coffee again.

"Jeez," Sadie muttered, "it's like pulling teeth."

"If you are looking for news I can update you on the security issue."

"Fine. Do that."

"The group who attacked Reynaldo all those months ago was led by the husband of a woman Reynaldo had… befriended. The husband had found out, fallen into the waiting arms of a cuckolded husbands help group, and in a frenzy of misguided support together they made the bungled attack."

Sadie blinked. "For *that* I nearly married you? I could kill Reynaldo right now. You know, if he was still alive." Then her eyes narrowed. "So what does this have to do with Amber?"

His clever friend knew him all too well. "There has been chatter since I arrived back home that something else was in the planning. The leader, the man who'd lost his wife, got it into his head that—considering my father's infamous infidelity and now my uncle's—I would be next to have a go at his wife. So they were planning to have a go at mine."

Neither Sadie nor Will laughed.

"Oh, Hugo. You must have been terrified."

Terrified didn't even come close. The shake in Hugo's hand still came over him every now and then when he thought about it.

"The leader now realises how twisted his thinking had become and is all remorse and apology. It's over. Happy ending all round."

Sadie looked to Will and mouthed something Hugo didn't catch.

"I saw that," said Hugo.

"What?"

He put down the coffee, cleared his throat, ran hard hands through his hair and looked at Sadie. This place, this turret, had been their favourite spot as kids. The place they'd run to when feeling hard done by, or in need of some peace and quiet; to sort out their heads.

In the days since Amber had left he'd wanted to move into the turret. Maybe for ever.

"If it's such a happy ending, why are you hiding on our turret?"

Good question.

"Only one way to turn that frown upside down. Go get your girl."

"She's in Serenity." Probably. "Surrounded by lavender fields and stingless honey bees, where she belongs. And if Serenity makes her happy then I'm not about to take it away from her."

"Right. Because you're in love with her."

Hugo kept his trap shut. The strength of his feelings for his wife did not matter—how he acted on them did. That was the lesson to be learned from all this.

The problems his uncle had left behind were due to him making the easy choices over the right ones, leading to blackmail, extortion and leaving behind his wife and young family. Hugo planned to fix it all.

"Don't panic. It's quite normal to be in love with your wife. Right, Will?" Sadie asked.

"So I hear."

"What are you talking about?" Hugo asked.

"What are *you* talking about?" she shot back.

"How I can best serve Vallemont, redeem the family name and sleep at night."

"By being a loving husband and father first, of course."

"Leo, for Pete's sake. Leave it the hell alone."

"Fine!" She threw her hands in the air and paced to the other side of the turret. "But just one last thing. She knows how you feel, right? Before she left you told her you loved her and that's why you had to let her go?"

Hugo turned and gripped the rock wall, looked over verdant farmland, craggy mountains, the road he and Amber had travelled from the airport. And he said, "Not in so many words."

"Okay, but you told her when you proposed to her."

Hugo kept his mouth shut again.

"How did you propose, Hugo? We never heard the story. Knowing how you proposed to me, I'm assuming you learnt your lesson and did it right this time."

Hugo thought back to the words he had used. The offer he had made. He tried to pretty it up but in the end simply said, "I made it impossible for her to refuse."

Sadie's face sank into her hand, her laughter rueful. "Hugo, Hugo, Hugo!"

"She prides herself on being pragmatic."

"Then that's why she agreed to marry you. But did you tell her why you wanted to marry *her*?"

"I don't understand."

"Of course you don't. And maybe I wouldn't have either before I met Will. Hugo, you're *in love with her*."

"Yes, all right, I'm in love with her. I've been in love with her since I first laid eyes on her, looking down at me with those wild whisky eyes, telling me off for invading her hammock, all the while looking at me like I'm a hot lunch." Hugo pressed away from the wall and paced about the turret. "I've never met anyone who makes me feel like I'm floating an inch above the ground while also so grounded in my own reality I can see it, smell it, taste it fully for the first time in my life. Who makes me feel..." He thumped a fist against his chest. "She makes me feel. And not having her near, not knowing when I'll see her again… I can't sleep. I can't function. I'm running on automatic."

Sadie sighed. "Was that so hard?"

"That was more difficult than you can possibly imagine!"

She gave his arm a squeeze. "And it didn't occur to you to lead with all that, when you asked her to be yours?"

"She prides herself—"

"On being pragmatic. Yes, so you said. So do we all, unless we are given reason to believe in the alternative. She might *want* to be pragmatic, Hugo. But what she needs, what all of us need, is affection, consideration, love. Some of us also need a rockin' hot prince. Or a puppy. Will, can we get a puppy?"

"We live in a construction zone, so no."

"Okay."

Hugo only heard the last of it in his periphery, for he was onto something. His brain having switched from automatic to clear and present. "A phone. I need a phone."

Sadie looked to Will, who was way ahead of her. He handed it over then took Sadie by the wrist, drawing her away, murmuring to her about giving him space.

Hugo called Prospero. The big guy answered on the third ring. Didn't wait for a hello before asking, "Where is Ned?"

A beat, then, "Your Highness?"

"If she went back to Serenity, Ned would be in quarantine. She would never have put him through that twice in such a short space of time. So where is she?"

But Hugo knew before he'd even finished the question.

"If you tell me she's been staying in the shack just up the road all this time, while I've been out of my mind worried about her, trying to run the country without her, I will send you on a mission to Siberia."

"Then I won't tell you that."

Hugo tried.

"I do like what you've done with the garden, Your Highness. Very Zen."

Hugo hung up, paced towards the exit, then turned to give Will back his phone. Then he was off, running down the winding staircase before he even had any semblance of a destination.

"Go!" Sadie's voice followed him.

She might have said, "Get our girl and bring her back," but Hugo's mind was otherwise engaged with thoughts of Amber.

He'd made the mistake of thinking he was a man who had it all, but he wasn't even close.

Not without her. She was his counterweight. The yin to his yang. The uptight hippy to his laid-back royalty.

And he loved her. Deeply. Ferociously.

Not because of the baby. Her child, their child, was important. But right now, it was only a dream. A fairy tale he hoped would come true.

Amber was his reality.

With that as his touchstone, Hugo hit the bottom of the stairs, sweat sliding down his face, his heart like a runaway horse, and burst out into the light.

Amber sat in the back of the town car, Ned sitting in the footwell, Prospero in the back seat with her, a strange smile playing around his eyes.

They came out through a copse that hung over the bumpy country road and the palace came into view.

"Are you sure about this, Your Highness?" Prospero asked.

She shot him a look. "You're the one who said Hugo sounded strange."

"Very strange."

"If you're pulling my leg and I drive up there and find

him sitting in his office surrounded by lackeys, I will find out if I have the authority to send you to—"

"Siberia?"

She'd been about to say Mongolia, but Siberia was close enough.

Staying in the shack, sleeping, reading books that weren't about princesses—mostly about what to do when you were expecting—and snuggling with Ned and talking to Sunflower and Johnno on the phone had been exactly what she'd needed.

Too long feeling like a car in need of a service—clunky and misfiring—she was now a finely tuned machine. Waking at six, yoga by sunrise, nap at three, bed by nine. Eating clean, drinking water like it was going out of fashion. She was the picture of hippy health.

And she couldn't remember ever feeling so miserable in her life.

The truth was, when she'd heard Prospero answer the phone she'd known it was Hugo on the other end. She so wanted to hear his voice, to make sure he was all right, perhaps even to fight with him a little so as to get her blood sparking again, it was a miracle she didn't tear the phone from Prospero's grip.

When Prospero had murmured something about the Prince sounding strange on the phone she'd practically grabbed him by the collar and dragged him to the car.

She might not have figured out what she'd gone to the shack to figure out, but she had discovered something. That she missed him. Missed his humour, his work ethic, the way he looked at her as if he'd never seen anything quite like her.

And that in the grip of old fears, she may have judged him too harshly.

The only way to figure out what they were to one another was to figure it out together.

Minutes later, the car pulled through the front gates of the Palace of Vallemont. It hooked around the back, heading towards one of the huge garages.

Prospero helped her out of the car.

She stretched her legs, looking into the garden leading to the forest. The one she could see from her balcony, where she'd seen Hugo wash Ned with his own bare hands and whatever methods she'd used to deny her feelings had truly dissolved away.

Hang on a second. What was that? A big white tent-type structure had been put up on the lawn since the last time she was there.

Curious, she took a few steps that way, only to see Hugo striding inside the thing as if his life depended on it, wearing what looked like an old knit jumper, dirty jeans and gumboots. His nose was pink, his beanie ragged.

He looked like a right royal mess. And she loved him more than anything.

Maybe that was what she'd figured out in the shack: that she could love their little family enough for the both of them.

Then suddenly Hugo was back at the entrance, what looked like a pile of weeds in his hand.

She saw the moment he clocked her.

She wasn't sure how he might react, whether she would get warm Hugo, or cool Hugo, or a whole new beast. Perhaps the Hugo she had left in the lurch.

But then he mouthed her name and soon he was running.

And she was running too, her bag dumped by the car.

And then she was in his arms, wrapped tightly. His face was buried in her neck, tears sliding down her face.

And then they were kissing as if they hadn't seen one another in weeks rather than days. And maybe they hadn't. Not really.

Amber slowly slid down Hugo's body, her feet touching the ground before their lips came apart. Then she blinked up into his eyes and knew. Something had happened to him in their separation as it had happened to her. Something magical.

"Hi," she said.

"Hi to you too."

His gaze slid past her shoulder to where Prospero stood on edge of the hill. Once Hugo gave him the all-clear he slipped into the shadows and was gone.

"What are you doing here, *miele*? I was just about to come and find you. If I'd known you hadn't fled to the other side of the world I'd have been there sooner. I'd have been there every day and night. Doing whatever it took to convince you that I want you here. With me. I want you at my side. In my bed. In my damn apartment. Or I'll move into your sparkly pink monstrosity if that's what it will take to show you I mean it."

She laughed at the words pouring from his lips. "Slow down before you hurt yourself."

"Too late," he said, reaching up to swipe her hair from her face. Then, realising he still gripped the weeds, he stepped back and held them out to her. "These were for you."

"Thank you…?"

"They're lavender seedlings. Not yet flowering, clearly. But with the bees at play we should see a good crop that we can plant along this patch of grass so you can see them from our window. *Our* window."

"Hugo?"

"Hmmm."

"I have no idea what you are talking about." Not that it mattered. He could have been talking wheat prices and sheep farming for all she cared. For he had his hand in hers, and the look in his eye made her feel faint.

"Right," he said. "Of course. Come on."

He took her by the hand and dragged her down the grassy slope. Up close, the tent was huge. Taller than a tree and half the size of a soccer field. With a half-smile, Hugo opened the flap with a flourish.

What hit her first was the heat. It was a hothouse. As humid and warm as an Australian spring. To go with it, a small forest had been planted in her absence. Wattle trees and banksia, liquidambar saplings and pots and pots of lavender. And buzzing around the lot were tiny little stingless Australian bees.

"Hugo, what have you done?"

"It's not finished yet. Not by a long shot. But it's a start."

"A start of what? Turning this into Australia?"

"Just this patch. Just for you. I realised that I had torn you out of your natural environment and stuck you in a cage when I should have been nurturing you. Nurturing *us*. I somehow thought that if I built this, a little patch of home, it might be enough to tempt you back."

He took her by the shoulders and moved her.

In the far corner, two huge trees had been transplanted into the soil. Mature gum trees, no less. And between them swung a hammock.

Seeing it, Amber burst into tears.

Hugo spun her around, stooped to look into her eyes. "Oh, hell, Amber."

Hands on her shoulders, he hustled her out of the hothouse and into the fresh air. "I'm sorry. Has it made you homesick? I can take it down. I'm not good at this kind of thing."

"What kind of thing is that exactly?" she asked, knowing but wanting to hear him say it.

"Romance."

She burst into laughter. "You toss a priceless family heirloom at me as if it's a trinket." She wangled her hand at him to prove her point. "And you romance me with a hammock."

He felt for her hand, held it up to the light. "You're wearing the ring."

"Of course I'm wearing your ring, Hugo. I've never taken it off. You could have given me the pull ring from a soda can and I'd still be wearing it. Because you gave it to me."

She grabbed him by the front of the jumper, a light glinted in his eye and he smiled. It was enough to push her over her last great hurdle. And once she leapt she felt as if she could fly.

"I don't need romance, you great big lug. Or crown jewels. Or a staff. Or a huge apartment of my own. I just need you." She breathed in, not sure if the words would come. But then it was as easy as breathing out as she said, "I love you, Hugo. I love you so much I'm willing to put up with your odd bodyguard and your family's strange obsession with the colour pink. I don't need romance, Hugo, I just need you." And with that she pulled him in and kissed him until she was about to faint. Then just a little more because it felt that good.

When she pulled back she was woozy with lust, and lack of oxygen, so she wasn't quick enough to stop him when he sank to one knee. "Get up."

"No."

She looked around to see a couple of gardeners watching from the hedgerow. A band of maids had congregated by the laundry door. Marguerite stood watching from a balcony on the first floor, her hand to her mouth. From that distance, Amber could have sworn she saw tears. "Hugo, please. I don't need this."

"Amber Hartley Giordano."

Amber looked down at the Prince and the rest of the world faded to nothing. "Yes, Hugo?"

"You may think you don't need romance, but I'm afraid that you live in a palace now, and you are married to a prince. Romance will from this point on be a given. Because I am besotted. Fuelled by desire. I am crazy in love. With you. I'd convinced myself it was dangerous to love that hard. But the only danger was the possibility of losing you because I never let you know it."

Amber was speechless, overwhelmed and so happy her cheeks hurt from smiling. "Right back at you. Now please get up."

"Not until you agree to marry me."

"I already did."

"Again. In front of your friends and mine. In front of God and country. And the world."

He was too big for her to lift, and too stubborn to convince, so she sank to her knees as well. "Okay."

"Really?"

"Why not?"

He leaned down, kissed her gently. Pulled back. "You like the hammock?"

"I love the hammock. I can't wait till everyone's asleep and we can sneak out to the hammock and…" She leaned in, whispering her intentions in his ear.

"I can order them all to bed now, you know. I have that power."

"No, you don't."

"You're right, I don't. So later, then?"

"It's a date."

"A date. I don't believe we ever had one of those."

"Now seems like a fine time to start."

Two weeks later, Marguerite got the wedding she wanted. Hugo had insisted on a no-camera policy inside the chapel, but the guest list was extensive and the decor extravagant.

The bride wore pink, because it was tradition. She was even beginning to get used to the colour.

"You look edible."

Amber turned to find Hugo leaning in the doorway of the anteroom in which she was getting ready. Then Sadie leapt in between them, waving her arms like a mad thing.

"Get out! It's bad luck to see her before the wedding. Your mother's family was dripping in bad luck, remember, Your Highness. Should you really risk it?"

"Bad things happen," said Hugo. "We do what we must to fend them off. Protecting those we love. It's been the way of things since the time of cavemen. Fending off sabre-tooth tigers with big sticks. It's not all that different now. Besides, if you don't remember, we're already married. You were even there."

"Oh, right. So this is all…"

"For the good of the country."

"I've heard that before."

"Mmm," said Hugo before taking Sadie by the hips, spinning her and pushing her forcibly out of the door, which he locked behind her.

Amber simply kept on pinning a silk peony rose she had unpicked from her coronation gown into her hair.

He moved in behind her, placing his hands on her gently rounded belly and kissing her on the neck. "Morning, wife."

"Morning, husband."

"Nearly ready?"

"I was born ready."

"Yes, you were. I had a quick look at the crowd."

"And?"

"Hell of a crowd. Nearly as big as my last wedding."

She caught his eye in the mirror. "Funny man."

"I try. When you get out there don't forget to check out the first few rows."

"Why?"

"Just do it."

"Tell me why. Right now."

"Fine, but only because I can't resist you when you get all bossy on me. On the right we have my mother sitting in a better position than Marguerite and clearly loving it, while my aunt looks as pleased as if she sucked a lemon. And on the left of the chapel, in a sea of hemp formal wear, half of Serenity."

"What? How?"

"We flew them in on a chartered plane yesterday." Hugo held out both hands, smug as all get-out.

"You really are a powerful man."

"Handsome too, don't forget."

"So handsome," she said, her finger climbing up the front of his shirt before popping a button.

"Oops," Hugo said with a smile.

When his hand went to her back, unzipping her simple, floaty dress in one fell swoop, there was no time for "oops". For soon they were both undressed, their wedding clothes strewn on the floor, and both glad Hugo had locked the door.

When the wedding start time came and went, the crowd did wonder if they might be about to see another exciting non-wedding at the Palace of Vallemont. But when the bride and groom took one another down the aisle fifteen minutes later, it was clear to everyone present how smitten they both were.

And that a new day was dawning in the story of Vallemont.

EPILOGUE

"AAAARGH!"

The midwife gave Hugo a look.

"Sorry," he whispered. "I stubbed my toe."

Amber rolled her eyes. Which was quite a feat, considering she'd been in labour for six hours and didn't feel as if she had the energy to breathe, much less express sarcasm in any meaningful way.

"I never imagined His Highness to be so precious," the midwife said to Amber, loud enough for Hugo to hear.

"It's a new thing. He seems to think I am made of glass and, in response, his tiptoeing skills have become excellent."

The tingle in the base of her spine, and the encroaching red at the edges of her mind, heralded another contraction. Amber closed her eyes, breathed gently and counted to fifteen. When she reached the peak, she rode the relief counting back down to one.

The midwife pottered about, doing her wonderful, calming, capable, midwifey things, and, after a glance to be sure Amber was back, said, "So how did you two lovebirds meet?"

"You really don't know?"

The midwife shot her a look.

"Of course you know. You're just trying to distract me. It's a long and winding tale," said Amber.

"We have time," she said, glancing at her watch as she checked Amber's pulse. "Not much, but a little."

Hugo caught Amber's eye, panic swirling about the hazel depths. "How little?" he asked.

"That's up to the little Prince or Princess." The midwife threw him a smile. Before patting Amber on the hand. "You are doing great. Textbook."

"Hear that?" Amber said as another wave of pain ripped through her body. "I'm a natural."

"You are perfect."

The midwife scoffed. "Don't ever let him forget he said that."

Amber smiled as the pain ebbed.

At which point the midwife had a look and a feel. She held Amber's eyes. "Are you ready to have a baby, Your Highness?"

Amber nodded. After months of nausea, followed by months of baby bliss, then months of swollen feet and arguments with Marguerite as to the nursery colours, she was so ready to have a baby, this man's baby, she could barely hold herself together. Her joy was such she felt as if she might split into a thousand pieces.

Hugo, on the other hand, groaned as if he might not last.

"Perhaps His Highness could go to the desk, track down another heat pack?"

Hugo wagged a finger at the midwife. "Not happening. I've spoken to other fathers. I know the tricks you lot pull when you think we're not handling things. I am fine. I will not miss the birth of my daughter."

"Or son," Amber said through gritted teeth as she hit thirteen, fourteen, fifteen, sixteen, seventeen… The pain was different now—bigger, broader—and she gripped the edges of her subconscious as it tried to disintegrate. Thankfully her body seemed to know what to do even if her mind was shutting up shop; taking over, bearing down.

And then…relief.

"That's right," said Hugo, suddenly at her side, holding her hand. Though his knuckles looked strangely white—bloodless, in fact…because she was squeezing the life out of them.

Amber let go. Or tried. But Hugo wrapped his hand around hers.

"We had a summer affair in a beautiful little country town in Australia," he said, eyes on hers. "Which ended when she kicked me out of her bed for no reason whatsoever."

Amber tried to open her mouth to disagree, but reality had taken a hike. Her head was full of stars. Her body felt as if it was floating above the bed, no doubt trying to escape the pain.

Hugo's deep voice was like a balm. "After that we got to know one another and discovered we actually liked one another. Knowing then I'd never met a woman of her like—fierce and fearless, loyal and lovely, bright and bold—I found myself terrified I'd screw up the best thing that had ever happened to me, so I did my very best to screw it up just to make sure."

Amber heard it all through the spangled depths of her brain as she came out of her next contraction. The urge to scream was stoppered by the stronger need to hear Hugo's words.

"The rest was pretty textbook. We found out we were pregnant; we got married; I was crowned; she became a princess; she left me; I willed her back." With his spare hand, Hugo pushed damp hair from Amber's cheek, tucking it behind her ear. "And somewhere in there we fell in love."

"And then…?"

"I'm hoping the 'and then' will be born pretty soon. Healthy, whole, and as beautiful as my wife."

Amber felt a tear running down her cheek even as she fell into the mental abyss that was birthing a baby. No matter how much she wanted to look into Hugo's eyes, to tell him how deeply she loved him, her eyes closed, her breaths came hard and fast and she dug deep, knowing she'd need every bit of energy she had to get through this.

The midwife's voice came as if down a tunnel. "I like it. Very modern. Though I'm not sure there's a greetings card that covers it."

"I'd expect not."

"Your Highness? Amber?"

Amber opened her eyes to see a team of people now milling about the room. The midwife clicked her fingers to make sure Amber was looking into her eyes. "The baby's head is clear, Amber. One more good push and your baby will be born."

Amber looked to Hugo. A matching tear left a track down his cheek too.

"You ready for this?" she asked. "For all of this? For us?

Hugo's smile was slow. Warm. Genuine. "I was born ready."

And somehow, Amber found the strength to laugh.

Half an hour later, after weighing and measuring and the most fundamentally soulful moments of Hugo's life to date—watching his wife smile and coo and glow as she enjoyed skin-to-skin time with her child—Hugo held a bundle of snuggly swaddled baby in his arms.

He kept his voice low so as not to wake Amber as he said, "I know I said your mother was perfect, and she'll never let me forget it, but I do believe I was jumping the gun. You," he said, looking down at the face of his baby daughter, "you are perfect."

Amber stirred and settled. Hugo knew she'd wake up grumpy, having fallen asleep and missed this, but after witnessing what her body had put her through for the past several hours Hugo did not wake her. Not just yet.

His daughter was sleeping too, still too squishy from her own recent ordeal to look much like her mother, but he could see the potential in the lashes brushing her cheeks, in the shape of her chin, the tuft of fair hair. Lucky girl.

Give her a day to grow into her new world and Princess Lucinda Sadie Sunflower Giordano would be the most beautiful child that ever was. And the most loved.

Princess or no princess, she had two parents who wanted her and adored one another so very, very much. Add an adoring dog, a dozen already besotted honorary aunts and uncles on the other side of the world, and a mini-hammock he had secretly hung in the hothouse as a surprise and Hugo knew this kid was as lucky as they came.

If Hugo had his way in the next session of parliament—and if that was what she wanted to be—he was looking upon the face of the girl who could one day become the first Sovereign Princess of Vallemont.

Shifting gently on his chair, instinctively mindful that not waking the baby was going to be a big deal, he leaned towards his wife and kissed her on the cheek. Then the edge of her mouth. Then her lips.

Her eyes fluttered open in surprise, before softening as she kissed him back.

"Lucy?" she said.

And Hugo shifted so she could see her baby.

"She has your nose."

"Poor kid."

"I love your nose," Amber said with a frown, so loyal to those she cared for she wouldn't even let him make a joke about himself.

"As you should. For it is the nose of princes and princesses."

"It's the nose of Hugo; that's all I care about."

"You did good, kiddo."

"I did, didn't I?"

"Did it hurt as much as it seemed?"

"More."

"Want to do it again?"

"As soon as humanly possible."

Hugo gave Amber a nudge and with a wince she scooched over so that the entire family could fit on the big hospital bed.

"But first, I want to talk to you about the nurses. I got talking to one when you were on a phone call earlier, about their working conditions. I believe we can do better for them. Job share for those who are keen. Add a crèche. I want to know more about mandatory breaks. I might even have offered to represent them…"

Hugo laughed. "Please tell me you're not about to call me out in front of parliament."

"Do the right thing and I won't have to."

"It's a deal."

Amber snuggled deeper into the bed, wincing again as she moved, but looking happier than he had ever seen her. "I'm going to like this job, aren't I?"

"Told you so. Vallemont has no idea how lucky it is to have you on its side, *miele*."

"Right back at you, My Highness."

With his daughter secure in his arms, Hugo leaned down and kissed his Princess, his wife, his partner, his conscience, his love. And the rogue Prince of Vallemont had finally found his way home.

* * * * *

FORTUNE'S HOMECOMING

ALLISON LEIGH

For my "forever" home.

Happy 10th.

Chapter One

"Holy cow. Is that who I think it is?"

Grayson Fortune heard the whispers start the second he walked into the office of Austin Elite Real Estate. He should have known better than to head straight there after the press conference. But going back to the hotel to change would have made him even later than he already was.

He hated being late. It was a product of his early years hustling from one rodeo to another, when being late could mean missing the event altogether. Wasted miles. Worse, wasted money.

"Ohmygawd. Is that Grayson? I just saw him on the news at noon. He's taller than I expected."

He didn't bother trying to locate where in the office the whispers came from. He just pulled off his black Grayson Gear cowboy hat and strode toward the stylish woman seated behind the reception desk. He'd had lots of practice ignoring whispers, and gave the receptionist his usual grin.

She was probably about his mom's age, and if she recognized him when she looked up at him with a friendly smile, there was nothing in her expression to say it.

"Welcome to Austin Elite." Her eyes were bright behind her black-framed glasses. "How can I help you?"

He heard another muffled laugh that might have been inaudible had the modern office possessed actual walls instead of a sea of glass partitions. *"I know how* I'd *like to help him."*

He'd asked his mother to find a real estate agent for him, and she'd set up the appointment. Otherwise he'd turn around and leave. He was used to public attention, but it was often a pain in the caboose.

"Do you suppose he's as good in the sack as the saddle? Imagine him tossing you down on the bed like—"

He focused harder on the friendly receptionist. "I have an appointment with Billy Pemberton. Sorry I'm late."

The receptionist consulted her computer, tapping a few keys. "Ah. There you are, Mr. Smith." She pressed a button on her phone. "Billy, your client is here." She looked up at him again with another smile. "Would you like something to drink while you wait?"

"Water would be great, ma'am."

"My pleasure." She came around the desk. "Make yourself comfortable." She gestured at the white chairs situated around an enormous world globe that sat right on the floor. Since the chairs looked like they came from outer space, he figured it made a weird sort of sense.

Two of the chairs were occupied and he took the one farthest away, nodding when the other people gave him sideways looks. Because they recognized him? Or because they'd heard the chair groan when he sat on it?

More than comfort, right now he just hoped he wouldn't end up on the floor.

He also hoped the real estate agent wouldn't keep him waiting long. But considering Grayson's tardiness, he didn't have much of a leg to stand on if the guy left him cooling his heels.

He'd expected a bottle of water, but when the receptionist returned, it was with a real glass filled with water, several sliced rounds of cucumber, some narrow ribbons of green stuff threaded on a wooden swizzle stick, all topped with a curl of lemon rind. A little overdone, but a nice touch, he supposed.

If you happened to like cucumber and unidentifiable green stuff. He did not.

He took the glass. "That's real kind of you, ma'am. Thank you."

"My pleasure." She started to turn back to her desk. "Oh, there's Billy now."

He wished the globe were a coffee table, so he could have set aside the water. Instead, he stood, turning in the same direction.

The real estate agent smiled at him, approaching with a hand outstretched. "Mr. Smith, I'm so sorry for keeping you waiting."

Not a Billy.

But a *Billie*.

And what a Billie she was. From the top of her gleaming hair to the shine on her shoes, every inch was… amazing.

He juggled the glass and his hat, and stuck out his hand, anticipating the feel of her palm against his.

Bam.

No disappointment there. No, ma'am. Her skin was as soft and smooth as kid leather.

"Darlin', you weren't the one making someone wait. That's all on me."

Her rosy smile looked a little nervous and she tugged her hand free. "Don't be silly. I'm Billie Pemberton."

He wondered if his mom had chosen the attractive real estate agent deliberately.

Considering Deborah Fortune's lament lately that he needed a good woman in his life? Probably.

"Let's go back to my office, shall we?" Billie's straight hair was long and deep brown, and she tucked one side of the sleek strands behind her ear. No earrings on her earlobe. Just a tiny sparkling stud high inside her ear and two equally tiny gold rings around the top edge.

He realized he was staring, as if he'd never seen an ear before. "Yeah." He gestured with the upturned brim of his hat. "Let's get on it."

She smiled again. Definitely a hint of shyness in those appealing eyes.

Too bad she also looked like she was young enough to still be in high school. She was a real estate agent, so he knew she couldn't be *that* young, but still…

Grayson liked women. Young women. Old women. Anything-in-between women. He liked the way they thought and the way they smiled and the way they smelled.

But he didn't mess with girls. Especially ones who looked like they came complete with starry-eyed visions of picket fences and babies.

So no matter what his mom was thinking when she'd set this up, *if* she'd set this up, she was on the wrong track.

Despite all that, he told himself there was no law against appreciating how the fat silver zipper running the entire length of the back of her short white skirt worked its way up from the hem an inch as she walked ahead of him.

"He looks older than I thought he was."

The whispers started up again as the two of them made their way along a glossy hall between glass panes. Or maybe they'd never stopped. He'd quit noticing anything when Billie had smiled at him. The whispers floating in the air. The aches and pains left over from his run a few days ago in Silver City, when he'd earned nothing but a bruised rib and a face full of dirt.

Billie stepped into a cube on her right. "I'm sorry it's so tight in here." She slid onto a rolling chair at the desk. Using the toe of one tall, neon-yellow high heel, she swiveled to face the two narrow chairs positioned adjacent to her. Her sparkling eyes met his, then danced away. "Sit wherever you like."

He chuckled and dumped his hat on one of the acrylic-and-steel contraptions, then took the other. It seemed sturdier than the chairs in the reception area, at least. "D'you mind?" He lifted the water glass slightly. She didn't have anything on her desktop other than a computer screen, a stapled set of papers and a desk pad that looked like clear glass.

He had a desk that he rarely used at the Grayson Gear office. It was nowhere near as neat.

"Not at all." Her eyes danced to his. "Nasty stuff, if you ask me. I have a drawer full of plain bottled water if you prefer."

He grinned. "If you're sure you don't mind sharing."

Those eyes danced away again. "I'm sure." She moistened her soft-looking lips as she leaned over to open the bottom drawer of a short cabinet wedged into the only free corner. Beneath her silky black tank top there was a glimpse of a black bra strap, but what kept drawing his attention was the translucent creaminess of her skin.

It made him almost thirsty enough to drink the cuke crud.

She moved his water glass from the desk to the top of the cabinet, nudging aside several photo frames to make room. Then she held out the slender water bottle.

When he took it, their fingers brushed.

She quickly swiveled back to face her desk and slid her papers squarely in front of her with one hand, touching the computer screen with her other. The blank screen leaped to life, showing the same logo that was on the front door of the office. She glanced at him. "I understand you're looking for a new home."

"Yup." He waited a beat. What the hell? "Can I ask you a personal question?"

"I guess that depends," she said warily. "Will you answer my questions?"

He spread his palms. "I'm an open book, darlin'."

As he'd hoped, her expression lightened. "Somehow I doubt that. But what's the question?"

"How *old* are you?"

Fortunately, she didn't look offended. "Twenty-four. I have a college degree and I've had my real estate license for several years. I assure you, I am perfectly qualified to represent your interests and—"

He lifted his hand, cutting her off. His mom wouldn't have sent him to an *un*qualified agent. "I'm not going anywhere. I just thought I'd ask." At least she wasn't *quite* fresh out of high school. But she was still too young for him to be as attracted to her as he was, even though he appreciated her ambition. "So, let's get on with your questions."

Her lips twitched faintly. "How old are *you*?"

He couldn't help grinning. "Thirty-seven and feeling every minute of 'em, darlin'."

Her eyes twinkled. Then she looked past him for a millisecond and sat straighter in front of her computer. "All right." She slid her fingers on the glass desk pad and the logo on the screen folded away, to be replaced by a form. "Do you have an existing home now?"

"Nope."

She slid her fingers again. The screen morphed again.

"Fancy desk pad you got there." The glass clearly acted as a computer mouse pad. "How do you type?" There was no visible keyboard.

"Here." She leaned back in her chair slightly so he could see her tap the corner of the glass. The faint outline of a keyboard appeared in it. She moved her fingers across it as if she were typing on the keys, and a line of gibberish streamed across the screen. "It's cool, but it took me quite a while to get used to it." Her smile stretched, looking more than a little impish again. "Nothing but the best and cutting edge here at Austin Elite."

He shifted on the chair, staring for a second at his water bottle. Damn. She was prettier than a spring filly. He took a healthy swig from the bottle, took his time capping it, and focused on the computer screen once more. "That's what my mom said when she made the appointment here. You were the best."

"Your mother?" She'd turned her attention to the screen, as well. "Will she be living with you also?"

Not unless he could change her mind. "I doubt it. She's my business manager." He waited for Billie to ask what his business was, because she'd given no sign that she knew who he was.

"Is there anyone else you'll be consulting with on your choice of a home?"

"Like who? A wife?"

"Or a girlfriend? Boyfriend? Psychic?"

He laughed silently. "Only one I've gotta please is me."

For a second, she looked disbelieving, but she moved on. "Are you working already with a lender, by any chance? I can give you a list of excellent choices if you're not."

Outside the clear cubicle, a steady parade of people kept going past, most sneaking a look their way. "No need. It'll be a cash purchase."

She was obviously accustomed to hearing that particular answer. "That makes things very simple. Is there some area of Austin that particularly interests you?"

"No, ma'am." Grayson Gear had claimed its headquarters in Austin since the start, though most of his involvement was conducted from wherever he was on the road. He'd competed in plenty of rodeos in the area, though he knew only certain parts of town, and generally liked what he knew. "My personal knowledge of the city is limited, actually. I'm not from here."

Her gaze slid his way again. "Is your relocation for business purposes?"

"Mostly."

She looked back at her computer. "And where are you coming from?"

"All over." That was true enough. His actual home was Paseo, Texas. But few people had heard of the minuscule town, much less knew where it was. Ever since news had gotten out that Gerald Robinson aka Jerome Fortune was his and his triplet brothers' absentee biological father, though, the journalists and the Grayson groupies had been getting too damn close to ruining the peace there that he was determined to protect. His employees at Grayson Gear had been operating just fine for years despite his frequent absences, but they could always be counted on to keep interlopers away from his door when he *was* there. Especially Gerald Robinson, despite him being a fixture on the Austin landscape.

Grayson's lack of a precise answer didn't seem to bother Billie. Her finger continued sliding on the glass as the form on the screen slowly filled. "Then you haven't looked at any houses already?"

"Nope." He shifted and hitched one boot on top of his knee. They were brand-new Castletons, and as fine as the custom boots were, he preferred the ones he tramped around in at the ranch in Paseo where he and his brothers had grown up. They were Castletons, too. Bought nearly twenty years ago out of his first big win and just getting real comfortable now.

He and his Grayson Gear manager, Jessica Monroe, had been working on establishing a line of Castletons specifically for the company. But progress was slow. Castleton was an old family business and getting in the door was difficult. Considering his numerous endorsement deals, the challenge with Castleton had only made Grayson more determined. He'd even enlisted his mother's help. Though she'd been managing his rodeo career since the get-go, she generally left Grayson Gear business to him. Always said she had enough keeping her busy without adding that to her plate. But since she happened to think Castleton was the best bootmaker around, he'd talked her around to it.

"Haven't worked with any other Realtor?"

His eyes drifted past his boots to land on the curve of Billie's hip where she sat. The chair was black, making the white of her skirt seem even whiter. Below the hem, her smooth thighs were golden. "No, ma'am. You're my first."

He caught a wisp of blush rise in her cheeks and saw

her moisten her lips again. He couldn't help smiling a little. Women often blushed around him, but none quite as charmingly as she.

Blushing or not, she stayed on course. "You're probably anxious to get on with properties to view, so we can finish up the rest of the details along the way." She tapped her glass-driven mouse and tiny images filled the screen. "Why don't you tell me what you're looking for? You want your forever home? Or something more short-term?"

Until Gerald Robinson came calling, he'd considered Paseo to be his home. "Forever."

Her smile deepened, as if his answer pleased her. "What kind of home? Single family? Condo? Any particular square footage in mind? Number of bedrooms? Lot size?"

"No condos. Only bedroom I care about is mine." But logic made him consider. He'd need more bedrooms if his brothers came to visit. Jayden and Ariana didn't have kids yet, but considering they couldn't keep their hands off each other, it was only a matter of time before they did. And Nathan and Bianca already had her little boy, EJ. Then there was his mom. He'd need a room for her, or even a guest house that she could call her own. One appealing enough to keep her safely away from Robinson.

"I guess six bedrooms ought to do. A guest house would be a plus." He banished Gerald Robinson from his thoughts. He was enjoying Billie's company too much to ruin it thinking about the bastard.

"Any deal breakers? Something that would rule out a property right from the start?"

"No property. I need acreage for my horses and stock. I can always build my own barn, but I'll need the land first."

"Would you consider undeveloped land? Build your own house, too?"

"I'm hoping for something that won't take that long. I'd like this wrapped up before summer's done."

She nodded. "Any particular features in the house that you require?"

"Like what?" He saw the same ripe blonde who'd already passed Billie's office several times make yet another round. Bolder than most, she gave him a direct smile and pressed her hands together over her heart. He automatically grinned a response and she stopped dead in her tracks. At least until an older man with a frown passed her, and she scurried away.

"If you prefer single-story, or must have a wine cellar, fireplace, pool," Billie was saying. "Things like that."

"I'm more beer than wine." He shrugged. "No particular preference. Just want a place I can put away the bedroll."

Her eyebrows lifted. "Bedroll?"

"Figure of speech," he said dismissively. Though it wasn't. He still traveled between rodeos with a bedroll in his truck. He could afford hotels now, but sometimes it was easier to bed down with the horses in the trailer, or under the stars. "I'm on the road a lot. Just need a place to land. And not too close to the city." He would never be able to replicate the ranch in Paseo, but he could try. "I like my space and my privacy. As for the house, I guess a fireplace for cold days. AC on hot." He grinned. "Running water and electricity."

Her smile edged toward impish again. "I've always thought they were convenient."

"'Course, that's when the fireplace comes in handy… good place to keep warm. 'Specially with the right company."

Her cheeks pinkened again. "And your budget?"

Did he have one? He supposed he should. He kept his eye on the broad levels, but Deborah kept her finger on all of the finer points. He knew he could walk away from rodeoing tomorrow and all of his resulting endorsements without personally missing the money a speck. Grayson Gear had become far more profitable in the last decade than anything else he did. But he had rodeoing in his blood. It kept Grayson Gear's name prominent, and as a result, he was able to keep his charitable efforts funded.

Which meant as long as he was physically able to rodeo, he would. Even if the rest of the rodeo world was starting to consider him ancient.

Billie was still looking at him inquiringly. Her hair had slipped free of her enticing ear and she tucked it there once more as she waited.

He felt thirsty all over again.

He tapped the toe of his boot. "Darlin', when I find the right one, no price'll be too high."

Her eyes did flicker at that. Still the model of decorum, though, she looked back at her screen and glided her fingers on her glass pad again.

"Does it get to you, working in a fishbowl like this?" He gestured at the clear, short walls, and the middle-aged redhead who'd been passing Billie's office with the speed of a snail suddenly picked up her pace.

Billie looked wry. "Everything here takes some getting used to. Particularly knowing the boss is always watching. He has a very strict code of ethics that I guess he wants to ensure we're all following."

"What does he expect to catch y'all doing? Stealing cucumbers and water?"

She smiled. "One of these days, I'm sure I won't even

notice all this glass at all. But it is very disconcerting when you first experience it."

"No kidding." His working life was fishbowl-ish, too, though it sure hadn't started out that way. Like a lot of the guys and gals competing in rodeo day in and day out, he'd done so in obscurity until a championship buckle was on his belt, and suddenly he had endorsement offers landing at his feet. "Probably not easy to get used to."

"No, but it's like what you've done in rodeo. You have a job to do and you get on with it."

His toe stopped tapping. "You *do* know who I am."

"It's hard *not* to know who you are. You've been on the news a few times this week. And then there are the Grayson Gear billboards around town." She smiled slightly. "Despite the impression of our local lookey-loos, you're not the first celebrity who's chosen to work with Austin Elite. All I care about is finding a perfect property for you, Mr. Smith." She waited a beat. "But if you prefer a more experienced agent—perhaps Elena. She's the blonde who has traipsed by a dozen times and she'd be entirely—"

"God, no. You, uh, you just surprised me for a bit." Bemused him, more like. "And it's not really Smith. It's Fortune."

She looked only mildly curious and he almost wished he hadn't said anything. Grayson Smith was simply the name he used on his professional bio. But at least his real last name hadn't raised any obvious flags for her.

Considering the way the Fortune name had been in the news since the revelation that Austin icon and bazillionaire Gerald Robinson was actually Jerome Fortune—an heir to even more millions who'd supposedly died a lifetime ago—it was a relief.

It was time to leave the subject of his name well

enough alone. "Mind if I pull my chair a little closer so I can see better?"

"Please do." She rolled her own chair a few inches over so he could edge nearer to the desk.

Nearer to her.

"I apologize again for the close quarters. I'm still the smallest fish in the pond here, so I don't get the pick of offices just yet. Or the pick of clients, so I have to thank you again for requesting me specifically, Mr. Fortune."

His mother had requested Billie, but who was he to correct her now?

"Just Grayson," he replied. He hadn't set out to be known only by his given name any more than he'd set out to be a celebrity. Over the years, it had sort of cemented itself in the public eye. But ever since his mother had admitted that she hadn't simply decided to use the last name Fortune because of her good fortune when she gave birth to healthy triplets, but had actually given them their *father's* name, he'd been increasingly happy not to use it.

Which was a line of thinking certain to put him in a bad mood.

And Billie—young or not—was too much of an unexpected pleasure for him to be in a bad mood thinking about the bastard who'd sired him and his brothers.

He maneuvered his chair almost next to her. It meant he had to stretch one leg out her office door, where someone might trip over it as they dawdled and gawked, but he didn't much care. "And I'm not complaining about the tight space." He nodded toward her computer screen. "All right, darlin'. Show me what you've got."

Chapter Two

Thirty minutes later, Billie watched Grayson stride out the Austin Elite front door. She held her breath and turned to face the receptionist.

Amberleigh Gardner was fanning herself. “That man makes even an old woman like me feel faint. And you’re the lucky girl who gets to work with him.” She winked. “You know he’s not married.”

Hoping that she was hiding the shakiness she’d felt since realizing that her prospective client Mr. Smith was *The* Grayson—famous rodeo rider, local business owner, endorser of everything from beer to saddles—Billie calmly started back to her office. “He’s a client, Amberleigh. No more or less important than any other client. His marital status isn’t relevant.”

Right.

Which was why she’d darn near tripped over her own feet in shock when she’d come out to greet her new client and recognized him. "Besides, you know the rules." No romantic involvement with clients. It was DeForest Allen's sacrosanct rule after having seen too many deals go south because of it.

"Keep tellin' yourself that, hon. Some girls would think losing a job over a guy like *that* to be well worth it." Amberleigh smiled knowingly as Billie passed her.

Once in the office that she'd been assigned three weeks ago when she began working with Austin Elite, she moved the chair Grayson had used back to its usual position before sitting down in her own chair.

Then it felt like all the strength in her body left her and she dropped her head onto her desk. Not caring if anyone *did* see.

From the top of his wavy, caramel-brown hair to the bottom of his expensive boots, Grayson was six-plus feet of drop-dead gorgeous.

Her skin felt flushed and her heart was racing.

She definitely needed to get herself under control before she met him the next day.

"How'd it go with the reigning King of Rodeo, Belinda?"

She sat bolt upright, assuming a confident smile for her boss. She didn't believe for one second that DeForest Allen had known *who* her prospective client was before Grayson arrived, any more than Billie had. "It went very well, Mr. Allen. I'm setting up a tour of six properties for tomorrow morning."

He nodded his silver head. "Close the deal quickly, Belinda. We don't want another Dickinson situation."

"No, we don't, sir." But inwardly, she'd tensed. She'd hoped by moving from Houston and back home to Austin, she'd have left the Dickinson situation behind her. She reminded herself that she'd been here only a few weeks, though. And trust took time.

Plus the proof of signed sales contracts. Dickinson aside, Billie had had plenty of those since getting her license years earlier. Reminding her boss of them, though, was probably not very politic. Despite her track record, she was still surprised he'd hired her. Austin Elite was the premiere agency in town. She'd never actually expected to be offered a position there.

He cupped the steel door frame of her cubicle, oblivious to the clear fingerprints he left on the glass. He was the firm's owner and broker, so they were his glass walls to smear up however he wanted. "Don't wait for the weekly status meeting to keep me posted."

"I won't," she promised.

She waited until he'd entered his own office before letting out another breath.

Did he think *she* wanted another Dickinson situation? Rhonda Dickinson, reeking of Texas oil money, had been a nightmare of a client, pulling out at the last minute on three different sales because she'd happened to find something that looked "just a teensy bit better" each time.

Of course, they hadn't been better in the end, either.

Ultimately, she'd blamed Billie—and subsequently the Houston-based agency she'd worked for—for her own inability to commit, and took her business to their chief competitor.

Last Billie had heard, Rhonda still hadn't signed her name on the bottom of a purchase contract. It was some small comfort, she supposed. If Billie would have been able to get the woman to commit, it would have been her largest sale to date. But now Billie had Grayson Smith—make that Grayson *Fortune*—as a client.

The Fortune name was a big one around Texas. She couldn't help but wonder if he was connected to it.

Her phone chimed musically and she automatically reached out to answer it. "Billie Pemberton."

"You goin' to Selena's birthday party this week?"

At the sound of her cousin Max's voice, Billie glanced at the photos sitting on top of her filing cabinet and plucked one from the collection, of Max taking down a steer. She'd used the excuse of putting Grayson's water glass there earlier to turn the shot of her cousin away from her new client's view. "I'm bringing the cupcakes and Mom's hosting, so yes. You?" Selena was the daughter of a mutual cousin.

Max laughed. "You know I'd skip it if my ma wouldn't make my life miserable for it. Too bad I'm not on the road somewhere."

"When are you heading out again?" Even though they each had four older siblings of their own, she and Max had been close as thieves their entire lives. Didn't hurt that their mothers were sisters, so they'd been raised more like brother and sister than cousins. Now, when Max wasn't out at some rodeo, he stayed with his folks, Mae and Larry. Billie had a one-bedroom apartment in downtown Austin, into which she was still moving her stuff from Houston.

She opened the bottom drawer of the cabinet and tucked the picture of Max inside. She'd leave it there, where there would be no chance of her newest client spotting it.

It was pretty unlikely the rodeo star would care that she had a photo of the young man who'd bested him in El Paso, but she wasn't going to take chances.

Nor was she going to take chances that Max would learn the identity of her new high-profile client. After what had happened earlier that year, he'd consider it treason.

"Coleman starts the day after Selena's deal, so we'll

drive over once it looks like I can git along without Mama getting ticked."

"Travis going?" When Max's buddy Travis Conrad wasn't competing in tie-down roping, he hazed for Max.

"Yeah. Hopefully, we'll still have enough time to catch some z's before slack."

"Slack," she knew, was the time scheduled for overflow contestants to compete, because they couldn't all be scheduled into the regular nightly performances. It was generally free to get into, whereas the performances were not. Fortunately for the competitors, a slack event counted just as much as a performance event. Like Max said, the paycheck was the same whether there were paying crowds in the grandstand or not.

Of course, a lot of times that paycheck was a big fat zero. Considering the entrance fees, as well as the cost of getting themselves, their gear and their horse, if they even had one there in the first place, rodeoing often meant cowboys headed on down the road already in the hole. Max loved it, though.

Personally, Billie liked having a bank account that wasn't always in need of life support.

She turned back to face her desk. "And after Coleman?" She tapped her glass keyboard, systematically printing off the listings Grayson had liked, as well as a few more to recommend if needed.

The Fourth of July was less than a month away and she knew Max would be particularly busy. "How many rodeos are you packing in this year?"

The few weeks in and around the Independence Day holiday were affectionately known as Cowboy Christmas because of the sheer number of opportunities a person had to enter the most rodeos for the most money.

"Long as my truck, trailer and gear hold out, seven,

including Reno. Got three saddle bronc riders plus Trav hitching rides with me. Helps a lot on expenses and the driving when we'll be covering some four thousand miles."

She grimaced, just thinking about five men packed into such close confines. She remembered one year after he'd returned from Cowboy Christmas. Ripe didn't even begin to describe the state of his truck. She wondered if Grayson would be caught up in the frenzied schedule, too. If he were, it would definitely put a crimp in his availability to see listings. "Going to Calgary?"

"The earnings don't count toward the standings. Cowboy Country's will. So that's where I'm planning to be. You gonna make it over for the rodeo?"

Her fingers paused on the glass. Cowboy Country USA was a popular Western-theme amusement park in Horseback Hollow, where their mothers had grown up. It was a good five to six hour drive. "Depends on work."

Max made a sound. "Everything depends on your work. You're gonna get old and dull, Bill. You need to get out and have more fun. And by fun, I mean sex."

Her fingers paused. "And the last time *you* had some fun?"

He snorted, laughing. "About a week ago. A chick I met at Twine."

"Obviously, you're not still brokenhearted from Bethany." Bethany Belmont was the barrel racer Grayson supposedly stole from Max back in March. Max claimed Bethany had been the love of his life until Grayson lured her away. It was then that Max had made it his goal to unseat the reigning rodeo champion.

"Being brokenhearted ain't got diddly to do with sex." Max's voice had gone flat.

She rolled her eyes and started typing again. If Grayson were still involved with the woman, he'd given no indication of it that morning. And she found it difficult to believe that her cousin had been as gung ho over the barrel racer as he claimed, since Max fell in love more often than Billie bought shoes. "I can't believe that of the two of us, *you* are the romantic."

"Yeah, well, you ought t' try it sometime. At least go out and drink a little. Dance a little. Never know where it might lead."

"Yeah, well, you know how I feel about that," she returned calmly. It wasn't that she didn't believe in love. Her parents had been inseparable since being childhood sweethearts. Billie just wasn't willing to sacrifice everything she wanted out of life because of it. She wanted her high-rise apartment that she could barely afford. She wanted her nice clothes and her interesting career and—one day—a bank account that allowed for more things than just the minimum daily requirements. So far, any relationships she'd had of the romantic variety had been decided letdowns in comparison.

"Look, Max, I've got stuff to do. Don't forget to bring Selena an appropriate gift. A bottle of hooch for a thirteen-year-old won't cut it."

"You give me no credit. Last time I did that was for Audie's eighteenth."

"Eighteen was still underage, Max," she reminded him before hanging up and turning her attention fully to the property listings once more.

When she met with Grayson in the morning, she wanted to be completely prepared. She'd been told to close the deal quickly, and that's exactly what she intended to do.

When the phone rang a few seconds later, she grabbed

it up again. "If you're calling to ask me to buy Selena's gift for you, the answer is still no."

A feminine laugh answered her. "Actually, I was calling to see if you were going to be in Houston this Friday."

Billie's fingers relaxed on her glass keypad again. "Well, if it isn't the soon-to-be Mrs. Zach McCarter." She grinned. "Or after enduring Schuyler's wedding last month, are you calling to tell me you and Zach decided to forgo all the hoopla and elope to Vegas?"

Maddie Fortunado laughed in her ear again. "We're still planning a wedding," she assured her. "So don't think you're getting out of attending. But I guarantee it won't be quite as over-the-top as my sister's come-one, come-all grand affair. So, are you going to be in Houston on Friday? We're trying out a new restaurant and I wanted to let you know in case you're able to join the gang."

Maddie was the newly crowned president at Fortunado Real Estate in Houston along with her fiancé, Zach, where Billie had gotten her start. She'd also been the one to invite her to join the "gang"—a group of young real estate professionals who met routinely to talk business and socialize.

"I hope to be," Billie told her. "I've still got a couple loads of stuff to move from my old apartment."

"Some people would just hire a moving company," Maddie pointed out.

Some people didn't have the extra money to do that. Billie kept the fact to herself. "I'm still helping the Montanegros navigate their home purchase in Houston," she said, which was true. "So I still have to be there occasionally, anyway."

"Oh, right. Your old neighbors. The ones you're forgoing your sales commission for."

"The ones who are storing my stuff in their garage,"

Billie added humorously. "It's the least I could do. So where's the meeting place?" She made a note when Maddie told her.

"How is business going at Austin Elite? Any new listings?"

It was all too easy to conjure Grayson's face in her mind. "No new listings. But a new client looking to buy came in today specifically asking for me."

"That's great, Billie! I knew it wouldn't be long before you were right back in the swing of things. Word gets around when you're a good agent. So what size fishy cracker are we talking?"

Billie chuckled. "He's a big one, if I haven't just jinxed everything by admitting it."

"He?" Maddie's voice piqued with interest. "Is he single?"

"Maddie! I don't know who is worse—my cousin with sex on his brain, or you with romance on yours."

"May I just say that those two elements *can* work quite well together? I'll take your nonanswer as the affirmative, though. So is the male big fish *eligible*? Do tell."

She could imagine Maddie's reaction if she knew just how eligible. "There's nothing to tell!" Particularly when DeForest Allen walked past her office again, giving her a close look. "I'll tell you as much as I can on Friday if I can make it. Right now, my boss is giving me the stink eye. And I've told you what he's like."

"That's what you get for defecting back to Austin," Maddie said humorously. "Fine. But I'm holding you to it, my friend. So be prepared with details the next time I see you!"

Grayson slid the key card over the lock on his hotel suite on the top floor of the Kimpton and pushed open the door. His mother, seated on a couch positioned to take in the lake view, looked up at him. She had her usual calendar spread in front of her, along with her phone and a foot-high stack of glossy Grayson publicity stills that she was signing.

"How'd it go?"

He dropped his hat on the table next to the stack. "Did you know that Billy with a *y* is actually Billie with an *i* and an *e*?"

"Don't let your sexism show, son." The fact that Deborah followed his statement at all was proof enough that she had known. She signed another photo with a flourish. "I can't help what you assumed."

"Then did you know how *young* she is?"

Deborah leaned back against the couch. As usual, her long brown hair hung over her shoulder in a thick braid, and she had another pen tucked behind her ear, almost hiding the few sprinkles of gray she possessed. "Everything I've heard about Billie Pemberton when she was in Houston is that she is an excellent agent. Astute. Hardworking, and most importantly—according to *your* specifications—*very* discreet. Why would you care whether she's twenty-one or ninety-one?" The fine lines at the corners of her eyes crinkled. "Or was she attractive, too?"

There was a price to be paid for having his mother act as his manager. When most men were off on their own, catching grief for not calling home often enough, Deborah Fortune handled almost every detail in Grayson's life. With finesse and grace when necessary, but more often than not with plain speaking and a no-bull attitude. It's how she'd raised him and his brothers when they were kids, and it was how things were now.

"Yeah, she was attractive." He sounded grouchy and

didn't care. He flung himself down on the other couch and started to stretch out his legs.

"Don't get comfortable. You need to sign some of these, too." She pushed a stack of stills toward him. She waited until he'd sat forward and grabbed a pen. "So you liked her."

After so many years traveling on the road together, they usually both knew how to give each other privacy and space. Evidently, this was not going to be one of those times.

He slid his gaze across the table toward her as he signed his name. Autographing the photographs they gave away during his appearances had gotten so mundane, he could do it in his sleep. "Like you said. She seems competent so far." And beautiful. Intelligent.

And sexy as all hell, the way the bridge of her nose wrinkled when she really concentrated.

He turned back to the stack of photos, but the image in his head was all Billie. "I'm meeting her tomorrow morning to look at a couple properties."

"Tomorrow." Deborah sounded surprised. "That's nice, but that's not what I was asking."

How well he knew it. "I'm looking for a new ranch, Ma. Not a wife."

Deborah clucked her tongue. "Don't be so reactionary. I'm not suggesting you get married tomorrow. I'm merely suggesting you don't have many opportunities to meet nice young women, and when you do, you should pay attention."

"I meet nice young women all the time. I don't need to be dating my real estate agent."

"So you've already thought about it."

His glare at her had no effect. So he gave up and

grabbed more photos from the stack. "How many of these did we print?"

"Five thousand. And usually, the women you meet are reporters and sales reps and buckle bunnies."

"Ariana's a reporter." Or a novelist. He wasn't exactly sure what Jayden's new wife was working on at the moment. "She wasn't a nice young woman?"

Deborah sighed noisily. "You know I already love Ariana and Bianca like daughters. And don't get me started on how EJ's already wrapping his hands around my heart."

"He *is* a cute little dickens." Grayson's brother Nathan would be a heck of a stepfather for the four-year-old now that he'd married Bianca. "I took out that rep from Change Sportswear I met a couple weeks ago. Dinner at a place with tablecloths and everything." Followed by a very entertaining evening in her bed. Like him, Livian Reed wanted nothing more out of their very brief acquaintance than that.

Good food. Good sex. Goodbye.

Just the way he liked it. No promises, no strings.

Too-young-for-him Billie Pemberton might be perfect in every way. But she wasn't a no-strings type. He hadn't even needed to see all the family photographs crammed on her filing cabinet to know it.

"Livian Reed's a buckle bunny, too. She's just dressed in Ann Taylor."

He couldn't help but grin. "And Livian would eviscerate you for the comparison if she ever knew."

His mother's expression turned dry. "Well, you're not going to see her again, I know that for certain, so I'm not going to lose sleep worrying that she'll find out."

"I oughta call Livian and take her out again just to make you sweat a little."

"Two dates with the same girl? The last time *that* happened, you were eighteen and hot after Bethany Belmont." Deborah laughed knowingly and pushed off the couch. "You've got me shaking in my Castletons, kiddo."

"Speaking of." He was glad to change the subject. "Any progress on that front?"

She opened the suite's minibar and studied the contents. "I'm still waiting for a call back from them. I'm not sure how much I can do, son, if the lure of The Grayson hasn't already impressed them."

He grunted. "Thanks."

"Want me to start pandering to your ego now? If this is a midlife crisis starting, just tell me now." She pulled out a bottle of fruit juice and eyed him with amusement as she shook it. "I'll head on back to Paseo most happily and leave you to your buckle bunnies, who will coo and awe your ego right up to its fullest—"

"Yeah, yeah," he said, cutting her off. She'd head back to Paseo and the ranch. Gerald Robinson might find out—God knew the tech giant had means that seemed to defy all imagination—and come sniffing around her and...no thank you, ma'am. From what Jayden had told Grayson about his last encounter with Gerald, there'd been real emotion on the man's face when he'd spoken of Deborah. Didn't matter that the man—whatever the hell name he was using—was married. Robinson's infidelities were the world's worst-kept secret. Grayson didn't believe for a second that their life would have been different if Gerald had known Deborah gave birth to his three sons. And Grayson intended to do whatever he needed to do to keep the man from ever hurting his mom again.

Fortunately unaware of his dark thoughts, his mother deepened her smile. "You know I'll always help you if you ask. But one of these days, son, you won't need me along to manage your rodeo career. Or you won't want me along. Or you'll realize it's finally time to give your body a break and retire from bulldogging. Neither one of us could have guessed how your teenage hobby would change our lives. But it can't last forever. And that's okay. Life moves on. As it should."

"I'm not retiring until I've got one more world championship to my name." The National Finals Rodeo would be held in Las Vegas in December. He was already tied for the most world championship wins ever. One more would set a new record. And *then* he'd retire from bulldogging.

Ego? Yeah. He knew he had more than his fair share of ego. But it was also calculated. Record-winning names faded from memory a little more slowly than also-rans. And the longer he could make money on his name, the longer he could put that money to good use.

"Well, I for one am glad you're already number three in the money," his mother said. "Between rodeoing, Grayson Gear and your charity appearances, you've worked nearly every day for the past year. One of these days, it's going to take its toll on you."

He wasn't worried about the toll. Aches and pains went hand in hand with rodeoing. "I'd be second in the standings if I hadn't bought it in Silver City and lost out to Max Vargas."

The entire season of pro rodeo was about the money rankings. Earnings were the only common ground on which to judge their success as they competed in rodeos throughout the country under every condition that could be had. If the Finals were the goal—and admittedly, for the majority of cowboys who competed it was not—then nearly every dollar earned paved the way there.

"Vargas can really run a steer," his mother pointed out mildly.

"And at the rate he's going, he'll be at the Nationals. But he's still a punk and I don't like losing to a punk."

Deborah looked amused. "There was a day when Joe-Don Gainer called you a punk."

"Yeah, and Joe-Don was right then. Same as I'm right, now. I'm not the saint that Joe-Don was, though. Hazing for me like he did even though he was a Hall of Famer?" Grayson shook his head. "Won't catch me hazing for Max Vargas. If his usual guy, Travis, isn't hazing for him, he treats the one who is like dirt."

A wrestler who didn't appreciate the contribution of his hazer—who rode on the opposite side of the steer, keeping him more or less straight and close to the bulldogger—was just damn stupid. Luck of the draw chose the steer. The hazer and the wrestler's skill together determined what they did with that luck.

"Don't go off on a tangent dissecting details of Silver City again," his mother warned. "The hour you subjected me to the other day was enough." She finally opened her juice and wandered to look out the windows. "I wonder if I should just show up at Castleton's doorway. Might be harder for them to ignore me in person. Red Rock's only a couple hours from here. I could rent a car and drive over and be back before we need to leave for Coleman. What do you think?"

"I think once the event tomorrow is finished, you could go to Red Rock, and from there head straight to Coleman." He gave her a look. "I can manage to get myself and the trailer and the horses there without you."

"I realize you're capable." Her tone turned dry again. "Whether you manage to do it all in time to not miss your event altogether is the question."

"Last time I did that was fifteen years ago."

"Because of a girl—"

"And I haven't been late once since," he said, cutting her off. "Even though you still harp on it often enough. Focus on Red Rock and let me worry about getting to Coleman." He lifted his pen. "We don't need five thousand of these things for tomorrow, do we?" The remaining unsigned stack was still a foot high.

"I think they're hoping for about a thousand to show."

He capped the pen and tossed it on the cocktail table, stretching his fingers. "What time's the deal supposed to start?"

"Two o'clock. I've personally taped up copies of your schedule this week in this suite. I told you that you didn't have to make the appearance tomorrow. If you hadn't, you would have had time with Billie to see more." She smiled knowingly. "More than just a couple properties, I mean."

He let that pass.

The library appearance had been added to his already busy schedule there in Austin at the last minute, and his personal appearance fee would go to local literacy. "It's a good cause." He hadn't taken the military route that Nathan and Jayden had. They'd been literally out saving the world. Instead, all Grayson could offer was his name and his money to support charitable efforts where he could. And he knew Deborah understood his motivations completely.

"I'll be finished with Billie in plenty of time to meet you here before the dedication." He pushed to his feet and stretched. "I'm going to hit the gym this afternoon and then see if I can scare up a massage somewhere."

His mom rolled her eyes. "Read your schedule!" She headed toward the connecting door that separated Grayson's suite from her own. "I've arranged a massage for you right here at four o'clock. Don't forget to tip your masseuse and don't forget to meet me at seven. We're having drinks with the Deckers at Twine."

He groaned. Claudia and Myron Decker had more money than Midas and could always be counted on to support his foundation, Grayson Good. But in the process, they definitely liked to trot him out as if he were their prized bull. Ergo the appearance the next day at the new library. "It's never just drinks with the Deckers."

"And whose fault is that?" She gave him one more pointed look. "They're bankrolling the event tomorrow, so wear a clean shirt and don't be late."

Chapter Three

Billie was wearing another short skirt complete with the intriguing zipper running right up over her backside.

Only difference today was that her skirt was black and the silky tank top that exposed her tanned shoulders was white. The high-heeled shoes were red, and the legs they showed off were still flat-out stunning.

She had her hair pulled back into a thick ponytail at the back of her head. The hairstyle not only exposed the trio of earrings on the upper curve of her ear, but the long, long line of her throat.

"Talk about perfect timing," she called to him as he jaywalked across the street toward the real estate office. She gestured at the dark gray luxury sedan parked at the curb next to her. "I just got here, myself." She waited until he reached her side of the street. "Where did you park?"

"I walked from my hotel."

Her bright smile turned stricken as she scurried to the

passenger door and opened it. "I'm so sorry. I should have offered to pick you up. It didn't even occur to me to—"

"No apologies, darlin'," he interrupted, looking at her over the top rims of his sunglasses. "I liked the walk." It was a good way to work out his muscle kinks and some of his hangover from the night before. "And it gave me a chance to get this." He lifted his oversize takeout coffee.

Her smile widened once more. She reached inside the vehicle, giving him an eye-popping view of her inner knee and thigh. Then she straightened and he belatedly noticed the identical cup she'd retrieved.

"If you tell me that's straight-up black coffee, I may have to marry you right now."

Her cheeks turned red, but she laughed. "Fortunately, all the hopeful women of the world can rest easy this morning. It's iced chai tea."

He made a face. "That's almost as bad as cucumber-laced water."

She laughed again and stepped out of the way. "Maybe I can redeem myself by offering plenty of legroom. Your chariot, Mr. Fortune."

"Told you. Just Grayson." He ducked his head and climbed into the passenger seat of the spacious car.

It was the kind of vehicle a wealthy grandmother might drive. Definitely not what he'd expect of a young woman like Billie.

He waited until she'd climbed behind the wheel and strapped herself in with the seat belt. "Company car?"

She laughed yet again, but wryly this time. "Don't I wish. I'd much prefer the payment to be on Austin Elite's bank account than on mine. But no." She patted the leather-wrapped steering wheel. "She's all mine. Or will be after six more payments to the bank. It's not the newest model, but it's comfortable and gets me where my clients and I need to go."

"Sort of how I feel about my truck." He'd had many over the years, but could easily remember when his truck had been his largest investment. "Not the newest but it gets me where my horses and I need to go."

"Wasn't a new truck one of the prizes last year at the Cowboy Country rodeo?"

Surprised, he gave her a look. Rather than settle her cup of nasty-ass tea next to his coffee in the console, she'd tucked it between her knees and was starting the engine. He *had* won the new truck, but had turned around and auctioned it off through Grayson Good for a children's charity. "You actually follow rodeo?"

"I come from a large family," she said. "They're into everything from baseball to zebra racing." Her cheeks still looked a little red as she pulled on a pair of gold-rimmed aviator sunglasses and checked the traffic before zipping out into it.

Given the sudden speed, he was glad he'd already fastened his seat belt. And also glad they were essentially driving around in a small tank.

"So..." She reached behind her seat and retrieved a fancy folder that she handed to him. "I've printed all the listings we reviewed yesterday, plus a few more that I think might be of interest, too. There's also a map if you're inclined to follow along." She nipped the big car between two semitrucks with about six inches to spare.

He grabbed his cup and wished there was something stronger inside it than just French roast.

She raced through a light more yellow than green, braked slightly around a curve and sped up a freeway on-ramp. "Is it too windy for you?" His window was halfway down and hers was all the way down, making her long ponytail fly around her head.

"Wind's good." Aside from the fact that she looked young and beautiful and vibrant, he was hoping he wouldn't have to hang his head out the window.

It wasn't that he was uncomfortable with her fast—make that maniacal, he decided when she shot across two lanes of traffic—driving.

It was more the combination of her obvious lead foot and the evening-into-night of drinks with the Deckers the night before. Then everything had gotten out of control, and the cops had been called, and a news crew showed up…

He planted his ball cap more firmly on his head and sucked on the coffee. He'd warned his mom that drinks with the Deckers was never a simple thing. Even when they were trying to do something good like sponsor the library deal. "Which place are we heading to first?"

Billie held the steering wheel and her tea in one hand and reached over to the folder she'd dropped on his lap, and he damn near choked on his coffee. But all she did was flip open the folder to reveal a colorful printed map.

"Property number one." She lightly tapped the page, then returned her hand to the steering wheel. Evidently, only to maneuver the car right back across the same two lanes of traffic.

He closed his eyes. Give him six hundred pounds of ornery steer any day.

"The properties are numbered in the order we'll see them," she said above the wind. "I know it's easy for the properties to blur together, which is why I've prepared the folio. You can make notes as you like."

She reached behind her seat again and produced a slender gold pen tastefully monogrammed with "Austin Elite" on the side. She handed it to him. "Three of the properties this morning are vacant, including this first one. I find my clients usually prefer visiting vacant properties. Makes it easier to imagine living there." She zipped around another semitruck. "Weather is supposed to be hotter than usual today. I have several bottles of chilled water if—"

He lifted his hand just in case she intended to reach behind her seat again. "I'm good for now. Thanks."

She sent him another smile. "Great. I love a morning drive." She changed lanes again. "Just gets the blood flowing, you know?"

He managed a smile. The only thing getting his blood flowing that morning was the vivid smile on her pretty face. That, and the knowledge that his life insurance was up-to-date.

Fortunately, the farther outside of town they traveled, the thinner the traffic grew. Then, at least, he didn't worry so much about colliding with other vehicles as much as flying off the highway curves. After about thirty minutes more, she pulled off the freeway and began working her way through the mercifully empty countryside to the first property.

Even though this whole thing was his idea, it still felt strange when she pulled to a stop in front of the first house.

"Here we are at last."

It was a brick two-story with two wings and not another house in sight. But imagining himself living there was beyond him.

"The property is on city water." She pushed her glasses up onto her head before gathering up the Magic Bag hiding behind her seat, then climbed out of the car. "As you can see from the printout, there is a little over five acres." She looked down at the ground beneath them, waving one arm. "The entire drive is covered in pavers—antique terra-cotta color, I believe. Very attractive." She looked up at him over the top of the car and he gave what he hoped was a suitable response.

Her sales litany didn't lose any steam, so he supposed it must have sufficed.

"The iron entrance gate was left open now for us, but it's electronically controlled. So you wouldn't have to worry about any Grayson groupies coming out to bother you."

He gave her a quick look. He hadn't used that particular term with her. "I don't have groupies." It was blatantly untrue, even though he wished otherwise.

"Sorry." She looked contrite. "I saw the news this morning about what happened at Twine last night. The term was just in my head."

He sighed. "Overeager fans who'd had way too much to drink. Unfortunately, it happens occasionally." Particularly when he was out in public with people like the Deckers, who felt compelled to make a big deal about their "celebrity" friend.

"Did that one woman actually punch the news cameraman?"

He grimaced. Two women from the bar, bolstered by booze and who knew what else, had been intent on joining their party. "Only after he told her he wasn't putting her on camera unless she put her shirt back on. It pretty much turned into a free-for-all after that."

"Did you really pay her jail fine?"

"It seemed the right thing to do at the time." He stared at the house. "Maybe an electronic gate would be a good thing, after all."

"Or maybe avoid places like Twine," she said humorously.

He grunted. "Ever been there?"

"A time or twenty. It's the best place for martinis and tapas." She gestured toward the house. "Would you like to see inside?"

He shrugged and closed the car door. "That's what we're here for."

She gave him a winning smile again. "Don't forget your folio if you want to make notes."

He reached back in for the fancy folder of information she'd prepared, and followed her toward the front door of the house.

"I haven't been here before, but I know it's on a lockbox." Her high heels clicked on the paver stones as she searched for the box holding the house key. "In addition to the three garages off to your left, there's a structure in the rear of the house that could also be used as a garage or for some other type of storage. Ah. There it is." She knelt down behind a tastefully positioned bush, and straightened a moment later, doing a little shimmy to push the hem of her narrow skirt back down toward her knees. She glanced his way as she unlocked the enormous front door. "The position on this hill gives a nice view. And I've heard that the adjacent land may be available for the right price. It's totally undeveloped and would mean an additional ten acres. Have any initial thoughts?"

The nice view he was looking at had more to do with her than the location of the house. Which wasn't exciting him in the least. The vegetation dotting the hillside was more cactus and scrub than grassland. "Let's just see what we've got inside."

She swept open the door and waited for him to enter.

He walked inside. The house might be vacant of occupants, but it wasn't vacant of furnishings. Beneath the vaulted entry, an ornate neon-green chandelier hung over a bright purple statue of a rearing horse.

For a minute, he wished he was back home in Paseo, where the only times you used the front entrance of the house—versus the back door—was if company was coming over for Christmas dinner. Where everyone in town knew who he was and didn't give two figs about his supposed "celebrity" status. And where anyone with two licks of common sense knew better than to hang a butt-ugly green chandelier over an even uglier purple horse.

"That's a bold design choice," Billie said faintly.

"It's ugly as hell," he said bluntly. "And I like horses."

"Just keep in mind that the furnishings aren't permanent fixtures. They'll all be leaving along with the owners. Do you want to see more, or shall we move on?"

Despite the hideous horse, the high ceilings and the view outside, the inside of the house felt like a cave to him. "Move on, if you don't mind."

"Of course not. You're the buyer, after all. Walking in the door should feel like home to you." She juggled the materials in her arm and came up with a business card. "I just need to leave my card. I'll meet you at the car."

He gave the hideous statue a wide berth and went back outside. He thought again about the ranch in Paseo. There, the house wasn't even a third of the size of this one, but it was surrounded by a whole lot more prime grazing land. Would he ever find a place that felt like home when he walked in the door, besides the house in which he'd grown up?

He headed back to the car and his now-cool coffee. He drank it anyway.

Within minutes, Billie had locked up the house again and they were off to property number two.

It excited him no more than property number one.

The land was decent enough, though still too little of it. There were two barns, and five bedrooms in the house.

Knowing that he'd given short shrift to property number one, this time he forced himself to traipse through every room of the streamlined home.

"No?" Billie gave him a questioning look as he paused in the state-of-the-art kitchen. It was all stainless steel, which he didn't mind here, but it matched the stainless steel and glass that dominated the rest of the house, too. Which he did mind.

Frankly, the place had the antiseptic air of a hospital. And having spent his entire adult life wrestling with horned beasts, he'd had more than his share of hospitals.

"Afraid not." He remembered his mom's admonishments to be polite when he'd set out that morning. "Sorry."

Billie waved away Grayson's apology. Seeing two houses without a spark of excitement wasn't anything to get worried about.

Yet.

"Don't be sorry," she told him. "Each time we see something, it helps me narrow down what you're really looking for." At least that was her theory.

She stepped around him to leave her card among the collection already sitting on the steel counter and led the way back out of the austere house.

Unlike the day before, when he'd walked through the door of the real estate office looking like the poster boy for professional rodeo, today Grayson wore slouchy beige cargo shorts, leather flip-flops and a Dallas Cowboys ball cap. The calves showing below the long shorts were just as tanned and muscular as the arms showing below the short sleeves of his gray T-shirt. His ridiculously handsome jaw was blurred by unshaved whiskers, and his dark eyes—visible in the few minutes when he pulled off his sunglasses—were clearly bloodshot.

He looked like he belonged on the beach sleeping off a bender. And he was still so mouthwateringly handsome that she couldn't keep herself from blathering on about every detail of the properties she was showing him, as if he couldn't see for himself the very things she was pointing out.

It was embarrassing. She was supposed to know the value of keeping quiet when she needed to.

They drove to property number three, only a few minutes later than the time she'd arranged with the owners the day before.

She expected them to be gone from the house by the time they got there, but the sight of the van still sitting in front warned her otherwise.

She hated showing properties when the current occupants were present. It never boded well. Nobody relaxed enough to properly give the house fair consideration. And she had high hopes for this particular listing.

She parked behind the van and looked at Grayson.

He was slouched in the passenger seat, cradling the coffee cup that she suspected was empty, the bill of his cap pulled low over his forehead.

"Why don't I check inside first? I think the owners are still here, and it's probably better if they don't realize *who* is looking at their house. More than once, I've had an owner try to drive up the price just because they think they've got a big fish on the hook."

He sent her a faint smile. "You're the expert."

That's what her business cards implied. But driving around "The Grayson" all morning—particularly after his name had been bandied about every fifteen minutes on the local morning news—was leaving her feeling more shaky than confident.

She grabbed her business cards and darted up the front steps to ring the doorbell.

The door opened so immediately, she suspected the owner had been waiting right behind it. "Good morning, Mr. Orchess." She stuck out her business card. "I'm Billie Pemberton with Austin Elite Real Estate. We spoke on the phone yesterday?"

The gray-haired owner smiled. "Come on in, little lady. Can't wait to show off my place here to you and your client." He made no secret that he was trying to see who was in her car parked behind the van, and she was glad for the tinted windows that gave no hint whether anyone was inside the vehicle or not.

"Actually, Mr. Orchess, my schedule has gotten out of hand this morning." It hadn't, but he didn't need to know that. "Is there another time I can bring my client back to see your lovely home?"

The man wrinkled his nose in thought. "Well, the missus and I have to be outta town for the next week or so, so that's out."

Drat, drat, drat. Mr. Orchess was clearly of the mind that he needed to be present, even though she knew very well he had a listing agent representing his multimillion-dollar property. "I don't mind showing your place to my client in your absence if you don't."

"But if I'm not here, I can't tell you all about the special details I've put in myself."

She nodded. "I understand your concern. What if I went through your home now with you and took careful notes? Then I could bring my client back another time and do my best to share all of the special details."

"I s'pose that'd be okay," he said, after giving it some thought.

It took twenty minutes before Billie was able to gracefully leave Mr. Orchess.

Inside, the house was a masterpiece. It also sat on a beautiful piece of property that she thought would be perfect for Grayson.

When she returned to the car Grayson was slouched in the front seat.

Snoring softly.

She almost wished, then, that she hadn't rushed Mr. Orchess quite so much.

She hovered outside the car for a few minutes, sighing. Grayson wasn't the first client to fall asleep on her. Rhonda Dickinson used to fall asleep regularly.

She sincerely hoped that was the only similarity between her new client and Rhonda.

Billie finally climbed behind the wheel of the car, closed the door softly and backed away from the house. Hopefully, he would awaken on his own before they reached the fourth property.

He did not.

Determination filled her. "You are not going to be another Rhonda," she murmured and opened her door. Then pulled it shut again with a loud slam.

Grayson sat up with a start. "What?"

She looked at him innocently. "Property number four is the smallest house we'll be seeing today, but has the most acreage. What do you think so far?"

He pulled off his sunglasses and blinked blearily at her. "I fell asleep."

"Did you? I hadn't noticed."

"I fell asleep with *you* driving."

She wasn't sure what to make of that, except to know

that it wasn't meant as a compliment. "Actually, you fell asleep while I was taking notes about the previous house."

"Thought you didn't notice."

She gave him a look that was hopefully far more congenial than she actually felt, before opening her car door again. "Nearly seventeen acres," she said, as she climbed out. "According to the map, there's a private lake in the middle of it. Do you like boating?"

"Doesn't everybody?" He grabbed a water bottle and seemed to stumble a little as he got out of the car. He swore softly.

She pretended not to see. "I've never been on a boat, myself." She headed for the front door of the house. She'd been through it once already with another client, so didn't have to hunt for the location of the lockbox.

"You've never been on a boat?"

"Nope." She crouched down and entered her access code. The box popped open and she pulled out the house key. "I don't swim." She straightened and smoothed down her skirt. "It doesn't make me a freak."

"Did I say it did?"

"No, but you'd be one of the few who didn't." Max was always riding her about it. She unlocked the door and led the way inside. "Mind the step down when you come in," she warned.

"I see it." He sounded grouchy.

Maybe because he'd just woken up.

Maybe because he was obviously still hungover.

Considering the high hopes she'd had for the morning, things felt on a downhill slide.

She crossed the scuffed wooden floor and opened the wooden shutters so that more natural light filled the living area. "The house was built in 1910, and has undergone a few renovations since. The kitchen has been modernized and two bedrooms were added on in the 1980s."

His expression was unreadable as he wandered around. But at least he didn't look entirely disinterested, as he had with the last house they'd toured. While he headed down the hall toward the bedrooms, she went to the kitchen to leave her business card on the counter. She gave him some time to explore on his own, then slowly followed.

She found him in the master bedroom.

"This one of the modernizations you mentioned?" He pointed his thumb upward toward the ceiling mirror positioned directly over the enormous bed.

Billie felt her cheeks heat. How she could have forgotten about that detail was beyond her. "Actually, the mirror dates back to the original house."

His lips twitched. "Interesting design choice."

"Better or worse than a purple horse?"

He slid his sunglasses down until his brown eyes met hers. "Now, darlin', do you really want me to answer that?"

She straightened her shoulders and channeled her mom's sternest expression. "Perhaps not."

He laughed softly. Which made mincemeat out of all of her channeling and straightening. Didn't matter in the least that he was a client and completely off-limits. Not to mention completely out of her league. He ruffled her.

She edged her way out of the bedroom. "Would you like to see the outbuildings?"

He seemed to consider it for half a minute. Then nodded slowly. "Yeah. I would."

It was more than she'd expected. And her enthusiasm for the morning came back brighter than ever. "All right, then. If you'd like to follow me..."

"Nothing I'd rather do, darlin'."

Chapter Four

"Come on. You can tell Uncle Grayson."

Billie rolled her eyes. "You're not my uncle."

His smile flashed and warmth filled her.

They'd seen two more houses after the one with the mirrored master bedroom and now they were sitting on the grass in a park not far from where she'd grown up.

All because Grayson had seen the circle of food trucks parked there and had decided he was starving.

Which was why she had her legs tucked to one side of her, with a huge paper napkin draped over her thighs to protect herself from the poutine she was eating. Because, evidently, she didn't know how to say no to him very convincingly.

"Okay, so I'm not your uncle. But you can still tell me."

She sighed around another bite of gravy-covered french fry. "This stuff ought to be illegal," she murmured, licking her finger. More to the point, *Grayson* ought to be illegal. "Why are you even interested?"

He pointed over her shoulder at the school field behind them. "You just told me you went to high school right there. That you ran track on that very field. You got me curious. So why not tell me what kind of student you were?"

"I told you I ran track. That's not enough?"

"I can imagine it, too. All long legs and big eyes and hair flying in the breeze."

She rolled her eyes, determined not to let his flirtatious words get to her. How he'd already gotten her to talk about herself was beyond her.

One minute they'd been discussing the merits of the sixth property they'd visited—namely, the accessibility of the acreage where he'd be keeping his livestock. The next thing she knew, he was buying her poutine—overriding her insistence that she pay for her own lunch—and getting her to talk about what it had been like growing up in Austin.

"I was an average student," she finally said, feeling more than a little exasperated. Mostly at herself. Because whether he was offering ridiculously flirtatious statements or not, the man definitely *got* to her. "Average in every single way."

"I find that hard to believe." He'd polished off his own double serving of poutine—which had come with a heart attack–sized serving of bacon atop the cheese curds and gravy—and was sucking down his chocolate milkshake. "There's nothing average about you. Tell me the real truth."

"That *is* the truth. I graduated smack-dab in the middle of my class from that high school over there."

"Then you ended up with a degree in economics from

Rice and are now working at the most prestigious real estate firm in the city."

She flushed. "How do you know I graduated from Rice?"

He tipped down his sunglasses and his warm brown eyes glided over her face. "I looked at your profile on the company's website."

Of course. Silly of her. She was glad that the newness of her college degree wasn't available online. The truth was, she'd gotten her real estate license well before she'd managed to finish her college degree. Mostly because she'd seen the kind of money to be made when she'd worked as a receptionist at Fortunado Real Estate in Houston, helping to pay her way through school.

"From what I saw on the site, you've got some hefty credentials."

"And I'm still the new kid on the block where my boss at Austin Elite is concerned." Then she wanted to kick herself. What good did it do to tell her *client* that? Why couldn't she tell Grayson about the deals she *had* closed? The kind of deals—Rhonda Dickinson aside—that were the reason DeForest Allen had hired her in the first place. "Speaking of my boss, he's going to ask how today went in terms of finding you the perfect property."

"Your boss with his strict code of ethics. What does that mean, exactly?"

If Grayson were anyone else, she wouldn't have even thought to mention Mr. Allen's rules that first day. But she had, so answering as if it was no big deal was the only course she could think to take.

She shrugged, supremely casual. "He discourages involvements between agents and clients."

Grayson's lips twitched. "What kind of involvements?"

She lifted her chin slightly, determined to keep her

wits about her. "Romantic involvements." She didn't allow a beat before returning to her original point. "So what should I say when he asks what kind of progress we made?"

He still looked amused. "Tell him it's a process."

Which told *her* nothing. Except that Grayson wasn't in love with anything she'd shown him that day. If he were, she had no doubt that he'd have said so.

She shifted restlessly on the grass and stretched her legs out in front of her. She should have taken off her pumps to save the high heels from sinking into the soft ground, but she had been afraid of being too casual.

Chowing down on poutine the way they were was bad enough.

"Break it down for me." He obviously wasn't going to let *his* original matter go, either. "What takes an *average*—" he air-quoted the word "—high school girl from point A to point B? Why real estate?"

She thought about lying, but she'd never been good at it. Which meant now would be a terrible time to start. "Know what it's like being the youngest of five kids?" She didn't wait for an answer. "Let's just say I got tired of hand-me-downs."

"So money drives you."

"That makes me sound very calculating." She nibbled her way through a french fry. "I prefer to think that financial security drives me. I've been fortunate. I worked at a very successful firm in Houston. First as a receptionist. Then as an agent. It helped give me a leg up."

"Not that I'm complaining, but what brought you back to Austin from Houston? Would have thought you'd have more business there with the larger population."

"Financial security is great," she admitted honestly,

"but ultimately, I came home to Austin because it's where my family is."

"Roots turned out to be stronger than you thought?"

She nodded, smiling ruefully. "Both my parents will be retiring soon. They drive me crazy sometimes, but yes. Those roots are strong."

"What do your siblings do? Are you close?"

"Two are schoolteachers like my parents. One is a stay-at-home mom. One is a social worker. That's Maggie. She's the next youngest to me, even though there's nearly ten years between us. My brother Ray is the oldest—he's only four years older than Maggie."

He grinned. "And surprise, along comes Billie?"

"Pretty much." Along came Billie…unplanned and the odd duck out for wanting a career that didn't come wrapped in do-gooder ribbon.

She focused on Grayson. "What were *you* like in high school?"

He grinned. "A hell-raiser. We all were."

"All?"

"Two brothers."

"Older or younger?"

"Same. We're triplets. You going to finish that?"

She realized he was eyeing her poutine. "Ah, no. I'm already stuffed."

He grabbed it and started in on the gravy-covered concoction. If she hadn't already seen how much her cousin Max could eat in one sitting, she might have been shocked by the amount of food that Grayson could put away. When it came to rodeo events, steer wrestling was known as the "big man's sport." And Grayson was big, but there wasn't an inch of spare weight anywhere that she could see.

She realized she was staring at his muscular shoulders

and quickly focused elsewhere. "You're one of triplets? That's not something I hear every day."

"We kept my mother busy, that's for sure."

"What about your dad?"

His expression didn't change, but she still sensed that she'd stepped into a conversational pile of doggy doo. "Never knew him. Left my mom high and dry before we were born."

Billie chewed the inside of her cheek. "I'm sorry. I should know better than to make assumptions."

"No reason to be sorry." He looked beyond her again. Along with the food he was voraciously consuming, his bloodshot eyes had cleared. "We had the only parent around who mattered."

It felt like a very good time to change the subject. "Did your brothers get into rodeo, as well?"

His smile returned immediately. "Hell no." His gaze roved over her face as he licked his thumb.

She suddenly felt as gooey inside as the poutine.

"Jayden was interested in getting out of Paseo, but not for every other weekend when there was a rodeo somewhere. He wanted long-term distance."

She frowned at the name of the tiny town. As an agent, she took personal pride in knowing the names of most every town, nook and cranny in the state. Which, considering the size of Texas, was no small feat. And Paseo truly was a tiny map-dot of a town. "You lived in Paseo?" She'd been certain she'd read somewhere that he was from Dallas. Of course, she'd also read somewhere that his name was Grayson Smith.

"Born and raised. Ever been?"

She shook her head.

"Most people haven't. Anyway, after a couple years of college to satisfy our mother, Jayden enlisted in the army. Got out a few years ago. Nathan took a similar path. Navy. He's out now, too. Do-gooders, both of them. Though they'll deny it still to this day."

She couldn't help smiling. "And you?"

He grinned and she felt the impact of it straight down to her core. "I didn't worry about doing good, darlin'. I was just good at…*doing*."

She kept her composure, though it was darned hard. The man was too sexy by far, and he knew it. "And so, *so* modest about it, too."

His smile widened. "You blush very easily."

A comment that made her cheeks turn hotter.

"And you clearly excel at teasing," she said tartly. "Did you start right out with bulldogging?"

"Either you've done your research or you know more about rodeo than I thought. Not everyone knows that's what we call steer wrestling."

She also knew steer wrestling was considered the fastest of the rodeo events, and that Grayson had set records—only to turn around and break those, too. She knew that he'd once competed in other events as well, namely saddle bronc riding and tie-down roping. That he'd been All-Around World Champion more than once, until he'd settled into just steer wrestling several years ago, after suffering some injuries during the Nationals in Las Vegas.

But to admit she knew all that?

She managed a casual shrug. "I told you that my family's big into lots of sports. Not a weekend goes by at my folks' place when there's not someone glued to the TV they set up in the backyard. But as it happens, when I was a student at that school—" she jerked her head toward the field behind her "—I did my share of volunteering at Rodeo Austin." Right alongside Max. "I picked up a few things."

"No kidding." He looked intrigued. "Volunteered doing what?"

"Shoveling a lot of horse pucky," she said wryly. "I tried my hand at barrel racing for a time but it never really stuck. Don't think it would have even if we could have afforded a horse of my own. I, uh, I think I saw you compete once, even." *Think?* If Billie wasn't careful, she'd be telling him about the calendar that he'd once autographed for her. The calendar that she still had.

And because she was afraid of that very thing, she made a point of looking at her watch. But what she saw genuinely surprised her. "I had no idea it was so late." When she'd made the appointment with Grayson the day before, they'd allotted only the morning hours. And it was well into the afternoon. "I'm afraid I've been greedy with your time."

"Pretty sure I'm the greedy one, darlin'." But he reached over and wrapped his long, sinewy fingers around her wrist and looked at her watch himself.

She tucked her tongue between her teeth and tried not to quiver.

"Damn." He sat up straighter. "It is late." He resettled his ball cap before gathering up their trash. "Can I borrow your cell phone? I need to make a call."

"Of course." She was surprised he didn't have one of his own. "It's still in my car. I'll get it."

"Thanks." He took her hand and pulled her so easily to her feet that her nose nearly grazed his chest.

She quickly crossed the grass, feeling her heels sink into the moist dirt with every step.

They were red suede. Not even real suede, and they'd never recover. But if she could get Grayson to close the deal on a property—any property—she'd consider the loss of the shoes well worth it. She reached the car and retrieved her cell phone, only to realize that Grayson had followed her to the car. He took the phone and quickly dialed.

"It's me," he said a moment later. "I'm running late, but you'll have to wait with the I-told-you-sos. We'll have to meet at the library. What's the address?" He'd paced away a few feet from Billie, but he suddenly looked her way. "Got a pen?"

She ducked into the car and retrieved a pen and paper.

He set the latter on the roof of the car. "Okay, repeat that." He scrawled the information on the sheet. "Yeah, I need clothes. My hat and my electric razor. Yep. Yep. I *know*. I'll be in a dark gray gunboat of a car. License plate B-P-REAL." He clicked off the phone and handed it back to Billie. "I'm not going to live this down any-time soon, I'm afraid."

She decided she was more curious than offended at his description of her car. "Live what down?"

"Being late." He held up the paper. His handwriting was bold and slanted, but clear. "Is that far?"

She thought for a moment. "That's the new library complex across town. Going to take at least twenty min-utes if there's no traffic." Considering his grimace, she decided not to point out that there was *always* traffic.

"Can I bribe you into driving me there? Or is that going to land you in *involvement* territory?"

"Mr. Allen's not against us being accommodating."

"S'long as there's no kissing."

He was teasing her and she was *not* going to flush. "There's no bribe needed." She reached to take the paper from him, and their fingers brushed when he didn't im-mediately release it.

"Seriously, I'll owe you one."

She felt all sorts of warm inside again. She tugged a little harder on the paper and he finally let go of it. "I'll collect when you sign a purchase contract." That would make her boss happiest of all.

"Deal." He opened the passenger door and got inside the car. "At least your lead foot will come in handy getting across town," he said when she had gotten in, too, and fastened her seat belt.

"I do not have a lead foot."

"Pretty as it is, it *is* lead," he said dryly. He pulled his cap farther down his forehead again and made a point of tightening his own seat belt. "Okay, Johnny Racer, let 'er rip."

"There's nothing wrong with my driving," she muttered under her breath as she drove out of the park. Just because she'd gotten a couple speeding tickets over the last few years…

Not that he could possibly know about *them*.

But the damage was done, and she couldn't help but feel self-conscious driving across town to the address he'd written down.

Even though she'd expected bad traffic, by the time they were within a few miles of the library, the streets were entirely congested. "I've never seen it this bad," she murmured, as she switched lanes yet again, trying to inch forward. "Whatever your meeting is, I doubt you'll be the only one who's late."

"It's not a meeting. It's a personal appearance." He was obviously paying close attention to their progress. He pointed toward a multistoried building about a mile away. "Is that the library?"

"Yes."

"Keep watch for a black pickup. She ought to be around here somewhere."

Billie started to smile, thinking he was joking.

This *was* Texas, after all. Pickup trucks were a dime a dozen.

But then he pointed again, this time at an enormous black dually parked on the side of the road. "There she is. Pull over."

There were cars on either side of them, so it took a little doing. By the time Billie drew next to the curb, though, the pickup's driver—a slender, brown-haired woman—had gotten out and was jogging toward them.

Grayson lowered his window and took the bulky bag of stuff the woman shoved in for him. Only then did Billie realize the woman was older than she'd initially appeared.

"Cutting it mighty close, son," she said before sticking her arm through the window and right across his nose. "Appreciate you playing chauffeur for Grayson. Would be pretty embarrassing for us if he didn't show up this afternoon."

Grayson had pulled an electric razor out of the bag of stuff. "Billie Pemberton, my mother, Deborah Fortune."

More than a little bemused, Billie shook the hand the woman was offering. "I'm happy to help, Mrs. Fortune."

"Just Deborah." The woman smiled and pulled back from the car. "Entrance is in the back of the library," she told Grayson. "The press is already there. No doubt hoping for something savory after last night's nonsense, so try to behave."

"Yes, ma'am." Grayson was wielding the buzzing razor over his bristled jaw.

Then Deborah was jogging back to her truck.

And it finally dawned on Billie that the increased traffic was because of *him*.

It was all well and good to assure him that he wasn't the first celebrity client she'd ever had.

Except that she'd been lying through her teeth. Oh, she'd had wealthy clients, to be sure. But not ones who literally stopped up traffic.

Still shaving, he tossed his bag into the back seat. Then he pushed open the car door.

For some reason, panic filled her. "Where are you going?"

"Rear seat." As quickly as he said the words, he'd climbed in the back of the car. "Roll up the windows, would you? Probably be a good idea if nobody catches sight of me like this."

Her fingers shook a little as she pressed the electric buttons. In seconds, the interior of the car was once more dimmed by the tinted windows. She looked over her shoulder at him. "Now what?"

He turned off the razor and ran his fingers over his now-smooth jaw. "Now you get me as close to the back entrance of the library as you can." Evidently satisfied with the shaving job, he tossed the razor down and upended the bag's contents and started yanking off his T-shirt.

She blamed her sluggish brain on the poutine.

The contents of the bag were blue jeans. Boots. Trademark black cowboy hat.

He wasn't sitting in the back seat of her gunboat of a vehicle because he wanted to arrive at his appearance "in style," but because he needed the space to change his clothes.

She jerked around until she was facing forward. But it wasn't fast enough to miss the amused look on his face.

Feeling hot, she abruptly decided against maneuvering her car back into the line of vehicles that wasn't moving anywhere, anyway. Instead, she used the empty parking lane to back up until she could turn down a narrow alley.

But not even the sound of gravel beneath her tires was enough to mask the rustle of clothing from the rear. "Suppose you have to, uh, do this a lot," she said a little too loudly.

"You do, huh?"

She heard the distinctive sound of a zipper and would have closed her eyes if not for the fact that she was driving like a madwoman down a narrow alley.

"At least there's more room back here than the last time I was pulling on my jeans in the back seat of a car."

Despite herself, her gaze flew to the rearview mirror. The laughter in his eyes captured hers.

You'd think she was still a virgin the way her cheeks felt perpetually heated around him.

She'd reached the end of the alley and quickly shot across the cross street, turning up yet another alley.

"You *do* know where you're going, I hope," he commented calmly. "Seeing as how we seem to be traveling away from the library."

"Short cut." Not by distance, but she was banking on the traffic sticking to actual streets, versus the back alleyways. As long as she didn't encounter a delivery truck or a garbage truck blocking her way, she knew she could make good progress. "In high school, my cousin Max and I delivered pizza around here. We had the best delivery times out of everyone." She cringed, realizing she'd mentioned Max's name.

But common sense reminded her that Grayson had no reason to connect Billie Pemberton's cousin Max with his rodeo competitor Max Vargas.

And Grayson was chuckling, anyway. "Pizza, huh?"

Despite her intentions, her eyes strayed to the rear-view mirror again.

She got an eyeful of bare, tanned chest before he started buttoning up his long-sleeved white shirt. And a moment later, just as she turned up yet another alley, he disappeared from view and suddenly a stocking-clad foot was hanging over the back of her seat while he tried to work on a gleaming cowboy boot.

It was accompanied by a lot of swearing that, surprisingly, had her relaxing a little.

She turned down the last alleyway, having bypassed all the traffic, and was now coming at the library from the opposite direction. She sailed past two television trucks and three police vehicles, nipped through the library's delivery entrance and finally came to a stop near the back door. She'd delivered her client safely to the drop-off point. But there was no sign of the black truck his mother had been driving.

When the car engine died, Grayson grabbed his cowboy hat and raked his fingers through his hair. It was starting to curl up at the ends, which meant it was past time to get it cut, though he wasn't sure when he'd find the time to fit it in.

Then he looked out the windows of Billie's car and was more than a little impressed. "We beat my mother here."

"Unless she parked elsewhere, it would seem so." Billie gave him a quick glance over her shoulder. "Do you, um, need anything else?"

"Jeans are zipped and shirt buttons don't seem to be mismatched, so I guess not." He said it for the pure pleasure of watching her cheeks turn pink. "I really do owe you one." He pushed open the back door of the car. "You want to come inside?"

She hesitated. "Are you sure it would be okay?"

He laughed at that. "Pretty sure." He climbed out and planted his hat on his head, then opened her door for her and held out his hand.

She stared at it. "Maybe I should just go."

"Oh, for God's sake." He reached in and took the keys out of her ignition, then closed his hand around hers. "Come on."

She had to scramble to keep up with him. Which was what he'd intended. He pressed the fob on the keys, locking her vehicle as he crossed to the back entrance of the library.

Deborah pulled up in the truck then, looking more frazzled. "This traffic is nuts," she said, as she joined them. She was carrying a box of the signed head shots. "Guess that's what happens when Grayson and the governor of the great state of Texas decide to show up together for the same event."

Grayson felt Billie's hand suddenly drag against his.

"Governor?" She looked stunned. "*What* is going on here?"

"Nothing," he assured her. But he could see Claudia Decker ahead of them, and knew whatever control he'd had that day was soon to be dust in the wind. She was the governor's sister and was positively gleeful over managing to get the two of them there for the opening of her latest literacy project.

He squeezed Billie's hand before letting go. "Stay with my mother. She'll protect you. And the two of you can figure out when I'm free to meet with you again. Got a rodeo in Coleman this weekend, then a quick trip to Montana for a couple days."

"But—"

"Grayson!" Claudia had reached him and presented

her expensively youthful cheek for his kiss. "I can't thank you enough for doing this for me. We're all set up in the new wing."

He dutifully kissed her cheek and let her lead him away.

But he couldn't keep from looking back toward Billie.

She was standing next to his mother, and for a moment, something strange inside his chest tightened.

Then the governor and his security contingent arrived, and he lost sight of them both.

But it was a long time before that strange feeling faded.

Chapter Five

Max took one of the few remaining cupcakes that Billie had set out on a platter in the middle of the birthday feast. "Your cake-decorating skills are improving."

Trust Max to notice. "I didn't have time to bake them," she admitted. Instead of taking a few hours that afternoon to shop, bake and frost the cupcakes she'd promised to bring, she'd hovered in the wings with Grayson's mom at the library dedication. By the time she'd been able to tear herself away from the fascinating spectacle, she'd gotten caught in rush hour traffic going back across town again. So instead of baking, she'd gotten store-bought.

Billie's mother, Peggy, had already given the cupcakes a disapproving look, but Billie knew that Selena hadn't cared. She was just thirteen. Her parents were perpetually broke which was why Peggy had insisted on hosting the party, and Selena loved everything pink and purple and glittering. And the cupcakes fit the bill perfectly.

Max didn't seem to care now, either. He peeled off the paper lining and swallowed an entire half in one bite. "Must be keeping you busy at your new agency," he said around his mouthful. "That's a good thing."

"I work on commission. It's only good if I close the deals," she said dryly.

Billie's mom brushed by her and began removing empty serving trays from the dining room table. "If you were teaching economics like your father and I planned, you wouldn't have to worry about working on a commission."

Long used to Peggy Pemberton's feelings on the subject, Billie just pinned on a smile and lifted one of the heavy trays out of her mom's hands. "Let me help."

Peggy blew a wisp of gray hair away from her forehead. "It's just so darned hot. We had the air-conditioning guy out last week and he tweaked things a bit, but obviously not enough."

"You need a new unit," Billie said. No amount of tweaking was going to keep the ancient thing alive forever. Fortunately, the birthday party had already spilled out onto the back lawn, because the small house wasn't really designed to accommodate the thirty or so family members who'd been crammed inside it for dinner.

"Yes, well, when it dies completely, we'll get one," Peggy said tartly.

Billie wished she'd held her tongue. The last thing she wanted to get into was another argument with her mother about money. Since she'd started earning real commissions, she'd tried more than once to help her parents with some of their unexpected expenses. And every time, she'd earned her mother's wrath. Peggy just wouldn't believe that Billie's real estate career would stay profitable.

Possibly because it was one of the careers that Selena's folks had both failed at.

She picked up another empty platter and followed her into the small kitchen. "I can wash all of this up. Go on outside with everyone else, Mom. It's cooler."

"There's too much here for one person," Peggy protested.

"Then I'll draft Max into helping."

Her mother's eyebrows shot up. "Oh, sure," she said with a dry laugh. But at least it was a laugh, even though she immediately wrapped an apron around her waist and started rinsing dishes at the sink.

Billie went to the doorway in time to see her cousin shoving another cupcake into his mouth. "Come and help me clean up so Mom can go outside with the others where it's cooler."

He looked at her as if she'd grown a second head.

Behind her, she heard her mother laugh again.

Billie gave up. When it came to her family, some things would never change. She moved her mother away from the sink and squirted liquid soap under the hot running water. To accompany the aging air-conditioning system—or rather to *not* accompany it—was the lack of a dishwasher. Not that there would have been any place to put one in the minuscule kitchen. And as the last remaining kid living at home, Billie had grown up with dishwashing duties.

The first apartment she'd gotten on her own hadn't had a separate bedroom, but she'd made darn sure it had a dishwasher.

"You ever think about living anywhere else, Mom?"

Peggy looked surprised. "You mean, like move back home to Horseback Hollow?"

The fact that—after more than forty years—her

mother still considered Horseback Hollow "home" probably had Billie looking just as surprised as Peggy.

"Your father would never leave this house," she said, before Billie could clarify. "And it's paid for." She narrowed her eyes, looking suspicious. "Are you that desperate for real estate clients that you'd expect us to sell your childhood home and buy something we can't afford just as we're about ready to retire?"

Billie winced. She wasn't sure what was more offensive—her mother thinking she needed to drum up business, or that she would look to her own parents to do so. "I'm not desperate for clients, Mom. In fact, I have a new—" She broke off. On those rare occasions that she spoke about clients with her family, it was only in the general sense. And there was nothing "general" when it came to Grayson Fortune.

"A new what?" Max had entered the kitchen.

Ordinarily, that would be a miracle.

"Client, I assume," Peggy answered. She plunked a stack of plates in the sink in front of Billie and tsked a little, adjusting the water temperature. "It doesn't do any good to wash dishes in cold water."

Long practiced, Billie bit her tongue as the hot water turned nearly scalding. Max, however, caught her gaze and grinned knowingly.

"I still don't know where you inherited this interest in real estate," Peggy said as she headed out of the kitchen, "when you could easily teach economics."

Billie quickly adjusted the water temperature again, flooding the sink with enough cold water that she could stand to put her hands in it. By the time her mom returned with another load of dishes, the sink was full and the water off.

"If I hadn't spent more than twelve hours delivering

you from my very own body, I'd think you were left on the doorstep by strangers." Peggy set the stack next to Billie.

It was definitely time to change the subject. "Max, what did you end up bringing Selena for her birthday?"

He made a face. "Only thing she begged me for was an autographed photograph from *The* Grayson."

The plate in Billie's hand slid out of her fingers back into the water, sending soapsuds cascading over the front of her.

"For goodness sake, Billie. Be a little careful! That's my grandmother's china."

Billie lifted the unharmed plate to show her mother, though she was focused on her cousin. "*You* got an autographed photograph from Grayson For—" She bit off the rest of his name, scrambling a little. "For Selena? I thought you hated the guy."

"Well, I damn sure didn't *pay* him for the thing. Guy's not getting any of my hard-earned money."

Peggy looked appalled. "Max, tell me that you didn't forge his autograph!"

"Didn't need to, Aunt Peg. Guy's got stacks of signed pics just lying around if you know where to look."

Photographs like the ones that had been available that afternoon at the library event?

Peggy was giving Max the same look that she'd been giving her seventh-grade math students for as long as Billie could remember. "Tell me exactly where you got Selena's gift."

Max sent Billie a "help me" look, but she was too curious to be of assistance.

He appeared increasingly harried. "It was Bethany's, all right? She left it behind when she dumped me for that cocky old bastard. She obviously doesn't need the picture now that she's got the real thing."

Billie refocused on scrubbing plates. She was increasingly doubtful that Max's feckless barrel racer "had" Grayson at all. Admittedly, she'd spent just one day with him, but the only woman he'd spoken of had been his mother. "I don't think Grayson is old." Or cocky.

"Don't tell me you're still crushin' on him? You made me wait in line with you for two hours back in the day for that dang calendar he signed. You know he still prints 'em?" Max made a face. "Greedy son of a gun, if you ask me. All he's about is making money and collecting other people's girls."

"I'm not crushin' on anyone." And she knew for a fact that Grayson donated all the money he earned from those calendars because the governor had talked about it that very afternoon.

None of which she could tell Max without him flying off the handle.

"You need to forget that Bethany," Peggy said tartly. "She was too old for you, anyway. Focus on meeting a nice girl to marry. Someone who'll give you lots of babies."

"Aunt Peg!" Max's horror was comical. "I don't have t'worry about all that for years yet."

"By the time Hal and I were your age, we already had two children." Peggy pointed her finger in Max's face. "And your mama had one on the way when *she* was twenty-four." Her pointing finger took aim at Billie. "I don't know why the two of you are so resistant to settling down."

"And I don't know why you and my ma are so insistent that we do." Max grinned and slid his arm around Peggy's slender waist. "Don't you have too many grandchildren already?"

Peggy's expression softened slightly. She'd always had more of a tender spot for her sister's youngest than she'd had for her own. "You obviously don't know that there can never be too many grandchildren."

Billie turned on the water to rinse the plates. "As long as you don't expect them anytime soon from me," she muttered under the sound of the water.

"I heard that, Belinda Marie. One of these days you'll fall in love, and you're going to eat those words. I know all about this life plan you think you have laid out for yourself, and I'm here to tell you that it doesn't work that way." Peggy pulled off her apron and tossed it on the cluttered kitchen counter. "Right now, you can just think about that while you take care of all this mess on your own, after all."

Max started to follow Peggy out of the kitchen.

Billie threw the wet dishcloth at her cousin's back. "Hey! Where are you going?"

He grinned, not slowing a bit. "You heard your mama. You can just think about that, Belinda Marie."

She looked back at the dozens of dishes yet to be washed and huffed out a sigh. "Only thing I'm going to think about is my very nice dishwasher at home," she muttered.

Her dishwasher.

And Grayson Fortune.

Two weeks later, Billie stood next to Grayson, looking at an enormous barn. "So, what do you think?"

It was the third time now that they'd been out to view properties, and after failing to catch his interest the last time, when they'd met to go back to the Orchess listing plus three others, she'd decided it was time to take a different tack.

Namely, *not* showing him the actual house until after he'd seen everything else the listing had to offer.

Despite his intention to purchase a new home, she could tell he wasn't quite ready to see himself living in any of them. But when it came to barns and good grazing land and accessibility and water? Those things he did care about.

She'd also realized that he didn't give two figs about her carefully prepared folios, which were generally so important to her other clients. She wasn't used to it, but it did save her a fair amount of preparation time. Which was a good thing, given his unpredictable schedule.

"When was the barn built?"

She scanned the information sheet she had printed out for herself. She didn't have a lot of confidence that he'd like the Harmon ranch, because it was so much more expensive than anything he'd expressed an interest in seeing before. It was also considerably farther away from the city and came with nearly a hundred acres. Yes, he'd said he wanted acreage, but this was on another scale entirely. But DeForest Allen had brought the new listing to her attention after the status meeting that morning. And so here they were. "The barn was built three years ago."

"It's not bad." He tucked his sunglasses in the collar of his navy blue T-shirt and thumbed back his black cowboy hat as he surveyed the acreage all around them. "It's on well water, you said?"

"Yes." Fortunately, she'd also gotten over the worst of her tendency to chatter nervously when she was around him, and she was able to leave it at that. She'd realized that when Grayson had questions, he asked them. And now, she was determined to remain quiet, leaving him to make his own observations.

On the *un*fortunate front, she was realizing that left her with plenty of time to just observe *him.*

And the more she observed, the more disturbed she felt. Because she genuinely liked him.

Liked him in a way that set all her nerves on edge.

Frankly, she blamed her mother.

Ever since Selena's party, when Peggy had harped on falling in love, Billie hadn't been able to get Grayson out of her head. Which would have been fine if all she'd been thinking about was finding him a property that he couldn't resist.

"Billie?"

She realized she'd completely missed whatever it was he'd said. She rustled the papers she was holding as if to blame her inattention on them. "Sorry?"

"The land does come *with* the house, doesn't it?" He'd taken off his cowboy hat and used it to gesture at the multiwinged stone structure.

She pretended her cheeks weren't hot. "Of course. The, uh, the house was built twenty years ago, but it was evidently renovated about the same time they built the barn." She quickly started toward the dwelling and eventually he fell in step with her. In the silence of the afternoon, their footsteps seemed loud as they crossed the brick-paved courtyard between the oversize barn and the mansion-sized house.

He resettled his hat on his head. "You seem distracted today."

"Do I?" She opened the lockbox. But the house key that was supposed to be inside wasn't there.

She frowned and pulled off her sunglasses, glancing around her. She wasn't so distracted that she would have accidentally tipped out the key without noticing, was she?

Grayson stopped next to her and his arm lightly grazed hers. "Something wrong?"

"Key's missing." She was already pulling out her cell phone. "I need to report it." Each time agents entered their unique code on the digital lockbox, the information was recorded. So it would be easy enough to determine who'd been there last. Plus, Billie wanted to make sure *she* wasn't blamed for the lapse.

Grayson didn't look particularly perturbed. "While you do that, I'm going to walk around and look in the windows."

It was apparent that they weren't going to be able to get inside anytime soon, so if he didn't like what he saw through the windows, they wouldn't need to waste time trying to come back.

She left a message with the listing agent about the key situation, closed up the lockbox again and went to find Grayson.

He was sitting on the built-up stone side of the glittering blue pool located at the rear of the house. His long legs were extended, boots crossed at the ankles.

"I left a message about the key." She slid her sunglasses back on. "We might as well head on to the next listing."

He patted the wide ledge beside him. "Sit."

She hesitated for half a second before complying. The stone was hot through the fabric of her skirt. But no hotter than the feel of him, even though she'd left a healthy space between them.

She shuffled her papers on her lap. "It's going to take us at least an hour to drive to the next listing. The asking price is definitely too high, but I've heard the owner is getting anxious, so I believe there will be some real negotiating room if it turns out to be the right property for you."

"What's wrong?"

Her shoulders felt stiff. "Nothing's wrong. Except for a missing key throwing a crimp in my plans."

He uncrossed his ankles and cupped his hand around the edge of the stone tile separating them. "Look, I know I'm not the easiest of clients."

She pushed to her feet, smoothing down her skirt self-consciously. "Don't say that. You've been an ideal client." Aside from the first day when he'd been hungover, his limited availability and his propensity to turn up his handsome nose at every sales listing she suggested, he was actually one of the easier clients she'd had. It wasn't his fault that she'd been having dreams about him. Day-dreams. Night dreams. Evidently, her overactive imagination didn't discriminate when it came to hours of the day.

"Even though I haven't found anything that says *home* the second we walk through the door?"

She squelched a sigh. "Some would say that's my failure, not yours." Some *had* said it. Namely, her boss at the meeting that morning. Fortunately, DeForest Allen wasn't a mind reader or he'd have also delivered a lecture on the importance of recognizing the fine line between making accommodations for an important client and being *too* accommodating.

"Grayson, we'll find the right fit for you. It's not as though you're looking to purchase a three-bedroom tract home. It just takes time."

"Time that I haven't given you much of. At least not since our first date."

There was no point in shivering over the word, when she knew good and well that he didn't mean "date" date. He just meant their first day of home touring. "I knew from the beginning that you have a tight schedule. Frankly, I was surprised you were even available today."

"Why's that?"

She spread her hands and the papers clutched in her right hand fluttered in the faint breeze. "Reno starts tomorrow. I know you're competing."

He lifted an eyebrow.

"Your mother told me," she added, lest he speculate that she'd been following his schedule out of more personal interest. All right. So she *had* been. But just because she knew he'd won at the Coleman rodeo—much to Max's consternation—then placed in Montana last weekend, and she'd seen his name on the roster for Reno, didn't mean that she needed to divulge the truth. "It's a couple days drive from here." Long days. Last time she'd talked to Max, he'd been on the road midway there. "I guess you must be flying."

"My mother wanted a quick visit home to Paseo before Reno, so my hazer, Lou, and another friend are driving everything out to Nevada for us. Her flight to Reno was this morning. Mine is tonight."

Considering his expression, he didn't look too happy about it. "Didn't you want to go to Paseo, too?"

"I had business to take care of here."

"Grayson Gear business?"

"Billie Pemberton business."

Her mouth went more than a little dry. She reminded herself that what he really meant was real estate business. Which, if he'd rather have been visiting home, might explain his discontented expression. She nudged up her sunglasses again. "Well, while I do have you, we should probably make our way to the next place instead of wasting time sitting here in the hot sun."

"It is hot. And humid." He looked over his shoulder at the glittering swimming pool. "Too bad you don't swim.

We could sneak in a dip." He gave her a quick look. "I could teach you how to swim."

He could teach you lots of things.

She kicked the sneaky voice inside her head right to the curb. "In someone else's pool?"

"Without their knowledge even." His expression had lightened and his lips twitched. "Lends a certain air of excitement, don't you think?"

"Lends a certain air of getting my rear end fired," she corrected. Getting just that right amount of dryness in her voice should have earned her an acting award.

"Only if your uptight boss found out."

"I should never have told you about that."

"Why?"

"Because it's not relevant."

Even with her sunglasses, his gaze trapped hers. "It's not?"

She felt a bead of perspiration slide down her spine. She swallowed and moistened her lips. "In any case, he's not going to find out for the simple reason that we're not getting in that pool. We don't even have swimming suits." She regretted the words as soon as she said them.

Because, naturally, Grayson's perfectly shaped lips spread slowly into a sexy-as-hell grin. "Well, hell, darlin', as far as I'm concerned, that ain't really a problem."

At this rate, she wasn't getting any closer to him signing a purchase contract. Instead, she was getting a whole lot closer to losing her willpower where he was concerned. Which was the height of stupidity. He flirted because it was his nature to flirt with *any* female.

She shook her papers at him. "We have places to go, Grayson."

"Fine." But he cupped his fingers in the pool and flipped water toward her.

She jumped back, but not quickly enough to evade the splash. She stared down at her thin silk blouse, which had started the day as a pristine white, but was now clinging almost transparently to her lace bra. She plucked the wet fabric away from her chest. "I can't believe you did that!"

He laughed. "Considering the way you drive, I can't believe you moved so slowly."

She was torn between embarrassment and the desire to laugh, herself. Even if the pool water ruined her blouse, the water did feel refreshing. And Grayson's laugh was low and sexy as all get-out. The sound of it made every nerve inside her tingle.

She crossed her arms and channeled her mother's best humorless glare, though it was difficult. "It's time to go, Grayson."

He made a face, but finally pushed off the ledge. "Did I tell you that the first crush I ever had on a woman was my third grade teacher, Miss Frost? She always used to cross her arms and give me that sort of look, too."

"If you're saying that to unnerve me, it won't work." Liar, liar, pants on fire.

"Just having a conversation, darlin'." He passed by her. "Your papers are wet, by the way."

"Gee. I wonder why." She waited until his back was turned, then dropped the wet pages and scooped both her hands into the pool water and flung it at him.

She was nowhere near as effective at it as he had been, but she did manage to douse the back of his shirt pretty well.

Enough for him to turn on a dime, giving her a surprised look.

She laughed.

He took a step toward the pool's edge. "Now you've done it."

She had the sense to be a bit alarmed and started to step away.

He dunked his arm in the pool and sloshed a wave of water toward her. It sluiced over the wide rock ledge, splashing her in the face and flooding over the toes of her shoes.

"That's three pairs of suede shoes I've ruined now because of you," she said, blinking against the water droplets. The second pair had fallen victim to the cow pie she'd accidentally stepped into while Grayson decided the Orchess land wasn't right for him, either.

"You don't swim," he reminded her as she leaned over the pool ledge.

"Doesn't mean I'm afraid of water." She sliced her arm across the surface, sending a jet of spray his way.

He took the water full frontal. He slowly pulled off his hat, and his smile flashed almost as bright as the beating sun. "Oh now, darlin', all bets are off."

She braced herself as he dipped his hat toward the pool. "Grayson…"

And then his hat filled with water and all bets were off, indeed.

Chapter Six

"Here." Billie handed Grayson a bath towel. "You're still dripping."

It was an exaggeration, but Grayson let it pass because he was preoccupied looking around Billie's starkly furnished apartment. She'd suggested dropping him off at his hotel, until he'd told her he'd already checked out that morning.

She hadn't been quite able to hide her consternation, then, as she'd brought him back to her place.

Far as he was concerned, they might as well have taken an illicit dip in that swimming pool. They'd ended up as wet as if they'd jumped in fully clothed. But they'd left a good portion of that moisture behind on Billie's car seats during the long drive back to Austin.

He flipped the towel around his neck and absently unbuttoned his clinging shirt as he approached the oversize windows that afforded Billie a decent view of the river.

Considering the location of the apartment building, it didn't take a genius to guess she was paying a hefty price tag for that particular view. It was almost as good as the view from his usual penthouse hotel suite. She even had a balcony furnished with a small, cushioned couch, a chair and a low, tiled table. Sitting on the table was a shallow wicker basket holding a couple glossy magazines.

The inside of the apartment wasn't quite so well equipped. Not unless she had a couch hiding in the brown cardboard packing boxes that were stacked against one wall. Aside from them, she had a dining room table with four chairs, a television that was sitting on the floor, and one leather chair.

He glanced at her. She was standing in the kitchen, but had kicked off her shoes in the tiled foyer.

It dawned on him then that he hadn't seen her without shoes until now. "You're short."

She paused in the act of twisting her wet hair up in a white towel, turban-like. "You're so good for my ego," she muttered and then straightened.

He wondered what her ego would feel like if he admitted that every time he looked at her, he wanted her. Too young for him or not, he wanted her. And it was a problem that kept getting worse. His stunt with the pool definitely wasn't helping things. "You're always wearing high heels," he said casually.

She returned to the foyer to pick up her discarded shoes. "Considering I seem to ruin a pair every time I take you out for a home tour, I'd do better to switch to rubber muck boots." She pointed the shoes at him. They'd been a brilliant peacock blue until the chlorinated pool water had had its way with them. Now they were splotched blue and white. "I'll be back in a minute."

She set the shoes on the kitchen counter next to his wet

hat before heading across the dark wood floor to disappear behind a door at the end of the short hall.

Where, no doubt, she would change out of her wet clothes.

He looked back at the window and lightly thumped his forehead against the glass. “Dumb move, Gray.”

Then he realized the windows were actually sliding doors, and after a second of hunting, he released the lock and slid one of the panels open, then stepped out. The afternoon sun was hotter than ever, but it didn’t quite reach all the way across Billie’s balcony. He closed the patio door behind him and shrugged out of his shirt and spread it across the back of the side chair. Then he sat on the couch and studied his Castletons. They’d fared better than Billie’s shoes, but then they were working boots meant to withstand some punishment.

He still had several hours yet before he had to catch his flight to Reno. His shirt would be dry for sure by then. As for his jeans…

He stretched out his legs across the entire depth of the small balcony. His jeans would have to dry *on* his stupid ass.

He hadn’t been sitting there five minutes when he heard the door slide open.

“Here.” Billie held out a tall glass. “Don’t worry. It’s plain old iced tea. No chai. No spice. Nothing but grocery store orange pekoe. No lemon, either, because I’m out.”

He’d automatically wrapped his fingers around the glass. But she didn’t immediately release it.

“Unless you prefer cucumber-and-basil-infused water.” A faint smile played around her lips.

He chuckled. “Not in this lifetime. Tea’s fine. Thanks.”

She released the glass and after a hesitation that he might have imagined, set aside the magazine basket and moved his shirt from the side chair to spread it out over the low table. "I do have a dryer," she said, sounding unusually diffident. "If you want to, um, dry your clothes in it."

"Sunshine and heat'll do."

She sat down in the chair and sipped her own glass of tea.

She'd changed into a faded blue T-shirt that said Rice across her breasts and a pair of shorts that exposed less leg than her usual short skirts. The towel was gone, and her hair hung in a damp-looking braid over one shoulder.

She looked about thirteen years old.

Except for the curves under Rice, that was.

He looked away, but his gaze landed on the magazines inside her wicker basket. An image of Ben Robinson was on the cover of the top one. Ben *Fortune* Robinson. A *legitimate* heir of Gerald Robinson.

And Grayson's half brother.

He stifled a sigh and focused on the ice cubes bobbing in his tea. "Why economics?"

"Excuse me?"

"Why'd you get a degree in economics?"

"My father teaches economics."

"So, following in his footsteps?"

"That's what my parents planned, anyway. They're not exactly thrilled with my real estate career choice." Her lip twisted as she took a sip of tea.

He gestured, taking in the balcony and view. "If it means you can pay for an address like this, what's the problem?"

"It's not what they had planned for me. You know how parents can be when they make plans for their children."

"Only things my mom keeps making plans for these days are grandchildren."

Billie smiled then. "A common affliction I am very familiar with, actually. My mother already has half a dozen grandchildren, but she thinks I'm disregarding my duties by not increasing their numbers." Seeming to relax, she stretched out her slender legs until she could prop her heels on the corner of the table next to his shirt.

Her toenails were painted in brilliant red. And she had a narrow black ring around her middle toe.

Then he looked closer, not caring that he was pretty much staring. It wasn't a plain black ring. It was a delicate, filigree design. "Is that a tattoo?"

She curled her toes, as if she wanted to hide the evidence. Her brown eyes skated over him, then away. "Yes."

He smiled slightly. "Well, you're just full of surprises, Rice."

Her cheeks were pink.

He supposed it might be because of the heat, but he doubted it.

"I got it when I turned twenty." She wriggled her toes again. "Seems silly now."

"Because…?"

"Tattoo on a toe? Hurt like the dickens." She shrugged. "But I was trying to impress a guy and I was young and stupid. Fortunately, I got over the habit."

He couldn't help chuckling. "Darlin', you may not be stupid but you're *still* young."

"You say that like you're ancient."

"And your point?"

She gave a huffing laugh. "Obviously, you're not."

"I've got thirteen years and a lotta miles on you, darlin'."

She rolled her eyes and sat forward to grab the glossy magazine from the basket. She flipped it open and waved it at him, tapping the photograph of him from the finals of Rodeo Austin. "And that's why *Weird Life Magazine* just named you one of the most eligible bachelors in Texas for the third time running. Because you've got so many miles on you." She closed the magazine and tossed it onto the cushion beside him. "Every time you come to my office, you send half the women there into palpitations."

"Only half?"

She chuckled, shaking her head. "You know good and well what your own appeal is. You don't need me stroking your ego."

"I could think of a few other things." He waited a beat, enjoying the way her cheeks turned red, then fed her own words back to her. "But that's not relevant."

Her eyes flew to his, then skittered away.

He changed tack. "What happened to the guy? The tattoo guy. Was he impressed?"

She spread her hands slightly, seeming to relax a little. "Briefly."

"No tears? No broken heart?"

Her lips curved ruefully as she shook her head. "Neither his nor mine."

"Ever had one?"

Her chin angled. "Have *you*?"

"Hell yeah. Miss Frost ruined me for years."

She laughed. When it faded, she looked reflective as she toyed with her braid. "I don't think I have ever cried over a guy. Much less had a broken heart. Disappointed heart?" She made a face. "That's pretty typical. My friends all think I'm a cynic."

"Are they right?"

Her shoulders shrugged. "Maybe. I don't know. I just know it's easier to focus on my work than my personal life. I like being able to depend on myself. If *I* let me down, it's my own darn problem."

He studied her for a long moment. “I doubt that happens too often.”

Her lashes swept down. Her cheeks looked pink again.

He shifted, and the magazine slid off the couch. He picked it up, closed it and tossed it back into the wicker basket.

“I didn’t graduate from college,” he admitted abruptly, though he wasn’t real sure why. Maybe because of that photograph of his übersuccessful half brother on the cover. The half brother he’d so far refused to meet. Even though both Jayden and Nate told him that Ben—as well as all the other Robinson siblings—were decent enough people despite having Gerald as a father. “I took classes now and then, but there was never enough time to do the job right. Which means you, young lady, are way more educated than I am.”

“Grayson Gear is turning record profits and I saw you rubbing arms with the governor.” Billie’s voice turned dry. “The lack of a college degree doesn’t seem to have held you back much.”

He grunted. Maybe there was some truth in that. To hear Jayden tell it, Gerald’s legitimate kids—all eight of ’em—were educated up the wazoo.

He rubbed at a sudden pain between his eyebrows.

“What kind of classes did you take?” she asked him.

He dropped his hand. Billie was looking at him.

“Agriculture. Animal husbandry.” He grimaced. “Marketing.”

She smiled slightly. “There’s nothing wrong with marketing.”

“There is when you’re pulling a D in it. Believe me, I wasn’t breaking any records when it came to my truncated college education.” He bent his knees suddenly and sat forward to grab the magazine back out of the wicker basket. "My sister-in-law used to write for *Weird Life*."

"No kidding? Small world. I sold the publisher's son a house in Houston last year. She doesn't write for them anymore?"

He shook his head. When Ariana met Jayden, she'd been writing a series on "Becoming a Fortune" and had been investigating all the deep dark secrets behind Gerald Fortune Robinson's sexual peccadilloes. More specifically, the results of those peccadilloes. She'd given up the series and her job when she'd fallen for Jayden, but that didn't make the things she'd uncovered go away. They were just being publicly dissected by other members of the media now. Scuttlebutt was that even Gerald's father, Julius Fortune, had been incapable of fidelity.

Made a man wonder if there was a faulty gene in the family. And God knew Grayson had never been interested in committing himself to one woman.

"You know who this is?" He tapped the magazine cover.

"The guy who runs Robinson Tech," Billie answered without hesitation. "Can't own a computer these days without knowing that. Not around these parts, anyway." She sipped her tea. "I helped one of his secretaries find a house my first week at Austin Elite. Nice girl. It was her and her husband's first home purchase. We're closing escrow on it soon."

"That guy's my half brother. We have the same father. Only, good old dad decided to marry *Ben's* mama even though he'd already knocked up mine."

Jesus, Joseph and Mary. He couldn't believe the words had come out of his mouth. What was wrong with him?

He tossed the magazine back in the basket and shoved to his feet. "I need to get moving." He grabbed his still-damp shirt.

Her brows pulled together. "I thought your flight wasn't until this evening."

It wasn't. But he was obviously losing his freaking mind.

She stood a lot more slowly than he had, looking wary and bewildered as she set aside her glass of tea. "Grayson—"

"I'll talk to you after Reno. I don't know when that'll be, exactly. Events go all week and it depends how my runs go. If I'll be home early—"

"—or staying through the final short round," she finished for him. "I know how it works."

He wished he could say he knew how his brain was working at the moment. "When I do get to town, I want to go back and see that place we were at today. If it's still available." He pulled open the slider and went inside.

She followed him, practically jogging across the wood floor to keep up with him. He grabbed his hat from the kitchen, and when he reached for the front door handle, she covered his hand with his. "Grayson, slow down. Let me get my shoes at least. I'll drive you to the airport."

"Don't worry about it."

She looked ready to argue.

"I'm supposed to meet up before the flight with an old friend." It was a true enough. He'd gotten an unexpected message at the hotel, though he hadn't intended to follow up on it. "I don't know if you follow barrels still, but maybe you've heard of her. She won last year's final in barrel racing. Lives here in Austin. Bethany Belmont."

Billie was silent for half a second before her slender hand moved away. "Never heard of her." She folded her arms across Rice. "I'll contact your mother about when you can fit in viewing the Harmon ranch." She smiled, though there was no humor in it. "If you want your *friend* to see it, feel free to bring her along."

He'd just dumped the truth in her lap about his being related to Austin's own version of royalty and she was going to be pissy about something as inconsequential as Bethany Belmont? "I think she could care less about it, but who knows?" He pulled open the door. "Sorry about your shoes."

"Get a decent draw?"

Grayson glanced at the young man who'd come up beside him on a good-looking sorrel. It was the first time Max Vargas had addressed him directly in months. "Decent enough." Shortly before their event, the draw had been made for the steer each bulldogger would run that morning.

He lowered the stirrup and swung up into the saddle. Vix shifted slightly, but soon settled, just as Grayson had known he would. "See you're on Deca," he said to Max. "He's a good ride. You been on him before?"

Max shook his head. His black hat was pulled low over his eyes, hiding most of his expression.

"He'll do everything right when you let him do it."

Max's mouth was still visible. It curled with obvious annoyance at Grayson's advice. "I know how to handle him."

Good enough. Max's first go would immediately follow Grayson's. Maybe that was the only point of the brief exchange.

Grayson dismissed the cocky young man from his thoughts as he looked toward his hazer. "You feeling good this morning, Lou?"

"Good as ever." Lou Blackhorn was a bulldogger himself, though he'd been sidelined for a few months as he recovered from an injury. But that didn't stop him from hazing. "Don't go breaking the barrier, now."

Grayson grinned. Long as Lou warned him not to

break the barrier—the breakaway rope stretched across the front of Grayson's box that couldn't be crossed before the steer reached its predetermined head start—he hadn't had a single broken barrier penalty. A bulldogger could have a smokin' fast time throwing down a steer, but it got shot to hell if he got hit with that ten-second penalty.

He rode Vix deep into the box and didn't even need to coax him into backing into the far corner, away from the steer's pen. As usual, he had his two best horses with him, but Vix always ran best first thing in the morning. Van, on the other hand, loved the night lights and crowds.

Grayson sat relaxed and easy in the saddle, but inside, he felt the familiar ripple of nerves. He considered those nerves to be a good thing. If he wasn't nervous, it was guaranteed he wouldn't have a good run.

Despite the fact that their first go was during slack, it was still a crowded affair, with the dozen or so officials and livestock handlers also packed into the area. And inside the metal pen between Grayson's box and Lou's, the steer was huffing noisily.

"Sounds like this ol' boy's anxious to be out this morning, too." The gray-haired man manning the chute grinned at Grayson. He'd wait until he got the nod from Grayson before tripping the lever that released the steer.

"That's the way I like them." He held the reins low and easy, catching Lou's eyes for a second. His blood thrummed in his ears and he looked down the arena for a moment, envisioning his ride. "All right, buddy," he murmured. Vix might not have been one of professional rodeo's horses of the year like Deca, but he was one of Grayson's best. "Let's show 'em how it's done." Then he gave the nod.

After that came the always strange fusion of blur and crystal sharp detail.

The steer bolting from the chute. Lou following a moment later. The snapping sound of the barrier releasing. The launch of horseflesh beneath him, going zero to thirty in the span of a second.

The steer was fast.

Vix was faster.

Then Grayson was sliding from horse toward steer, catching one arm around one of the fast-running beast's horns and wrapping his hand around the other horn.

He felt his heels dig good and deep in the dirt and he wrangled the steer around until the animal was on the ground, four hooves pointing the same direction.

It was textbook perfect.

The moment Gray let the steer go, the animal was back on his feet, chasing around in circles, frisky as all get-out. That's the way it usually went.

Grayson didn't even know what his time was, except that it'd felt decent. Mostly, as he rolled to his feet and brushed the dirt off his hands, he was feeling that immediate satisfaction of knowing he'd just thrown a good steer that was twice his weight. His rib wasn't hurting. His thigh wasn't aching.

If he didn't let himself think about the look on Billie's face when he'd left her apartment the day before, it was pretty much a perfect morning.

"And we're off to a fine start, folks," the announcer was saying. "That's the Big G outta Texas with four-point-two-o-o seconds! Grayson's an old-timer out here, showing all them young bucks how it's done."

There was a smattering of laughter and applause, more from the other bulldoggers and hazers waiting on their go-round than from the small crowd of onlookers sitting in the bleachers around the arena.

Grayson waved his hat once as he jogged to the edge of the arena, where Lou was already waiting with Vix.

"Good run, Gray." Lou handed over the reins.

"Only 'cause you kept that son of a gun where I needed him." He swung up into the saddle again, intending to hang around to see how everyone else did. Plus, Lou had already told him he was hazing for a couple other guys.

Including Max Vargas.

It was a common enough occurrence. A good hazer was worth his weight in gold and typically got a nice cut of the bulldogger's payoff when he was in the money. But out of the dozens of entrants, only a handful would end up in the money. Even when Lou did compete himself, he also did a lot of hazing because he had two ex-wives and four kids he was supporting.

"And up next in the box is Max Vargas," the announcer was drawling, "outta the fine capital of Texas. Max is standing at number seventeen in the world right now and he's on last year's horse of the year, so let's see what he and Deca can do-o-o."

Max's nerves as he and Deca settled back into the corner of the box were easily visible to Grayson. He was holding the reins tight and high. Exactly the way Deca didn't like.

"Come on, Max," Grayson murmured. "Loosen up."

There was no possible way the other man could have heard. Too much distance. Too much noise. Too much distraction.

But Max suddenly rolled his head around. He planted his hat down harder on his head. Then he lightened up the reins and with a nudge of his boot had Deca shimmying sideways back into the corner.

Less than half a minute later, it was all over.

"And *that's* Max Vargas with a four-point-three-e-e,

ladies and gentlemen. And we've got ourselves a fine start here this morning in Reno. Folks, let's not let this cowboy outta the arena without a little love."

Aside from noting the time, Grayson paid little attention to the announcer or the applause he was coaxing from the crowd. Instead, he watched Max say something to Lou that had his old friend's expression tightening before Max stomped out of the arena, leaving his hazer to deal with Deca.

Without thinking too much about it, Grayson casually moved to one side, knowing that he'd be blocking Max's exit if the kid ever looked beyond himself.

"Good time," he said, a second before Max would have plowed over him.

Max's head came up. He glared at Grayson. "Would've been better if my hazer woulda done his job right." His voice was tight and low. "As usual, everyone's loyalty is to *you*."

Grayson clamped his arm around the shorter man's shoulders, pulling him close. "Kid, you've got talent, but you've got a helluva lot to learn if you think a pro like Lou doesn't do his best every single ride no matter how much of an ass you are. You've been at this long enough to know there are three things that matter in bulldogging. You. The steer. And your hazer." He ignored Max's effort to shake him off. "You want a better time? Stop blaming someone else and stop straightening your legs so damn much every time you throw the steer. Standing up that much just adds time on the clock."

"If I wanted your advice, I'd ask." Max shoved his way past Grayson.

He took a step after the kid, only to stop short when he spotted his mother sitting in the stands. He hadn't seen her since arriving in Reno.

She gave him a smile and a thumbs-up.

All normal stuff.

What *wasn't* normal was the glimpse Grayson got of a man sitting about a dozen rows from Deborah who'd just risen and was walking away.

The man wore a ball cap on his head, a dark colored T-shirt and jeans. But Grayson could swear the man was Gerald Robinson.

Grayson's hands curled into fists as he squinted, trying to see the man better before he moved out of sight. But Deborah had risen, too, and was heading down the bleachers toward Grayson.

If she knew the man who'd left her pregnant and abandoned was anywhere near, she gave no sign of it.

And when Grayson looked back to where Robinson had been—if it *had* been Robinson—the man was gone.

His mom's smile seemed perfectly normal when she finally reached him. "Good time." She was carrying a printed list that he knew would be his schedule for the coming week. "How's the rib feel?"

"It's fine. How was Paseo?"

At his abrupt tone, her eyes narrowed. "It was fine."

"Was Robinson there?"

She frowned. "What are you talking about?"

He scanned the arena yet again. "Forget it. Nothing." He plucked the list from her hand and studied it. Autographing session at noon. Conference call at three about Grayson Gear's proposed collaboration with Castleton Boots.

His mom snatched the list back, giving him a close look. "Nothing my fanny."

He exhaled. "It's not unheard of. He's shown his miserable face in Paseo before. As Jerome Fortune, the guy faked his death a long damn time ago and recreated himself as Gerald Robinson. Now that he's found you, who knows what else he's capable of."

"I should think you'd know what *I'm* capable of. Just because I wanted to go home and catch up with my other sons, you start thinking the worst?"

"He's a married man with more kids than he can count."

Temper filled her eyes. "That sounds like you're warning me, son."

"I'm not warning. I'm just… I just don't want him hurting you again."

"Oh, for heaven's sake, Grayson. I was in love with Jerome once, but that was a long time ago. It happened too fast, and maybe if I could turn back time, we could have found our way. But I can't turn it back and I'm no home wrecker. If you're intent on worrying about something, worry about yourself."

"What do I have to worry about?"

"Making more out of your life than work! Finding someone who'll keep your bed warm at night. I mean the *same* someone who'll be there night after night after night. Look at your brothers—"

"I'm not my brothers." He cut her off before she could head on down that road again. Since he'd learned about his biological father, his worst fear was that he'd turn out to be more like Jerome/Gerald than like his own brothers. Neither Jayden nor Nathan had ever shared Grayson's proclivity against entanglements. "Only thing *I* need to worry about is showing up on time where I'm supposed to show up." He tried to take the list from her again. "I'm gonna need that, you know."

She tossed the paper at him, obviously still annoyed. "Autographing and press conference today. Grayson Good session with an elementary school tomorrow and a senior center the next day. I'll work out the rest of the week when we know your next go-round." She waited a beat, studying him closely. "You saw Billie yesterday, didn't you?"

He picked up the list from the ground where it had fallen. "I looked at a *house* yesterday with my real estate agent." Spilled half his guts with her, too.

"With Billie."

He folded the sheet and shoved it in his back pocket. "Dammit, Ma. Would you give it a rest?"

Her eyebrows rose. "I'll give it a rest when you tell me what's really got a burr under your saddle."

He pinched the bridge of his nose. There was no way he was going to tell her he thought he'd seen Robinson in the arena. She'd be upset that he was hallucinating, or upset that he wasn't.

But he was even more reluctant to talk about Billie. It was a guarantee that Deborah would make too much of anything he said. And it was hard enough not thinking about Billie, particularly after the way he'd left.

From the corner of his eye, he saw Max Vargas stomping around, still peeved. It was a toss-up who the young man wished six feet under more—Grayson or Lou, as the hazer passed nearby, still leading Deca.

His mother was still giving him the stink eye and Grayson threw out a Hail Mary. "I saw Bethany Belmont last night before my flight. She's pregnant."

His mother's eyes widened with dismay. "With your—"

"Hell no." He'd never slept with Bethany, even back in the early days, though he'd given it his best shot for a time. "She didn't say who the father was."

Deborah looked confused. "Then why'd she tell you?"

He spread his hands. "I guess she needed someone to talk to. She's got no family. Or maybe because we both grew up in Paseo. Take your pick. You were single and pregnant once." He looked over the bleachers again. "What else should I have done? She asked me for a job at Grayson Gear. She's thirty-six years old and pregnant. She can't compete right now. She's behind on her bills."

His mother's lips compressed. Then she sighed. "Even after all these years, I remember what that's like. What did you tell her?"

"To talk to Jessica on Monday." He'd already told his manager at the company to find a spot for Bethany. "Meanwhile, I gave her about five hundred to tide her over."

"She might use it for an abortion."

"I doubt it. She was anxious about finding a job, but still seemed pretty happy about the baby."

"Hey, mister." The greeting was accompanied by a tug on his shirt and Grayson looked down to see a young boy holding an autograph book and wearing a hopeful expression. "Can I get your autograph?"

Glad for the interruption, Grayson crouched down until he was at the boy's level. He had dark brown hair and dark brown eyes and looked about five. "You bet. What's your name, cowboy?"

The boy beamed. "Billy."

"Billy, eh?" Grayson had always suspected the universe had a strange sense of humor. He took the book and opened it to a blank page. "I knew a Billy a long time ago." That was true enough. "Billy Wood was a great bronc rider. Taught me a lot back in the day. How old are you?"

"Six." The boy preened. "I'm gonna be a mutton buster!"

Grayson smiled as he scrawled his autograph across the page.

"You know, that's how Grayson started," Deborah told the boy. "Mutton busting."

Billy looked at Grayson, awed. "Really?"

"Sure did. But you know, every mutton buster needs a good hat on his head."

The boy rubbed the toe of his scuffed boots in the dirt and looked toward a dark-haired woman standing protectively nearby. "My mama said I could get boots or a hat but not both."

"My mama used to tell me the same thing." Grayson smiled at Billy's mom as he returned the autograph book. Then he took his hat and plunked it on the boy's head. "Hold on to that, cowboy. One day it'll fit you just fine."

Billy's eyes widened like saucers. He clamped one hand down on the oversize hat as though Grayson might change his mind. "Thanks, mister!" He raced back to his mama, who beamed and mouthed a "thank you."

Deborah waited until they'd moved out of earshot. "That was a nice thing. But you gave him your favorite hat." Her eyes were speculative. "You've never done that before."

He shrugged. "Kid reminded me of EJ."

"Sure it wasn't the boy's name?"

It wasn't often he lied to his mother. But he lied then. "Positive."

Chapter Seven

Stepping off the elevator on her apartment floor, Billie juggled her purse and the bag of groceries with her keys while she listened to her phone messages. She'd spent most of the afternoon pinch-hitting for Elena, who had scheduled three different open houses all at the same time, and the rest of the day trying to save a sales contract for one of her own clients from falling through because of a disagreement over carpet.

It was nearly eight at night. She was tired. Her feet ached. All she wanted was a cool bath, half the package of peanut-butter cookies inside her bag of groceries, and a glass of wine. Not necessarily in that order.

But the sight of Grayson sitting in the hallway with his back against her door made her forget all that. A large paper shopping bag sat on the floor beside him.

She stopped short and had an overwhelming desire to hurry back to the elevator and make her escape.

But he'd already noticed her and was rolling to his feet.

He was dressed in full-on "cowboy" from the snaps on the front of his torso-hugging shirt to the oversize championship belt buckle, drool-inducing blue jeans and gleaming boots. The only thing missing was his trademark black cowboy hat.

She knew he hadn't busted out already in Reno, because one of her voice messages had been from Max as he'd ranted about losing to Grayson by a fraction of a second in their first go-round.

She dropped her phone inside her purse and gave him a sideways look as he shifted so she could put her key in the door lock. "Aren't you supposed to still be in Reno?"

"I have to go back for my second go."

What she really wanted was an answer to what he was doing there outside her apartment, particularly after his abrupt departure the day before. But since she didn't want to ask the question outright, she supposed she deserved what she got.

"Let me help you." He didn't wait for her permission before taking the heavy grocery bag from her.

She turned the key and pushed open the door, going inside. He followed. Again without permission. He set the grocery bag on the counter in her kitchen. "You always work this late?"

"When I need to." She dumped her purse right beside the groceries, before crossing her arms and leaning back against the cupboards.

He still didn't provide an explanation for his presence. Instead, he started removing the items from the grocery bag.

Tall bottle of chardonnay.

Lavender-scented bubble bath.

His gaze roved over her. "Expecting company?"

"Is that so surprising?"

He didn't reply as he turned once more to the grocery bag. Of course she knew what was coming. But short of making a big deal about it, she didn't figure there was anything she could do to stop it.

Out came the giant-sized package of cookies. The small vat of ice cream.

The industrial-sized box of tampons.

"You plan to make a meal on this stuff?"

"Well, not these." She tapped the tampon box, damned if she would be embarrassed. Instead, she picked up the ice cream and stuck it in the freezer, where it could keep company with her ice tray.

He folded up the bag. Without asking, he opened her refrigerator door and plucked out the container of Chinese takeout that sat on the empty shelves alongside a withering orange and two green apples. He opened the container and gave it a wary sniff. "And not that, either." He stuck it back in the fridge. "It occurred to me," he said, as he shut the refrigerator door, "that we sort of had our first fight."

"No," she retorted, before she could stop herself, "you dumped a load of obviously personal information in my lap and then ran." Not to mention running straight to another woman.

His lips compressed. He turned on his heel and left the kitchen. But he returned a moment later with the bag from the hall. "And it occurred to me that I probably owed you an apology." He set the shopping bag on top of the neatly folded grocery bag, pulled out what looked like a boot box, and handed it to her.

"What's this?"

"Open it and see."

She flipped off the lid, half expecting to see a pair of Grayson Gear boots inside.

But she was wrong, and despite herself, she felt a smile start to tug at her lips. She lifted one of the tall rubber muck boots out of the box. "At least you know better than to take me for the glass slipper type."

His expression lightened a little. "I don't know about that." He pulled out another shoebox. This one was cashmere-tan in color, much smaller, and had a very famous name printed on the top.

It was ridiculous the way her mouth went dry as she unsteadily reached for the box. "You didn't really bring me Christian Louboutin shoes."

"I didn't?"

She swallowed and carefully lifted off the top. The patent high-heeled pumps inside were black. Peep toe. Deathly high heel. With the kind of brilliant red sole that she'd seen only in magazines and on Rhonda Dickinson's feet. "You...you shouldn't have." She put the lid back on the box and nudged it with the tip of her finger toward him. "I can't possibly accept them."

"What's the difference between them and the rubber boots?"

"Besides *several* hundred dollars?"

He nudged the box back. "You like shoes."

To be accurate, she loved shoes. But she never spent a fortune on indulging that love, primarily because she ordered all her dress shoes off the internet at a discount site she'd discovered years ago.

Once more, she pushed the box toward him. "They're too expensive. And—" she kept pressure against the box before he could slide it back her way "—how would you even know what size to get?"

"I'm a good guesser."

"I can just imagine how you got good at that."

He lifted one of the ridiculously beautiful shoes out of the box and suddenly crouched in front of her. "Let's test it out."

It was galling to feel a little light-headed, seeing him kneeling that way, and she pressed a steadying hand against the counter beside her. "Grayson, I—" Her words strangled in her throat when he wrapped his long fingers around her bare ankle.

"Lift."

Knowing she ought to resist him was a far cry from being able to do it. She lifted her foot and he slid off the neon-yellow pump she had on.

"You were wearing these the first day we met," he murmured as he set it aside.

"Was I? I, uh, I don't remember." Her lie sounded as strangled as she felt. She swallowed hard and looked away from how his hair waved against the back of his neck. Her fingers curled against the cool granite. But her imagination was conjuring warm skin and thick hair.

He slid the peep-toe creation on to her foot.

Where it fit perfectly.

Then he was rising, and for a moment, his fingertips trailed lightly along the back of her calf, skipping away before he reached her knee.

The damage was done, though. Warmth was flooding through her every nook and cranny.

"Seems like a good fit to me," he murmured. "What d'you think?"

She thought he was standing much too close. She thought that, even with the addition of a five-inch heel, he still towered over her by half a foot. And she thought that he might well be worth her chancing her job. "I think you guessed well." That wasn't her voice, was it? All breathy?

He shifted and the minor distance separating them became nearly minuscule. She could make out every single one of the lashes thickly surrounding his dark eyes. "If you don't accept them—" his voice dropped "—then we've got a problem."

"What problem?"

His gaze roved over her face, seeming to settle on her lips. "I'll have to find another way to apologize." He shifted again and she felt something hard and intrusive nudge against her midriff.

She moistened her lips. "Grayson—" Then some kernel of common sense rescued her. It was the other *shoe* he was holding between them.

What was wrong with her? Had it been *that* long since she'd felt such a visceral attraction to a man?

Yes!

She ignored the answer circling inside her gut and took the shoe as she edged away from him. Feeling almost grief-stricken, she leaned over and slipped the beautiful shoe off her foot. She set it and its mate inside the box and carefully placed the lid back in place. "There's no need for expensive apology shoes because there was no fight."

"Felt like it to me." He waited a beat. "You know, there's nothing going on between me and anyone else."

She couldn't help herself. "Does Bethany Belmont know that?"

"And that's why it felt like a fight." He lifted his hand and she froze when he slid his fingers through her hair, tucking it behind her ear. "She's just an old friend, Billie. We grew up in the same town and both ended up in rodeo. It's nothing more than that."

Her mouth was dry all over again. "This entire conversation is—"

"Necessary?"

"—inappropriate."

"I'll keep it between the two of us, if you will."

She felt like her entire body was buzzing. "Grayson—"

"Is that your phone?"

"What?" Feeling stupid, she looked toward her purse sitting only inches away from her. From inside came a distinct vibrating buzz. She plunged her hand inside and grabbed the cell, silencing it even before she pulled it out to see the screen. Max.

She dropped the phone back into her purse like the hot potato it had become.

"Tell you what. You think about the shoes while we have dinner."

She looked at the wine and the package of cookies.

"While we go *out* and have dinner. There's a new place I've been hearing about and I'm starving."

So was she, but quite probably not in the way he meant. "A *business* dinner." The emphasis was as much for herself as for him.

His gaze roved over her face again. "Sure." There wasn't an ounce of conviction in his response.

God help her. She had no willpower whatsoever.

She jabbed the tip of her finger against his chest. "I mean it, Grayson. I'm going to—" She realized her finger was still pushing against him and quickly pulled her hand away. "I'm going to find some new listings to show you. And we'll review the ones you've already seen. Just in case."

Now, he looked amused. "Whatever makes you sleep at night, darlin'."

If she could sleep at night without dreaming about

him, she would be a whole lot better off. She was weak-willed where he was concerned, clearly, but she wasn't so far out of her mind to admit *that*. "Fine." She started to walk away, only she still had one yellow shoe on and one off. She quickly shoved her toes back into the shoe, where they throbbed and cried a little at the discomfort, particularly now that they'd brushed so briefly against Louboutin heaven. "I'm going to change," she told him.

He held up the tan box. "Don't forget these."

She gave him a look and marched into her bedroom, closing the door.

The bed, made neatly that morning like she did every morning, seemed to stare back at her.

A shiver danced down her spine. Glancing back at the door, she let out a deep breath, giving her bed a stern look as she walked around it and into her closet. She changed out of the blouse and skirt she'd worn all day for work and pulled on a pair of black jeans and a silky purple blouse. She traded the neon-yellow pumps for a more comfortable pair of high wedges and went into the bathroom.

There was too much color in her cheeks, but since nature seemed determined to put it there whenever she was around Grayson there wasn't much she could do about it. She brushed her teeth and brushed her hair. Smoothed on some lip gloss, then tucked her hair behind her ear.

Her fingers froze as she stared at herself in the mirror. She felt Grayson's fingers slipping behind her ear all over again…

And something inside her belly dipped and swayed.

She grabbed the brush again and quickly worked her hair back into a high ponytail, where she could be certain there'd be no need for tucking stray strands behind any ears.

"*Business*, Belinda Marie. Just because flirting is as natural as breathing to him, this is just business. Remember that."

Her reflection nodded back at her and she went out to brave the evening.

All too soon, her intentions went awry. In fact, they didn't even make it out of her parking garage before Billie knew she was swimming in waters too deep for someone who didn't even swim.

Grayson stood beside her car with his hand outstretched.

"You want my keys?" she asked him.

"Yes. I want your keys."

"But nobody drives my car but me."

"One day I'll let you ride Vix. Nobody rides him but me. For tonight, though, *I* want to arrive someplace with you without me sprouting more gray hairs."

She immediately looked at his thick hair. It was a little overlong. And not a single gray that she could see.

He hadn't lowered his hand. "Please?"

It was okay to be accommodating for an important client, she reminded herself. Just not *too* accommodating.

She dropped the keys in his palm. His fingers closed over them, catching her fingers, as well.

"That wasn't so hard, was it?" Still holding her hand, he opened the passenger door for her and didn't release her until she'd slid down into the seat.

The only times she'd sat in the passenger seat of her own car was when she took it to the self-serve car wash and was cleaning out the inside.

He rounded the vehicle and reached down to adjust the power seat before he even tried to sit behind the wheel. When he was in, he adjusted it even more. He fastened his seat belt and started the engine. "Seat belt, Billie."

She shook herself. What was so fascinating about him driving her vehicle? She fastened her own belt and looked through the side window as he drove out of the parking garage.

He cast a sidelong look at her. "You're too young to be such a control freak."

"You try being the baby of a controlling family for a while and see how you turn out."

"What's controlling about your family?"

Her gaze drifted back toward his hand on her steering wheel. "What isn't? I didn't even choose my own college degree."

"You didn't want an economics degree? What would you have chosen instead?"

She crossed her legs against the imagined feel of his fingers drifting up the back of her calf. "It was never an option so I don't even know."

"But you *did* choose to go into real estate."

Right. That had definitely been her own choice. She reached behind the seat and retrieved her phone from her purse and pulled up her Austin Elite app.

"Calling someone?" he asked her.

"Checking for the new listings this week. We can go over them during dinner. What's the name of the place you've been wanting to try?"

"La Viña. It's the restaurant at Mendoza Winery. Been there?"

"Just once. I went to a wedding there not too long ago. The sister of a friend of mine invited me." That was one way to describe Schuyler Fortunado's joyful "the more the merrier" inclusion of everyone working at her father's real estate office, which Maddie now headed. Billie had gone to the wedding only because there hadn't been any tactful way to get out of it.

"Good food?"

"Good food. Good wine." Billie didn't want to think about the wedding bouquet that she'd unintentionally caught when Schuyler's flowers separated midair. Maddie had caught the other part and at the time had said it was a sign. A fact that Billie promptly dismissed where she was concerned. As for Maddie, it had been obvious even then that she and Zach were already head over heels for each other. No magic wedding flowers involved at all.

"The winery is a pretty setting." She was glad her outfit wasn't any more casual than it was, though. "And the restaurant's a popular one. I'm not sure we'll get in without reservations."

She caught his grin.

"Oh. Right. I imagine that's not a detail you have to worry about too often."

He chuckled softly and the sound of it flowed over her like warm honey.

She looked out the window again. Definitely, the waters were way, *way* too deep.

Predictably, when they arrived at the crowded restaurant, the maître d' did a double take when Grayson—after tugging Billie past the people already waiting to be seated—stopped in front of him. He obviously recognized Grayson, though, because he immediately showed them to a cozy table near one of the tall windows reaching from floor to ceiling. "It's a pleasure having you dining with us, sir. My son was one of the participants at the riding clinic you held last year. He still talks about it."

"What's your son's name?"

"Carmelo."

Grayson grinned, nodding. "I remember Carmelo. He was fearless once he got on a horse. Tell him I hope he comes back next year. We're expanding the clinic to include high schoolers and he'd be that age now, right?"

"Yes." The maître d' beamed as he opened the heavy menus and placed them in Billie's and Grayson's hands. "Your waiter tonight will be Alfonse, but please let me know if there is anything I can do to make your evening even more perfect."

"It's mighty perfect already," Grayson drawled, giving Billie a sideways look that made her want to squirm in her seat. "But I appreciate it."

Instead of squirming, she looked around the candlelit tables surrounding them. Even when it wasn't being used as a wedding reception site, the restaurant was unabashedly romantic.

The press of Grayson's thigh alongside hers wasn't helping any. She stared blindly at the menu and tried to focus, and when Alfonse appeared a short while later, she gladly agreed to his suggestion that they ignore the menu altogether and instead enjoy the chef's "special selections."

The waiter moved away again and Billie looked at Grayson. Despite the crowded restaurant, their table still had the feeling of intimacy. "I suppose this happens a lot for you."

"Getting into restaurants without a reservation?"

"That. And the chef's special attention."

She looked up when the maître d' appeared again, this time to introduce them to the sommelier, who proceeded to present them with one of Mendoza Winery's finest. "With our compliments, of course."

With flair, the wine was poured, and once again Billie and Grayson were left alone.

He lifted the long-stemmed wineglass and tilted it toward Billie. "Yeah, and sometimes I'd just like to take out a beautiful woman and be left alone. To peace and quiet and, hopefully, a good steak."

Afraid she'd break the delicate stem of her own glass because her fingers were so shaky, she lifted it toward him in return. "You do know that I'm vegetarian, right?"

Even in the candlelight, he looked surprised. And consternated.

She grinned and sipped the wine, which bloomed against her taste buds as promised. She leaned forward, conspiratorially. "I'm kidding. I'm strictly a 'give me steak or give me death' kind of girl."

He chuckled. "I like to think I'm a live-and-let-live sort of guy, but between the chai tea and no steak, I'd be lying if I didn't say I was relieved."

"Can't have a real estate agent whose palate differs from yours?"

He waited a beat while his eyes captured hers. "Sure."

She stiffened her back against the shiver sliding down it. Sliding into Grayson's appeal would be oh, so easy. And oh, so pleasurable. Until he got bored and moved on. "I didn't know you did riding clinics. Grooming the next crop of rodeo riders?"

"Not quite. We set up the clinics through Grayson Good for kids dealing with various challenges. Physical. Emotional. Financial. Any kind of background. Program's doubled in the last year."

"Here in Austin?"

"All over. About half the towns where I'm rodeoing. I don't even have to twist too many arms anymore to get some of the other guys and gals competing to come on out and help." He smiled wryly. "When we started out five years ago, though, it was a little harder."

"How many kids do you end up with?"

"Depends. It's elementary-school age through junior

high kids, but we kept having to turn away kids once they got too old, so I found another sponsor to kick in so we could go through high schoolers. I suppose we average about fifty to sixty kids at each deal."

She did a little math in her head. "And you remember Carmelo?"

"Might have been harder if he'd been named Jacob. You know how many thirteen-year-old boys are named Jacob?" His lips tilted up as he shook his head.

"Nathan? Is that— Oh." A strikingly beautiful blonde stopped next to their table and propped her hand on a hip that was lovingly outlined by a bandage of a red dress. "You're not Nathan," she said to Grayson, "but you're definitely Billie. Pemberton, if I remember correctly." Schuyler Fortunado Mendoza's vivid gaze bounced from Billie's face to Grayson's and back again. "How the heck are you, sweetie?"

Still bemused as she was by what Grayson had told her, it took a minute before Billie remembered that Schuyler hadn't only married Carlo Mendoza, who was one of the winery founders, but that she worked there, as well. "I'm great, Schuyler. Marriage must agree with you. You look more amazing than ever."

Schuyler grinned. She was even shorter than Billie, but she had a personality as big as Texas. "Marriage suits me *very* well." Her gaze took in Grayson with undisguised curiosity. "So. Let me guess. You're the other brother. The rodeo one."

Grayson returned her smile, though a little less naturally than Billie was used to. "You've got one up on me, I'm afraid," he said.

Right. Billie mentally shook herself. "Schuyler Mendoza, this is Grayson F—Smith. Grayson, Schuyler was the bride at the wedding I mentioned on our way here. Now she's the special events coordinator for the winery."

Schuyler looked pleased that Billie knew that detail, and extended her hand to Grayson. "So nice to meet you, Grayson Fuh-Smith." Her smile widened as she winked. "I've met your brother Nathan, hon. I know all about you Fortune boys."

Billie thought Grayson's expression looked a little doubtful about that, but he shook the bright-eyed blonde's hand without comment.

"How do you like the merlot? We're pretty proud of it, if I do say so myself."

"It's everything that your sommelier promised," he assured her. "Truth is, though, by nature I'm more of a beer kind of guy."

Schuyler laughed. "Sugar, I've heard that your tastes are wide and varied." Her humorous gaze took in Billie as she said it. "Well, you have one of the finest tables in the house and Alfonse is one of our best. He'll take good care of you, I'm sure, so I'll stop intruding on your evening." She bussed Billie's cheek with a quick kiss before sashaying away.

"Good friend of yours?" Grayson asked after they were alone.

"Schuyler's good people. She treats everyone like they're her dear friends. But I really only knew her because I worked with her sister." Billie toyed with her wine stem. "She sure seems to know about you, though." She finally lifted the glass and took a sip. "Fortune boys?"

Grayson grimaced. "I'll have to call Nathan to see what that was all about."

Billie hadn't eaten since that morning and her few sips of wine were already going to her head. Almost as much as he was going to her head. "Being triplets, I imagine you're all pretty close."

"Close enough. I haven't talked to either one of my brothers in a few weeks." His gaze turned to where Schuyler had stopped at another table across the room, where an attractive older couple were seated. "I wonder what her deal is," he murmured.

Billie didn't have to wonder what he was thinking. Schuyler was stunningly beautiful. "She's married," she reminded him.

His dark eyes slid back toward her and he smiled slightly. "And not my type, anyway."

"Not wide and varied enough for you?"

The amusement in his eyes glinted in the flickering candlelight. "My tastes have been narrowing down to more of a fine point lately."

"Well, I hope you're not going to be as picky about real estate as you are about women, or you'll never find your forever home." She couldn't believe the words came out of her mouth.

He let out a bark of laughter.

"It's the wine," Billie muttered, feeling the glances his laughter had drawn their way, and pushing her glass toward the middle of the table. Since the table seemed about the size of a postage stamp, that wasn't very far. "Keep that stuff away."

"I don't know about that. It's helping me get a glimpse into what you're thinking."

She frowned at him. Without her noticing, his arm had gone around the back of her chair and his fingers were flirting with her bare shoulder. "What I'm thinking is that this is supposed to be *business*."

To prove it, she pulled her phone out of her purse and brought up the new listings again. She scrolled through several, dismissing them out of hand because they didn't have any land. When she was finished excluding the unsuitable ones, there were only a few remaining, one of which was the Harmon ranch.

"Here." She set her phone on the table between them so he could see the display. "Three possibles. How much time do you have before you need to be back in Reno? I'm sure I could schedule—"

She broke off when he took her phone and turned it upside down on the table where she couldn't reach it. *"Grayson."*

"Billie."

"You're far too used to getting your own way."

He just smiled slightly and placed her wineglass in her hand. "Indulge me with dinner and I'll look at your listings over dessert."

"You're making that sound like I've invited you to see my 'etchings,'" she grumbled into the wineglass.

He leaned closer until his lips practically brushed her ear. "Is that an offer?"

"Belinda, I thought that was you."

She nearly choked when DeForest Allen stopped next to their table. "Mr. Allen!" She set aside the glass again and it would have tipped right over if not for the smooth way that Grayson caught it. "What a surprise. You, ah, you haven't actually met my client Grayson Smith yet, have you." She quickly made introductions.

"What a surprise, indeed." Her boss's smile looked tight as he shook Grayson's hand. "Anita and I are here celebrating our anniversary."

"Our twenty-fifth." Anita Allen patted her husband's arm. "I insisted on a romantic dinner and DeForest didn't fail me. La Viña is simply wonderful, isn't it?" She leaned closer to their table. "I was going to insist that DeForest take a walk with me in the vineyard, but I just couldn't tear myself away from the excitement." She gave a meaningful little nod toward the table where Schuyler was still talking with the older couple.

Billie had no idea what Mrs. Allen meant, but she was more concerned with the conclusions her husband might be drawing about the cozy picture she and Grayson made, particularly with his arm still around her the way it was. She wiggled her shoulder once, hoping he would take the hint, but he didn't.

"She's just as elegant in person as I thought she'd be." Anita's voice was hushed. She was still looking toward that other table.

"My wife is fascinated by all things royal," Mr. Allen said.

Anita lightly slapped his arm. "Tell me *you're* not impressed that an honest-to-goodness British royal is sitting right over there as normal and natural as you please." She focused on Billie and Grayson again. "I imagine that's Lady Josephine's new fiancé with her. I don't care that nobody really calls her that anymore. She's still a Lady to me. He's a Mendoza, you know. I wonder if they'll have their wedding here? The Mendoza Winery has become *the* place for weddings."

"I don't know about weddings," Grayson said, holding up Billie's phone, "but so far it's been a great place to sit and talk about the ranch I want to buy while we grab a bite. She's been showing me places on her cell." He set the phone down again.

"You're discussing business, then." DeForest didn't look entirely convinced, but his smile was a little less stilted.

"The Harmon ranch is one of the places," Billie added quickly. "So far, Grayson has only seen the exterior."

Her boss's expression cleared and his smile warmed noticeably. Maybe at the thought of the cut he'd be taking if she were to make such a sale. "The Harmon ranch. That is a special property. You'll want to take particular note of the wine cellar—" he gestured toward the wine bottle sitting on their table "—since you obviously have an appreciation." Then he took his wife's arm. "We'll take that walk, dear, and leave these two to their business."

Billie didn't exhale until she saw them walk out of the restaurant. When they had, she reached for her glass of wine and gulped it down.

"You suppose that's the last of our interruptions?"

"I hope so." She set down her empty glass. "Thank you. I believe you just saved my bacon."

Grayson's grin turned wicked. "I have a pretty good appreciation for bacon."

"Don't start," she warned, and flipped up the phone so they could see the display again. "Mr. Allen once canned an agent right on the spot when he was caught playing tonsil hockey with his female client."

Grayson tugged lightly on her ponytail. "We're not playing hockey."

She ignored that. "When *do* you need to be back in Reno?"

He pulled the phone away from her again. "Later." Then he refilled their glasses. The moment he'd drained the last drop, Alfonse whisked the bottle away and replaced it.

"Did you know who she was talking about?" Grayson eventually asked. "Lady Whatsername?"

"Not a clue." Billie picked up her glass. She didn't recognize the slender, silver-haired woman sitting across the restaurant, though she did have a distinctly classy look to her. "If you'd give me my phone back, I could look it up on the internet. Give me five minutes and we'll know all about her."

"Not a chance, darlin'. I'm just a simple rodeo cowboy and I've had more than my fill of internet gossip about me. 'Spect a person like Lady Whatsername has it even worse. Don't feed the beast."

"Simple. Oh yeah, sure."

He settled his arm on the back of her chair once more. "Relax. Drink your wine. The food'll be here soon, and nothing else could possibly go wrong tonight."

Chapter Eight

He was wrong.

Not about the food, which was excellent. As was the second bottle of wine. And the dessert Grayson ordered was mind-bogglingly good. Having him coax her into tasting the chocolate confection right off the tip of his own fork might have contributed to the mind-boggling part, but the restaurant's pastry chef deserved some credit, too.

No. The wrong came about when they actually left the restaurant.

No sooner were they walking out the front door, with Grayson's hand lightly on her waist, than a blinding flash hit them in the face.

Billie instinctively threw up her arm to shield her eyes, belatedly realizing it was a camera flash.

"Whoa, that's Grayson! Almost didn't recognize you without the cowboy hat. Yo, Big G!"

Grayson grabbed her hand and pulled her past the photographer, who'd obviously been camping out in front of the restaurant.

Dizzying strobes followed them. "Who's the new lady? Is she the reason for the five million dollar house you're buying in Austin?"

"Y'all know me better 'n that." Grayson sounded easygoing despite the way he hustled her along the sidewalk toward the parking lot. His stride was so long that she had to jog to keep up. "It's just business."

She heard the photographer laugh. "You gonna take home another win in Vegas this December?"

"You know it, buddy." They'd reached the parking lot, where her car seemed to be parked in the farthest possible slot.

"Just one shot of you and the lady?"

"Only if you promise you're not gonna follow us any farther."

The photographer snickered. "Yeah, sure. Just business, right?"

She felt the sigh work through him, but his smile was pure "Grayson" as he stopped for a few seconds, just long enough for the camera to capture them again. Then the strobe ceased and she blinked against the darkness as she heard the retreating footsteps.

Grayson took her arm again and started walking once more. "Sorry about that."

"You've already bought a five million dollar house?"

"Yeah, that's why I haven't kissed you already. Because I'm working with someone else on a secret real estate deal. You can't listen to stuff like that, Billie. It's all horse pucky."

Her vision was starting to clear. They'd reached her

car. "What do people like that do? Just camp out places hoping to get some little salacious tidbit?"

"Who knows? Maybe he was there for the royal Brit and got a twofer." Grayson unlocked the car and opened the passenger door for her.

One part of her mind wondered if she ought to argue about that, but the more sensible part said she'd had several glasses of wine over the course of the night. "Maybe we should call a taxi. Uber it or something."

He brushed his finger down her nose. "You're the lush. I didn't finish my second glass. In you go, now."

She sank down into the passenger seat. There really was something awfully nice about having someone else take care of things.

Not just someone else.

Him.

When he drove out of the parking lot, she saw bright flashes of lights going off near the restaurant entrance. "Lady Whatsername?"

"Probably. Have you thought more about those shoes?"

"Grayson—"

"Keep thinking." He closed his free hand around hers. "I'm a patient guy."

She let out a short laugh at that. "In what world?"

His teeth flashed in a quick smile.

She leaned her head back. "Where *is* your hat, by the way?" He always wore that black cowboy hat. Except when he'd been in hangover mode, and then it had been a ball cap. But today was the first time she'd seen him without any kind of headgear at all.

"Gave it to a kid wanting an autograph."

She angled her head until she could watch him. "Good thing Grayson Gear sells hats. You probably go through a lot of them if you give them away all the time."

"I don't give 'em away all the time. But this kid was particularly cute. Name was Billy-with-a-*Y*."

Not for a second did she believe the name had prompted his generosity. "I bet you *do* give away a lot of hats."

His lips twitched. "Not my favorite one."

She was suddenly so tired it felt like she was melting into the comfortable seat. "I am going to look up Lady Whatsername," she told him.

"Knock yourself out, sweetheart."

Sweetheart.

If she were in her right mind, she'd never admit how much she liked the sound of that.

Instead, she hugged that secret to herself through the drive back downtown to her apartment building. But when they neared, she made herself stir. Think practically. "I should drop you at your hotel."

"Or…not."

Slippery warmth flowed through her. If she let on how tempted she really was, he'd take that inch and pull her along for a mile. "I should drop you at your hotel," she repeated more or less steadily. "I'll pick you up in the morning."

His smile flashed again as he drove into her parking garage. By the time he parked in her assigned spot, her heart was pounding so hard it was probably visible through her blouse. "I'm…I'm not inviting you up, Grayson."

"Okay." He climbed out of the car and came around to open her door.

"I mean it."

"Okay." He leaned over her just long enough to unclip her seat belt.

But it was long enough for her to inhale the warm

scent of him and her mouth went dry. When he took her hands and gently pulled her out of the car and onto her feet, she was painfully aware that she was on the cusp of letting herself be talked into something that she would ultimately regret. She might be more infatuated with him now than she had been at sixteen, but his business was flirtation. To him, every female walking was *darlin'*.

He closed the car door. Locked it. Then took her elbow and walked with her to the elevator. He pushed the call button. "Give me your hand."

Her legs felt unsteady and she was pretty sure it wasn't the wine. She gave him her hand.

He turned her palm upward and dropped her keys into it. She closed her fingers tightly around them, as if the feel of the jagged edges would help her keep hold of some bit of sanity.

His gaze was steady. "I'll see you after Reno."

It was the last thing she expected him to say. "You're leaving?"

"I've got to catch the red-eye back to Nevada."

She blinked, trying to make sense of it. "You came back just for one evening?"

"I came back just for you."

Her heart skittered around like water on hot oil. "But…but *why*?"

"I told you." He slowly drew his thumb along her jaw. "To apologize."

Her head swam. "You could have done that over the phone."

"I don't particularly like phones."

"Is that why you don't have a cell phone?"

"I have a cell phone. I just rarely use it. Particularly when face-to-face communication is called for." His gaze dropped to her lips and she knew, just knew that once he kissed her, her life was never going to be the same again.

"H-how are you getting to the airport?"

"I'll call a taxi." He smiled faintly. "Or Uber it."

The elevator door slid open.

"Without a phone?"

"I'm a big boy." He gave a quick wink. "I can manage." He nudged her into the waiting elevator, leaned inside and punched the number of her floor. "I'll see you after Reno."

She blinked, watching the doors slowly close. Okay then. The whole kiss thing was her imagination.

But then his hand came up and stopped the doors from closing.

She moistened her lips, her heart charging right back up into her throat.

"Billie?"

"Yes?"

"Think about the shoes." Then he moved his hand away and the elevator doors shut.

She exhaled shakily as the elevator lurched gently and started to climb.

It wasn't the extravagant shoes she was having such a tough time resisting.

It was him.

"Man, it's going to be a helluva week," Max crowed in Billie's ear two days later. "If I do as good in the short round as I just did in my second go, I could walk away from Reno with more 'n ten grand!"

Holding her cell phone to her ear, Billie smiled. She was keeping an eye out for Grayson, who'd arranged—via Deborah—to meet her at her office. It was Sunday afternoon, and even though the Reno rodeo was still going strong until the following weekend, Grayson wasn't waiting that long to see the Harmon ranch.

At least that was the plan. Right now, he was a good twenty minutes late.

She scanned the sidewalks, figuring he'd show up on foot, like he typically did, but there was still no sign of him. And Max was still jabbering away, ninety miles a minute. She waited until he stopped to draw breath. "So where are you heading after Reno?"

"Pecos. Man, I can't wait to see his face when they hand *me* the trophy next weekend. Doesn't matter how good he throws from here on out—it'd take a miracle for him to shave off enough time to beat me on the average! And there ain't anyone else in the lineup who's ever beat my last time on the clock."

She spotted Grayson down the block and felt excitement slide through her veins. He was wearing an off-white cowboy hat. "Who's face?"

"Criminy, Bill. Are you listening or not? I just told you. Grayson's face. He won't be leaving town with his toothpaste-endorsing grin in place when that happens, I can tell you."

"Congratulations. But listen, I've got to run." Grayson had seen her, too, and lifted his long arm in a brief wave as he jaywalked across the empty street, his long, jean-clad legs making short work of it. "I'll talk to you later." She didn't wait for Max's response as she disconnected and pushed her phone into the back pocket of her jeans. Her heart was thumping like mad and she pulled in a deep breath, trying to calm down.

It had been only two days since he'd left her in her parking garage.

Left her in a shaking mess.

He was smiling when he reached her car, and he pulled

down his sunglasses, giving her a once-over. "Nice boots," he drawled.

She looked down at herself. The rubber boots he'd given her reached nearly to her knees. "It's been raining here since you left." She felt oddly shy and half regretted her impulsive decision to wear them. "I'm afraid it might be muddy when we get out to the Harmon ranch."

He looked amused. "Wouldn't want to ruin another pair of high heels."

She moistened her lips and opened the passenger door for him. "Let's get going before someone puts in an offer on the place while we're standing around here on the sidewalk."

The lines beside his eyes crinkled as he pulled off his hat and ducked his head to get into the car. She quickly went around and slid behind the wheel, then started the engine and moved away from the curb. With traffic as light as it was, it wasn't going to take as long as usual to get to the property. "How was your flight?"

"Bumpy." He stretched out his legs. "How's your weekend been going?"

She didn't dare look his way. She'd spent way too much time thinking about him. "Busy. I signed two more new clients yesterday."

He propped his cowboy hat over one knee. "That's great. Congratulations. Good weekend for both of us, then."

She couldn't help glancing at him. "Have you had your second go-round, then?"

"First thing this morning. Got outrode hard by a guy I can hardly stand, but I've still got a chance of making it to the final. Won't know until later this week. More importantly, though, Grayson Good gained another corporate sponsor yesterday to the tune of several thousand dollars."

If he was worried at all about the rodeo, it sure didn't

show. She still couldn't help being concerned that the guy he couldn't stand might be her own cousin. She should have just told him in the beginning. It would have been awkward, but at least it wouldn't feel like a lie the way it did now.

"And now I'm sittin' next to the prettiest girl I've seen all week."

She turned onto the interstate and picked up speed. "I saw the photos last night on the internet of you posing with the rodeo queen, so I'm not falling for *that* line," she said lightly.

He gave her a long look. "Internet, huh? Find out anything interesting?"

She could feel her cheeks reddening. She couldn't tell if he was amused or annoyed. "Merely professional curiosity about a client. I did see a video of your ride there last year. You'd have won if you hadn't had a broken barrier penalty in the final round. Must have been frustrating for you."

At that, he did smile. "It's all part of the ride, sweetheart."

She wished her cousin subscribed to that theory.

While she'd been poking around on the internet, she'd also found out who Lady Whatsername was, but decided to keep that to herself. Lady Josephine Fortune Chesterfield.

For all Billie knew, the woman might be some distant relation of Grayson's. The more she'd read about the Fortune family, the more confusing the connections had become. Particularly when the only detail she knew for certain to be true was what Grayson had told her himself. That Ben Fortune Robinson was his half brother. Gerald Robinson—or Jerome Fortune—was his father. The man whom Grayson said had left his mother high and dry before Grayson and his brothers had been born.

That was pretty much the only nugget of gossip that *hadn't* appeared on her computer screen when she'd made the mistake of following Gerald Robinson's name. The man had founded Robinson Tech and turned it into a household name, but he'd evidently also turned a lot of women into mommies along the way. Women who were not his equally moneyed, society wife, Charlotte. There'd been dozens and dozens of news mentions about his affairs.

Billie's parents might drive her up a tree, but at least they weren't internet fodder like that.

The only complications going on with her family right now were strictly attributed to Billie representing her cousin's competitor and not telling either Max or Grayson.

Her fingers tightened on the steering wheel. She glanced at him from the corner of her eye. "Where's your next rodeo after Reno? Assuming you go back for the short round, I mean."

"I have to go back to Reno even if I don't because there're a few more charity events going on. But the following weekend is Cowboy Country over the Fourth of July. I have to go Red Rock before then, though, to take care of some business. Not sure how many days it'll take. We're not announcing it yet, but I'm close to inking a deal with Castleton Boots to do a line for Grayson Gear."

Her eyes instinctively darted to the cowboy boots he was wearing. She didn't know much about Castleton except they were Texas-based, expensive as all get-out and—according to Rhonda Dickinson, who'd worn them with everything from Daisy Duke shorts to evening gowns—supposedly worth every penny. "That sounds impressive."

"It'll be impressive when we finally come to terms. You ever been to Red Rock?"

"Once. I went to a real estate conference at the Red

Rock Inn. *Trés chic.* I know the real estate market there is healthier than ever these days. Have you been there?"

He smiled lazily. "Honey, I've crisscrossed this state so many times, there aren't many towns I haven't been to. Red Rock's nice. It's no Paseo, though."

She couldn't help but chuckle at that. "Right. Red Rock with its famous ranches and fancy resorts versus Paseo with what? Lots of grass?"

He didn't take offense. "Don't knock all that grass until you try it. Paseo may only have a handful of people calling it home, but that's the way we like it. Won't find Paseo in the news the way you might places like Red Rock or Horseback Hollow, even."

"Didn't you have a tornado in Paseo last year? That made the news."

"Yeah. We were lucky. Didn't have too much damage at the ranch. Nothing major, anyway. That's how Jayden met his wife."

"Wind blew her in?"

He chuckled. "That's more accurate than you know. We all think Paseo is about the most perfect place on earth."

"I'm surprised you chose Austin, then. I know Grayson Gear's office is here, but if you love Paseo so much why make the change?" She was genuinely curious. "Why not move your company to Paseo instead?"

"Be careful before you talk yourself right out of a real estate commission there, sweetheart." He was silent for a while. His long fingers tapped the crown of his hat. "Not a lot of modern technology in Paseo. Keeping a growing business going would be tough. And my twenty-some employees would balk if I asked 'em to leave all that Austin has to offer."

"So it makes more sense for you to come here?"

"Basically."

It wasn't quite the question she'd asked, but they'd arrived at the turnoff for the Harmon ranch, anyway.

The gate was open and she drove through, going slowly to afford Grayson a good look. "I have two more listings to show you after this one."

"Afraid it won't say *home* to me when we walk in the door?"

She sent him a wry smile as she parked near the barn, the same way she had the last time they'd visited the property. "I'll take the fifth on that, if you don't mind."

He gave a bark of laughter and climbed out of the car.

She'd made the excuse about the recent rains to justify wearing the muck boots he'd given her, but she was soon glad for them when he decided to explore outside again before heading to the house. After pulling her foot from yet another sucking hole of mud, she propped her hands on her hips and stared after him. "Grayson, I'm pretty sure we don't need to walk all the way to the lake! Are you just avoiding looking at another house?"

He turned back, gazing at her over the rims of his sunglasses.

She could imagine the sight she made. Mud reaching halfway up her boots. Mud on her butt from when she'd slipped. Mud on her hands from when she'd tried to catch herself. "At this rate, I'm going to have to hose myself off."

"Shouldn't have turned up your pointy little nose when I offered to hold your hand, then." He headed back toward her, grinning. "You could always jump in the shallow end of the pool. I'd make sure you wouldn't drown." He wrapped his hand around her waist, lifting her from the muddy patch as if she weighed no more than a child. "All right, then. Let's get on with it. Walk ahead of me, though, so I can see if you land in quicksand."

He was the quicksand.

When he'd set off on his little walking tour, she *had* avoided the hand he'd offered her. It surely would have been no more disturbing than to have him lift her the way he'd just done.

She rubbed her dirty hands on her jeans, pretending that her entire body wasn't feeling jarred as she picked her way back over the uneven ground. The rain they'd had the day before had cooled the air a few degrees, but she was still grateful for the shade provided by the oak and mesquite trees, even though she cursed the twisted Texas cedar that kept catching the toes of her boots. Fortunately, not all the acreage was so heavily wooded. There was plenty of cleared range just ready for grazing.

By the time they made it back to the outbuildings, her T-shirt clung to her spine and her ponytail to her sweaty neck. On top of the entire mud thing, she was having a hard time maintaining some positivity.

Grayson, on the other hand, just looked damnably sexier than ever. The sheen of sweat on his brown throat. The way he'd rolled up the sleeves of his plaid shirt to his elbows. The only mud drying on him was on the soles of his Castletons and a smear along the bottom of his faded blue jeans.

There were no longer any animals occupying the pens and stalls as they went through the largest of the barns. Primarily, the air was fresh, but there was a distinct undertone that spoke of the days when the pens and stalls had not been empty.

It wasn't unpleasant. Reminded her of when she and Max had spent so many hours hanging around the fairgrounds as teenagers.

She and Grayson passed from the barn back out into

the sun. "Hold up there, sweetheart." He gestured when she glanced at him. "Got a hydrant here."

She turned on her mud-caked heel and joined him where he'd stopped near a tall standpipe sticking out of the ground, topped by a complicated looking spigot. He turned it on and water gushed out. Holding his arm for balance, she stuck one foot, then the other beneath the stream until her boots no longer wore two inches of caked-on mud. Then she washed off her hands and swiped them dry against the back of her T-shirt as she moved out of the splash zone. "Thanks. Water felt good." Almost as good as the pool water had felt the first time they'd been out here.

"Yeah. Hold this." He pushed his cowboy hat into her hand, then ducked his head and pulled his shirt right off over it, buttons fastened and all.

She nearly dropped the hat.

Fortunately, he didn't notice, since he'd basically bent in half so he could sluice water over his head.

Then he straightened, slicking his hair back with his fingers.

She swallowed hard, watching water slide down his roping shoulders and creep along the hard plane of his chest. Then he swiped his hand down to his belt buckle and she swallowed, finally managing to look away. She expected him to pull his shirt back over his head, but he didn't. He just held it bunched in one hand as he took back his hat and settled it once more on his head. "Much better." He waved his shirt in the direction of the house.

She made a strangled sort of sound and started toward it again.

This time, when she opened the lockbox, the house key was there. She opened one side of the hand-carved wood double doors for him, then pulled her feet out of the boots before following him inside. Even though most of the mud was gone, she didn't want to track water inside the house. And at least the boots had done their job; her socks were dry and her jeans from the knees down where they'd been tucked into the boots were cleaner than the rest of her.

He noticed. "Hell. I should take off my own boots."

She shook her head. Heaven help her if he took off even more. "No need. Your boots weren't as bad as mine." She gave him a wide berth as she entered the spacious foyer. Even though she'd studied the listing in preparation, the sheer amount of gleaming hardwood and rough-textured stone was astonishing.

Even Grayson seemed awed. He pulled off his hat and looked up at the exposed beams overhead. "Damn." He dropped his shirt on the foyer table, not seeming to notice when it slipped off the edge and onto the gleaming tile floor.

For the first time since she'd begun showing him properties, she felt a bite of excitement over his reaction.

She plucked his shirt off the floor and set it back on the table, following him silently as he made his way through the house. Unlike most of her clients, who either headed first for the kitchen or the bedrooms, Grayson went for the stairs. Not the grand stacked-stone staircase leading up from the large foyer, either, but the mildly more modest brick staircase leading down from a wide window-lined hall that overlooked the pool.

It was hard not to be sidetracked by all the beauty on display—not the least of which was a shirtless Grayson himself.

But she was supposed to be a professional, so she

made a mental note of a couple obvious flaws. Several cracks in the highly polished Saltillo tile. A faint discoloration in one of the walls that could have come from water damage at one point.

When it came to flaws where Grayson was concerned, there were more than a couple.

A scar beneath his right shoulder blade. Another on his left side, right above his belt. Two more on his ridged abdomen.

They didn't do a darn thing to lessen the overall perfection of him.

It was almost impossible not to gawk at him, but she did her best to focus instead on the house. She followed him blindly through another doorway, and had to stop short just to keep from plowing right into him.

"Suppose the bottles are included with the price tag?"

She looked beyond the bronzed skin three inches from her nose to the wine cellar they'd entered. More stone. More exposed wood beams. And three walls of racks holding what had to be hundreds of wine bottles inset into the brick walls. And in the center of the room a high, thick plank table surrounded by four simple wooden bar stools.

"This is nicer than some wine tasting rooms I've seen," she said.

"Room must have a separate temperature control. It's cooler in here than the rest of the house." His arm brushed against hers as he pulled a bottle from one of the racks. "What d'ya say?" He nodded toward the table. "There's a wine opener lying right there." He gave her a devilish look. "Might be wrong, but nobody'll know but us."

She wagged her finger at him. "I'm onto you, Grayson Fortune. I think there is probably very little that you do that is actually *wrong*."

"Yeah, or I'd have fired you as my agent as soon as I learned about your boss's stupid ethics rule." He reached out and touched her chin, closing her mouth. "Don't look so horrified, Billie. I've been thinking about kissing you since the day we met. But firing you just so that I *could* would be wrong." He slid the wine bottle back into the rack. He picked up the opener and tapped it twice against the wood table. "Besides. I'm a beer guy."

Her heart was racing. "I like beer," she said after a moment. "And, um, and muck boots."

He gave her a long look. "And high-heeled apology shoes?"

She swallowed. She'd obviously lost her mind. But right then, she wasn't sure she cared. "I like those very, very much, too."

With slow deliberation, he placed the wine opener down on the table, and with just as much deliberation, placed his hands on her waist, sending her nerves into a frenzy.

"And if I kissed you?"

She looked at the faint cleft in his chin. At his perfectly molded lips. His deep brown eyes. She couldn't lie to save her life. "I think I'll like that more than apology shoes."

His fingers tightened slightly, drawing her closer. "Not afraid of what your boss would say if he knew?"

She moistened her lips. "Not…not right at the moment."

He smiled slightly as his head lowered toward hers. "When's the last time you kissed someone, Billie?"

"I can't remember," she breathed.

Then his lips met hers. Brushed lightly. Cautiously.

Her head still spun and it felt like the earth was falling away. But then she realized he was lifting her onto the table. Bringing her up to his eye level. Her knees just sort of naturally parted to allow him to step even closer.

She wasn't even aware that she'd lifted her hands until she felt his warm, bare skin against her palms. She pressed her fingertips against his chest muscles. "When's the last time you kissed someone?"

"Strange," he whispered back. "I can't remember, either."

Then his mouth lowered again, and this time, there was nothing cautious about it at all.

Sensation grabbed her by the soul and shook her hard. So hard, that when he lifted his head again and lightly rested his forehead against hers as they both caught their breath, she knew that if ever there was a good excuse to get fired, being kissed by Grayson Fortune was it. It was all she could do not to tug him down on top of her right there on the tasting table.

"Well, that seals it," he said huskily. His fingers trailed lightly up and down her spine, sending all manner of shivers dancing through her.

"Seals what?"

"I have to buy this place now."

It took a minute for his words to make sense. But when they did, she planted her palm against his chest and pushed him back a few inches. "What?"

"I'm going to buy this place."

She blinked. "Just like that?"

"Just like that."

"But...but all you've seen of the house is the wine cellar!"

His lips curved. "Doesn't matter. It's my lucky house." He brushed his thumb over her lower lip. "It's where I got to finally kiss you." He dropped another mind-melting kiss on her lips, then pulled her off the table. He didn't seem to care that her legs were almost useless as he nudged her toward the door "Now get on it, sweetheart. Go make the deal!"

Chapter Nine

Thirty minutes later, it was done.

Billie wasn't sure if she felt faint because she'd just negotiated the largest deal of her career, or if it was still the aftereffects of kissing Grayson.

Either way, it didn't really matter.

"Thanks for your time, Bob," she said to the seller's broker. "I'll get the paperwork over to your office as soon as we're back in town."

"Your client's getting a heck of a deal," he said in return. "You ever decide you want to get out from under DeForest Allen's thumb, I'll have a desk waiting for you here at Crenshaw."

She was smiling as she ended the call and went to find Grayson, who'd tired of pacing around the enormous living room while they waited for the seller's response to the offer he'd made.

She found him stretched out on the wide ledge of

the swimming pool. Cowboy hat propped over half of his face. Still shirtless. One arm trailing in the glittering water.

She was still wearing only her socks, so there was no way he could have heard her footsteps as she neared.

But he still moved his hat and swung his feet down as he sat up, his sinewy muscles bulging, his abs rippling. "Well?"

He was everything the good Lord must have intended when designing a man.

She managed to drag her eyes up to his.

"If they're balking because we offered a hundred thousand less than they were asking, tell 'em I'll give 'em full price *and* buy their dang wine to boot." He pushed to his feet.

She shook her head. "They accepted your offer. All we have to do now is get it in writing."

It seemed to take a moment to sink in.

But then he whooped and swung her right off her feet, spinning her around in a circle.

She laughed, caught in his infectious exhilaration. He finally set her back on her feet and grabbed her hand to pull her back into the house. She automatically turned to head for the front foyer, but he had different ideas.

"I want to look at the rest of my house."

She thought of the paperwork that needed to be done as quickly as possible, and dragged her heels. Which, considering they were covered in cotton socks and the floor was covered with slick tile, turned out to be fairly ineffective. "You should have looked while I was on the phone with the owner's broker. A verbal agreement can still go awry, Grayson."

"It won't." He'd pulled her, sliding along the floor, right to the rear staircase that led to the upper floor. "I told you. This is my lucky house. Either pick up your feet, darlin', or I'll pick 'em up for you."

She knew the basement contained the wine cellar, a workout room and another all-purpose room. The main floor had the kitchen, living and dining areas. The upper, the bedrooms.

And after that kiss in the wine cellar, she wasn't sure it was all that wise getting anywhere near a bedroom. The house might be vacant, but it still had enough furnishings so that it showed well to prospective buyers. It was entirely likely there were beds in the bedrooms.

"Grayson—"

"Too late. Seconds are money in my business, sweetheart." He picked her up as if she weighed nothing and tossed her over his shoulder before starting up the stairs.

"Grayson!" Her head bumped against his back and she tried to lever herself up, but his arm was clamped over her backside, keeping her firmly in place. "I'm not a sack of potatoes!"

"I am well aware." He patted her rump.

She couldn't help herself. She giggled. Gave a silent apology to independent women everywhere, then giggled some more and stared down at *his* very fine jean-clad rump.

If her boss were to see her now, he'd be apoplectic and she'd be looking up Bob Crenshaw for a place to hang her real estate license.

Fortunately, DeForest Allen wasn't ever going to know about any of it. At least not before the deal was done. And then she'd have such a whopping commission to her credit it would all be moot.

When they reached the top of the stairs, Grayson pulled her slowly down from his shoulder and she forgot all about giggling. Even though every cell in her body was singing from the contact, she quickly evaded the hands he tried to loop around her waist. "You can look the rest of the house over, but then we really *do* have to get back to my office."

"Your fishbowl, you mean." He hooked her around the waist from behind and kissed the back of her neck.

She shivered and wriggled out of his hold again. "This isn't a rodeo, Grayson. Come on."

"Killjoy," he said, grinning lazily. He waved his hand. "Let's get the thirty-second tour so we can get on to your all-important paperwork."

She gave him a look. "It's *your* paperwork," she reminded him. "I'm not buying a house, two barns, a guest house and a hundred acres. You are."

Grayson's brain still felt rattled from the wine cellar. "Speaking of which. I'd better warn my mother so she can set the money part in motion. She's still in Reno, hanging out with some old friends until I go back." Before he could ask, Billie gave him a knowing look and handed him her cell phone. He placed the quick call as they made their way around the upstairs. There were four bedrooms, each one larger than the last, until the master suite.

Then he stood there in the center of the enormous room, staring out the wall of windows that afforded anyone lying in the bed opposite an unfettered view of rolling hills and pristine lakefront. "Damn. That's a helluva view."

"That's *your* view." Billie padded across the plush carpet and into the en suite bathroom. "Damn."

Her soft exclamation drew him. "What?"

"Three closets." She gestured. "You can pack a lot of pairs of Castletons onto those shelves."

He briefly stuck his head inside the closets, which all led off a bathroom the size of his bedroom back in Paseo, then tapped the toe of his boot against the claw-foot tub situated in a bay of windows. "Nice."

"Wouldn't have taken you for a bath guy."

His imagination didn't need a lot of encouragement when all he had to do was look at Billie to get ideas. She was such a slender thing, they'd both fit in the tub just fine. With only enough space to make things really interesting. "I guess that depends on the company."

Her face flushed. But she didn't look entirely disinterested. He started to reach for her again, but she stiff-armed him, and sidled away. "You've seen the bedrooms. Nothing alarming that makes you want to back out?"

Still smiling, he shook his head. She had no way of knowing he wasn't thinking about the house, at all.

"Okay, then. We have *got* to go." She aimed straight for the stairs and practically skipped down them. She was either afraid to let him get too close or really was in a helluva rush to get to the paperwork end of the real estate deal.

In the foyer, she grabbed his shirt and tossed it at him, and was sitting outside pulling on her rubber boots by the time he joined her. Then she locked the house and stuck the key back in the box.

"What happens to the lockbox now?" With an agreement to his offer to buy the house, he didn't particularly want anyone else having access to the place.

"The seller's agent will pick it up." She started walking toward the car.

It was a toss-up which preoccupied him more. The sight of her denim-covered rear end sashaying ahead of him, or the reality that he was really buying a new home. It was no longer just an idea circling in his head.

Which had him also thinking about the other ideas that had been in his head, too.

He'd just agreed to spend a truckload of hard-earned money. Yeah, he could afford it. But it made a man tend to rethink whether he ought to give up one of the sources of his income or not. Bulldogging was going good. He wanted another championship to his credit, but he didn't *have* to give it all up once he'd achieved it.

They'd reached Billie's car and he looked at her over the roof of it. "What happens after the paperwork?"

"Your earnest money will be deposited in the escrow account while the title company does their thing." She got inside and started up the engine and turned on the AC. "We know the sellers are agreeable to the short escrow you want, and unless something comes up during title or the inspection, you should be able to take possession within a few weeks."

He was the one who'd insisted on the short time frame, so he knew there was no point feeling skittish now. "Middle of next month." After the Cowboy Country Rodeo, he was going to be busy as hell. His rodeo standings were good right now, but that didn't mean he could sit back on his laurels. Not when there were others right on his heels, ready to take his place in the rankings if he gave 'em even half a second. "I won't be able to be around much," he warned her.

"I know," she said calmly. "Cowboy Christmas and all. Don't worry. It'll work out."

He gave her a sidelong look. "What if I need to sign something important and I'm way the hell out in Timbuktu?"

"We *can* do digital signatures these days, you know. All you need is your computer."

He grimaced.

"Oh, what? You don't like computers as well as cell phones?"

"Not much, since I learned the founder of the company that makes both happens to be my old not-so-dear dad."

She lightly touched his hand. "If there is any paperwork that requires your signature, I'll have it messengered to you. Simple enough?"

"Or *you* could bring it." He turned his hand, capturing hers. He ran his thumb over her smooth skin. "Better yet, just come with me."

She gave him a startled look. "Come with you where?"

"Back to Reno. On the road. I'd sort of planned on retiring from bulldogging after this season, but now I'm rethinking it."

She pulled her hand from his, placing it back on the steering wheel. "You're not serious."

"About retiring? Or about having you come with me?"

"Either. Both."

"Never more so. For either. For both." On the other hand, she looked fit to strangle the steering wheel.

"And what would I do?"

He discarded the flippant "me" that was the easy response. "Whatever you like." He offered a grin. "Even on a Robinson Tech device."

"Grayson, I have a job. I can't very well do that if I'm… I'm on the road with you."

Shrugging just then was no harder than it had been six years ago after his final saddle bronc ride, when he'd had to push to his feet from the dirt and wave his hat to a crowd of fifty thousand people even though he'd just cracked two ribs and separated his shoulder. "Yeah, sure. It's not for everyone."

She looked dismayed. "It's not that I don't appreciate the—"

He waved his hand. "Don't worry about it, darlin'. It was just a spur-of-the-moment thought."

She didn't look convinced.

And why would she, when he couldn't remember spewing such bull before?

She was silent for a long moment. "You're still good on buying the ranch, right?"

He barely hesitated. "A deal's a deal."

She smiled slightly. "Okay. Good." Her fingers wrung the steering wheel a few more times. "Great."

He looked out the side window and for once was glad for her lead-foot driving.

The office was empty when they got there. It meant there weren't any lookey-loos watching their every move, but considering everything, he almost wished there had been. At least it would have provided a distraction.

Instead, he paced the hallways while she prepared the paperwork he needed to sign. There were a lot of offices. He wondered if his deal would bump Billie into one of the larger ones.

He wondered if he'd read too much into things. If the universe was finally paying him back for all the times he'd kissed and moved on without a second thought.

He wondered if she'd gone along just for the sake of a freaking real estate deal.

"Grayson?"

He looked away from the office obviously belonging to her boss. She was walking toward him, carrying a thick packet of paper.

Maybe her boss's rule against romantic entanglements wasn't so far off the mark, after all.

"Are you ready to do this?" She held up the pen.

He'd walked into this office with the intention of finding a ranch of his own, he reminded himself. Nothing had changed since then, even though Billie had worked so far beneath his skin he'd let himself forget all his basic rules of life. "That's what I'm here for." He took the pen and walked into the nearest open door—clearly a conference room.

She set the packet down on the long table, explaining each item with painful detail. He wished for some of the speed she saved for her driving. But finally, they got to the part where he needed to sign. And as soon as he did, he handed her back the pen. "Congratulations."

"You're the one who should be congratulated. This is an exciting day for you."

"Finding my *forever* home?" He managed a smile. He could always turn the wine cellar into a trophy room. If he was lucky, maybe a complete remodel would get rid of the memory of kissing her. That wouldn't dissolve the images from their water fight at the pool, though. It wouldn't eradicate the sounds of her laughter, or the intense notion of looking out at that lakefront view from the master bedroom with her lying by his side. "Maybe it'll get you into a bigger office, at least."

"I don't know about that, but it might make up for the Dickinson situation."

"What's the Dickinson situation?"

"It doesn't matter anymore." She toyed with the pen. "Grayson, about your offer..."

He wasn't a teenage kid. He shouldn't feel like everything inside him froze, waiting for her next words. "I told you—"

"I know. Spur-of-the-moment." She moistened her lips. "It's just, well, I'm flattered and...and tempted, frankly. But my job—"

"Tempted." He latched on to the word. "Are you saying that because you were afraid I'd back out of the contract?"

She looked troubled. "No. Of course not."

"You don't even look convinced of it."

"Grayson." She made a frustrated sound and tossed the pen onto the conference table. It rolled off the other side. "I've worked really hard to get to this point in my career. I didn't plan any of this. I don't know if you entirely realize what a whirlwind you are. Walking away to go on the road with you isn't the kind of decision that I can make at the drop of your cowboy hat. I've made commitments here. I have bills and—"

He cupped her shoulders and she broke off, staring up at him with her pretty brown eyes. "Then put a pin for now on the road part. After I'm done in Reno, come to Red Rock with me while I deal with the Castleton folks." He could see he was making headway and pressed his advantage. "It's only a couple days. And you can think about the rest. I've already got a suite reserved at La Casa Paloma. It's a resort. You've got pools you can dangle your pretty toes in. Spa treatments. Anything you like. The suite has two bedrooms. You can lock your bedroom door if you're worried about your virtue."

Her soft lips parted. "And if it isn't *my* virtue I'm worried about?"

He leaned down until his lips brushed her earlobe. "If it weren't for the security cameras around this place, I'd show you." He straightened again.

Her eyes had darkened. Rosy color rode her cheekbones. "I'll think about Red Rock," she said huskily.

He drew his finger along her cheek. "There's a great Mexican restaurant there called Red. You can wear my apology shoes."

"I said I would *think* about it!"

Despite the cameras, he leaned down again and brushed his mouth over hers. Not as long as he wanted. Definitely not as deep as he wanted. But it was still enough to leave her breathing unsteadily.

Then he straightened, because they both heard the chime of the front door as someone else entered the office. A second later, her boss came into view through the glass walls.

Grayson went around the table to retrieve the pen.

Then, intent on keeping the progress he'd made from slipping away again because of her boss's untimely arrival, he handed her the pen.

Their fingers brushed.

"I'll be thinking about it, too, Billie," he promised softly. "I'll call you from Reno."

Then he left, giving DeForest Allen a brief nod when they met in the hallway. "She deserves a bigger office," he said without pausing. "Particularly when my Western-wear company starts looking for a new commercial space later this year."

He'd just reached the front door when he heard Billie's exclamation. "Commercial space!"

Smiling, he headed out into the afternoon sun.

"Are you thinking about Red Rock?"

Billie was sitting on the love seat on her terrace, watching the sunset. She cradled the phone against her shoulder and slid down a little until she could prop her bare feet on the table. If she stretched, her toes would brush the cashmere-colored box containing the apology shoes.

"Who is this, now?"

The sound of Grayson's low chuckle made her shiver. "Funny girl."

"Oh, that's right." She curled her toes and the tattoo ring temporarily disappeared. "The guy with the dimple in his chin who doesn't like phones. Whose phone are you borrowing this time?"

"There are still such things as pay phones, sweetheart."

She immediately imagined him standing next to some old phone hanging on the wall, his cowboy hat dipping as he fed coins into it.

"So, are you thinking?"

It had been forty-eight hours since he'd left her office. Forty-eight hours of thinking about him. About Red Rock. About the fact that—wise or not—she wanted to go with him and she had no intention of locking her bedroom door when she did. "Yes, I'm thinking."

"So am I." His deep voice dropped even deeper. "Want to know about what?"

He was over a thousand miles away, but he might as well have been sitting right next to her. Every cell in her body hummed. "How about I tell you how your escrow is progressing?"

"Some might consider that a buzzkill."

She smiled into the sunset. Her terrace was peaceful, but in Grayson's background, she could hear music on the loudspeakers and the rodeo announcer's voice. "Some might. I've scheduled the inspection for tomorrow."

"Thrilling."

"It will be once you know you won't be looking at replacing a roof the second you move in, or dealing with a foundation leak or something just as bad."

"It's my lucky house. Everything is going to be fine. Don't be a worrywart."

"It's my job to be a worrywart on behalf of my clients. Particularly ones who were ready to plunk down a fortune on a property as is. And you know, you really threw my boss into a tizzy with that line about Grayson Gear needing new space. It's all he's talked about for two days."

"We do need new space. Ask my manager, Jess. She's been harping on it for over a year."

"I haven't done a lot of commercial real estate. You'd be better off with one of our associates who has."

"I don't want one of your associates. I want *you*."

Her stomach swooped, taking the words in an entirely intimate way. Her brain, however, was determined to stay the course. "I wouldn't want my inexperience to adversely affect your company."

"You don't want the business?"

"Well, of course I want it. But—"

"If anyone else but me dangled that in front of you, would you hesitate?"

She couldn't help but smile wryly. "No."

"Well, then, sweetheart, buck up. One of the first things I liked about you was that you've got grit."

"Oh. Flattering. Compare me to John Wayne, why don't you."

"John Wayne doesn't turn me on like the thought of you going all 'real estate' on me." He waited a beat. "What're you wearing?"

She had to take a second to catch her breath. But two could play that game. "Maybe I'm lying in my bathtub, surrounded only by bubbles."

"Ah, sweetheart," he drawled. "You're killing me. But I'll bet you're really sitting on your patio wearing cutoffs and a Rice T-shirt, with a bottle of wine and a package of cookies on the table in front of you."

She laughed softly. The wine was there. As yet unopened because he'd called her before she had a chance to use the corkscrew. But a pair of outrageously expensive shoes replaced the cookies of his version.

It was silly that she'd brought the shoebox out and set it on her coffee table. The truth was, though, that she'd been keeping the box close by no matter where she was in her apartment. And it wasn't so much the shoes themselves, but more what they represented.

Or maybe even *who* they represented.

No matter how tempting, the shoes inside the box felt unattainable.

The same thing could be said of Grayson.

Despite his persistent pursuit, she was afraid to let herself believe anything long-term would come out of it.

"I'm right, aren't I? See how well we've gotten to know each other?"

"Let's just say you're close." She decided it was safer not to tell him that the cutoffs and T-shirt were in the dirty laundry, so she was wrapped in a silky robe that didn't do a darned thing to soothe her hypersensitive nerves.

She stretched out her foot a little farther and nudged the lid off the shoebox. The red soles inside beckoned. She leaned forward, intending to grab the wine bottle and opener. Instead, her fingers drifted to the shoes. And it was a foregone conclusion that they'd end up on her feet from there.

Propping her high-heeled feet up on the table, she eyed them and sighed a little. It was much too easy remembering the feel of Grayson's long fingers on her ankles when he'd slid them on to her feet.

"Now what're you doing?"

A hot flush ran under her skin. She quickly slid the shoes off again, tucking them safely right back into the box. "Nothing."

She could practically hear the slow smile on his face. "You're wearing the shoes."

Her bare toes pushed the box a few inches away as if he could see her. "No, I'm not."

"You might as well accept it, sweetheart. Those shoes are meant for you."

Like he was meant for her?

She tried to banish the fruitless thought, but it wouldn't go. "They're too extravagant and I *will* be returning them to you. So accept it. *Sweetheart.*"

"Aww. That's your first 'sweetheart.' You're making my heart go all pitter-pat."

She laughed. "You're nuts."

"Well, I could get serious and promise that one day, you'll wear those shoes and nothing else while we make love." He paused, making her wonder if he could hear the sound of her pounding heart right through the phone line. "But…I wouldn't want to scare you off. Not when you're supposed to be thinking about Red Rock."

Her head fell back against the cushion. "You're relentless."

"When there's something I want? That's what has got me where I am today, sweetheart."

"In Reno. A thousand miles away."

"Closer to two. It's only a plane ride, Billie." He sounded serious. "Say the word. And I'll get you here in a matter of hours."

Word.

She closed her eyes. "The inspection is tomorrow. And after that, I have to go to Houston."

"What's in Houston?"

"The rest of my furniture."

"So you *do* have more than boxes?"

She smiled. "I have a couch, even. It's been stored

in my old neighbors' garage. But they're moving into a house soon that I helped them find, so one of my brothers, Ted—he has a pickup—is going with me to get the last of my stuff. It won't take us long. What about you? Will you have a lot of stuff to move to your new place?"

"I've got my horses, my gear and my bedroll."

"Sounds like you'll be doing some furniture shopping, then."

"Maybe for a bed." His voice dropped a notch. "It'll go against the wall where it'll overlook the lake. What do you think?"

"I think we should talk about something else."

He laughed softly.

She cleared her throat. "Why are you reconsidering retiring? Why were you even considering it in the first place?"

"*That's* what you want to talk about?"

It was a safer subject than her future, which seemed so much less certain than it had just a few weeks ago… before he'd walked into her office. "I've got you on the phone," she said lightly. "I figure I'd better take advantage of it."

"I'm thirty-seven, Billie. Bulldogging's hard work."

"There've been successful steer wrestlers older than you."

"And there've been unsuccessful ones, too. I've been thinking about it for a long time. If I'm gonna quit, I want to quit on top."

"On your terms." Ego, she understood. "When did you start reconsidering?"

"When I found myself buying a ranch twice as big as I'd figured I'd want."

All because he'd kissed her in a wine cellar. As romantic gestures went, it was a pretty huge one. "You need the money. If you've changed your mind about buying the ranch, better to do it now, rather than later."

"I *want* the money. No offense, Billie, but you of all people should understand that. You told me yourself you chose your career because of the income potential."

She'd told him she was tired of hand-me-downs. But the bottom line was the same. She wanted—needed—to be self-sufficient. Trotting after him on the rodeo circuit flew right in the face of every goal she'd ever had. "What you're spending on the ranch will take more than a few years at the top of the money rankings to recoup, won't it?"

"It's not the rodeo money. It's the endorsement deals I have as a result. Billie, I can afford the ranch. I could afford two of 'em and not really sweat it. But I spent more of my life *not* having money than having it. So it's kind of second nature for me to hold on to it when I can."

Except when he was donating small fortunes to help fund the work that his foundation did.

"You're an interesting man, Grayson Fortune."

"Well, hell, Billie. Next thing you'll be saying is that I'm a good friend."

She smiled slightly. "From your tone, I take it that is bad."

"It is when it's coming from the girl I'm tryin' to woo."

Her smile widened. "I've never been wooed before."

"Not even by the guy who inspired the toe tattoo?"

She wriggled her toes. "Not even by him."

"Does it earn me any points?"

She stared out at the glorious sunset. Imagined the same view from a lakefront bedroom with him by her side. "You're sure not losing any."

Chapter Ten

"You know he got her freaking pregnant, right?"

Billie nearly jumped out of her skin at the sound of the furious voice. "Max! I thought you were still in Reno!"

Her cousin stepped into her office cubicle and planted his hands on her desk, leaning toward her. "Did you hear what I said?"

She looked nervously at the glass walls surrounding her. It was Wednesday afternoon and the office was hopping. "Keep your voice down. There are people here trying to conduct business." She pushed him toward her side chairs. "Sit down."

He didn't budge. "How could you, Bill?"

"Who is pregnant? And what do *I* have to do with it?"

"He'll just use you, same as he did her. And then he'll throw you away, same as he did her."

"What are you talking about?" But her stomach was already sinking.

"Who do you think? Your new boyfriend, Grayson the Great. What the hell, Billie? Did you forget what loyalty to your family was all about?"

She hopped up from her chair and it rolled back, knocking noisily into her filing cabinet. "Keep your voice down!" She grabbed his arm and hauled him down the hall and into one of the conference rooms. It was surrounded by glass, too, but full walls of it that afforded a fair measure of soundproofing. She pushed the door closed and looked at him. "Grayson's a client." It was the understatement of the year. "And how'd you even hear about that?"

He shoved back his cowboy hat. "Are you kidding me?"

She frowned at him. "Did Grayson tell you?" They were both competing at the rodeo in Reno. She still hadn't given Grayson any reason to connect her with Max, but she had no idea what kind of conversations went on between men when they were hanging around waiting to wrestle an enormous animal to the ground.

"Like I'd listen to anything *he* said." Max's voice was filled with disgust. He'd pulled out his cell phone and was fiddling with it. "There." He flipped the phone between his fingers so she could see and hear the video playing on the screen.

"Is she the reason for the five million dollar house you're buying in Austin?"

"Y'all know me better 'n that. It's just business."

With a swipe of his finger, Max silenced Grayson's words. "Two of you didn't look like you were doing much *business*."

It was from the night they'd been to La Viña. It seemed so long ago, but had really been less than a week. "Where did you find that?"

"I didn't have to find it. It's all over the news that

he's buying that big ol' Southfork-sized ranch outside of town." He made a face. "'Is Grayson finally settling down?' That's the question the media keep asking. Geez, Billie, I knew you were still crushin' on him. I can't believe you worked with the guy after what you know about him!"

"I had a job to do, Max. It's not like I can afford to pick and choose who my clients are!"

He waved his phone in her face. "And you can't choose who you're hitting up the latest hot spot in Austin with?"

"It was a business dinner," she said through her teeth. *The business of you falling for Grayson, maybe.* "Look, Max. I'm sorry if you think I've betrayed you, but none of this was about you!"

His look turned pitying. "You still don't get it. She. Is. Pregnant."

"She *who?"* Even as the exasperated words burst from her, she realized the answer. "Bethany."

"Bethany." Max rubbed his hand over his face.

But she still saw the gleam of moisture in his eyes and her shoulders suddenly fell.

This was the boy she'd grown up with. The one who was more a brother than a cousin.

"Oh, Max," she breathed. "You really loved her."

He dropped his hand, glaring at her. "I told you I did. You think I made it up?"

"No, but…" She spread her palms. "You've never been serious before about anyone and I thought—we all thought—it was just another fling."

His jaw worked. He grabbed a chair several spaces down the table and sat in it. "It's his, you know. The baby."

Her stomach clenched. "Grayson's not involved with Bethany. They're just old friends. He told me."

"And you believed him, Little Miss Don't-Believe-in-Love." He snapped his fingers. "Just like that." He leaned forward. "He gave her a job. He gave her money."

Billie didn't want to believe it. "How do you know that?" She couldn't imagine Max actually talking to Grayson about it. Not the way he felt. "Did Bethany tell you?"

His lips twisted. He looked away. "She won't see me."

"Then how—"

"Heard it from his hazer." He made an impatient sound. "Lou Blackhorn. He's Grayson's regular hazer and he's been filling in for Trav for me in Reno."

"This Lou…he told you specifically that Grayson paid Bethany money because she's pregnant with his child." Saying the words made Billie more than a little nauseated.

"No, he didn't tell me specifically, but I heard it all the same. Your boyfriend got her knocked up and now he's moved on to you." He pointed his finger at her.

She shook her head. "You're wrong."

"He's not trying to get into your pants?"

She flinched. "Don't be crude."

Max snorted. "Right." He shoved out of the chair. "Well, next time he does, just remember what I said. He'll use you, same as he used her. And when he's finished, he'll move on to the next and the next and the next." He yanked open the conference room door and stormed down the hall out of sight.

She exhaled shakily, lowering her forehead onto her hands while Max's words rang insidc her mind.

"Billie?" A tentative voice interrupted her misery. She looked up to see Amberleigh's concerned face. "Are you all right, hon?"

She lowered her hands to her lap and nodded. "I'm fine, Amberleigh. Just…just family…stuff."

The older woman nodded sympathetically. “Your two-o’clocks are here to sign papers. I came to find you when you didn’t answer your line. I can see if someone else can handle it. Elena’s in this afternoon, I think—”

“That’s okay, Amberleigh.” Billie pushed to her feet. “The Nguyens are my clients.” Lana Nguyen was also the secretary of Ben Fortune Robinson that she’d mentioned to Grayson.

The same day he’d told her Robinson was his half brother.

“I was just printing out the rest of their paperwork when I got interrupted,” she said around her tight throat. “I’ll be there in a minute.”

“Okay.” Amberleigh gave her an encouraging nod. “Family stuff works out, hon. Don’t forget that.”

Billie smiled sadly. She was sorry that Max was hurt, but she knew that eventually, everything between them *would* work out.

Grayson, however, was another situation entirely.

Why on earth had she ever let herself believe that he would be different? That he was worth risking her entire future on?

He was Grayson Fortune. Flirtation was his stock-in-trade.

Amberleigh’s gaze dropped to Billie’s feet before she started walking away. “Meanwhile, those are some pretty spectacular shoes. They ought to make everything feel better. Are they real?”

Billie looked down at the red-soled pumps. “They’re real,” she murmured. She followed the receptionist out of the conference room. “But they’re going back.”

She just had to figure out the proper way to do it.

* * *

"Just another picture, folks. Grayson, why don't you put your arm around our rodeo queen here?"

It was the same routine he'd followed at hundreds of rodeos. Holding the championship spurs in one hand. Dropping his other arm around a beaming rodeo queen. He'd even done it more than once right there in Reno.

Only difference this time was that Billie was here.

He'd spotted her beyond the glare of the grandstand lights. She hadn't made any move to approach him yet from where she stood off in the shadows, but he'd still recognized her. She wore jeans and a short jacket—not much different than a lot of women there—but he would recognize the shape of her anywhere.

"That's great now, folks. Grayson, how about—"

He lifted his hand, cutting off the photographer. "Sorry." They'd already gotten plenty of pictures. "Have someone I need to see." He tipped his hat to the rodeo queen and headed off to Billie. Anticipation made short work of the walk across the arena.

Until she stepped out of the shadows and he saw the shoebox she was holding.

The leap inside him didn't fully nosedive, though, until he saw the unsmiling look on her face.

He closed the rest of the distance. Ignoring the shoebox, he reached for her shoulders, dropping a kiss on her cool cheek despite the stiffness he felt in her. "This is a surprise. When did you get here?"

"In time to see you win the final round. Everyone thought the numbers were against you, but you surprised them all."

He'd surprised himself, too. Breaking his own fastest time. Setting another record. "If you'd have told me you were coming, I would have made arrangements—"

She shook her head before he could even finish. "I didn't plan at first to come." She looked away. "But I couldn't just send these by messenger, either." She held out the box.

There was no question that it contained the red-soled apology shoes. He didn't take it. "Those were a gift."

"I told you I couldn't accept them. And now…" Her lips twisted. She shook her head again and her sleek hair slid down over her cheek.

"And now…what?"

"Yo, Big G. Sweet run, man." A man in clown makeup brushed past them as he jogged into the arena, where two women on horseback were circling the arena with flags, preparing the boisterous crowd for the next event while rock music blasted from the loudspeakers.

The interruption had been brief, but Billie had still backed away from him even more.

He stifled an oath and closed the distance again. "Let's go somewhere more private."

"It's really not necessary." She sidled away again, holding out the shoebox.

"It damn sure is if you think I'm going to let you shoe and run without at least tellin' me why first." He took her elbow, and steered her around a bunch of giggling teenage girls carrying sodas and cotton candy.

"Hi, Grayson," they chimed like a chorus.

He tipped his hat. "Ladies." But he didn't slow his steps. Nor did he release Billie's elbow, despite her effort to pull free. He aimed away from the lights and the crowds, bypassing the animal pens and heading for where his own trailer was parked out on the dirt. The people they were likely to encounter here were more interested in loading up their horses and their gear and pulling out for the next stop than they were with Grayson and Billie.

"All right." When he reached the side of his horse trailer, he turned to face her. "What bee have you got in your bonnet? Last time you and I talked, you were all but set to go to Red Rock with me."

Her jaw worked from one side to the other.

"Dammit, Billie!" He grabbed the shoebox and tossed it onto the open tailgate of his pickup. "Just talk to me."

Without the box to clutch to her waist, she folded her arms tightly over her chest. "I know about the baby, okay? I know!"

He stared hard. It was nearly dark and there were more shadows than there was light shining from the lampposts. "What baby?"

"*Your* baby!"

He felt a jolt deep inside his gut. No matter how randy his past was, he'd always been damn careful. Considering his upbringing, he knew better than to carelessly make a baby that way. "If I had a baby, I think I'd know about it, darlin'."

"There's no reason to hide it. Max told me. You and Bethany—"

"Max." His brain felt sluggish, trying to keep up. "Max Vargas*?*" He knew Bethany had briefly dangled the younger man from her strings. "How—"

"Max is my cousin." She cupped her elbows, looking miserable.

Whether she was as miserable as he felt seemed debatable at that point. "Your cousin." He waited a beat. "And you're just now thinking to mention it."

"I didn't think it was relevant—"

"Relevant." He'd told her about Jerome Fortune/Gerald Robinson being his father. But she couldn't mention that the guy who'd been dogging his heels for months was her cousin. Grayson resettled his hat, trying to contain his temper. It wasn't often that he lost it, but he knew he was as close to that line as he'd ever been. "When did you think it *might* get relevant?"

"It doesn't matter anymore."

"The hell it doesn't."

"Grayson? Everything all right here?"

Billie startled even more than he did at the sound of his mom's voice. He hadn't heard her approach.

His jaw felt so tight it was hard to speak. "Yeah." He looked from his mom to Billie. "You remember—" Billie, he'd been about to say. But he was too damn mad. Instead he added, "—my real estate agent?"

Deborah smiled, though he could see the concern behind it. "Of course. Billie and I have talked many times since we first met."

"She's Vargas's cousin," he said abruptly.

Deborah's eyebrows rose a little, but she didn't seem to be anywhere near as annoyed about it as he was. "I've always thought it was a small world. Grayson didn't mention that you'd be here. Is everything coming along with the ranch contract?"

Billie tucked her hair behind her ear. She didn't look at him. "Yes, it's progressing just fine."

"Good to hear." His mom gave Grayson a searching look. "Do you want me to start loading up Vix and Van?"

He shook his head. "I'll get to it in a few."

"Well, I'll leave the two of you to it, then." Deborah started walking away.

"I'm not staying," Billie said quickly. She started edging back.

He blocked her path. "You're damn sure not going," he said in a low voice. "Not without explaining yourself."

"Explaining *myself*?" Her gaze darted to his. "What about you and Bethany?"

"I told you we were old friends." He grabbed her arm. "Wait. You think her baby is mine. Because your cousin Max spewed a load of BS about it."

Billie's chin came up. "You deny giving her money?"

"No, and that doesn't mean a damn thing. Neither does my giving her a job at Grayson Gear. She's not pregnant with my kid. If she were, I'd be the first one to tell you. Not Max." He spread his arms. "You know what? You're right. There is no reason for you to stay. From the start, I've been an open book with you. Instead of just telling me the truth about your cousin, though, you'd rather believe whatever line he's feeding you. You want to think the worst of me, you go right on ahead, darlin'. Frankly, I'm too old for that crap."

Even in the thin light, he could see the sheen in her eyes and steeled himself against it.

"Don't worry, though. Your precious real estate deal is still safe. You'll earn your sales commission."

She winced. "I'm not worried about the commission."

"Then why didn't you just tell me about Max?"

"Because at first it wasn't important! You were a brand-new client and that's all." She visibly swallowed. "And by the time it was important," she said in a lower, raw-sounding tone, "I didn't know how."

"What's so tough? 'Hey, Gray. Funny coincidence. One of the guys gunning to dethrone you is my cousin.'"

"Easy for you to say now!" She looked away, folding her arms again.

"You could've trusted me."

Her jaw worked. "We hardly knew each other."

"Bull."

"It hasn't even been a month since we met!"

"I don't care if it's been a week or a year." He pointed at her. "You're the cynic. Expecting the worst when it comes to anything but work. Bethany's baby isn't mine," he said flatly. Clearly. "For the simple reason that I never slept with her. Not even back in the day when I was trying to do exactly that. So next time you talk to your cousin, maybe you can suggest he stop tossing blame around when he oughta be looking in his own backyard."

"You think the baby could be *his*?"

"I don't know. At this particular moment in time, I don't much care. That's their deal." Grayson waved his hand between her nose and his chest. "This, though? The fact that your first reaction is to think the worst about me? That's our deal. Which, as far as I'm concerned, means there is no deal." He reached around her and grabbed the shoebox. "You might as well take 'em, darlin'. They don't mean jack to me." He pushed the box into her hands and turned away.

"Grayson." Her voice sounded thick. "For what it's worth, I *am* sorry."

His steps barely hesitated. "So am I, Billie." Pushing the words out was a helluva lot harder than it should have been. "So am I."

"Anything you want to talk about, son?"

"No." Ignoring his mother, Grayson kept guiding Van into the trailer, where he'd already loaded up Vix. When he'd walked away from Billie to get the horses, he'd known she wouldn't be there when he returned more than an hour later.

And he'd been right.

Considering her anxiousness to leave, she'd probably turned tail and bolted the second he'd disappeared from view.

Knowing he'd told her to go didn't make up any for the sting of knowing she hadn't cared enough to stick around and fight for them.

"You sure?" His mother held up a red-soled shoe.

Even though Billie had left, she *still* hadn't taken the damn shoes.

"I don't want to talk about it."

It was either that or succumb to the urge to punch his fist through the side of the trailer. Which he couldn't do for several reasons.

One, he'd end up breaking his hand.

Two, he'd up having to answer even more questions from his mom.

He ran his palm over Van, needlessly checking the wraps on the horse's legs.

"Grayson."

"I don't want to talk about it, Ma."

"I know those are the shoes you bought for Billie."

That's what he got for having his personal manager write most of the checks to pay his bills. "I said I don't want to talk about it." He'd never once had a woman refuse a gift.

But then he'd never once bought a woman infernal apology shoes, either. Or gotten involved with someone determined to have so little faith in him. Or gotten involved, period.

He climbed out of the trailer again to where his mother was standing. "Throw the shoes away. Give 'em away. Either way, I don't care."

"Grayson, you don't mean that."

"The hell I don't." He closed the trailer doors and secured them. "I want to get on the road. It's a long haul to Red Rock." Made even longer by the fact that he was pulling a trailer and two horses that periodically needed a decent break from the ride.

They took care of him in the arena. It was up to him to take care of them outside of it.

Deborah tucked the shoe back into the box with its mate. "Maybe I should go with you."

"Why?" They'd already made the travel plans. She was flying back to Texas in the morning, with the intention of spending a few days in Paseo before meeting him in Horseback Hollow for the rodeo next weekend.

"Because you're obviously upset. Clearly, Billie is special to you."

"Might be time for a vision check." He dropped a kiss on his mom's forehead just to reassure her. "I'm pissed off, but I'm not gonna drive a fortune in horseflesh and equipment off the road because of it."

"But—"

"Ma, enough."

She exhaled noisily. "It's not a sin to admit you're hurt, Grayson. I'm not so old that I don't remember how it feels."

"You'll never be old." He started walking around the trailer, automatically checking every latch.

Deborah's voice followed him. "If you think that's flattering enough to distract me, you're wrong."

He ignored that. She was standing right where she'd been when he made it around the trailer. "You going to be okay getting from the hotel to the airport in the morning?"

She made a face. "Strangely enough, I think I will be." She was having a late dinner with a group of rodeo sponsors, and she had her own rental car. "Don't worry about me. Worry about what's going on between you and Billie."

"Nothing's going on. Not anymore." His lips twisted. "If it ever had a chance, her habit of thinking the worst took care of it." He shot his mom a look. "And I am *not* talking about it."

"I don't know whose stubbornness you inherited more of. Mine or your—"

He raised his palm. "Don't even say it."

"Well, unsaid or not, it's still true. If either one of us had been less stubborn, who knows what might have happened."

God help him. At least with hours on the road ahead of him, he wouldn't have to listen to anyone or anything but his own thoughts.

And those he could drown out thanks to the miracle that was satellite radio.

Chapter Eleven

"You're dating Grayson?"

"Can I meet him?"

"Why haven't you been returning my calls?"

Billie had barely arrived at her parents' annual Fourth of July barbecue when the questions started accosting her.

"Happy Fourth," she said in return as she placed the tray of brownies she'd brought onto the table set up in the grass near the back door.

"Belinda Marie!"

She ignored her mother for the moment and bypassed the inflatable kiddie pool filled with teenagers as well as kiddies, then weaved around the others sprawled in lawn chairs near the television that had been dragged outside, and finally made it to her father, where he was tending the meat sizzling on the grill. She kissed him on the cheek. "Hi, Daddy. What you got cooking there?"

He waved his long-handled tongs. "Usual ribs and chicken. How's work?"

She thought about the check that she'd received the day before. The check that was still sitting in her purse.

The sale on the Harmon ranch had gone through in record time. And the payment was her share of the commission.

"Closed on a property just yesterday."

"Get enough commission to pay your rent?" He winked through the barbecue smoke swirling around him.

"A few months." It was a wild understatement. Hands down, it was her largest commission yet. But she'd never been less excited about a sale closing since she'd first gotten her real estate license. Even the new, larger office that Mr. Allen had assigned to her hadn't generated any feeling of accomplishment.

"Good for you, baby. Run and get me another beer, would you?"

"Sure." She headed for the insulated cooler that was sitting in the shade of a tree, where her eldest brother was stretched out on a lounger. As she bent over the cooler, she could see the television screen several feet away. From experience, she knew the channel wouldn't stay the same for long. Between the Cowboy Country rodeo, baseball and NASCAR, there were a lot of things they'd be watching.

She looked the other way and plunged her hand into the ice and water filling the cooler. She had no intention of even inadvertently catching any of the rodeo.

"Hey, peanut." Her brother barely moved the cowboy hat covering half his face. "What's the deal with the rodeo king?"

"Not you, too, Ray."

He lifted his hat far enough that he could give her a

stern look. "I'm not sure I like the idea of you sleeping with that guy. He's got quite a reputation."

"According to who? Max?" She pointed her finger at her brother. "First, I'm not sleeping with him, but even if I were, it's none of your business."

"You're my baby sister. That makes it my business."

She gave him a look. "Interesting, when you've never seemed to care in the least who I might have been sleeping with before now."

He looked pained. "My ears! You're too young to be sleeping with anyone. Especially a walkaway Joe like Grayson. He's a rodeo rider, peanut. And to hear Max tell it—"

She raised her hand. "Max is misinformed." She would regret to her dying day assuming Max was correct about Bethany's pregnancy, even though it didn't change anything. "Grayson's also a business owner and a philanthropist, in case you're interested in the facts. None of which matters because I'm *not* involved with him!"

Her voice rang out in the sudden silence that just naturally had to fall right then.

She looked at the expectant faces around her.

She focused first on Selena. "I'm sorry, sweetheart. But I don't think I'll be able to introduce you to Grayson. My business with him is done." And after the things they'd said in Reno, she had no expectation of seeing him again now that the real estate deal was concluded.

She hadn't even been present at the closing, as was her usual practice. Instead, the final paperwork had been handled two days ago, entirely in Horseback Hollow, where he was staying for the three-day rodeo.

Selena looked disappointed. "I tried to get Mom and Dad to go to Cowboy Country for the rodeo finals today, but they didn't want to drive that far for just a day 'cause it's too expensive. And I couldn't just go with Aunt Mae and Uncle Larry, 'cause I'd a' had to miss school. Otherwise Max could have introduced us." She waved at the television. "We're stuck watching it on TV."

Billie smiled sadly. "I don't think an introduction would have happened, even if you had found some way to be at the rodeo. Max and Grayson don't exactly get along."

"Why not?"

She exhaled. How much could she explain to a thirteen-year-old?

"'Cause Max wants to be better than Grayson," Peggy said tartly as she joined them. She plucked the forgotten beer out of Billie's hand and stuck it back in the cooler, pulling out a bottled water instead. "Take that to your uncle Hal," she said, handing the water to Selena. Then she wrapped her no-nonsense hand around Billie's arm.

"I don't appreciate you ignoring my phone calls." Her mom pulled her toward the house.

"I wasn't ignoring them." It was an outright lie. "I've just been busy with work."

"Pfft," Peggy said dismissively. She hauled Billie into the oppressively hot kitchen and crossed her arms. "Well?"

"Well what?"

"Don't take that tone with me, Belinda Marie."

Exasperated and miserable, Billie threw out her arms. "What do you want me to say, Mom? Grayson was a client."

"That's all? That's not what the news people have been saying."

She opened her mouth to deny it, but the words wouldn't come.

She swallowed and looked away. "Nothing they're saying in the so-called news is accurate except that Grayson was buying a ranch. It doesn't matter now, though. He thinks I don't trust him because I didn't tell him about Max, and Max hates me because I didn't tell him about Grayson."

"Because of that Bethany Belmont business?" Peggy's lips compressed. "Mae told me everything."

"From her son's viewpoint, I'm sure," Billie muttered. "Max is always quick to overreact."

"He's really hurt this time. He cares more about her than we thought."

"And are you hurt?"

"That Max is mad at me?"

Her mom gave her a look. "Over Grayson."

"It doesn't matter, Mom. Grayson just wanted me to go on the road with him."

Peggy's eyes widened. "He proposed?"

Was her mother listening at all? "Propositioned, more like." She didn't want to think how close she'd been to joining him in Red Rock. Because from there, how easy would it have been to agree to all the rest? "But don't worry." Her throat felt tight. "I know better than to become a Grayson Groupie."

Peggy didn't look convinced. "I think you're still crazy for him. Same way you were when you were Selena's age."

She'd been sixteen, not thirteen, but she knew there was little point in correcting that particular detail.

"Grayson was only a client." Maybe if she said the words often enough, she would start to believe it. "And now he's not. There's nothing more to say about it." She reached for the door once more, only to have it fly open before she could touch it.

Selena grabbed her arm. "Come on. You gotta see."

"The only thing I've gotta do is get something to drink," she countered.

But her young cousin held on. "No, you gotta come." She was aiming toward the inflatable pool where Ray's oldest, Meredith, was floating on her back in the two feet of water.

"Hi, Aunt Billie." Meredith kicked her legs, splashing water over the side of the pool as well as Billie's T-shirt. "Oh, sorry."

Billie managed a smile. There would come a day when she wasn't reminded of Grayson everywhere she turned, but it certainly wasn't going to be that day.

Selena kept pulling her past the pool to the folding chairs surrounding the television propped on its usual sawed-off tree stump. It was the same stump that had supported a TV even when Billie was Selena's age.

"Watch." Selena pushed her toward one of the empty chairs. "They'll show it again, for sure."

Billie resisted. She really, really didn't want to see any of the rodeo. And that could be the only reason her cousin was so insistent. "When did you get taller than me? I'm sure you weren't as tall as me at your birthday party."

"Peanut." Ray had joined the others around the television and he put his hand on her shoulder. "Maybe you should watch."

Billie's mouth felt dry. But the only thing she saw when Selena crouched down on the grass near the television and turned up the volume was a beer commercial. At least it wasn't one of Grayson's. "Thrilling." She tried to turn away.

"Wait."

She exhaled impatiently. "Look, guys. I don't want to see Grayson beat Max. Or Max beat Grayson. Or anyone else beat both of them. I do *not*—" She broke off when the commercial ended and a shot of a rodeo arena filled the screen.

Her stomach tightened.

But it quickly became obvious that it was the tie-down event that was under way. Not steer wrestling at all.

The knots in her stomach began to ease up. "Travis Conrad," she said, as she recognized the competitor. "Max's buddy. Oops." On the screen, the calf had escaped his ties.

"No time for Travis. Bummer." The double zeros flashed on the screen while the rodeo announcer stirred up the crowd to applaud anyway as Travis rode out of the arena.

Before Billie had a chance to look away again, the image flashed to a picture of an ambulance pulling out of the dirt arena. "That there's the fine folks who're gonna transport another one of our Texas boys to the hospital," the announcer drawled. As she watched, the image of the ambulance was replaced by another video clip.

And then she *couldn't* look away.

Just stood there in horror, watching.

Grayson. Flying through the air as he slid from his horse toward the running steer. Only the steer stopped short, and instead of finding purchase on the animal, Grayson slid right past him, landing in a tangle of racing horse legs and steer horns. The hazer's horse went down, rolling right over him, and both animals became even more frenzied as they tried to get away from each other, from Grayson and from the riders who raced in trying to separate them all.

And once they succeeded, instead of rolling to his feet the way she'd watched in countless videos, Grayson just lay there on the ground.

"There's a steer-wrestling wreck if there ever was

one," the announcer said as the very worst of the video started playing again. As if once wasn't enough. "Now, folks, we all know accidents can happen despite everything we do to keep our rodeo athletes safe, but you combine a five-hundred-pound steer and horses going thirty miles an hour and—"

Billie's head seemed to fill with a roaring sound as the video went to slow motion on his cowboy hat rolling from Grayson and finally falling flat amid a cloud of dust.

"—all remember six years ago, Grayson used to compete in saddle bronc, until injuries during the National Finals in Las Vegas sidelined—"

She bolted away from the rodeo announcer's voice and ran into the house, where she'd left her purse.

"Belinda—"

She ignored her mother's call. Once inside, she fumbled in her purse for her cell phone, only to finally upend the contents right on the kitchen counter. Her keys, notes about property listings, lipstick and commission check all scattered. She snatched her phone from the midst of it and quickly found Deborah Fortune's number and dialed.

She wasn't even aware of her mother hovering beside her as the phone rang, until Peggy pushed a chair against the back of her knees and made her sit on it.

Finally, the call was answered. "He's okay, Billie," Deborah said in greeting, sounding breathless.

Billie's insides liquefied. She leaned over, until her head was near her knees. "You're not just saying that? I saw the replay on television."

"The doctor at the arena is pretty certain he's broken a bone or two. But he was conscious and, of course, mad as hell at himself. There's a pilot here who is giving us a lift to the hospital in Lubbock."

She was still ready to think the worst. "He *was* conscious?"

"They've given him something for the pain," Deborah said. She sounded far calmer than Billie felt. "He was asking for you."

Billie lifted her head again. "What?"

"Honey, I know it's a lot to ask, but would you consider meeting us at the hospital?"

Her knots tightened up again. "Why would he a-ask for me? The ranch sale is complete."

"There was a time when I was as single-minded as you." Deborah sounded disappointed. "I guess I wanted to believe there was more between the two of you than—"

"I can get to Lubbock." The decision came out in a rush, so easily it was really no decision at all. "I'll fly or drive. If…if you're really sure he wants me there."

"I'm very sure." Deborah didn't wait a beat. "We'll be in Lubbock within the hour. If you do drive, be careful yourself. The last thing we want is another accident."

"I'll be careful. Mrs. Fortune—Deborah—thank you." Billie's hands were shaking as she ended the call and opened the flight app on her phone. The next flight to Lubbock didn't leave for a few hours, and it was routed through Houston before backtracking to Lubbock. Meaning it was unlikely she'd save any time at all traveling by air.

She pushed to her feet and slid her phone into her pocket. "I'm driving."

"I'll go with you," Peggy said quietly.

Tears burned in her eyes. "Mom."

"You're not driving all that way when you're this upset." She began shoveling the contents of Billie's purse back inside. When she reached the commission check, she hesitated, her eyes widening when she saw the amount. She carefully tucked the check inside the purse and then cupped Billie's chin in her hand. "I warned you that life doesn't follow all the little plans we make."

"The day isn't complete without an 'I told you so' from Mom," Ray said as he walked into the kitchen.

"Because so many days go by when I'm right about so much," Peggy retorted. "Now, I'll just go tell Hal and we'll get on our way."

"It's okay." Billie swiped at her face. "You don't have to ride with me, Mom. We'd just have to figure out how to get you back home again. You know you hate to fly." She gave Peggy a tight hug. "But thank you for offering." She kissed her cheek. "I'll call you when I get to Lubbock."

Peggy looked like she wanted to argue. But then, surprisingly, she subsided. "All right."

Billie couldn't contain her surprise. "That's all you're going to say?"

"Well." Her mother handed her the refilled purse. "When all this is over, I guess maybe we'll let you buy us a new air-conditioning unit, after all."

It was nearly dark by the time Billie reached the emergency center parking lot in Lubbock. She'd made the drive in just under six hours. But before leaving town, she'd gone to her apartment to throw some clothes in an overnight bag. She'd phoned Amberleigh from the road to have her reschedule her appointments for the rest of the week, and only thoughts of Grayson's comments on her lead foot kept her from hitting the gas pedal even harder.

She'd kept the radio on the news stations the whole while, but didn't hear anything at all about him. Not that it surprised her. A rodeo accident generally didn't garner the same media attention that other sporting event catastrophes did. Which meant that for a good portion of her drive, she was entirely out of touch with both ends, Lubbock and Austin.

She locked the car and hurried through the emergency room doors. She figured that she'd have to ask someone to find Grayson's mother first, but the moment she walked through the waiting area to the information desk, she stopped in her tracks, hopeful emotion flooding her at the sight of him standing right there. "Grayson?"

As soon as she said his name, the tall man turned to look.

Disappointment flooded through her. How stupid of her.

It wasn't Grayson at all. Just a near identical version of him. His brother. Either Jayden or Nathan.

The man headed toward her, one hand outstretched. "You're Billie."

She nodded. She felt more than a little punch-drunk with the combination of worry, the long drive and now, feeling like she was seeing double. "You're—"

"Jayden." The man smiled faintly as he squeezed her hand. He hitched his thumb toward the carbon copy who'd walked up beside him. "And this is Nate."

She looked from one face to the next. They were equally as handsome as Grayson. But she didn't feel a speck of the pull that their brother held for her. "How's Grayson?"

"Loopy as all hell," Nathan answered. "He just got out of surgery and the anesthetic's still wearing off. Keeps talking about getting some damn shoes or something."

"Probably got the deal he just inked with Castleton Boots still on his brain," Jayden surmised. "Anyway..." He turned his attention to Billie again. "Mom sent us down here to wait for you. There's not a lot of space in the recovery room." As if he recognized the fact that her knees had turned rubbery, Jayden slid a supportive arm around her shoulders. "They had to put a pin or two in his leg and he's got a concussion. Docs say he might not remember everything that's happened, but he'll heal up okay."

"Except he's not gonna be bulldogging for a while," Nathan added. His voice was a little deeper than Jayden's. His expression a little more closed. "Not the rest of this season, anyway."

She realized that as the men had talked, Jayden had steered her to the elevators.

"He's not going to be happy about that," she said faintly. "I don't think he's ready to retire, even though he's been thinking about it."

"Retire!" Both brothers looked shocked, and she caught the glance passing between them as she stepped into the waiting elevator.

"He's talked to you about that?" Jayden punched the button for the third floor as the doors slid shut.

"I didn't know it was secret."

"It's not," Jayden assured her. "Just didn't know he'd talked to anyone about it besides me and Nate and Mom."

Billie chewed the inside of her lip. She wasn't sure if Grayson's brother was happy about that fact or not. And it made for a very slow climb from the first to the third floor as silence bounced around the elevator car.

Finally, the doors opened again, and the two men waited for her to exit first. Then took a circuitous route until they stopped outside one of several curtained cubicles fanning out from a central nurses' station.

Billie's nerves were at fever pitch. She started to reach for the curtain, but her hand froze in midair. People said all sorts of things when they were under the influence of painkillers and anesthetics.

"You all right, kiddo?"

She looked up at Jayden. "When my dad had shoulder surgery a few years ago, he thought he was an astronaut on a space mission."

His expression softened, making him look even more like Grayson. "You've come this far."

"Might as well go the distance," Nathan added.

She swallowed. "I hate feeling like a ninny," she muttered.

"You're not a ninny. It just ain't all that easy falling in love with a Fortune."

Startled, she stared at Jayden. Nobody had said anything about *love.* "I've only known your brother for a few weeks."

He definitely wasn't cowed by her stare. If anything, he looked like he wanted to smile. "Sometimes that's all it takes."

Nathan nodded toward the curtain. "We're not here to make you go in, Billie. If you've changed your mind, change it now rather than later."

He couldn't have chosen better words to straighten her shoulders. She pulled back the edge of the curtain far enough to see the foot of the hospital bed. A lot of thick white cast extending up and over his knee. A lot of bare, masculine thigh. And a very little bit of white sheet between thigh and hair-dusted chest.

She felt perspiration break out along her spine.

Then Deborah stepped forward, rounding the end of the bed and catching Billie's hands in her own. "Billie, hon." She brushed her cheek against Billie's. "I'm so glad to see you." She gently tugged her into the curtained room.

Billie decided then and there that Grayson's brothers looked more like him than he did lying there right now. His eyes were closed. His face was so pale that the bruises on his temple and his cheek looked purple in contrast.

Deborah drew her unresistingly to the side of the bed. "Grayson, honey, look who's here."

Billie swallowed her instinctive protest not to wake him, and felt afraid to breathe as she waited for Grayson's eyes to open. Waited for him to look at her with the same anger that he'd felt for her in Reno.

"Mom." Jayden quietly caught Deborah's attention. He and Nathan were still standing just outside the border of the cubicle. They'd been joined by an older man with salt-and-pepper hair who struck Billie as vaguely familiar. "Orlando is flying back to Horseback Hollow. Now that everything's stable here, we figured we'd hitch a ride with him and leave the truck here for you."

"Excuse me, hon." Deborah left Billie's side and joined them. "I know you want to get back to Ariana and Bianca." The curtain rattled softly in its track as she pulled it closed behind her .

Billie tuned out their low voices, which were still audible despite the impression of privacy afforded by the curtain, and sank down on the chair next to the bed. She moistened her dry lips, looking from Grayson's ashen face to the monitors surrounding him. One beeping softly. One humming monotonously. He had an IV taped to one arm and some sort of sensor clipped over the tip of his index finger. The leg with the cast from the knee down was suspended several inches off the mattress by an overhead contraption.

"Grayson," she whispered tentatively.

He didn't stir.

Her eyes burned and it felt like a vise had tightened around her throat. "I'm so sorry I didn't tell you about Max. That I didn't believe he was wrong about Bethany without you having to say it. I'm sorry I didn't tell you that I would have gone to Red Rock with you." Unable to help herself, she leaned even closer to the bed. "Or anywhere else," she added hoarsely. "Just open your eyes so I know you're really okay." She slid her hand beneath his on the mattress and her heartbeat stuttered when his lax fingers seemed to tighten against hers. "Grayson? Wake up, sweetheart, please."

"Anywhere." His lips barely moved.

She could hardly breathe. "What?"

"You'll go anywhere." The words weren't much more than a mumble. His thick eyelashes lifted only long enough for her to glimpse a thin slice of dark brown.

But it was enough.

Tears burned in her eyes and she pressed her forehead to his hand, aching sobs jerking through her body.

His hand moved. Pulled away from hers. But only to touch her hair. And then he was still again. When she looked at him, his eyes were closed once more.

But the monitors were beeping softly. Humming reassuringly.

She wiped her face, but the tears still flowed. Not because she'd been saving them up for so many years.

But because he was the kind of man who really could—and would—break her heart.

Chapter Twelve

"Say hello to Selena." Billie turned her phone to face Grayson so that her cousin could see his face.

Grayson offered his trademark grin. "Hello, Selena. How's the riding clinic going?"

On the small screen, Selena's face was beaming. "Great! I'm trying to talk my mom and dad into buying a horse, but they keep saying no way."

Billie tapped her fingers against the edge of Grayson's cast, which was propped on the chair next to her. They were sitting at the kitchen table at his family ranch in Paseo, as they had each morning since he'd been released from the hospital. "I warned you that she'd end up wanting her own horse," she stated. He'd helped her young cousin get enrolled in one of Grayson Good's ongoing riding clinics in Austin.

"I do, but it's okay," Selena said. "Long as I get to ride Molly at the clinic, I'm still happy. She's the best horse ever! My mom and dad said I had to write you a thank-you letter." She held up a small rectangle that had a big pink heart drawn on it. "But I already did. We're gonna mail it today."

"I'm glad you're having fun, darlin'."

The sun could have taken lessons from the wattage in Selena's smile. "Are you gonna be back in Austin soon?"

Billie chewed the inside of her cheek, waiting for Grayson to answer. Even though Mr. Allen was salivating over Austin Elite handling the commercial property search for Grayson Gear, she figured her boss's good graces would only go so far. She'd already been away from the real estate office for nearly a month now while Grayson recuperated. His purchase of the Harmon ranch was complete, but the house was still empty, and he'd chosen to come back to Paseo. It was just easier, he'd said.

Privately, Billie had wondered if he was testing her to see if she really would go with him.

If so, she'd wanted to pass that test. So when he'd been released from the hospital, she'd offered to drive him the long way to his hometown of Paseo. He'd be more comfortable in the big back seat of her car than in the pickup or the private charter plane that Orlando Mendoza—who'd been the one to fly him from Cowboy Country to Lubbock—had offered.

It was only later that Billie had realized why he'd looked familiar.

Because he'd been the man with Lady Whatsername at La Viña the night she'd had dinner there with Grayson. Lady Whatsername who was really Lady Josephine Fortune Chesterfield and a relative of Grayson's, albeit a distant one.

That hadn't stopped Lady Fortune Chesterfield and her fiancé, Orlando, from inviting Grayson and his family to their wedding, being held in a few weeks. The invitation was taped to the old-fashioned white refrigerator because Deborah had already accepted. They owed Orlando a debt of gratitude, she'd said, considering the way he'd helped after Grayson's accident.

It was one small mystery solved. But after three weeks of being in Paseo, a larger one loomed. Because she didn't really know why Grayson wanted her there.

And she couldn't help but feel increasingly antsy.

Deborah told her to have patience. That Grayson had never trusted easily, and the fact that he'd wanted Billie with him in Paseo meant more than any words he wasn't offering.

She hadn't known what to expect when they'd arrived at the remote ranch. She knew that Jayden and his wife lived there. As did Nathan and Bianca and little EJ. And Deborah. If Billie had thought all the bodies there would mean little extra space for her, she'd been wrong.

Grayson hadn't even suggested that she sleep with him. Instead, she was in a small room of her own that had a chair and a window. She'd spent a lot of long nights sleeping alone in a narrow bed, knowing he was only a few doors away.

She looked at him now as he spoke with her niece. "We'll be in Austin next week," he answered Selena. "Have an appointment with the orthopedist."

"Are you gonna get outta your cast?"

He made a face. "Probably not just yet. But maybe they'll give me a smaller one." His gaze slid over Billie. "Something easier to maneuver around with."

All sorts of warmth sprang out inside her, but she knew better than to get too excited, considering he'd been treating her pretty much the same way he treated his sisters-in-law, Ariana and Bianca. Like a sister.

It was maddening.

Frustrating.

And confusing as anything in her life had ever been.

"That'd be cool," Selena was saying. "When will you be able to start riding again?"

Billie tucked her tongue between her teeth. She was more anxious to hear the answer than Selena could possibly be.

"I'd ride right now if I could get myself on the back of a horse, but the crutches tend to get in the way."

Selena giggled. "I mean *rodeo* riding."

Grayson's grin stayed in place, though Billie thought it looked forced. "Don't really know, Selena. That's up to the doctors, still."

The girl made a face. "Well, I hope it's soon. You know Max's head is getting, like, *this* big." She held her hands in the air, so wide apart the phone screen couldn't capture them. "He's winnin' every week, seems like."

"Good for him," Grayson said smoothly.

"He'll never be as great as you, though," Selena assured him, ever loyal despite being related to Max.

"Never say never," Grayson warned. "Your cousin's just startin' out. And I'm..." He shrugged. "Well, I'm laid up with a dang cast on my leg that's itching me like crazy."

Selena wrinkled her nose. "My dad had a cast on his arm last year. It got stinky, too, 'cause he kept getting it wet. Billie, you're not letting Grayson's cast get wet, are you?"

"Grayson's a big boy." Billie ignored the flush in her face. "It's up to him to keep his cast from getting wet."

"But I thought you were there helpin' him."

"She is," Grayson answered easily, into Billie's stymied silence. "In fact, she's gonna help me out to the barn now because whether I can ride 'em or not, I've still got to take care of Vix and Van. So say goodbye to Selena, Billie."

"Goodbye, Selena," she said obediently.

Her cousin waved at them, smiling broadly. "Bye, Billie. Bye, Grayson." A moment later, the screen went black.

Billie set aside the cell phone. "Thanks for not badmouthing Max to Selena." He still wasn't talking to her, no doubt even more entrenched in his opinion since she'd run to Grayson's hospital bedside.

Grayson's lips tightened. "Do you think I'd really do that?"

She handed him his crutches. "I don't know what I think." She moved over to the kitchen door and looked out. She could see the barn that Ariana had told her had been damaged the year before during the tornado but now looked in perfect condition. It was going to be hot that afternoon, so the doors were closed to keep in the air-conditioning. But she could still hear the tinkle of the wind chimes hanging near the door that Jayden kept outside to help orient his blind dog, Sugar.

As she watched, she saw the dog and EJ both running across the patch of grass growing on one side of the barn.

Grayson's new nephew was four. He was a brown-haired ball of energy and Billie wasn't the least bit surprised when she saw Bianca running after her son a few moments later. Then Nate caught them all, and soon they were tumbling on the ground, rolling in the grass.

The three of them so clearly belonged together, the sight made Billie ache inside. Even though both Ariana and Bianca had been incredibly welcoming to her, Billie still knew that *they* belonged here in Paseo, in this incredibly charming but modest ranch house, with their husbands.

Billie was just…she didn't know what.

She looked back at the man responsible for all the uncertainty stirring inside her. If he'd made even a single attempt to kiss her, or to touch her, just once in the last twenty-one days, she wouldn't have felt so adrift. But he hadn't. And it wasn't because he was too unfit with his broken leg.

For heaven's sake, just yesterday afternoon she'd watched him working alongside his two brothers, tossing bales of hay that outweighed her, keeping pace with both of them. All three men had been shirtless and sweating. The only difference was that Jayden and Nathan each had two good jean-clad legs. Grayson had a casted leg sticking out of the jeans he'd torn up one side to accommodate the bulk, while the crutches he was supposed to be using had been tossed aside.

Ariana, who'd been washing dishes at the sink while Billie dried, had nearly been drooling as she'd watched her husband out the window. "Hard to believe there are three of them, isn't it?"

Billie hadn't even been able to articulate agreement.

"Three, four, five, six," EJ had chirped from the table, where he and his mom were looking at a picture book.

Ariana and Bianca had laughed. Billie had had to excuse herself to go off and take a walk. It was either that or a cold shower. And she'd figured a walk would draw less interest, considering how many people shared the limited number of bathrooms in the house.

She could still hear EJ's peals of laughter from outside now as she watched Grayson stand up from the table, fitting the crutches under his arms before heading toward her. Toward the door.

But when she didn't move out of the way, he raised an eyebrow. "What?"

Her heart suddenly felt like it was beating inside her throat. She reached up and slid her hand behind his neck, pulling his head down to hers, boldly fastening her lips to his.

She felt his surprise.

Then his resistance.

Determined not to quail, she added another arm around him, fitting herself tightly against him.

Then he swore, angled his head a little and kissed her back.

One of his crutches clattered noisily against the kitchen counter and bounced off onto the ground as his hand slid behind her back. It traveled beneath the edge of her T-shirt and splayed hotly against her skin.

He tasted like the coffee Ariana had made that morning. Like the peach-studded pancakes that Bianca had prepared. Like maple syrup and the kind of hope that made Billie long to roll around laughing in the grass with him and a boy of their own.

His other crutch clattered against the tile and his hands grasped her arms.

At first, she thought it was just to keep his balance. But she realized quickly enough that he was pulling her hands away. That he was dragging his mouth from hers. Putting distance between them.

His overlong hair was messed, his dark eyes burning between his thick lashes. But it was her breath that was coming fast, as if she'd been running sprints.

Which pretty much described how she'd felt since meeting him. One breathless sprint after another.

"What am I doing here, Grayson?"

His brows pulled together. Instead of answering, he

leaned down, balancing on one leg, and scooped up a crutch, which he stuffed under his arm. Then he reached around her to pull open the door. She knew he wasn't unaffected by their kiss because she could see the evidence for herself. "Horses need exercising." His voice sounded gruff.

She opened her mouth to protest, but didn't know what to say.

Instead, she just watched him clomp out the door, then down the porch steps and toward the barn, seeming to barely even nod an acknowledgment when he crossed paths with Bianca, who was heading for the house.

Billie nudged the door closed and turned away, trying to gather her composure before Bianca could see her.

She might as well have tried jumping over the moon.

As soon as Grayson's newest sister-in-law floated into the kitchen and saw Billie, her eyebrows pulled together. "Honey! What's wrong?"

Billie sank down onto a chair, covering her face. "Nothing." Ever since she'd cried at Grayson's bedside, her tears came much too easily. "Everything."

Bianca snatched a napkin from the holder on the table and pressed it into her hand. "You want to talk about it?"

Billie knew that Bianca was only a few years older than she was. That she already had one failed marriage under her belt, and that she was the little sister of Nathan's best friend, who'd died while he and Nate had been in the military together.

"Not really." Billie swiped at her cheeks, her nose. Then she crumpled the napkin in her fist and proceeded to talk, anyway. "I don't understand him." She grabbed another napkin. "At all. People say women are complicated. But our sex has *nothing* on men."

Bianca smiled sympathetically. "Particularly Fortune men."

"At least Nathan made it plain what he wanted from you! You're married. You and EJ are making a family with him."

"True, but it wasn't as if he just arrived at that conclusion all that easily." Bianca tucked her long hair behind her ear. "At first I didn't think he wanted me, even though he took EJ and me in when we had nowhere else to turn. We lived here in this house with him, but he never took advantage of it. He was very…old-fashioned about it at first."

Billie studied the other woman. "Old-fashioned. As in…"

"He didn't touch me for what seemed the longest time," Bianca said. "Didn't matter how much chemistry we had. Not that I was anxious to move too fast, either, but—" She broke off, smiling ruefully.

"Is it a family trait, then?" Billie scrubbed her cheeks. "Or is it just that Grayson likes the chase better than the actual catch?"

"I can't speak for Grayson, obviously. I'd barely even met him before he was injured. Nathan and I had some stuff to work through. With my brother's death. Then my ex-husband. Ariana and Jayden, too, had to find a way through the fact that she was planning to write about them being the latest secret sons of Gerald Robinson. But the point is, we all found our way."

"How?" Billie pushed to her feet and paced the length of the kitchen and back. "I don't know how to reach him if he won't talk. Or touch."

"The only thing I know is you can't give up when something really matters." Bianca pulled a few juice boxes from the refrigerator. "Does Grayson really matter?"

Billie exhaled. "More than I want him to."

"There's your answer." Bianca held up the juices. "Nathan and EJ want to go for a walk. You're welcome to join us."

Billie managed a smile. "Thanks, but you guys go." She knew it wasn't all that often that Nathan or Jayden had any downtime around the ranch. "Enjoy."

Bianca gave her an encouraging smile. "Keep your chin up, Billie. When things are meant to work out, they seem to do just that."

And when they weren't meant to?

She kept the thought to herself as the other woman left, then nearly jumped out of her skin when the wall phone rang shrilly.

There was no one in the house besides her. Deborah had gone into town before breakfast. Ariana and Jayden had gone off after breakfast to visit some people who lived nearby. "Nearby," Billie had learned, was a relative term, since nothing was really nearby in this remote area of the world. The only reason Billie's cell phone had worked since coming to Paseo was because the town had recently bowed to pressure from some of its residents to put up a cell tower. Until then, the area had been a landline-only sort of place.

The phone kept ringing and she finally reached out, plucking the old-fashioned receiver off the hook. "Fortune residence."

"May I speak with Grayson, please?" The voice was feminine. Throaty. "This is Bethany Belmont."

Billie's fingers tightened on the hard plastic receiver. "He's not in the house right at the moment. Do you want to hold on while I get him?"

"No, that's okay. Is this Deborah?"

"No. She's out, too."

"Oh, well. Would you be able to take down a message for me?"

Billie's jaw felt so stiff it was hard to speak. "Sure."

"Tell him it's going to be a boy. And I, uh, I've thought about what he told me and decided he's right. He'll know what I mean. Have you got that?"

Just what she wanted to do. Deliver messages with inside meanings. "I've got it."

"Thanks. And tell him thanks, too, will you please?"

Billie twisted the coiled cord in her fist. It was wrong to imagine it was Bethany's hair she was pulling, but she did so, anyway. And she wondered what Bethany would say if Billie told her she was Max Vargas's cousin.

"I'll tell him. G'bye." She quickly hung up before her baser instincts took control. Grayson was right—whatever had gone on between Max and the pregnant barrel racer was their business.

Billie exhaled and went outside to deal with her and Grayson's business.

When she reached the barn, it was pretty obvious that he'd had no intention of waiting for her or anyone else to help him with the horses. Because there he was, leaning on one crutch while still managing to wield a pitchfork to spread straw across a stall. Nearby was a wheelbarrow full of the manure and straw he'd obviously already mucked out.

She went over and took the pitchfork from his hand. "You're getting your cast filthy. What if you get an infection or something?"

"We'll never know, 'cause I'm gonna saw the damn thing off if it doesn't stop itching me."

"Maybe your skin wouldn't itch so much if you didn't insist on being Mr. Ranch Man right alongside your able-bodied brothers! You're a terrible patient, you know. Your mom warned me before we left the hospital, and she was right."

Billie finished spreading the straw and turned to the next stall. She grabbed the shovel and scraped it along the floor, dragging out the mess that needed to be cleared first. "Bethany called to tell you that it's a boy." *Scrape, scrape.* "That she thought about what you said and you're right." *Muck, muck.* "You'd know what that meant. And thanks." She pitched the crap into the wheelbarrow and went back for another shovelful.

He was looking at her warily. "That's it?"

She dumped the second shovelful, as well. "Are you expecting another meltdown from me?"

"I'm not sure what to expect from you."

She smiled humorlessly. "That makes two of us, then." She went back for a third shovel, scraping the ground meticulously clean before considering it ready for fresh straw. Doing exactly what she'd learned all those years ago when she'd worked at Rodeo Austin, hoping for a glimpse of the Big G. The Great Grayson.

"You know," she said, as she dumped the last shovelful and grabbed the pitchfork, "I still have a calendar that you signed for me when I was sixteen. I remember everything about that day as clearly as if it were yesterday."

"I'm glad I don't remember."

She winced. "Well. Thanks for that."

"It would just remind me how young you are."

She propped her arm on top of the pitchfork handle and eyed him. "I'm no younger now than I was a month ago when you were trying seduction by shoe. Pretty effectively, too, except that I didn't want to get my butt fired from my new job. The job I've now basically put on hold for you, anyway. Do you want me here or don't you, Grayson? Because I honestly don't know!"

He grabbed the pitchfork, looking impatient. "If I hadn't wanted you here, I would've said so."

"But I have no purpose here!" She waved her hand at him. "You're clearly not in need of a nursemaid. Even if you were, you'd blow it off because you're *The* Grayson. Gotta prove you're all manly-man, even when you've still got bruises from being trampled by two horses and a steer. And you're clearly not in need of a bedmate, or you wouldn't have put me in a separate bedroom!"

"For Christ's sake, Billie. My mother lives in this house, too. What do you want us to do? Get down and dirty right on the kitchen table? I've never let another woman come here with me. Not like this." He raked his fingers through his hair. "You know I want you. But I also don't want to make a mistake that'll end up hurting you!"

She stared at him. "You think I'm not afraid of making a mistake?"

"You've got a normal family, Billie. You don't have to worry that you'll turn out like your bastard of a father!"

"Grayson!"

At the sound of a new voice, they both whirled, to find Deborah standing in the doorway of the barn. She looked pale. But no more so than the tall, commanding-looking man with a head of thick gray hair and Grayson's brown eyes standing there with her.

Billie's stomach fell to her toes as she looked from Gerald Robinson's face to Grayson's.

"What the hell are *you* doing here?" he demanded.

Gerald looked at Deborah.

She lifted her chin slightly. "I invited him," she said clearly.

Grayson's knuckles were white where he was clenching the pitchfork. So white that Billie took a concerned step toward him. Whether because she was afraid he'd pitch the thing across the barn at his father, or because he was still recovering from surgery he'd had less than a month ago, she didn't know.

But it didn't matter.

Because the second she took that step, his head swiveled toward her. *"Don't,"* he gritted.

She froze. "Don't what? Don't touch you? Don't worry for you? Don't love you?" Her eyes flooded with tears and she spread her hands. "Too late for that mistake. Too bad that you asked for me in the hospital. All of this could have been avoided." She'd still be wishing for things that would never be, but at least she'd have never fallen in love with Paseo and the rest of his family, too.

"You're the one who came to the hospital," he said through his teeth. "I woke up and there you were. Strange, but I thought that meant something."

She heard a rushing sound in her head. The only other time she'd experienced it was when she'd been watching the replay of his rodeo accident on television. "You didn't ask for me..." A part of her was aware of Deborah walking toward them.

"Grayson, honey, you had a concussion. They said you might not remember everything that happened that day. But you most certainly did ask for Billie."

He glared at Robinson, who'd followed Deborah. "I remember *he* was in the grandstands. Just like you were in Reno," he said to the man. "Weren't you?"

Gerald inclined his head slightly. "I was there."

Grayson rounded on his mother. "You told me you hadn't seen him in Reno."

"She hadn't." Gerald put his hand on Deborah's shoulder, which seemed to infuriate Grayson even more.

Despite everything, Billie edged closer to him, touching his arm. "Grayson, why don't you sit down?"

"Dammit, Billie!" He shrugged her off. "This doesn't concern you!"

If he'd physically slapped her, it would have hurt less.

She swallowed hard. "You're right." She'd known he would be the kind of man who could break her heart. And even knowing it, she'd still let it happen.

She gave Deborah a painful smile and stepped around her and Gerald.

The only thing she could concentrate on was escape.

So that's what she did.

"You're making a huge mistake, son."

Grayson's molars ground together. He looked from where Billie no longer was to his mother. "The mistake was thinking that *you* would never lie to us. But you did. First about us not having a father. Second about our last name. Third—" he gestured at Robinson, whose presence there was enough to make him want to choke "—about getting involved with him again!"

"We're not involved." His mother's voice was tight.

"Really?" Grayson looked at Gerald's face. "He know that?"

"I know you're angry, Grayson," he said.

At least the old man hadn't called him *son*. "You think?" He threw the pitchfork aside and the sharp prongs dug into a wood post.

"I never knew that your mother was pregnant with you. If I had—"

Grayson cut him off. "And you never knew about all the other women you left pregnant, either, I bet." He advanced on Gerald, moving unevenly because of the damned cast. "The women who started coming outta the woodwork as soon as your favored son, Ben, started looking for all of us poor slobs who got left out in the cold once everyone learned you weren't who you said you were. *Jerome*."

"Grayson—"

"Just because I never talk about it doesn't mean I didn't listen. You didn't want to marry any of 'em except one. The fair Charlotte Prendergast Robinson who—after you'd already abandoned *my* mom—gave you eight legitimate little Robinsons. Or are they really Fortunes, since that's who you really are? It's a little hard to keep straight." Grayson stopped when he got six inches from Gerald's nose. Looked him straight in the eye. "Not my mom. Not Nash's mom. Or Amersen's. Or Chloe's. How many others are there, *Dad*?"

Deborah pushed between them. "Stop this right now! You don't know the whole story, Grayson."

"I don't need to know." He looked at his mom. She'd been the linchpin of their family. Made of leather and steel. Jayden said she'd always had to be, raising three sons on her own in Texas the way she had. "You didn't know he was in Reno. Fine. Did you know he was at Cowboy Country?"

He didn't need to hear the answer when he could see it in her eyes.

"Yeah." He shook his head. "That's what I thought."

Then he, too, limped out of the barn.

He intended to head to the house.

Mend fences with Billie. If he could.

But the second he left the barn, he knew he'd lost that chance, too.

Because her big, old-lady luxury car was gone. And knowing the way she drove, she'd be outta the county in minutes.

His leg ached and his balance wobbled. He threw out his arm, intending to grab the side of the barn.

He got human instead of wood and he swore all over again.

As soon as he'd steadied him, Gerald stepped away. "I didn't intend for you to see me in Reno *or* Cowboy Country."

"Too freaking late."

The older man's lips tightened. "I hope that wasn't a factor in your accident."

"The only factor in my accident was thinking about a woman when I should've been thinking about the steer."

"The woman who just left?"

"I'm not talking about Billie with you. I'm not talking about anything with you."

Gerald nodded. "Fair enough. I'll just tell you one thing. I heard what you said. That you don't want to be like your bastard father. Then don't be like me. If you really love this girl, go after her. Or spend the rest of your life like I have, chasing a taste of happiness that, unfortunately, you'll never find again."

"If that's supposed to mean you loved my mother, sell it to the next guy. I'm not buying."

"You don't have to buy it, Grayson." Gerald looked to where Deborah had come out of the barn, as well. Her arms were folded across her chest and her expression said she wasn't particularly pleased with either one of them. "But it doesn't make it any less true."

Chapter Thirteen

He saw Billie the second he walked into Twine.

Hard not to, when she was in the middle of the dance floor, a blur of short white dress and flying dark hair as she jumped up and down to some song that he'd never heard before. Aside from the visceral appeal of watching her move the way she was, he pretty much hoped he'd never hear the song again. 'Cause it would just remind him of the leer on the face of the guy who *was* dancing with her.

It had been only five days since she'd driven away from him and Paseo. Five days for him to sulk, as his mom had plainly put it. More like five days for him to get over the burning anger he felt every time he thought about his mother actually inviting the man who'd betrayed her to their house.

At which point, Deborah promptly pointed out that the Paseo ranch was still her home and she had every right to invite whomever she wanted. Particularly when

Grayson had a new home that he needed to be concerned with. Including the fact that, if he didn't get over his almighty sulk where Billie's leaving was concerned, he'd be living in it all alone.

He waded into the fray of writhing dancers, cursing under his breath when someone gasped and grabbed his arm. "Ohmygod. You're Grayson!" The someone was red-haired and dancing so frenetically her dress was practically falling off her shoulders. She shimmied even closer to him and he hastily sidled away, not moving as quickly as he wanted because of the stiff boot wrapped around his new half cast. He bumped into a tall guy who didn't even seem to notice, then finally managed to make his way to Billie.

She stopped dead in her tracks when he stepped between her and her dance partner.

One glance and it was obvious that she'd been drinking. Not that it took much. He'd learned that the night they'd been at La Viña. Two glasses of wine was all it had taken and she'd been toast.

"What're you doing here?"

"What do you think?"

She turned up her nose and her back, and started dancing again. This time with the two women behind her.

Once again, he stepped in her way.

She glared and shoved her hair out of her face. It was loose and straight and slid silkily down her back, just waiting for his hands to tangle in it. "How'd you know I was here?"

"Max."

That, at least, gave her pause. For about ten seconds. Then she turned her back once more and started dancing yet again.

He sighed, wondering how long it would be before

the song ended. Only to realize quickly enough that the song wasn't going to end for the simple reason that the DJ spun straight into another hard-beating tune.

Grayson had spent the morning with the orthopedist talking his way around to the walking boot. Then signing autographs at a Grayson Gear-Castleton Boots event where his manager, Jess, had decided it was a brilliant idea to have the newest up-and-comer, Max Vargas, also sign autographs. As a marketing ploy, Grayson could understand it.

Out with the old. In with the new.

But what he hadn't been able to understand was Max willingly participating.

That is, until he'd seen Bethany, looking way more pregnant than she had the last time he'd seen her, standing in the wings. Then he'd remembered the message that Billie had relayed that last day in Paseo. That Bethany had decided he'd been right.

The only thing he'd told her was that it wasn't fair for a kid to never know his dad.

Which meant Max, ready or not, was going to be a father.

When Max had sat down at the table beside him, his apology had been begrudging. But Grayson had to at least give the kid credit for offering it.

He wasn't sure he'd have done the same in his position.

When Grayson had finally peeled away from the event, he'd wished them both good luck. Bethany had kissed his cheek, still grateful for the job at the Grayson Gear office. Max had told him that Billie had taken to going out to Twine every night. Then he'd shoved his hands in his back pockets and told him that if Grayson hurt his cousin more than he already had, all bets were off.

Billie was gyrating in front of him, her short dress

barely skimming the backs of her smooth thighs. And he'd had enough.

He wrapped his arm around her and flipped her up and over his shoulder.

"What the *hell*!" She thumped his back. Hard. "Put me down."

He clamped his arm over her thighs, holding her sorry excuse of a dress down over her butt, and started working his way off the dance floor. One young woman looked startled, then handed him a tiny purse that he assumed—hoped—was Billie's.

The music screeched. Or maybe that was just the sounds the shocked people made as he passed them by.

He didn't know if he ought to be grateful or disgusted that nobody tried to stop him. But then, he thought about the last time he'd been in that very bar. The night before he'd gone out house-hunting with Billie that first time. The topless woman. The cops.

Maybe his hauling Billie out the way she was wasn't so shocking, after all.

He'd seen her car parked in the lot, but he didn't head toward it. Instead, he dumped her on the front seat of his pickup truck and tossed the tiny purse onto her lap.

She crossed her arms and glared at him. "If you were trying to embarrass me in front of my friends, you did a smashing job of it."

"Some friends. They didn't make a move to stop me. What're you doing in a place like that, anyway? It's a meat market."

"Maybe I was hungry!"

"And maybe you should be a vegetarian after all." Because he wasn't sure that she'd do it for herself, he strapped the safety belt across her chest and clipped it in place. When he started to straighten, he hesitated, his mouth close to hers. She smelled like wine and temptation.

He straightened and slammed the door shut. Rounded the truck and got behind the wheel.

At least she hadn't tried to bolt when she'd had the opportunity.

"If you think I'm going to let you tuck me in," she said when he started the engine, "you've got another think coming."

He ignored her and worked his way into the traffic surrounding the popular club. Instead of heading toward her apartment building, though, he headed to the highway.

He knew she realized it when she stiffened. "I don't know where you think you're taking me, but you can just turn this truck around right now."

"We're going home."

She snorted. "Your home? And do what? Sit down on the floor and drink tea from invisible cups?"

He ignored that, too, picking up speed as the traffic thinned a little.

She huffed and turned to look out the side window. They'd gone about ten miles when she finally spoke again. "You got a new cast."

"Yep."

"Suppose you'll ruin that one, too, soon enough."

"Probably."

She fell silent again.

His radio was turned off. The only sound was the lull of his steel-belted radials against the road.

"You hear that hum?"

Billie grunted. Not exactly an answer, but he decided to take it as one.

"It's a sound I'm comfortable with. The sound of most of my adult life, spent on the road, traveling from one rodeo to the next." His thumb tapped nervously against the steering wheel. He glanced at Billie. At the faint gleam of the three earrings on the upper curve of her sexy ear. "And now I'm looking at changing all that."

She was still. Not responding.

He could deal with that. Figured he more than deserved it, considering how he'd treated her in Paseo that last day. "I always thought my roots ran really deep in Paseo. But…" He shook his head. "They're not. Not like they are for Jayden and Nate." Just like when they'd both gone into the military the second they'd been able to, his course was taking a different route. A route that kept bringing him back to Billie.

"I need to put down new roots," he admitted. And even having rehearsed it more than once on the long drive from Paseo to Austin, he found his throat still felt tight around the words. "I've already got the lucky house. The only thing I need now is the reason it's lucky at all. You."

She didn't answer.

He stifled an oath. "You're gonna make me beg, aren't you?" He'd reached the turnoff for the ranch and he slowed. "Fine. I'll beg. But I'm not gonna apologize for not sleeping with you in Paseo. Sex has always been too easy for me. And whether you want to hear it or not, you started to mean more to me than that."

He parked in front of the house. "Dammit, Billie. Say something, even if it's telling me to go to hell." He touched her arm.

She finally moved, her head turning his way.

She was sound asleep.

Snoring slightly, even.

"Well. *Hell.*" Shows what he knew about women. Pouring his heart out while she quietly passed out on probably two glasses of wine.

He turned off the engine and got out of the truck, leaving the headlights on to see his way up to the front door and unlock it.

There wasn't any furniture inside the house. But he always had his bedroll in the truck.

When he checked Billie, she'd shucked off her seat belt and snuggled down in the seat, her cheek pressed against her clasped hands. Looking about sixteen, except for the long, shapely legs on display.

He reminded himself that he wasn't low enough to take advantage of an inebriated woman—even if he did love her—and grabbed the bedroll from the back seat. He carried it into the house, flipping on a couple lights as he made his way up to the master bedroom.

There, he spread out the bedroll, right where their real bed would someday be, and went back out to the truck.

She still hadn't moved.

His leg was aching from all the activity—just as the orthopedist had warned—but he ignored it and lifted Billie into his arms. No fireman's hold this time.

He cradled her against his chest and shoved the truck door closed with his shoulder. He didn't worry about the headlights. They'd turn off automatically before long.

He carried her inside the house, then up the stairs and to the bedroll. Lowering her onto it took some doing considering the immobility of his left leg in the boot. But he managed.

Her long hair slid over his arms and she sighed, one hand slipping around his neck. "Where're we?"

He smiled slightly and kissed her forehead. Her nose. Her lips. "We're home, sweetheart."

He hadn't turned on a light in the bedroom, but there was enough moonlight shining through the big windows to see that her eyes were open. Dark and gleaming.

He stretched out next to her and propped himself up on one arm. “Are you awake this time?”

“This time?”

He ran his fingers through her silky hair. He leaned down and brushed his lips against her triplet earrings. “How much did you have to drink?”

“A glass and a half of wine, smart aleck.”

“Smart aleck, nothin’. You’re the one who passed out on me in the truck. If I’m gonna pour my heart out to you, I’d like to know you’re conscious enough to hear it.” He propped himself on his arm again.

“You don’t pour your heart out to anyone. You flirt.”

“I’m not flirting now.” He discarded the rehearsed speech and just pulled the ring out of his pocket. The ring he’d chosen that afternoon, after the orthopedist and before the autographing. “I love you, Billie Pemberton. Have pretty much loved you since that first day when you rescued me from cucumber-and-basil-poisoned water. And the deal was sealed for good when I woke up in the hospital with you crying by my side.”

Her lashes dipped. He saw the gleam of a tear on her cheek and his chest tightened all over again as he gently thumbed it away. “If you marry me, I promise that I’ll love you harder than anyone else ever could. But you need to understand that *you* are the catch. Not me. I’m just an old bulldogger with no chance of another championship this year, if ever. I’ve got a chip on my shoulder when it comes to my…when it comes to Gerald. Or Jerome. Or whoever the hell he is. And even though I’ve got a business with an office, I can guarantee that there are gonna be days when I want to still be on the road. Listening to the hum of the tires, going from rodeo to rodeo. Whether I can compete or not. It’s just a part of who I am, sweetheart, and—”

Her fingertips touched his lips. "You love me?"

He caught her fingers in his hand and kissed them. And because she still hadn't said yes, he simply pushed the diamond ring on her finger. She'd either let it stay there for the rest of her life or he'd spend the rest of his life talking her into it. Either way, he wasn't taking it back. "I said so, didn't I? Do you want me to say it again?"

She nodded. "Again." She lifted herself up and kissed him slowly. "And again." Then she pushed on his shoulders until he rolled onto his back. She slid over him. "And again. Every morning." She pulled her short dress up and over her head and let it fall from her fingertips with a soft slithering sound. Her creamy shoulders gleamed in the moonlight. "And every night." She unclipped the wisp of lace that masqueraded as a bra and let that, too, fall to the side.

Then she leaned forward, cupping his face between her hands. "Can you handle that, Grayson Fortune?"

He grasped her hips, dipping his fingers beneath the flimsy sides of her skimpy panties. "S'long as you agree to become Billie Fortune." He slipped his hand between her thighs and couldn't help groaning when he found her wet heat.

Her breathing deepened. "Belinda Marie Fortune, if—ah—" She arched against his hand and started fumbling with his belt. "If we're going to be strictly accurate."

"By all means." He caught her lips with his. "Let's be strictly accurate." Before she could get too far, he flipped her until she was on her back. He peeled her panties the rest of the way down her smooth thighs, thoroughly exploring every inch of skin along the way. Until she was writhing against him far more enticingly than anything she'd done on the dance floor at Twine.

This dance was strictly for him.

He didn't have a hope in hell of quickly undoing the complicated straps holding the molded boot around his broken leg. "We were supposed to be doing this with *you* wearing the shoes," he murmured, as he pulled off his shirt, only to suck in a hard breath when her fingers trailed down his abdomen.

"Next time," she whispered huskily, peeling open his fly to work her hand inside his jeans.

He nearly came unglued. "There's a condom in my pocket," he said with a rough laugh.

"Engagement rings *and* condoms. The things you carry with you."

"I won't lie. The condoms were routine." He tried to put on the brakes. But her fingers were circled around him. Drawing him to her. Brakes were child's play. "The ring's a first."

"That's good. I want something to be a first for you." She slid her legs along his thighs, taking him in with a quick arching movement.

His heart nearly jumped out of his chest. He hadn't had sex without protection, ever. "You're on the Pill?"

She shook her head and brushed her lips over his. "Not since I was twenty."

"Holy—" He kissed her hard. "The toe tattoo guy was the last time?"

"Mmm." The tip of her tongue flirted along the edge of his ear. "Was no need after that. Don't worry. I'm perfectly safe. No dreaded diseases." She undulated against him, letting out a low, shaking sigh that was so erotic he had to count backward in his head just to keep some control.

"I'm safe, too," he managed to tell her. "But what if—"

"What if?" She was panting harder, her hands racing

from his hips, up his spine and back again. "You want to plant roots? Plant the first one now. Right now. With me."

His head went still, even though the rest of him was set on pursuing perfection inside her. "You were listening."

She twined her arms around his shoulders. "I was listening." Then she kissed him again. Tasting like wine and seduction and forever, while her body tightened so sweetly, so responsively, he couldn't do anything but rush headlong into the waves of her splintering around him.

The sun was coming up over the lake when Grayson next had a coherent thought.

He looked at Billie lying beside him and woke her with a kiss on her shoulder. "You never did say yes," he murmured.

She turned on her side, snuggling back against his chest and pulling his hand over her waist. "Maybe I'm still thinking about it."

He laughed and lightly swatted her bare butt.

Billie giggled, feeling happiness flood through her as she kissed his knuckles. "Yes. That doesn't, however, mean I'm waiving any of my commission when I find Grayson Gear's new corporate home. I mean, I'm not a pushover like someone I know."

"I'm not a pushover."

"Please." She twisted in his embrace and looped her arms around his neck. "You, who never met a cause he could resist? Admit it. The only real reason you want to make money at all is so that you can give it away to someone who needs it. It's one of the things I love most about you. That big, squishy heart of yours."

He made a face. "I like my comforts, too, sweetheart. The Harmon ranch? That's a lot of evidence."

"You would've been just as happy with the Orchess place. Half the price."

"Half the land," he countered immediately. "And no wine cellar where I can make love with my new fiancée. Speaking of which." He pushed to his knees and then to his feet. She'd helped him get rid of the rigid boot and his jeans before they'd made love a second time, and the sight of him in the dawn light was enough to make her catch her breath.

He was perfection personified.

"The wine cellar? Now?" She laughed softly as he limped into one of the large walk-in closets. "Pretty sure there isn't a secret staircase leading down there from the master bedroom closet, Grayson." But curiosity got the better of her when he didn't respond. The white shirt he'd been wearing the night before was lying in a heap next to the blanket he'd rolled out on the carpet, and she slipped her arms into it before heading after him.

If there'd been any shred of her heart that wasn't already melted into a Grayson puddle, it would have melted then.

He smiled at her, his rumpled hair sticking out around his handsome face. "What d'you think?"

She walked into the oversize closet. Slowly took the red-soled apology shoes off the fancy, lighted shelf where they'd been displayed. "You kept them."

"Only because every time I tried to get rid of them, they kept ending up right back in my possession. Reminding me of you. You still want to return them?"

She shook her head, set the shoes on the floor and slid her bare feet into them. They fit just as perfectly now as they had the first time he'd tempted her into trying them on.

"Come on, Billie. Tell me what you're thinking."

She smiled slowly. "Hopefully, the same thing you're thinking." She slid his shirt off her shoulders again and held out her arms to him. "That you have another promise to keep."

His smile was slow. Not at all trademark Grayson. But entirely *her* Grayson.

For now. And forever.

Epilogue

"You may kiss your bride."

Laughter and cheers followed, as the groom's handsome head lowered to his beautiful bride's and the two kissed. Probably a little longer than some might think appropriate.

Billie couldn't help but grin.

Lady Whatsername was now Mrs. Orlando Mendoza and Billie was pretty sure a bride had never looked as happy as Josephine Fortune Chesterfield did.

She leaned her head closer to Ariana, who was sitting beside her on the white chairs set up in pristine order among the ornamental grapevines at the Mendoza Winery. "Did you ever figure out just how they're all related?"

Ariana shrugged slightly. "I started a family chart once when I was planning to write the book about the Fortunes, but I gave up. Too complicated."

Grayson's hand covered Billie's. "We could have our wedding here at the winery, too," he murmured from the side of his mouth.

She shook her head. "We may not have agreed on a date yet, but we *have* agreed to have our wedding at home." Their home. Where they definitely wouldn't be having as large a guest list as Orlando and Josephine did, even though the Fortune ranch could have probably accommodated it.

There were almost as many people here now as when Schuyler had married Carlo. All the Mendozas who'd been present then were back. And there were Josephine's children from her prior marriages, as well as their spouses and their children. Plus Orlando's daughter and sons and all their families.

To say it was a huge crowd was putting it mildly.

Even when the wedding itself broke up and people started milling about as waiters circulated, bearing hot and cold hors d'oeuvres, the size of the guest list seemed to be one of the favorite topics. Either that or the designer duds that the bride and her daughters were sporting.

And Schuyler was clearly in her element in the winery as she flitted around, making certain that everyone had their glasses and plates filled. That everyone knew everyone else.

Billie was glad that there was at least one person not present. There was no sign whatsoever of Gerald Robinson, even though several of his children—Grayson, Jayden and Nathan aside—were present. But Deborah also had chosen to forgo the wedding, and Billie knew that Grayson feared the absence was too coincidental. He was clearly anxious to get away from all these people with whom he was even tenuously connected.

All she could do was hope that he'd be more accepting of his Fortune ties when they started *their* family.

He seemed to read her mind. "We can sneak out anytime you want," he murmured.

"Oh no, you don't," Schuyler said, overhearing as she personally topped off their glasses of champagne. "Not before the toasts at any rate." Her smile sparkled as she moved away.

Grayson looked pained. Billie knew it wouldn't be because of his leg. He was supposed to use a cane for the next two weeks. But of course, he wouldn't. "How long is this thing gonna last?"

Billie chuckled. "Hopefully not as long as Schuyler and Carlo's wedding did. I caught the bouquet. Well, half of it, anyway." She scanned the faces of the bridal couple's families and friends. "Wonder who'll catch Josephine's bouquet."

"Wonder if anyone cares?"

Billie bumped his arm. "Hush." Standing on the other side of Grayson, his brothers covered their smiles, and she gave them both a look. "You're not helping."

"Give up," Ariana advised. "When the three of them get going…" She shook her head. "No way of stopping." She hushed when Orlando and Josephine stepped onto a small dais near the winery entrance.

The couple held hands. "We're not going to stand up here and make long speeches," Orlando said. He smiled self-deprecatingly. "At least I won't subject you to mine. My wife, on the other hand—" he kissed the back of Josephine's fingers "—is much more graceful in front of a crowd than I." He shared a smile with his elegant bride. "I'll keep it short."

He held up his glass. "I wish for all of you to be as sheltered by love as we are today by your presence with us. People say you toast the bride and groom. But I say that we toast all of you." He raised his glass. "Cheers."

The sentiment resounded throughout the room as glasses clinked and people drank.

"And now, as promised, I will put a lock on it." Orlando mimed locking his lips together. Even across the distance, Billie could see the smile in the man's eyes.

"My new husband exaggerates greatly," Josephine said in her crisp British tones. "And I love him for it, particularly when he tells me I am more beautiful than the sea."

Orlando laughed and Josephine smiled. She definitely was comfortable in front of the large crowd. "I think we can all agree that the Fortune families and the Mendoza families have a long, storied history together," she said. "Some of our stories are longer. Some are shorter." She lifted her glass toward her groom. "But each is special. And unique. And joined by love. And I am so very grateful that I have been welcomed by all of you. As so many of us have learned, there is nothing more important than family."

Billie's eyes blurred a little. She reached out and found Grayson's hand with her own.

"Whether it's the family you've been born into or the family you've chosen, it all boils down to one thing. Hold on to those who love you. And let them hold on to you." She raised her glass one more time. "To all of you. Our family. Thank you for making this day even more special for us by taking the time to be here."

Ariana swiped at her eyes with the edge of her cocktail napkin. "Sheesh," she whispered, sharing a look with Billie. "Tear fest."

"And now, I, too, will be quiet," Josephine said with a soft laugh, "so we can get on with the food!"

Carlo walked to the front of the dais. It wasn't entirely

surprising, though Billie had sort of expected Alejandro—Orlando's son—to speak. "Actually, there's just one more thing we want to say before we begin this party in earnest." He nodded toward his uncle. "If you'll forgive me hijacking the schedule for a moment."

Bianca looked at Billie. Her eyes were dancing. "Ten to one, Schuyler's pregnant."

Billie wasn't going to take that bet. Because she'd immediately thought the same thing. And when Schuyler stepped beside Carlo and took his hand, she was certain of it.

"I'm glad that my new aunt-in-law spoke about the importance of family," she said. "Because there's actually more family here than any of you know."

"When's the due date?" someone called out.

Schuyler laughed and propped her hand on her spectacular skin-hugging dress. "Now, y'all. Seriously. Do I *look* pregnant?" She grinned. "Carlo and I have lots of time to make babies."

Billie caught the way Carlo squeezed her hand encouragingly. *"Go ahead,"* she saw him mouth.

"Actually..." She took a deep breath and let it out in an audible rush. "It's me. And my brothers and my sisters. We were born Fortunados. But under that, we're Fortunes, same as a lot of you. Our daddy's daddy was Julius Fortune, Jerome's father." She suddenly looked toward where Grayson and they all stood. "Same as your granddaddy." She looked over to Alejandro and his wife, Olivia Robinson Mendoza. "And same as *your* granddaddy." She spread her arms wide. "And *boy* is it a load off my chest to finally admit it to y'all!"

Far from looking upset, Josephine merely stepped off the dais and hugged Schuyler. "Once again," she said, so brightly that people laughed rather than gasped, "there's simply no end to this dynasty. Mark my words, we need a Fortune family reunion—"

"Fortune family meet-and-greet," someone called out with a laugh.

Josephine's smile widened. "—and soon!"

Grayson wasn't laughing, though. "Are we sure that there aren't cousins marrying cousins or something?"

Ariana heard him. "Fortunately, back when I was trying to map it all out, none of that ever happened."

"Small wonder." He looked around them. "Any other secrets coming out today?"

"Just one." Billie knew one sure way to clear the discontented look from Grayson's face. "Maybe Schuyler's not pregnant, but—" she shrugged slightly and met his eyes "—I am."

His jaw dropped. "It hasn't been that long since—" He broke off. Swallowed. "How do you know?" He swept his hands down the sides of her purple dress. The fact that they weren't exactly steady made her love him all the more. "Are you sure?"

"The home test I did seemed pretty sure."

He threw back his head. Let out a whoop and lifted her right off her feet, swinging her in a circle. "Sweetheart, I don't care what you say." He set her back on her feet. "We are out of here." He grabbed her hand and pulled her past the ornamental vines.

"And that there's Grayson, folks." Jayden's pseudo-rodeo announcer's voice followed them. "Breaking yet another timed record…this one the fastest wedding exit ever!"

Laughing breathlessly as they raced across the green, green grass, Billie pulled on Grayson's hand to stop him. "You're really okay with this?"

His eyes softened. "Planting roots with you? Belinda

Marie soon-to-be Fortune, don't you know the truth by now?" His hands cupped her face. "*You* are my forever home."

Her eyes flooded. She didn't think her heart could be filled any more, but it was. "Grayson."

His eyes weren't exactly dry then, either. "*Now* can we get outta here and go set a dang wedding date? We've gotta tell your folks. Tell my mom. Sweetheart, there's stuff to be done!"

She laughed. Leaned down to slip off her red-soled shoes, then she held out her free hand to him. "Let's go."

He closed his hand around hers. And they went.

* * * * *

MILLS & BOON

Coming next month

REUNITED AT THE ALTAR
Kate Hardy

Cream roses.

Brad had bought her cream roses.

Had he remembered that had been her wedding bouquet, Abigail wondered, a posy of half a dozen cream roses they'd bought last-minute at the local florist? Or had he just decided that roses were the best flowers to make an apology and those were the first ones he'd seen? She raked a shaking hand through her hair. It might not have been the best idea to agree to have dinner with Brad tonight.

Then again, he'd said he wanted a truce for Ruby's sake, and they needed to talk.

But seeing him again had stirred up all kinds of emotions she'd thought she'd buried a long time ago. She'd told herself that she was over her ex and could move on. The problem was, Bradley Powell was still the most attractive man she'd ever met – those dark, dark eyes; the dark hair that she knew curled outrageously when it was wet; that sense of brooding about him. She'd never felt that same spark with anyone else she'd dated. She knew she hadn't been fair to the few men who'd asked her out; she really shouldn't have compared them to her first love, because how could they ever match up to him?

She could still remember the moment she'd fallen in love with Brad. She and Ruby had been revising for their English exams together in the garden, and Brad had come out to join them, wanting a break from his physics revision. Somehow he'd ended up reading Benedick's speeches while she'd read Beatrice's.

'I do love nothing in the world so well as you: is that not strange?'

She'd glanced up from her text and met his gaze, and a surge of heat had spun through her. He was looking at her as if it was the first time he'd ever seen her. As if she was the only living thing in the world apart from himself. As if the rest of the world had just melted away...